Before turning to crime, **A.M. CASTLE** was a national newspaper feature writer. Her first psychological thriller for HQ Digital, *The Perfect Widow*, is an Amazon number one bestseller in Noir Crime, and a top-selling audiobook. She also writes cosy crimes as Alice Castle. She lives in south London with her two daughters and two cats and, when not dreaming up new ways to kill people herself, is usually glued to a whodunit on TV.

Also by A.M. Castle

The Perfect Widow

The Invitation

A.M. CASTLE

ONE PLACE. MANY STORIES.

HQ
An imprint of HarperCollins*Publishers* Ltd
1 London Bridge Street
London SE1 9GF

www.harpercollins.co.uk

HarperCollins*Publishers*
1st Floor, Watermarque Building, Ringsend Road
Dublin 4, Ireland

This paperback edition 2021

1
First published in Great Britain by
HQ, an imprint of HarperCollins*Publishers* Ltd 2021

Copyright © A.M. Castle 2021

A.M. Castle asserts the moral right to be
identified as the author of this work.
A catalogue record for this book is
available from the British Library.

ISBN: 9780008364748

MIX
Paper from
responsible sources
FSC
www.fsc.org
FSC® C007454

This book is produced from independently certified FSC™ paper

to ensure responsible forest management.

For more information visit: www.harpercollins.co.uk/green

Printed and bound in Great Britain by
CPI Group (UK) Ltd, Melksham, SN12 6TR

To Ella and Connie, with love

Prologue

Tregowan Castle, Mount Tregowan, 1st November, Midnight

The glare, when the lights suddenly go back on, is worse than the total blackness moments before. The guests blink as four huge chandeliers blaze down on them. The table, dead centre in the vaulted baronial dining hall, is covered with the detritus of their long, indulgent reunion meal: crystal glasses, fine china, empty bottles of Champagne and Barolo. From the looks of things, it's been quite an evening.

A bewildered murmuring starts. Everyone is in identical Halloween costumes, though some have ditched their orange wigs. Then someone gets up to see what caused the power cut, almost tripping on the long black and red velvet cape. But, before they've even reached the light switch, they begin to back away, colliding with chairs and table, pointing wordlessly. The others follow the direction of that single, shaking finger.

Someone is face down in one of the sumptuous gold dinner plates, wig askew, shoulders hunched. *Who could possibly have slept through all this?* they ask each other.

No one, it turns out. The blinding light catches something. A shiny metal skewer, sticking straight up from the back of that still neck.

As a second horrified silence falls, a red bead wells up where the skewer has entered the body. It traces the nape, languid as a lover, and trickles off the table. On the floor a pool, rich and red as the Barolo, is rapidly gathering.

Then the screaming starts.

Excerpt from *Yes! Magazine*, November Issue

It's two short months since Lady Tregowan, better known as heiress and socialite Rachel Cadogan, threw her magnificent castle open to us.

Forty-four-year-old Rachel, who tied the knot with Lord Tregowan in a glittering New York ceremony at her family's Cadogan Museum, home of her internationally renowned art foundation, had additional receptions for several hundred guests in London and Paris.

'I'm eager now just to enjoy my new life with Ross and my adorable stepchildren, Penny (46) and Roderick (43), over simple family evenings like this one,' she explained graciously.

Resplendent in the Tregowan pearls and a full-length Oscar de la Renta evening gown, Rachel was standing in front of the mantelpiece in Tregowan Castle's Great Hall, emblazoned with the family's crest.

'It's a sabre rising from the castle itself, with the motto underneath, "My Revenge is Swift." How fun is that?' smiled the radiant newlywed.

PART ONE

Chapter 1

Vicky

Central London, 5th September

Don't get me wrong, I love Gita, and our lunches. But I sometimes wonder how much there is to talk about, every single month. Especially as we can never discuss the real issue: her marriage. Christ, if I'd been stuck with Tom and his wandering eye, he would have been six feet under long ago. But Gita always pretends everything is great. I find it a strain; I suppose she'd say I'm a typical plain-spoken Northerner.

That's one of the reasons it's been three times as long as usual since we've made this journey into Soho. My fault; I was in charge this time and I, erm, let things slip.

Now, on this crowded Saturday tube, filled with tourists beginning to wonder why they picked this rainy capital in autumn, I wish I'd carried on postponing. Never mind. Nearly there now.

It's chilly. I pull up the zip on my jacket, sympathising with the Japanese guy in shorts. He's going to suffer when he gets above ground. But I don't let on. I may give away my roots every time I open my mouth, but I have a proper Londoner's transport face.

My job is numbers, and thank God they don't talk back. Opposites attract, I suppose. Gita has a constant need to 'communicate' as she puts it. Take her Instagram. It's a waterfall of beautiful family pics. Her sheaf of blue-black hair and those Mata Hari eyes. Tom, still far too handsome for his own good. And their three girls, showing off top-notch genes from both sides. It's more carefully stage-managed than an episode of *Keeping Up with the Kardashians*. I don't know when she even sees them to take the snaps; she's working at the newspaper all hours of the day.

Still, she loves that job. 'Can you see me as an accountant or a lawyer, the way Mum and Dad wanted? I was so lucky I could say no.' She's always reckoned her parents' scandalous divorce saved her. 'If it hadn't been for the fuss, I'd have been under their thumb forever. But what could they say, afterwards?'

One evening we'd both had too many, and I finally had the balls to come out with it. Why, after her dad scarpered, did she ever decide to marry someone like Tom? 'Love,' she hiccupped. 'And,' she said, lowering her voice, 'at least I know Tom and I will last. Unlike my parents.' My double take must have been comical, but she was looking the other way. It's amazing what you can convince yourself of – if you try hard enough. Usually it's him I want to kill but sometimes it's her. Deluding herself is bad enough; inflicting it on me and everyone else is hard to take.

No wonder it's been so long since we met. Poor Gita. She's had to crush it on all fronts, to prove herself to everyone. Newspapers instead of a profession, and then Tom on top. And, despite his electrical engineering degree, he 'only' went into the police force. Fast track, fair dos, but still not the kind of job a family like Gita's would ever rate. No wonder she's got a million perfect photos to try and prove how brilliantly everything is going.

Truth is, nothing much has turned out the way either of us expected. We were going to have it all: careers, men and kids. No problemo. Ha!

Oh well. We're fine. I'm fine, I am. Really. Well, I miss my lad,

Raf, I can't deny it. Like that sore place on the back of your ankle, from high heels. Sometimes you hardly notice it. But then it'll rub itself raw and it's all you can think about. Like now, when I see a kid the same age as Raf opposite me in the tube carriage, sitting plugged into his phone, bobbing his head to some phantom beat. I gaze out of the window for a moment, though the only view is of darkness whisking past us.

Somewhere out there are secret tunnels beyond the tube tracks, places where people hid during the Blitz, and where they stuffed our art treasures until victory was won ... I know everything there is to know about my adopted city. Our friend Rachel Cadogan's family collection was stashed down here, along with the Elgin Marbles and half the National Gallery. Everyone's heard of the Cadogan Foundation, even the likes of me. It's been world famous forever, long before Rachel decided to slum it with us at uni.

Where was I? I'm seeing Raf next weekend anyway. It's my turn, though at twenty he's too old to be passed between me and Bob like a parcel. And he has a bad habit of postponing. Wonder where he got that from.

When I emerge at Leicester Square, the crisp, blue skies cheer me up. I dodge the homeless, feeling the usual guilt. I make a monthly charity donation to shut my conscience up. Better than pressing cash into outstretched palms. Too much temptation – I should know. We all have our secret vices, don't we? Gita has her blinkers. And yes, I have a weakness of my own ... But I shan't dwell on that now.

I peer into furniture shops instead, wishing I was good at that design stuff, promising myself a trip that will never materialise. Maybe Raf would stick around, if I made the place more homey? In Shaftesbury Avenue, I inhale as I pass Lisle Street, breathing in five-spice, admiring the red paper lanterns around the Chinatown sign.

I check my watch and speed up. When I arrive, I pull open the Club door before the man has a chance to get it, and shift

7

from foot to foot as the fourteen-year-old with the iPad checks the seating plan. In the end, I read it upside down and point to us on the diagram. 'They're already here,' she trills and sashays away in front of me.

They. I'm just processing the word when I see Gita waving, her pretty face alight with smiles, long dark bob swishy as a shampoo ad. She's never understood what a stunner she is. But wait, who's that sitting next to her, a beam of sunlight almost making a halo out of bright blonde hair?

My God, it's *her.* Actually her. Did I conjure her up, thinking of her art, hoarded in those dark tunnels? I kick myself. This lunch just got a whole lot harder.

All right, we've seen each other at the big events, over the years. Gita's parties; Christmas and New Year, christenings, birthdays and whatnot. And sometimes Gita has had an invite to some enormous Cadogan Foundation thrash, and I've tagged along as a plus-one. I've glimpsed that famous face, hobnobbing with the great and good. But I can't remember the last time we sat down for a casual meal. It might even have been over the chipped Formica of the uni canteen. Gita's seen much more of her – but then, she has no reason not to.

I suppress a shiver, stick on my best smile, and step forward to greet her. The one, the only, the amazing – Rachel Cadogan.

Chapter 2

Gita

Central London, 5th September

Vicky doesn't do it on purpose. Well, I'm pretty sure she doesn't. But when she isn't happy, she somehow lets everyone know, without a word being spoken. And then she refuses to discuss it.

Today, even the way she stands and looks at us both, with her back very, very straight and her smile so rigid, makes it plain that something is up.

Communication. I always come back to that. It's crucial. I know she's still smarting at her long separation from Raf. She's probably been longing to discuss it. She's no doubt heard he's round at ours a lot at the moment. Maybe she's angry? But we're his godparents. And he's been chatting to Tom about the police force, fitness, potential careers. Surely she'd be glad about that? With Rachel here, it's impossible to broach the subject. Vicky would never admit to that sort of pain in front of anyone else.

I feel terrible. Seeing Rachel again after all this time should have been such a brilliant surprise. But Vicky has been so … off recently. Perhaps I should have known better. She flicks her eyes from Rachel to me, and then submits to Rachel's hug, still as unbending as a lamppost.

A couple of minutes in, and, thank God, Vicky is beginning to rise to the occasion. Things are suddenly going with the swing that I first envisaged. It's down to Rachel, of course.

She always assumes people will be thrilled to see her. And then they are. She's the one to watch, the punchline of the joke, the Viagra in the pensioner ... no, where is my mind even going? But it's true that Rachel makes people sit up and take notice. Maybe it's apt after all.

'It's been, what? So long, love. *Too* long. I can't believe it, you look so ...' Vicky says.

And Rachel does look *so*. Indefinable things have gone on, and she looks amazing, miraculous. Neither young nor old, but suspended between the two. She shrugs and hits back the compliments faster than Novak Djokovic. I wish she'd spill the beans. I'll need to start getting a few tweakments soon. Policemen may be getting younger every day, but so are policewomen – and Tom works with way too many of them for my liking. It's not a question of trust, exactly. Men can just ... have their heads turned. It's up to me to keep young and beautiful, as they say. I'll have to ask Rachel another time. There's something she *does* want to show off about, though. The massive new ring weighing down the third finger of her left hand.

'Christ, Rach. I didn't think I'd need my shades in September.' Vicky takes Rachel's hand as though she's going to check for occlusions like a Hatton Garden jeweller. It's a safe bet that there aren't any. No one can say Rachel has lived a flawless life. But this ring is bound to be perfect – the real thing.

Vicky's second question is typically blunt, but I admit I was wondering myself. 'Did you buy it, or did he?'

'Oh *he* did, darling, of course,' Rachel says, though all three of us know she can lie for Britain, or anywhere else she touches down, if the occasion demands it.

'So who is he, where did you meet him and, most importantly, why didn't *I* meet him first?' Vicky's smile doesn't quite go with her eyes.

Is she still smarting over Bob? But they were never right for each other; they never really communicated. Vicky's focus has always been on making it big, while Bob was all about the pro bono cases. She used to say he was the only lawyer she knew who made a loss. She should be over it by now. Of course she's not. Bless her, she holds grudges like it's an Olympic sport. But today I want to concentrate on Rachel.

'Come on, we want to hear all about this proposal,' I say, even though I'm kicking myself. I spiked a story that Rachel was engaged only last week, on the grounds I'd have been the first to know. I'm going to look a prize idiot in the office.

'I'm sorry I didn't call you right away,' Rachel says, searching my face. 'It's been a whirlwind. But now I'm going to tell you *everything.*' She leans forward with a gust of perfume, a glimpse of still-firm décolletage and a discreet clank of her Tiffany bangles.

And she's off.

It's quite a tale. *Klosters, Bequia, Monaco, Meghan, Amal and Reese.* 'Christ, you never bump into anyone in Tesco Metro, do you, Rach?' says Vicky. But Rachel doesn't get it; for her this is normal life.

When the waitress first starts hovering, Rachel waves her away, though Vicky has her mouth open, ready to order. The next time the girl appears, I make sure to grab her myself and then turn swiftly to Vicky. Once she has a bottle of red coming her way, her shoulders finally relax.

Both of us raise our eyebrows when Rachel goes for the lobster starter and then a complicated squid ink risotto. *Allow twenty minutes cooking time*, it says on the menu, which means half an hour at the very least. But I smile reassuringly. Vicky probably (hopefully) won't remember the way Rachel always toys with her food, shifting it from three o'clock to nine o'clock and back again, as though that's the point of mealtimes. One of six brought up on benefits, Vicky still clears her plate as though food is going out of fashion. Worse still, Rachel confided to me before Vicky arrived that she's just had a gastric bypass. 'Only a precaution,' she explained.

'But you're skin and bone! And isn't it really dangerous?' I was agog. 'I thought it was an absolute last resort. For people with, you know,' I sketched a ghostly paunch.

Rachel just laughed. 'You're so funny, Gita.' Apparently, money not only talks, it also gives you the second opinion you require.

Thank God, the bread comes quickly. Then the wine. Vicky ignores the fresh sourdough and the dainty dipping saucers of truffle oil, chopped rosemary and salt, and goes straight for the red, wrapping her hands around the glass as though it's her long-lost child.

I turn and ask Rachel about her new man. 'So his name's Ross and he's wonderful. But what does he do?' For a second, I could kick myself. *Silly question, Gita.* Rachel's other friends, the rich ones, don't 'do' anything, they just … are. Drifting across the oceans, in search of pleasure. Or, as Vicky might well say, a purpose in life. But Rachel dives in happily.

'Oh, you have to come and see. He's got the most amazing place. Or it very soon will be, when I've finished with it. He avoided it for years.' She breaks off, looks around and lowers her voice. '*Family tragedy,*' she explains in a stage whisper. 'His first wife died in a horrible road accident. So awful – his daughter was in the car. So he left his son to run everything – or run it down, more like. But now we're taking it on together. I'm going to turn the place around.'

I feel a fleeting sympathy for this unknown son. He won't know what's hit him. But Vicky waves her glass at Rachel. 'Cheers to that, love. Where is it?' She drains her glass and waves to the waiter for a fresh bottle.

'Cornwall. You may have heard of it? Mount Tregowan.'

There's a brief moment when you can almost hear pennies dropping. I'm first. 'Not *that* Mount Tregowan? The castle on the island?'

Then Vicky chimes in. 'Where they shot the smuggling mini-series? With that guy with the six-pack? Isn't it owned by some lord or other?'

Rachel's laugh is delighted. 'Yes, yes and yes! That's Ross's place. Ours now. So you'll come? I'm thinking of the end of October – you know how I love Halloween.'

Vicky and I look at each other. 'Who could forget?' she says. But I'm so excited, I just leap straight in. '*Of course* we're coming!' I say.

'Well – if that actor's still there,' says Vicky. But now she's beginning to grin. What an invitation! We both need this break. Tom and I, well, some time together would be good. And it'll give me a chance to keep an eye on Vicky, too, see how she's doing with her little … problem. It will be great, having our trio together again. Like old times. I love my lunches with Vicky, and I always try and grab Rachel when she's in town, but getting the two of them in a room is like herding kittens. And we always had the most fun when we were together.

Things weren't the same, when Rachel left uni in the middle of our last year. Vicky's other friend, Jane, started coming round much more. Nice enough but always looking as though she'd seen a ghost. No one could hold a candle to Rachel, of course. But Vicky needed the support. And now Jane has buried herself out in the country with her lawyer husband, Geoff. Bit pompous, but harmless enough. I suddenly wonder. 'Will you be inviting Jane?'

'Oh, why the hell not?' says Rachel expansively. Then she holds forth for the rest of our lunch about how amazing and fabulous her life suddenly is, thanks to this new man – like her life wasn't amazing and fabulous yesterday, and won't be tomorrow.

I can sense Vicky shifting next to me from time to time. It's always been more difficult for her to accept the usual Rachel tsunami of wonderfulness. And, as the years have rolled by,

Rachel's life has not diminished one jot in sheer glamour, while ours have inevitably been constrained. Work, men, children – however wonderful, they do take a toll. Vicky must be finding it hard to keep it zipped.

Finally, Rachel draws breath, looks fondly from me to Vicky, and claps her hands together like a child.

'Brilliant to catch up! And I can't wait for you to come to the island. Because, as soon as we're all there together, I've got *the* most amazing secret to share. I'm dying to tell you.'

Chapter 3

Tom

London suburbs, 27th October

Something funny happens today. I am trekking to the gym, as usual, when I catch sight of my reflection in a shop window. For a second, I don't even recognise myself. No word of a lie, I look decades younger. I've been slumped over a desk forever, but now, striding out, kit bag over my shoulder, I'm different. Taller, broader, fitter. My hand reaches out of its own volition and claps this stranger on his flat stomach. It's the round of applause I deserve, sharp and hollow. Couple of months ago, it would have been muffled by flapjacks. Ironically, I'm now the type of plod a lot of my colleagues really respect – someone who wouldn't break a sweat, chasing a villain across an estate.

A lot of coppers still think a degree is, well, lipstick on a pig. And the public agrees. They want bobbies on the beat, not my uni dissertation on electrical circuits. They don't understand how much can go on behind the scenes, without even getting near street level. You have to be tech savvy, though. Rules out a lot of my colleagues.

I've got it covered both ways now. Chiselled down into myself, built myself back up from the bottom. Sometimes Gita looks at me, full of sweet concern, all 'Would you like a cup of tea, darling?' even when she's been the one out at work. I'm hard pressed not to laugh in her face.

This weekend, she wouldn't hear of me being left behind. 'I don't want you to brood, all on your own.' I wouldn't have done – my conscience is clear. But I agree. It's definitely for the best, me coming along.

Don't get me wrong, hanging out with Gita and her mates holds no appeal. And seeing how the other half lives, meeting Rachel's sucker of a new husband, gawping at what she's done with his ancestral home, all the other stuff Gita is gagging for? Way too much celebrity flim-flam for me. But she's shown me a few pictures of the island, and I've had a google. Looks just the spot. Mount Tregowan piques my interest, so to speak. Distinct possibilities, once we're all there. And I'll bet my own little secret is nothing, compared to what's weighing down some of the others. Vicky, for instance. But Jane, too. I'll have my eye on Geoff, that husband of hers.

Gita's dying to see Vicky and Rachel. Always pretends they're some kind of sisterhood. She's told me she wants this weekend to be 'unique, truly memorable'.

She really needs to be careful what she wishes for.

Chapter 4

Vicky

Cornwall, 30th October

As soon as Rachel buggered off that day – late for something much more exciting than lunch with us girls – the second thoughts kicked in. I turned to Gita but her palm was already up, the lollipop lady of the group, keeping us all in order. Or trying.

'Before you even start; yes, I know Rachel has talked us into stuff that … doesn't always play out brilliantly. But we've got to accept this invitation; we really do. You need a break, Vicky. When's the last time you took any kind of holiday?'

While I was sifting back through the months, she struck again – right in my weak spot. 'And what about Raf? You could ask him, spend some time together. You know you'd love that. It's outdoorsy, the sort of thing he's into. He could actually surf in Cornwall – it's really big down there.'

'In October?' I pretended to be sceptical, but Gita had chalked up a hit. I've spent hardly any time with my lad in the last year. It's got to the point where I've found myself sitting in his too-clean room, on his too-smooth bed, clutching one of his sweaters. Even

17

though they don't smell like Raf anymore. The bloody cleaner is much too thorough.

Gita fiddled with her phone. 'Look at this site, "top ten surfing beaches in Cornwall", she said, holding up a photo showing a lad like Raf, charging through the waves, board under one toned arm, blue skies overhead. 'And this was Christmas.' Gita smiled widely, Santa Claus offering the best present ever.

Still, I hesitated. He might refuse. That last phone call … Bob saying smugly, 'Just give him time, Vicks.' Christ, there are moments when I hate my ex-husband even more now than I did when we were married.

'And what about Jane? When did you last see her?' Gita asked me earnestly. Ding, another hit.

Jane is the fourth in our gang, promoted to third once Rachel left uni, sweeping off in her cloud of glitter. I really needed her, in those last months before we graduated. Quiet and shy in her twenties, Jane isn't much louder now. The only downside is her husband. Jane hasn't got kids, so bloody Geoff has expanded to fill the space. She never seems to leave home without him. Geoff is fine, if you like obscure bits of law, or being informed of his views on them. If you'd rather manage without, you're in trouble.

'She really needs a holiday, I know that much,' I said slowly. Last time we'd met, there had been something wrong somewhere, but I couldn't tell whether Geoff's golf handicap had slipped, or whether the whole house had burnt down; she's always so restrained. I love that, of course. As Bob would say, it gives me the space to dominate.

I looked away and shrugged. 'Oh well, I suppose it might be fun …'

Gita whooped, *'Yes!'* and I let her. 'It'll be a fresh start for all of us.' She smiled. 'Everyone's been out of sorts. This will be a reset. You'll see. We'll come out of this better friends.'

I smiled and drank but I had my doubts – and they've grown every day. There could be advantages, sure. Time with Raf, time to find out whatever ails Jane, time with Gita, yes, those are good things. And Rachel is certainly never dull. But what about everything that happened before? After her Halloween party, at uni. Can we really pretend none of it mattered? That there weren't consequences, for any of us? Surely even Rachel's money can't paper over cracks that big?

But Gita was triumphant. 'Let's stay and have a pudding!' I couldn't say no. I relaxed back into my velvety seat. The weekend was still ages away, then. And, after Rachel appearing and disappearing like the genie from the bottle, I deserved a massive drink. I chucked the last of the wine into our glasses – happy to finish Gita's if she couldn't – and obediently clinked.

'Face it, you can't resist, can you? You want to know what on earth Rachel's got herself mixed up in now, don't you?'

I met Gita's eyes over the wreckage of the lunch: Rachel's untouched, fifty-quid risotto, and my own scoured plate. The waiters cleared the table and brought our chocolate mousse. One pot of temptation, two spoons. My resistance was very low that day. I dug in.

She was right, of course. Even now, after years making – as Bob pointed out in the divorce – a 'fucking fortune' of my own, there is still something fascinating about a silver spoon the size of Rachel's. I own my Canary Wharf apartment, and it's pretty jammy too – but Rachel could buy my block, the street, and half of New York, Paris and Rome on top, if she felt like it, from petty cash. Yes, I admit it, I wanted to see her latest acquisition, this island she'd just got her hands on. And the man who came with it.

So, there was curiosity. But my few friendships are important, too. Gita was right, everyone had been a bit off recently. Evading phone calls, dodging invitations. *Secrets.* Big, heavy secrets, which took up our time and made us hard work to be around. It wasn't just me. All of us needed to put things right.

When I braced myself to ask for the bill, the waitress smiled. 'Your friend has taken care of it.'

Gita and I exchanged glances. I'd really begrudged Rachel that bloody lobster. Then I whispered, 'Is it awful that I wish we'd ordered another bottle? Or two?' Gita giggled. But it was typical Rachel. If she'd said she was paying, I wouldn't have had to spend so much time resenting the mouthfuls she didn't take.

The five-hour train journey to Cornwall wasn't as bad as I'd feared – thanks to Gita. 'Sandwich, anyone? Now then, who's for cheese and onion crisps?' she kept on saying at just the right moment, delving into a massive cool bag. She really has that suburban uber-mum act down. That, and playing I-spy with her girls, got me and Raf over any soul-searching we might otherwise have had to do.

'Something beginning with … D,' said Ruby, the little one. We were all stumped as ditches, diggers, dells and doors flashed by and she turned the lot down. I swear, it was at least an hour before we gave up. 'Jumper!' she cried triumphantly.

'I'm getting a refund from that effing school,' Tom grumbled darkly. For once I sympathised with him.

Now I'm here on this godforsaken Cornish beach, and I still can't quite believe it. Mount Tregowan is opposite us, surrounded by sea. The wind is whipping through my hair. My posh new winter jacket, bought for going from desk to bar in Canary Wharf, is about as much use here as a tutu in a tornado. I should have known better – but I've never been this cold before down south. The sky is iron-grey and the sea's a match, while my face is being sandblasted to the colour of smoked salmon.

The island is a lumpy-looking stack of boulders, the sort of thing Raf used to make with his Lego years ago. It was forever embedding itself in the soles of my feet. I was that happy when he outgrew it. Now I look at him, silky dark hair ruffling in the breeze, and wish both my lad and his Lego were back. 'Let's make the most of this weekend, love?' I say to him, but the wind steals my words.

That must be Castle Tregowan, on top of the pile of rocks.

Little Ruby next to me shivers in her cagoule. I tut and reach down to drag her zip up to her chin. For all Gita's Mary Poppins ways, the kid, like me, needs a better coat. 'No, no, I'm not cold.' Ruby fights me off. 'I just don't like that place. It looks like where the bad fairy lives.'

She's right, it's Cinderella's palace gone to the dark side, with that turret, jet-black against the dying light. 'What's Rachel doing in a place like this?' I hiss to Gita. She could have afforded Versailles, all gilt and mirrors.

Gita shrugs. 'You know she's always had a soft spot for a bit of goth.' How could I forget? Yes, she's got the golden hair and wall-to-wall tan, but she actually prefers black magic. Like that dreadful party, when Gita and Tom had just got together. That was a Halloween thing, too.

Here we all are, twenty years later, turning up to another of Rachel's dos. I look down the line of us strung out on the beach, the girls rushing this way and that in a game of tag. For a second, it's idyllic. Then Ruby falls over and wails. The older girls ignore her. I throw a conspirator's smile Raf's way, but he's turned to help Ruby up. Gita and Tom have their heads down, oblivious, striding silently into the wind. And I suddenly get a really bad feeling.

'Is this all a terrible idea? It's not too late, is it? To go home?' I yell over to Gita. The gale does its best to gag me, making snakes of my sharp new haircut.

'What?' Gita struggles to hear, holding on to the ends of her scarf for dear life. Tom stomps off alone. 'No, no. Come on, Vicks. It's going to be *fun.*'

She grabs my arm and leads me forward, but I can't shut out her tone of voice. I'd been half-joking, after a bit of reassurance. But gone is her pretence that this is just a jolly weekend do. There is something much grimmer behind her words.

If I didn't know better, I'd think she had some kind of plan. Is it to do with Tom? Has she seen through him, at last? I glance

21

over and, of course, he's staring at me, a leer behind his eyes. I curse myself for looking and turn back to Gita as quickly as I can. Her expression is flinty for a second, then she grins widely. Is she trying to convince herself, or me?

All of a sudden, I shiver in earnest – and not just because of my useless coat.

Chapter 5

Rachel

Mount Tregowan, 30th October

I'm overdoing it. I always do. But this time even darling Ross, who never questions me, gave me a look when the last crate had been unloaded at the dock. 'Are you trying to drown them in champagne?'

Am I? Am I actually trying to atone, for that party long ago? But I dismiss the thought. No, I have something completely different in mind for this weekend. Something spectacular, and long overdue. A reckoning. And why shouldn't I be lavish if I feel like it? I can afford it. It is a mantra I've repeated so often over the years it might as well be tattooed across my forehead. But I never once say it aloud. I'm like the Little Mermaid. So much can never pass my lips.

That's the deal, with extreme wealth. I've got used to the burden, and not least to the fact that I can never identify it as such. *Burden* – no, that can never be said. No one outside the charmed circle can understand why it's almost a handicap, being born into what I have.

People assume I should constantly thank my lucky stars. They think money breeds money, stacking up like the gold coins in Aladdin's cave. Not so. I have to work to be this rich. I have to question the credentials of every adviser, check the share prices, select the paintings ... I never leave anything to chance, to fate. And I must never speak about any of this, to anyone. Money has its own *omertà*. 'Never complain, never explain' – that was about the one coherent sentence my mother left me with.

Then dealing with staff is, to be frank, a pain. Yes, it's nice not having to cook, for example. But first, catch your chef, as they say. Then things get formal; background checks, contracts, non-disclosure agreements ... It might be easier if I knocked up my own *coquilles St Jacques*. Though obviously that's not going to happen.

And that's leaving aside the issue of trust. Plenty of trust funds, precious little of the actual commodity. It's the one luxury denied me. Are my friends here because I've bought them, or because they actually like me? Welcome to living without ever really knowing.

That's why I've always been fond of Vicky. Respected her, even. I bet she was genuinely surprised the other day, when I paid for lunch. Admittedly, I used to mock her behind her back, laughing with Gita. I'd make jokes about her family having a bath full of ferrets or her daddy labouring down the black pudding mines, in an absurd fake Northern accent. Nowadays that's probably a hate crime. But all the time, I rated Vicky's ingrained resistance to the idea of my being born into staggering wealth. And she has remained true to her roots. Her City flat, once a warehouse, may be gentrified to the eyeballs, but her voice is not. Despite all her years in London, for Vicky 'baths' will always rhyme with 'maths'.

Now here they both are, Gita and Vicky, trudging up the path towards the castle. I'm watching them through the oriel window in my turret, the place where I've created my bedroom. Mine and Ross's. As soon as I saw it, I thought of Rapunzel. And I had to have it. Ross's daughter Penny didn't mind, not really. All right, it's a stretch, to picture Ross scaling the walls with my blonde hair wrapped round his wrists – I smile at the thought – but what he might lack in youthful athleticism, he more than makes up for. In other ways.

Gita and Vicky are chatting now as they follow the path. Behind them trails their baggage, real and metaphorical. Tom's in charge, with Vicky's Raf as his number two. They both have that musclebound build, perfect for shouldering luggage. Funny to think I once quite fancied Tom. Well, we all did. The three of us met him at one of the endless series of uni house parties we went to in those days, in scruffy bits of south London. For me, they are still some of the most exotic safaris I've ever undertaken. He was doing biomedical science then, before he swapped courses.

'What are you going to do with that?' I asked naively, when Tom grabbed my bottle of rather nice Châteauneuf-du-Pape the moment we crossed the threshold.

'Come and see,' he said with a wink over his shoulder. And I trailed behind him into the stinky kitchen.

'Ever seen anyone make a cocktail?' he asked. I suppressed the thought of the little beachside bar in St Kitt's that I'd rather taken to over the Christmas holidays, and of the staff at home for that matter, and I shook my head the way he wanted me to. He pushed the cork down into my bottle. I suppressed a wince. 'Couldn't be simpler,' he said, glugging the contents into an enormous pan, which looked like something Vicky's granny might have boiled her smalls in.

Then he added two litres of own-brand lemonade, chucked in a sprig of mint, scooped some into a plastic cup, and passed it over. 'Glass of Pimm's, milady,' he said, holding my eyes. Funny how sexy it seemed, for a minute. We were all so young, babies really. Tom already had that confidence, some indefinable air of command. No wonder he went for a job with a uniform.

I look at him now, manhandling the suitcases. He isn't in bad shape for his age. No dad bod there.

25

Back then, I could have sworn Vicky was keenest on Tom. But it was Gita who got him, and who now has those three girls to show for it. Tasha, the eldest, is as tall as her mother, and has her grace. She keeps a little distance between herself and her younger sisters.

Meanwhile, Vicky and Gita march on, oblivious to Tom's efforts to keep the youngest girl's case clear of the water. Now he's telling my favourite – sulky, gawky middle child Nessie – to keep up. I wonder if I'm going to regret extending the invitation to children. Ruby, the littlest, is really too young to join in with all the fun I have planned, but I couldn't exclude her. I didn't want to give Gita any excuse to duck out. Besides, Ruby does make up the numbers.

I laugh to myself, enjoying my private joke. I'm expecting Vicky to get it; she's the one with the talent for figures. But it'll go over the heads of the rest. And having drinks tonight will help disguise it. It won't be until we sit down, tomorrow night, for the Halloween feast, that they'll discover we are a very special group indeed. Thirteen of us, to be precise.

Lucky for some, they say. Not for others. I narrow my eyes at the group, focusing, assessing. Yes, this invitation was long overdue.

Gita and Vicky are laughing now. I hope they are excited; as excited as I am. I wonder what they make of my causeway. I adore the way it's revealed by the ebbing waters. It's so beautiful, now I've had it restored. And the way it leads straight to me, and Mount Tregowan, makes it a delicious cross between the parting of the Red Sea and the Yellow Brick Road. The thing I love most is its disappearing act. Twice a day, the relentless tides cover it, cutting off my castle completely.

When Ross told me the way the sea severs us from the mainland, I nearly swooned at the romance of it all. If he'd asked for my hand right there, right then, I'd probably have said yes. And it wasn't long after that he actually did. I had no doubts, none at all. When I look into his eyes, I'm home. He knows what it is to be surrounded by rumour and gossip, to need only a few loved ones to feel secure. That whole business with his first wife, for instance. The way he had it covered up. He's never discussed it with me, and I like that steadfast loyalty, reaching even beyond the grave. But it's still the talk of his little social circle here, and it didn't take long for me to glean the necessary. Bless Ross, thinking no one outside the family knows, believing this island keeps his secrets safe. He's such an innocent. I love that about him. And I'm so glad we've found each other, at last.

Of course, my splendid isolation is an illusion. You can always reach the island by boat, no matter how deep the sea lies over my causeway. Well, except in the most awful storms. It's a short hop. You need to be an experienced sailor, to weave between the rocks, but thanks to me, we now have the best mariner on the mainland at our beck and call. There are ways round anything and everything, always. But I won't be letting on about that. It breaks the spell of Tregowan; the legendary feel of a place that no one can leave – until I say so.

I step away from the window. I don't want Gita and Vicky to see me too soon, though I suppose it might feed into the Rapunzel theme, my blonde hair cascading from the oriel. But no, I want to be in full-on chatelaine mode when they finally make it up to the castle. I'll greet them at the heavy oak door, banded with iron bars. It opens with a groan from rusty hinges, swinging back on the splendour beyond. Yes, I could easily have it oiled, or plane the bottom of the door where it catches the stone, but there's no drama in that. Creaks and clanks go with an old castle. I'm only sad there's no portcullis to lower, no moat around us here.

What am I thinking? The sea is my moat. It will be rising up behind Gita, Vicky and the rest right now, a dark green wall, my careful restoration job a fathom deep by the time they're halfway up the hill. I love the way I've got the hang of the tides so quickly; it makes me feel part of the place. A rightful queen.

My dress for tonight reflects this. I've been torn, I admit, between wanting to lay down my position immediately and trying to avoid any derision from Vicky. But in the end, I know Vicky will always find something to be sniffy about; that chip is even more a part of her shoulder than Tom's epaulettes. So I've picked a simple, flowing Dior number that drapes with every move. Best of all, it billows behind me when I walk, like my own in-built train. I smile at the thought of pageboys to carry it for me. I would have loved that, but God, Vicky would have a field day.

The shame of it is that Vicky and I find the same things funny – but we can't ever acknowledge that we both find my situation absurd. I have to revel in it, as far as Vicky is concerned, and Vicky has to hate it, as far I am allowed to see. Maybe this weekend will finally be our chance to put all that behind us. We could become the true friends we always should have been. Or, just maybe, we could turn into sworn enemies.

So much is going to shift in the next forty-eight hours, so many secrets will finally come to light, thanks to me. I'm looking forward to putting my world to rights at last.

I'm going to make it a healing, positive experience, whether the others like it or not.

After all, what doesn't kill us makes us stronger. Doesn't it?

Chapter 6

Geoff

Mount Tregowan, 30th October

It is somewhat unfortunate, but yes, we did arrive late for Lady Tregowan's drinks. My fault entirely. I'm afraid I chanced on a bookshop, not far from the island, and I persuaded Jane that it would be a good idea to pop our noses round the door. 'I've clean forgotten to bring anything to read, and you can't pretend your Rachel is a books person,' I said. At that point, needless to say, we knew nothing of Lord Tregowan's library.

'She's not *my* Rachel, but fine,' said Jane. 'I told you, you should have let me pack.' I wasn't too worried by her expression; she loves a bookshop as much as I do. We weren't disappointed; it was an independent outlet with a good selection of ordnance survey maps. I'm researching our next walking holiday at present.

Jane made straight for the children's section, of course. Oh, not for our own little ones; we've not been blessed in that department. But Jane is an author. *The Melford Mice*? Tiny dancing rodents, who live in a house and garden very similar to our own. They have long been a favourite with the nation's offspring.

29

Jane often feels a little awkward amongst groups of mothers. I'm afraid females don't always grow out of silly, cliquey schoolyard behaviour. I include Rachel and her coven in this. But sometimes it can be good to confront one's fears. Anyway, when I looked over, Jane seemed happy enough amid the Kate Greenaways and there were only a few fractious toddlers playing nearby.

I was soon deep in my maps, lost to the world. It wasn't until Jane coughed by my elbow that I realised how much time had ticked by. One look outside confirmed the worst; the tide had turned and we'd missed our chance with the crossing.

For a happy moment, I thought I'd been let off the hook, and we could return safely home, with only the minor inconvenience of purchasing a new rail ticket to show for the weekend. But no; Jane had a plan B. She's very efficient, my wife.

I was rather appalled when we finally tracked down the boatman on the pier. Not only had the wind got up, adding a distinct chill to proceedings, but the boat he indicated didn't look particularly seaworthy. You would think, with the Cadogan millions at her disposal, that Rachel would have bought a nice new vessel. But no. We had to lurch aboard a leaky old skiff and sit amongst lobster pots and nets festooned with defunct sea life. I did quip to Jane that we might not arrive scented with the sort of *eau de toilette* that Rachel might expect. But she didn't seem to find it amusing.

At first I thought our skipper was going to row, and I believed we might miss most of the first night's festivities. But he soon got an outboard motor to splutter into life and then we were zipping along like billy-o. Jane certainly perked up, and I resigned myself to the approaching ordeal, her smiles a recompense for all I was sure was to come.

I've never much enjoyed the company of the Rachel set over the years, even at the most propitious of times – the usual slew of gatherings, drinks parties and the like, that keep the social wheels turning. And, with everything that's transpired recently,

I can truthfully say I am not looking forward to this at all.

However, with my good wife at my side, I am confident we will get through the event and emerge at the end of the weekend, as Henley put it in *Invictus*, 'bloody but unbowed'. Of course, Rachel's island isn't going to match the rest of that poem, and turn out to be a 'place of wrath and tears', full of 'the horror of the shade'.

Or at least, I certainly hope not.

Chapter 7

Jane

Mount Tregowan, 30th October

So we finally arrived half an hour late for the drinks. It was Geoff's fault. It usually is. I love him dearly, but what did I expect, marrying a lawyer? In his funny old head, he's always right.

As soon as I saw the bookshop, I knew there'd be trouble. And it was a mistake, saying we had to cross Rachel's blessed causeway at a certain time. That's Geoff for you. He doesn't much like deadlines, unless they're his own.

It's been a while since I've got up the courage to visit a bricks-and-mortar children's section. I always feel a fraud, as though the parents there have X-ray vision, and can see my withered, incompetent womb. They might force me out with pointed sticks, these mums and dads, if they knew the horrible truth.

But someone up there with a rare sense of humour has decreed that my mouse stories 'delight generations of little girls,' as it proclaims on my covers. So I have a legitimate reason to be there, keeping an eye on the competition.

Five years ago, the room I'd earmarked as our own nursery

finally got converted into the second study neither of us wanted, needed or could bear to look at, let alone work in. We didn't say a word as we slapped a coat of grown-up greige over the joyful yellow walls.

It's one of the reasons I can't ever get cross with Geoff. He's gone through so much for me. Well, we've both been through hell, but many men would have given up long since, decamped for the easier shores of a partner with a functioning uterus, her sturdy child-bearing hips the pathway to family life. Never mind, we've got dogs. I think of Dolly and Molly, our two little wire-haired Dachshunds, with the sitter at home. Though my heart pretends they're not substitutes, my head tells me differently. I can only just about resist the temptation to knit them bootees.

There's never a reproach. I must live up to his forbearance, I must deserve his tolerance. It's not easy. A lot of the time I want to hit things, including him. The worst bit is my dirty secret. *It's all my fault.*

I worry this lovely weekend is going to tip me over. I see Vicky every now and then, and she's casual about Raf, though I know he's the light of her life. I still feel proprietorial about him, having helped Vicky so much before and after his birth. That was when I still thought I'd have children of my own, some day.

Gita, meanwhile … Well, her Instagram is about as much of her as I can usually cope with. That beautiful string of daughters, they seemed to pop along at my worst moments, every time our hopes of a family were being dashed. Do I really want to see them in the flesh?

But Rachel – childless, haphazard Rachel. She will be a comfort. She's never been the maternal type. Now she's married a much older man, all that must be done and dusted. I don't suppose she cares a jot; kids would just get in her way. I can imagine her losing one at an airport, then deciding to board the plane anyhow. I must try to be more like her.

'Don't worry.' I smiled, as Geoff looked gloomily at the feet of water covering the island causeway. In theory, he's the details man, the punctilious lawyer advising clients on obscure pitfalls. And I'm the ditzy creative. But in fact, I deal with the day-to-day stuff. It makes sense. My books might sell for £20 as lavish hardbacks, for Granny to give to her favourite granddaughter as a disappointing birthday gift (even I know any child would prefer the latest gadget to rodent romps), but my share of the spoils is pennies. So I take up the household slack to make my contribution. Today that included knowing about the boatman.

I'm looking forward to seeing Vicky. Last time we had lunch I had a lot on my mind. She's super-busy and super-successful, and was even harder to reach than usual behind her financial wizard facade. 'What are these weekends of which you speak?' she said when I suggested she visit us. 'It's work, work, work, Jane. You know that.' I felt guilty taking up her time, when I wasn't making the most of it. Something was eating her up. I wonder if it was, you know, her *usual* problem. Even back at uni, she was always first in the queue for the bar.

I also know she feels she's failed with Raf. 'He'll be back. Once the novelty of living with his dad has worn off,' I said. Mind you, it's been well over a year now.

I've never been as close to Gita. Her friendship with Rachel was so intense, when Vicky and I first met, that it was easy to avoid her, even if I hadn't had good reason. When Rachel jetted off, we all plodded on, then graduated and scattered anyway. Gita was in the thick of her fling with Tom by then. Who'd have guessed it would actually end in marriage? And one that seems to be lasting, too. Then those three little girls, their adorable hand-knitted jumpers and long shiny plaits. 'More pictures,' Geoff would warn me, opening all envelopes from her. What would she do if she knew those photos ended up ripped smaller than confetti, and thrown in the bin? But now they are teenagers. You can't be jealous of someone's spotty, mulish brat, can you?

Of course they're not going to be like that, Gita's girls – they'll be slinking through adolescence as painlessly as their mother no doubt did. 'Are you sure you want to go on this jaunt? We can always turn down the invitation,' Geoff has said, more than once. But I'm braced. And Raf is something else again; Gita, Tom and I are all his godparents, and I've become one of his many devotees. He's a lovely boy; gorgeous, so sporty, a real credit to his mum. And his dad, I suppose.

By this point, Geoff and I had made it over to the boat. Now that I looked at it, the peeling paint, the interior coiled with ropes, the way that it swayed under the heavy-handed slaps of the water all around, I did feel a bit peeved about that nice dry path. But Geoff was mouthing *sorry* to me even as the boatman helped me clamber aboard. Once I'd got used to the rocking, I was a bit calmer. Geoff came to rest heavily beside me, with our bags, and I snuggled gratefully into his side. We cast off.

When we were clear of the jetty, the engine started and it was all rather fun. The wind whipped through my hair – farewell to my non-existent chance of giving glamour puss Rachel a run for all that money – and the little village receded. The waves were heavy, a deep grey-green that reminded me of Kipling's Limpopo River. I had a beautiful edition of the *Just So Stories* as a child – it was one of my inspirations when I started out. I turned and Geoff was yelling something. I'm pretty sure it was, 'Isn't this marvellous?'

I nodded and wrinkled my nose at him, remembering in a rush why I love him. And why I worry about him. I hope he's going to take advantage of this weekend to come clean. Finally. Otherwise, I'm going to have to say some things to him that we might both regret. If Vicky was distracted, then Geoff has been positively haywire these last few months. It's got to stop. He needs to open up. Otherwise, how can I help him?

Once we were safely across, with me just about hanging on to my lunch, we then had to get ourselves up to the top of the hill. I felt like Dorothy in *The Wizard of Oz*, contemplating the path between the overhanging boulders. Close to, the rock was black, volcanic possibly, porous-looking like a bath sponge, rather amazing. I was itching to sketch it. But by the time we'd slogged our way up to the top, I was regretting my sedentary life in front of a drawing board, and the way I threw that Fitbit tracker Geoff got me for Christmas into a drawer. I'm sure he meant well.

The first sight of the castle made up for it. Looming straight above us, it was even more imposing from this angle than from the shore. Sheer drama, *very* Rachel. The walls are surprisingly well pointed for a structure built in medieval times. Maybe the Tregowans have Rachel's trust fund to thank for that.

So, basically, there's no time to change before the drinks – and no opportunity either. The front door (it should be a grander word for a castle, shouldn't it?) opens straight into a magnificent hall, where everyone has gathered. We more or less fall in on the assembled guests, in my case looking like the wreck of the *Hesperus*.

My hands go automatically to my hair, but once I've touched its tangles, I really wish I hadn't. They're almost crispy after their battle with the winds and water. My jeans are wet around the ankles, thanks to being hauled in and out of the boat, and my fleecy jacket is many years old, on the naff side of serviceable, and had no claims to fashion even when brand-new. Geoff isn't quite as windswept – having significantly less hair has played in his favour for once – but I sense his minor country squire get-up of cords and sleeveless Puffa won't cut it with Rachel either.

There's a startled silence, then Rachel, like a mermaid in sea-green bias-cut satin, shimmers towards us. 'Jane! Both of you! How wonderful.' She couldn't be more welcoming, but now I really wish I'd shooed Geoff out of the bookshop earlier. I look as though I've come to unblock her drains, not rub elbows with her friends.

But, after the year I've had with Geoff, the mysterious silences, the broken nights when I've awoken to find his side of the bed empty and heard him pacing downstairs, I thought a weekend away would be the break he needed. So I didn't follow my first instinct and turn it down flat.

I take a breath. It doesn't matter if we're bedraggled, surely. This, according to the schedule one of Rachel's underlings emailed over, is the 'welcome drinks and buffet supper' before the formal 'Halloween Feast' tomorrow night. Shambling in like this, I'm just making Rachel look even better. If that's possible.

Rachel doesn't seem to have any of my doubts. She throws her arms wide and I melt into a wonderfully scented embrace. Her flesh is warm and yet smooth as marble against my cold (and probably now smelly) polyester fleece. I can't tell where her skin stops and the satin of her dress begins. Even Geoff's eyes seem to light up at the sight of her. Only to be expected. She's always been made for the three-syllable *a-ma-zing*.

I now have two questions I urgently want to ask, but can't frame out loud: how come she looks younger than when we were at uni – and why isn't she dying of hypothermia? The cold is still biting through my horrid jacket. Before I can protest, a uniformed (yes, really) maid steps forward and strips it off me, revealing an old T-shirt, which is worse if anything. But she gives me the consolation prize of a glass of champagne. It's so perfectly chilled that I can see a bead of condensation dripping down it, and without thinking I lick it off, raising my eyes in time to see Tom smirking. I turn. Time to take stock of the rest of the gang.

They all got here in time to change, I can see that much. Gita is in one of those 'desk-to-date' Ponte numbers, jazzed up with jewellery. It suits her neat figure, and the fig shade is perfect with that cloud of black hair. I usually think of her as our bombshell – but not when Rachel is in the room. She can't mind, they've been friends forever.

Vicks is in something pricey but uncomfortable, as per usual, her hair cut in a rather mannish crop. I wish she'd let me go shopping with her, like I used to. You'd never guess it from my

37

fleece, but I can tell what looks best – on other people, anyway. I'm an artist after all. There's no chance at the moment, though. Vicky doesn't want to let me, or anyone else, in. Oh well, a jacket with angles suits her personality, if not her looks.

Those willowy girls leaning over the minstrels' gallery above our heads must be Gita's trio. Each looks dressed for the event she'd rather be at. Tasha, the eldest, in shorts, tights and boots, is festival-ready; Nessie, the middle child, is awkward in voluminous clubbing black; and Ruby, the little afterthought at just nine, is like the fairy on top of the tree in a sticky-out skirt and purple top. As I watch, she sneaks her thumb into her mouth. Tasha is leaning over the balustrade, very intent. I hope some of Rachel's millions have gone into making sure that gallery is secure, it's a ten-foot drop to the floor.

There's Raf, over in the corner. He's doing his duty, good boy that he is, talking to an elderly patrician gentleman – who must be Rachel's new husband, I realise. God, he's *that* old? Not for the first time, I wonder what Rachel is up to. Flanking him are an odd pair, a middle-aged man and woman. She is as tall and thin as her companion is wide. The stepchildren, I reckon. The son is at least our age, the woman looks older still, with those big raw wrists you see on skinny women. And there's Tom again, now saluting me with his glass.

I turn on my heel, take a massive glug of my own drink, and gravitate towards Gita and Vicky, expecting Geoff to follow. 'Oh, I'll just say hello to Tom,' he says. 'You know, work stuff.' Oh God, I hope Geoff isn't going to pretend to be some legal eagle. Tom, now a high-up in the Met, must know Geoff spends most days fussing over which cats' home benefits from Great-Aunt Maud's will.

Couples with children have more camouflage for their faults, don't they? If it's just the two of you, with no small person running interference, then you soon know your partner inside out, shortcomings and all. But I wouldn't swap life with Geoff for anything. Except a child, of course. But that ship, like the little boat back to the mainland, has already sailed.

I insert myself into Gita and Vicky's chat. Both of them have at least five inches on me; I feel like a Babybel rolling between two elegant slivers of Brie. 'When did you get here? God, I feel such an idiot turning up in this,' I say. Immediately Gita does all that kind female twittering to make one of the flock feel better. 'Sorry, I interrupted. What were you talking about when I came over?' I ask, looking from one to the other. From the way they blink, I know for certain it was child-related, and therefore I am excluded. I sigh inwardly. Vicky is the least maternal woman I know, yet even she is within the magic circle I'm forever shut out of.

'Um, we were just saying, how fabulous is all this?' Gita says, her gesture covering the castle, the island, and Rachel too, her roll of the eyes drawing me into their little gang and away from my lamentable shortcomings.

I giggle along, but I'm thinking maybe, just maybe, now that we're all of a certain age, my childlessness should matter less. Things *are* getting easier. The time of disappointment is over – the years calculating my cycle, tempting Geoff to perform, then scrutinising my body like a forensic pathologist. IVF, acupuncture, mindfulness and Chinese herbs have all been binned. We're even nearing the end of other people's obsession with nappies, schools and unis. Soon we'll be able to talk to adults about grown-up things again. But not yet. I know what's expected of me.

'Your girls are looking so gorgeous,' I say to Gita. 'Chips off the old block.' Gita tries not to, but she preens. 'Did I tell you, Geoff's nephew – *our* nephew – has just done his Cambridge interview. Is Tasha at that stage yet? I've lost track.'

'She's applying for art schools, isn't she, Gita love? Gap year to get her portfolio up to scratch,' says Vicky.

'Really? Let me know if I can help at all,' I say to Gita, though I hope I haven't lumbered myself with tons of thankless work. I did look at the drawings by Tasha and Nessie she used to send with her Christmas cards, and they weren't too promising – but they were younger then. Girls seem to stop drawing when hormones kick in. All except me. Maybe that meant I never had the right hormones? I dodge the thought.

There are so many advantages to childlessness. No worries about what to do when they misbehave, for example. Ruby is demonstrating this nicely, getting fractious, bored as only an aspiring tween can be. She's made pellets out of tissues and is letting them drop accidentally-on-purpose from her balcony. Gita looks up anxiously, then glances over at Tom. Naturally he's turned his back on the problem. And I can do the same, chat away with Vicky, pretend I haven't seen. Another pellet plops at our feet. Gita breaks away with a tut to sort things out.

Vicky is just taking a deep breath – I can tell she's got something big to impart – when Rachel glides past Tom and Raf, towards us. She singles me out. 'Vicky, you won't mind if I borrow Jane for a second?'

I don't know which of us is more surprised. I'd thought that initial greeting was probably my lot. I was quite stunned to be asked to the island at all. I assume I made up a job lot with Gita and Vicky, with Geoff even lower down the pecking order. Rachel did look at him in slight confusion earlier, as though wondering who the hell he was. He'd be happy enough to tell her, given the chance. I mean, she's Rachel, she's irresistible. But it's me she's beckoning to, her lovely satin shifting and glinting in the firelight. Vicky is looking boot-faced at being abandoned by me and Rachel, and follows aimlessly.

'Funny how both Raf and Tom have blue eyes, isn't it?' Rachel says dreamily as she draws me closer to the fireplace, her glance flicking over the boy as we pass. 'And Vicky and Bob have brown.' Behind me there's a clattering sound; I turn to see Vicky quickly righting a vase that has toppled over on a shiny oak sideboard. Gita rushes over to help her. Ruby, looking thrilled, escapes from the dressing-down she's been getting from her mum. Rachel seems to be waiting for a reply, but I just shrug. I've been avoiding looking Tom in the face for years. I'm much more interested in this fireplace. It's big enough to roast a whole suckling pig at a village fete, though I'm sure the Tregowans have always been too posh to chow down with the locals. Judging by her husband's patrician looks, it's been swans and venison all the way.

I'm really impressed by how beautifully the place has been restored; the high ceilings, the tapestries, the ancestral portraits, even the rather horrible spears crossed high up on the walls. It's all exactly what you'd think of, imagining an ancient castle. I tell Rachel so, hoping I'm not gushing too much.

'Oh, I'm so glad you love it too,' she says, truly looking as though I've given her the best present ever. Her face is creamy and flawless in the flickering glow from those huge logs. 'Thank you! And I *adore* your books, I always buy them for Rupert's kids.'

I wonder for a second who on earth Rupert is. From her expectant air, I realise she is not only certain I'll know, but also thinks I should be hugely flattered. Then I remember – her ne'er-do-well cousin. There was endless tabloid coverage of his wedding to a supermodel, followed swiftly by an equally well-documented acrimonious divorce. I didn't realise there were children involved. I wait for the usual stab of envy, that this feckless pair – in the short, turbulent time they were together – managed to produce what Geoff and I have not, in all our loving, steady years. But maybe the champagne has deadened things. It's certainly slipping down nicely.

'Funny how you got into children's books, isn't it?' Rachel says conversationally.

'What do you mean?' I ask lightly as I can. But suddenly I am on red alert.

'Oh, you don't have to pretend with me, Jane. I know you got that termination in our final year. And what happened after.'

Rachel says it as though it's of no consequence, as though I'd nipped out for groceries one day on a whim. She doesn't even lower her voice. Now there's a ringing in my ears. God, am I going to faint?

I certainly haven't forgotten, the day I came back to my hall of residence room to find her sitting there, cool as you like, idly glancing through my bank statements – my private papers! 'I was looking for Gita,' she said, as though that explained her presence. And then she cocked an eyebrow and said, 'Snap! I see we've just been to the same clinic,' as though we were both members of some secret club. She left uni soon after, thank heavens. Why is she mentioning it now?

I look around wildly. Where is Geoff? Has he overheard? No, he's right at the other end of the room. But Gita and Vicky are much too close for my liking. Vicky is looking over at us. What's that expression on her face? No, no. Surely I'm being paranoid. But I'm gripping my champagne flute so tightly I'm worried it's going to shatter into a million pieces.

'Oh, don't fret, silly, I've never breathed a word,' Rachel says, seeing my face. And then she laughs. Her throat is so white, her neck so fragile. 'It's no biggie, is it?'

My mouth is open. I'm trying to assemble my scattered thoughts. *No biggie?* My life has been lived in the shadow of that day, that trip. The worst thing that's ever happened to me.

'Sorry,' she says, putting a hand on my arm for a second. 'You're upset. But all that was *years* ago, darling. Blood under the bridge. Let's change the subject. Gita's girls are so lovely, aren't they?'

I stare at her. Now, of all times, she mentions blood. When so much has been sluiced from me. And I can never bear talking about other people's children. Why would I want to now?

I've got to think of a way of getting Rachel off this topic, right now. I have to shut her up.

Forever, if necessary.

Chapter 8

Vicky

Mount Tregowan, 30th October

Did Rachel really just say that? About Raf? *Shit.* After I fumble her stupid pot upright – what a place to put it, right on the edge of this table – I stare into my glass, hoping I've just had a drop too much fizz, imagined the whole thing. But I know I heard her right. Yet when I dare to look back over at her and Jane, they're just carrying on chatting. Not rushing up to Raf, or staring at Tom. Doesn't either one of them understand?

I sidle over as subtly as I can. I don't generally go in for eaves-dropping – I'm upfront, me. But on the other hand, I need to keep tabs on this situation. That's how I hear what comes next. Rachel has what they call a carrying voice. I put it down to generations of her lot having to shout at each other across their grouse moors or in great barns of places like this one. Whatever, she virtually yelled it out across the room. Jane had a termination.

I have two reactions; wow, I can't believe it. And, thank God Rachel has come up with this now. Jane definitely won't be worrying about anyone's eyes for a bit. I can breathe again.

Jane's so shy, I really thought bloody Geoff was her first and only boyfriend. What on earth was she up to at uni? And as for who with ... My mind's a blank. There were boys around, sure, but they were mostly Rachel's. Or Gita's. I had my own long-term obsession, the less said about that the better. But Jane. I thought she was our vestal virgin. There wasn't a sniff of a lad, all that time. She'd go bright red whenever anyone (usually me) mentioned S-E-X. Just goes to show. Spot on, all that about the quiet ones.

I take a slug of my champagne. As Rachel is hosting us, this is the good stuff. I can't get my head around this Jane business. Not least when I think about all I've had to listen to, for so many years, from Jane and Gita. How much Jane hates children, from Gita ('she's never shown a blind bit of interest in my girls,' she's told me incredulously) and how much Jane would actually like to get pregnant ('another miscarriage. And I was so sure this time,') from Jane. Both have sworn me to secrecy. And I've actually managed to keep my mouth shut this time – unlike some people. I look over to Rachel, but she doesn't show a shred of awareness that she's dropped two bombshells. She just looks bloody fantastic, as usual.

Must be Geoff with the problem, then. Makes sense. Looks like he couldn't mount a rice pudding, that one. He's talking to poor old Tasha and she's clearly on the brink of dropping dead with boredom. For a second, I consider going over to save her, then I decide to save myself instead. I glance back at little Jane.

Yep, looks like she's trying to get Rachel off the subject of dead babies as best she can. I can see from her face the lass has had the shock of her life. I know how she feels. Poor thing is gesturing frantically at the fireplace, asking something. Her finger is actually trembling. Surely that's not going to work? Since when did Rachel care about fixtures and fittings?

But no, as I watch, I see Rachel's face light up. She's *loving* talking about the fireplace. I'd be a lot more interested in hearing about the abortion – who the father was, for instance – but I'm still trying to pretend I'm not listening. I'm nodding away as Gita starts filling me in on every single thing that's happened at the paper since we last met. Thank God she can talk for Britain.

Ah, I get it now. Castle Tregowan must be Rachel's new hobby. She had a stack of them, when we all lived together. At one point it was Esperanto, she was going to become fluent and get the family businesses to use it too. That lasted about a week. Then she wanted to be a Tantric healer. But that was so she could have a fling with the instructor – fair enough.

Poor Jane. She looks like a rabbit in the headlights. God, I bet she's regretting setting foot on this island. I'm with her on that one. Raf hasn't come within a mile of me yet and I can't face being the one to eat humble pie, sucking up to my own lad. When Tom's tongue isn't hanging out at Rachel, he's giving me weird glances. Geoff is Mogadon on legs, Ross Tregowan's 'kids' are a right barrel of laughs and the groom himself looks as old and dry as a stack of firewood. If he stands too close to the mantelpiece, someone might throw him on it.

Is there anyone sane on this island? Apart from me. Christ, what a party.

If I don't get another drink soon, I'll die of thirst.

Chapter 9

Jane

Mount Tregowan, 30th October

My heart is hammering. I gaze at the mantelpiece, seeing nothing, but after a while its beauty does the trick, and calms my frantic mind. Gradually, my panic recedes, my pulse slows. *Yes, Rachel knows, but she's known for years. She won't say anything. She's promised me. She doesn't even think it's a big deal.* I take a breath, steady myself.

Thank God I hit on the right thing, asking about the fireplace. I'd never have thought Rachel would have been so expert, but I suppose she's picked up some art history via that foundation of hers. If I wasn't still feeling sick with horror, I might even be impressed.

The fireplace is surmounted by a sort of huge cartouche of finely wrought plaster. There'll be a special word for it, but I don't dare ask. If Rachel's knowledge doesn't extend that far she'll be riled, and then who knows what she'll blurt out. I'm going to spend the rest of this weekend walking on eggshells – that much is plain.

I tune in to what she's saying, try to nod intelligently. 'It's a relief of the Tregowan coat of arms, of course.' Her smile is just the tiniest bit smug, as I scan her face anxiously. But she's only thinking of her new family's past. Not mine. 'I love all those lances, a bit like giant skewers. And what do you think of the castle in the background?'

I mumble something back, and my answer must have passed muster as she carries on blithely. I peer more closely. It's Castle Tregowan, but a curiously titchy version. Maybe this was the medieval equivalent of a humblebrag? Maybe the plasterers were really bad at perspective.

Or perhaps it was just a question of getting the emphasis right. Because, plunged right into the centre of the little castle, is another thin but deadly-looking sword, standing upright and proud. Your eyes go straight to it. You can almost see it quivering. And, as I lean forward, I imagine that, if you ever removed it, blood would well up, run down the castle walls, and pour into the sea.

Rachel's looking at it like the cat that got the cream, but I try and control a shudder and look away. Everywhere my eyes rest, I now spot another instrument of war. Spears, knives, hatchets. They are in the paintings, in the mouldings, even displayed in patterns on the wall. And there are definitely daggers in the eyes of Rachel's stepchildren.

Geoff is always saying I'm an utter wuss, when I turn down the opportunity to watch yet another war film with him. But I don't like it; I don't. I hate violence, pain, blood, I'd do anything to avoid confrontation. Look at me, even now. I can't slap Rachel round the face, for her horrifying, casual indiscretion, as I'd like to. I can't run screaming from the room. I can't go up to Vicky, who keeps staring at me, and tell her she's heard wrong, it isn't true. I'm not sure I can even trust Vicky to keep quiet. She's always had a habit of putting her foot in it, after a certain point in the evening. She once told Geoff loudly how much she preferred Peppa Pig to my mice. And once told me how boring he was. I suppose I'm just going to have to hope she's learned. Either that, or I'm going to have to shut her mouth for her. Oh, God, this is already getting horribly complicated.

I wrap my arms around myself, but it's no longer the temperature in the room giving me chills, or even my jeans, which are nearly dry now. The fire is scorching. I don't know how Rachel can stand so close to it, but then it looks as though she has nothing on under that Great Gatsby frock. Her body is amazing, for her age. Well, any age. I try and stand up a bit straighter, aware of my illustrator's stoop, about to go full-on hunchback any day now.

I glance over to Rachel's husband, head of this spear-happy clan. He stands in the shadows with his middle-aged children. I wonder if he actually wanted us all to descend on him this weekend. Does he like parties as much as Rachel? They seem to be unavoidable in their sort of set, so he's probably used to it. Even at uni, Rachel always loved to throw what Vicky would call a 'drink spotty,' mocking Rachel's cut-glass accent – though Vicky's disdain didn't extend to turning down the free booze.

Looking around gives me the chance to work on my composure. And the place is worth the scrutiny. The carpet I'm standing on is lush, the thickest Persian I've ever walked across. I've got a couple at home, but they're more hole than rug. The oak settle at the side of the room is glossy as a mirror, a genuine Tudor rose carved in its centre. Even now, I'm longing to run my hands over it.

'So, you like what I've done with the place? It's nice to have an artist's view.' Rachel leans forward and despite everything – her indiscretion, her knowledge of my darkest deed, her casual contempt for other people's privacy – I feel the seismic pull of her charm. What must it be like, to be so beautiful, to be in possession of so much power? Her silky hair tickles her almost-bare shoulder. The tiny satin strap slips down her arm yet again. Her green eyes are merry, as though we two are alone and in on a spectacular secret. I suppose we are.

'Oh, I *love* it,' I say, knowing I'll probably come over as envious. But that's exactly the response Rachel craves. Bowling people over with your wealth and taste ought to get tired. Yet Rachel is as childishly pleased as she ever was. I look over at the old man she's married. That's cruel, but he must be nudging seventy. And Rachel herself is so full of vitality, everyone around her seems a little greyer. As I scan the room, I see Tom staring at her with a strange look in his eye, almost avid. But what man wouldn't feel something, looking at Rachel's creamy bust rising and falling in scarcely adequate satin.

I realise I'm staring myself and decide to leave her orbit. 'I'll just, um …' I trail off, gesturing towards Geoff, who's somehow cornered young Tasha, descended from her Juliet balcony. It's vital that I double-check he was too far away to hear Rachel just now. Tasha is looking fixedly at the floor, the walls, the ceiling, her sisters or Raf, anywhere but at Geoff. Oh dear. Raf is chatting animatedly with Tom, both broad backs to the flames.

Vicky used to tell me it drove her mad, the way Raf had converted his room to a semi-gym, but still paid full membership at some city fitness centre. Well, it seems to have paid off – he's a personal trainer now, and apparently earning a fortune. Vicky is proud of that, even if her heart aches at his absence. Strange she's not chatting to him now. You'd think she'd be all over him, the way she's missed him. Maybe she doesn't want to crowd him.

I wonder what Tom and Raf are talking about at such length? Maybe Tom's trying to get some fitness tips. I smirk at the idea, though he's leaner than when I last saw him. He was sporty at uni, flexing that body all around our flat when he finally took up officially with Gita. But he was cerebral too, constantly looking for someone to have 'deep' philosophical debates with. He surprised us all, going into the Met's fast-track scheme. But he was like a bullet from a gun, even doing a stint in the armed police. I would have been beside myself, if it had been Geoff, but Gita seemed to take it in her stride.

Or maybe she did her usual, dangerous trick. Just ignoring things she doesn't like.

Chapter 10

Geoff

Mount Tregowan, 30th October

I'm a little surprised that Jane didn't give me the proverbial 'heads-up' about Tom and his career progress. I was under the impression he was still making his way through the lower echelons of the force. As a result, I felt quite wrong-footed when I attempted to enlighten him on one or two matters of criminal law I thought he'd find of value. I found him not only well-versed in such subjects, but apparently a presence on various task forces on the Police and Criminal Evidence Act. He wasn't averse to filling me in on the extent of his influence. Once he had held forth, I regret he showed lamentably little reciprocal interest in my own legal practice and instead scouted out Vicky's boy, the rather muscle-bound Raf.

They are now hugger-mugger in the corner, presumably comparing their biceps or some such nonsense. I must say I find the current obsession with fitness a little baffling, and Jane is of the same mind. I saw her looking askance at young Raf earlier. Though, when I cast an eye over our hostess, I suppose I do see the point of *some* exertions. I would not wish Jane to flaunt herself in such a way but it behoves me to acknowledge that Rachel can certainly carry off that frock she is, ahem, almost wearing.

As I am wondering whether it is the right moment to approach Rachel – I have, let's say, business matters I really should discuss with her this weekend – Gita's daughter Tasha appears at my elbow. Of course, I am more than glad to give her a little steer on future careers, finding she is at that interesting stage between A levels and university.

Running through the steps I took myself twenty years ago to achieve my degree and establish my practice seems the very least I can do to set the girl on the right path. I have barely reached the zenith of the story of how I qualified as a solicitor when Jane pops up at my elbow. She seems a little agitated, as she often does. When I met her, she was getting over some failed love affair at university and, even after all this time, she's a martyr to her nerves. I wonder if it might also be, well, a question of hormones. I find with the ladies, it so often is.

It's a relief, at this point in our lives, that she seems to have abandoned the quest to reproduce. It has certainly taken its toll, physically, mentally and, dare I say it, financially. When I think of the money we have lavished on the most invasive techniques … IVF does *not* come cheap. It's fruitless to think of the staff I could have taken on, the premises we could have moved to … It was my bounden duty to do my utmost in this matter, regardless.

Of course, it was Jane who suffered the most from all those procedures. The worst I had to cope with was a humiliating tryst with a plastic pot, with medical professionals tapping their feet outside and only a well-thumbed magazine for inspiration. And, of course, writing those hefty and distressingly regular cheques. Even as I think back to that grim time, Rachel flits past me, laying a distracting hand on my arm, and I quite forget my difficulties.

Where was I? Poor Jane. But when I turn to her I see she's perked up considerably since coming over. She really looks as though a load has been taken off her mind. I am gratified; I thought she had perhaps heard the expatiation I am giving young Tasha one too many times. Nice to know that she still appreciates my skill as a raconteur.

I take a sip of champagne to ease my dry throat and Jane leaps in. 'I hear you're keen on art. We should chat about it,' she says to Tasha.

Immediately the girl sidles away. 'I must just get a refill for Mum, looks like she's gasping,' she says. I should talk to Jane at some point about hogging the conversation. But now is not the moment – a gong is sounded somewhere. The summons to our repast, I assume. I look around eagerly. My discourse has given me quite an appetite.

Rachel raises her glass. 'Drink up, everyone. Dinner's ready.' Then she pushes back a velvet curtain and leads the way through a Gothic arched door.

I turn to Jane, but she's looking a little distracted again. 'Everything all right, my dear?' I enquire.

'Oh, I so wanted a chance to get changed. I feel ridiculous like this. I'm the only one who's underdressed.'

'Apart from me,' I remind her gently, but she only rolls her eyes.

As we follow the others through the doorway, Jane darts a glance at Ross Tregowan. 'Shouldn't he be inviting us all to dine? It is his castle, after all. That mouth of his looks just like a letterbox.'

I am about to remonstrate with her – the man deserves some respect, after all – when Penny slaps her glass down on the mantelpiece and strides past us. 'Well! That was a glance that could strip paint,' says Jane, a little more quietly this time.

Now Vicky is bustling ahead too. Maybe, like Jane, I am becoming oversensitive, but to me it looks as though she turns and gives us a very searching look. Meanwhile Tasha edges past me, following her siblings, who I regret to say are bickering again. Gita runs after them, with a rather cross look at Tom, if I'm not mistaken.

'Come on, darling. We don't want to be last *again*, do we?' says Jane. Obligingly, I pick up my pace.

But, if I had known that there would be so many peculiar undercurrents at play at this gathering, I doubt I would have let my dear Jane persuade me to make up the numbers this weekend. I need to have a word with Rachel – that is incontrovertibly true. Yet I am beginning to believe that having so many discordant elements around me while I do it, will not be conducive to the outcome I require.

I can't help giving my wife a tiny reproachful glance of my own. What on God's good earth has Jane got me into?

Chapter 11

Gita

Mount Tregowan, 30th October

I was so enthusiastic, when Rachel first came up with the invitation. A free break in Cornwall. All right, high summer would have been better. But October still sounded fun, and as we're a bit stretched financially at the moment, it seemed like the answer to all kinds of problems. Getting the girls through half-term, with Tasha needing to work on her art and Nessie approaching the dreaded GCSEs at warp speed. Keeping Tom busy. Not to mention taking my own mind off so much. And a break for Vicky might help her finally heal the rift with Raf. I've had less to do with Jane, over the years, but I've heard from Vicks how much she and Geoff could do with brightening up a bit.

Most of these problems aren't mine to solve; I realise that. It's just what I do, day in, day out at the paper. Sorting, smoothing, squashing all the bumps in the road. I come home, cast an eye over my brood, and I go right on thinking of ways to fix stuff. I know I shouldn't. But it's a hard habit to break.

It's like the way people always fall in with Rachel. I'm as

bad as anyone here; she suggests something, and immediately it sounds like the best idea in the world. Because, if she's involved, it will be. 'She's dangerous; you want to do what she says, but she doesn't hang around for the consequences.' Vicky first said that to me twenty years ago, when we'd only just met her. Before any of it, really.

But it was already too late. As soon as I met Rachel, I realised she was even better than me at getting stuff done. I communicate, try and broker compromises – she just leaps into action. It's a gift. And what a relief, to relax and let her do her stuff. I find it intoxicating. Until I have to deal with the fallout. But there won't be any this time. We're all older, wiser. Nothing bad could possibly unfold here, on this extraordinary island, in Rachel's lovely castle.

I hope Vicky will behave. She's quite the recluse, these days. Since Raf left. But she agreed to accept Rachel's hospitality. Now all she has to do is have an amazing time. I rely on my girls to be polite at all times and I'm expecting no less from Vicks. I hope she won't let herself down. Or me.

Anyway, here we all are. I hate being caught in the middle, but as usual I feel opposing forces gathering on either side of me. Tom's been in a weird mood since … well, a while now. For such a big tough guy, he's very sensitive. I wonder if one of the girls has said something to him today. They might easily have done. They're barely speaking to one another. That's nothing new but I worry it's more obvious here, out in the open as it were. Meanwhile Jane looks so sad in her fleece. I don't know why Rachel didn't send her up to change; it would have been kinder. But I suppose the drinks were in full swing.

God, a moment's inattention, that's all it takes. There's Nessie, swiping an abandoned champagne flute from the mantelpiece. I march over and she gives me the big eyes. 'What, Mum? I really wasn't going to …' But I don't wait for her to finish, I just snatch the glass – and drain it myself. She wasn't expecting that. Then we walk through the archway, the velvet curtain now swept back by a brass curlicue that looks authentically medieval.

I must say, Rachel has done a brilliant job with this place. It's Hogwarts gone mad. Ruby is in heaven, probably expecting to see Dumbledore any moment. My mind flashes to Ross Tregowan for a second, and I suppress the thought. *Not* fair to Rachel.

Even Tash, who these days does her best not to be impressed by anything, is staring as though memorising every detail. This passageway goes on and on. I'm not much into interiors – I got our news editor's wife to do up our house, in return for plugging her decorating business in the Sunday magazine – but even I can see every detail is perfect. Just as I'm wondering if we'll ever come out alive, we emerge into a room even more spectacular than the one we've just left.

Everyone's gazing round, saying 'wow' with their eyes, but terrified of looking like bumpkins in front of Rachel. But I don't care, I go over to her and slide an arm round her tiny waist. That gastric bypass is definitely working. 'What a fantastic place,' I say, gazing up at the distant ceiling. Four huge chandeliers dangle over the long table but there's more than enough light from all the sconces set into the walls. 'You've done an incredible job.'

I'm awed by the sheer grandeur. Even Jane looks dazed, and art and design is her thing. We once saw tapestries like these at Hampton Court Palace, on a family outing. I remember thinking how boring and dusty all that old embroidery looked. I was astonished at the little plaque saying it was priceless. These look like the rest of that job lot, to my very untrained eye. I hope Rachel didn't spend too much on them. On the plus side, they probably warm the place up a bit. I can't see any radiators, but there's a massive fireplace at each end of the room. I hope the girls are sitting near one. Ruby's had an awful cold.

'I'm so glad you like it,' Rachel whispers in my ear, and then beckons her husband over. Suddenly her arm is snaked round him instead and I feel the chill. But it's quite right that they should be entwined, like a formal welcoming committee. They've only just got married, after all.

To be honest, I don't think Vicky or Jane expected an invitation to the wedding – but I was a little sad. Fair enough, we had that lunch when she told us about the engagement. But then she shut me – us – out of the do itself. It was splashed all over my own paper. She could have given me a heads-up, if not asked me outright. The editor gave me a sideways glance, as if to say he now thinks my occasional references to Rachel – and obviously I'm no name-dropper – have been a bit exaggerated. The pictures showed *thousands* of guests. But that's by the by. And, being Rachel, she's atoning in style. Not that she really needs to. It was just a miscommunication. I'm sure of it.

Now, after smiling round at us vaguely and saying 'splendid, splendid' a few times, Ross stalks over to the plates set out at the side of the room. Everything's been organised as a buffet. With those long thin legs, he keeps reminding me of a praying mantis. But don't they get murdered by their mates? I must stop it. Rachel may be a diva sometimes but she's never yet ripped someone's head off and eaten it. I suppress a smile. That would be quite a Halloween spectacular, even for her.

Ross couldn't have been nicer when we reached the castle, though he does seem a little vague. It's probably the only way to get through things like this, meeting Rachel's many friends. His children are like a praetorian guard. Even now, Penny slides automatically into place by his side, and looks as though she intends to be glued there all evening. Shouldn't that be Rachel's spot now?

I glance at Rachel but she's fine, heading for the opposite end of the long room, having a word with one of the unobtrusive serving staff. The newlyweds are now so far away from each other they'd have to shout to be heard, or send a carrier pigeon across the cavernous hall. But then I see Rachel blow a kiss to her husband, and he taps a hand to his heart. It's quite sweet. I turn away. Roderick, Ross's son, is right behind me, looking like he's eaten a wasp. 'Stubbed my toe,' he explains. I look down at his shiny brogues and up again. There's nothing but carpet around us.

'We haven't met properly yet, I believe,' he says in a careful high voice. 'I understand you work for *that* newspaper.' My smile becomes fixed, and I look around instinctively for Tom. Defending my tabloid's reputation definitely gets old. Everyone has a view on red-top papers; I'm not sure why they think I want to hear it, though. Some assume I can single-handedly bend our editorial stance around to reflect whatever their personal bugbears may be. Newsflash – I can't. There's a limit to the problems even I can solve.

'And what do you do?' I deflect. I've now located Tom; he's with the girls, getting plates and persuading Ruby that yes, she will need a napkin. He's not close enough to help me. But I've seen off similar onslaughts often enough.

'Do?' Roderick looks dumbfounded and I realise my mistake. He's another lotus eater, of course, not so very different from Rachel's other friends. But then he confounds me. 'Oh, I manage the estate here,' he says.

Even with zero knowledge of tourist attractions, and this island in particular, I can see this would be quite a job. The place is usually open to the public. Rachel's closed it, especially for us. The girls thought that was super-cool when I told them. I was hoping there'd be those scarlet ropes hanging across doorways saying 'private', so we could breeze through. I knew they'd love it and to be honest I would myself. I haven't spotted any yet but I live in hope.

So normally we'd be dodging the crowds, eager to see the self-same tapestries that I'd put in the next parish jumble sale, given half a chance. With my management hat on, I ask Roderick what the entrance fee is, and the normal number of visitors at this time of year.

I wonder if it's the thought of the revenue being lost this weekend that's making him and Penny so sour. Or is it the way their dad has landed Rachel on them?

I catch Roderick darting his father another vicious glance as the old chap blows another kiss at Rachel. He carries on giving me succinct answers about the running of the estate, though. Not revealing too much, but showing me that he's definitely not a figurehead; he knows what he's doing.

'And is Penny part of the family firm?' I ask. Roderick looks alarmed at the very idea.

'No, no ... er, it's not her sort of thing,' he says quickly. 'She did some nursing, of course, after all the ... but then, well. She, I suppose you'd say, she's retired.'

Retired? She's older than us, but not by much ... I smell a story, but I'm too canny to pursue it. I'm off duty. We all are.

Though, having said that, no one looks relaxed. Even Vicky's Raf, who's usually so laid-back he's moments from unconsciousness, is standing bolt upright over by that pillar. He's been dragged into a conversation with Penny and Geoff. I can't imagine him loving their company.

What on earth is Tasha up to? She's taken a plate, and put a few of the fancy canapés on it, but she's holding it at such a rakish angle that everything's going to hit the floor in a second. I can't stop myself; I shout over, drowning out Roderick's painstaking explanation of the tides and rather underlining the fact that, though I've been nodding along like a good girl, I basically don't care how often the waters come and go. Tasha flushes bright red at my intervention, but thank goodness the snacks haven't hit the floor. Vicky looks over and we exchange a wry smile.

Once Tasha's colour is back to normal, I turn back to Roderick and set him off again, this time talking about the landscaping of the island. When we clambered up to the castle, there seemed to be solid rock as far as the eye could see, so I'm not quite clear what his efforts contribute. But I look interested, even while I'm scanning the room for Tom. It's become a reflex.

It's OK, Tom doesn't see. He's down the other end, still with our girls clustered around him. I'm glad they're getting proper time with him, but he ought to circulate. Normally he needs no bidding. I wonder if he's feeling all right. And the girls should chat to other guests, not clump together.

Nice that Raf and Tom get on so well. Raf's spent a bit of time at our place since moving out of Vicky's. He must have really missed having a male role model at her place. She isn't exaggerating when she calls Bob a tosser. I smile mechanically as Roderick comes to the end of a spiel about the special conifers that grow in the region, and make some 'gosh, really?' noises.

As Penny is already munching one of those long grissini breadsticks, I figure it's all right to start eating too. It's usually up to the hostess to give some sort of signal, but Rachel is fully occupied. She's finally made it back to her husband's side and I sort of wish she hadn't. They're smooching. Ugh, I hope that's not 'tongues', as the girls would say.

Vicky's over near Jane now, talking animatedly to Geoff. Wonders will never cease. She's already waving her glass at a server for a refill. I hope she's going to pace herself. Rachel has disentangled herself from Ross and drifted over to Tom. 'What's up with your, um, stepdaughter?' I hear Tom ask Rachel, cocking his head towards Penny. 'Looks like she's seen a ghost. And not a friendly one.' I stare at Tom. Sometimes he forgets he can't just interrogate people when he's off duty. Rachel isn't bothered, though.

'Oh, you'll hear about it. Everyone still talks about it. There was a car accident here years ago, killed her mother. Penny's never been the same since,' Rachel says casually – and a little loudly. Penny is talking to her father but I see her head swivel immediately. Oops. It's the cocktail party syndrome. I wrote an article about it years ago. People can hear their own name even through a babble of conversation. I do hope Rachel knows what she's doing; she doesn't always take other people's feelings into account. But the next moment Penny has turned away.

Out of the corner of my eye, I see Ross has stalked over to Geoff and Vicky. Now Penny walks abruptly over to Jane, bumping into a side table as she goes. Part of me is amused at the Tregowans' innate politeness, doggedly tolerating their guests, circulating as best they can. They're probably trained at birth to allot ten minutes to everyone at dos like this.

Well, I've had enough of standing, even if everyone else is on their feet. These kitten heels are murder. And I can't eat and chat and stand all at the same time. I drag out a heavy chair and sink gratefully onto the rush seat. It's not nearly as comfortable as it looks. That's antiques for you. I turn to Roderick, who is now towering above me. I hope he's not going to go through the island plant by plant.

But just as I'm preparing myself to brush off more journo skills, get him onto a more interesting tack, Rachel sits next to me, alighting like a gorgeous hummingbird, and puts her hand on my arm. I notice her nails have been done to match her dress, some sort of aquamarine. It's a reminder of all that water outside, which by now must be swirling not far below the castle's windows. See, I was listening to Roderick's tide explanation really. A bit. Rachel's eyes look all the brighter against the shade.

'I'm so glad we could do this, aren't you?' she says. Immediately, I feel as though we're twenty-one again, in a conspiracy against the rest of the world, and I can borrow some of Rachel's delicious certainty, the way I used to slip into her Chanel shoes. That assurance that success is coming, is just round the corner. Sometimes I think I've got it. Job, children, husband. Tick, tick, tick. As long as I don't look at any of it too closely. I've made my way in the world, the way I wanted to when we were young. But not, of course, to the extent she has.

'So, Lady Rachel at last?' I whisper to her. It was always one of our little jokes, via our mutual passion for *Love in a Cold Climate*. For me, Nancy Mitford was as far removed from real life as any other fairy tale, but for Rachel it was like flipping through the family album. I always teased her that she was Debo Devonshire, holding out for 'the Duke of Right'.

'Lady *Tregowan*,' she corrects absently. Just two words, but they sting. After a second, I say with a laugh, 'Sorry, milady,' and tug my non-existent forelock. I'm sure I now know more about Burke's Peerage than she does. For years I had to make sure it was applied properly across all our papers, whenever anyone with a title popped up. I thought she realised. I turn to Roderick.

Then her soft hand comes down again on my wrist and presses warmly. I turn back, leaving Roderick to chunter on about igneous rock. I'm not sure he'll notice I'm not listening.

'I'm a bit tense tonight, I don't know why,' Rachel says, eyes wide. 'Tomorrow's the big feast but everyone seems a bit ... off, you know?'

'It's funny you should say that ...' I start, but Rachel's away. Sometimes she's even more of a communicator than I am.

'I just want everyone to have a good time, and fall in love with this place – the way I have,' she says. For a moment I think she's smiling at me, then I realise she's twinkling right over my shoulder to Ross at the far end. He tips his glass towards us.

'I'll drink to that,' I say anyway, and we do a little clink.

Before I have a chance to take a sip, she's spotted Jane fidgeting on the fringes of Raf and Penny's conversation. She calls over. 'So Jane, come here, tell us all your secrets.'

Am I imagining it, or does poor Jane tense up even more? 'I'm worried about her, she's really looking ... unwell,' says Rachel under her breath. Jane's put her fleece back on and I detect Rachel's faint wince. Jane walks slowly, almost reluctantly, towards us.

'I have to squeeze in the gym and the odd haircut between everything else, but *I* manage,' Rachel whispers. Briefly I remember the bypass, which must be helping – just a little. I suck my own stomach in. Despite the bulletproof lining of this dress, three children take a toll.

'Come *on*, hon, over here,' Rachel does reeling-in gestures to Jane and she speeds up, still as though she can't believe she's in

Rachel's spotlight. Finally she's chugged over to us and Rachel has pushed out another chair, though I'm sure she'd prefer we were all standing and mingling effortlessly, like people do in films.

'What about your latest book?' Rachel says excitedly. 'When's it going to be out? I want to be first with the news for Rupert.' The words are flattering enough, but Jane, in the middle of taking a sip of her champers, splutters. Nessie, who's walking past, turns to pat her on the back but I catch her eye. Thumping a sister is fine; not an adult she doesn't know. I hand Jane a napkin from the table. 'Oh God,' says Rachel, clapping her hand to her forehead. 'I'm so sorry. Penny has a friend at your publishing house and she said there'd been a few authors axed recently ... Not you, surely?'

Unfortunately, no one else is really talking much. The room is suddenly hanging on Jane's response.

'Not that I know of,' Jane says eventually, cheeks scarlet. 'Just a tiny delay, my editor says. It'll be out soon.' She narrows her eyes at Penny.

I plunge straight in. 'Tell us about your honeymoon, Rach,' I say. It's not that subtle, but Rachel has just said she wants everyone to get on. After a beat, Rachel takes the bait, then bats her eyelashes at Ross, who promptly blows yet more kisses to her across the room. It's been years since Tom and I were at the lovey-dovey stage. I take a big sip of my drink.

Rachel's on her feet now and gliding over to her man. I'm not mistaking the look Penny gives her when those silky bits of dress flick out and inadvertently catch her shins. As soon as Rachel's level with her new husband, she dips one hip so that she can rest her head on his shoulder.

I hadn't noticed before, but the Lord of the Mount isn't that tall. Like his son, I suppose. He just appears it because he's so – forgive me – skinny. And, next to Rachel, so beautiful and vivacious, he looks like he could do with a bit of a check-up from one of his wife's doctors.

I turn back to Roderick, wondering what on earth I can find

as a topic that will span both his interests and Jane's. I don't suppose he cares about publishing, and she's too airy-fairy for the nuts and bolts of business. Yet, when I see his face, I realise it's a wasted effort anyway. He's staring over at towards his stepmother, and her new husband.

His expression is intense. I've heard the phrase before, but I've never known, until now, exactly what it meant. *If looks could kill.*

But which of them is he glaring at?

Chapter 12

Vicky

Mount Tregowan, 31st October

Jesus Christ. I lie in bed for a full five minutes or so, wondering why someone is hitting me repeatedly over the head with an axe. Then the usual realisation sets in. And the backwash of remorse, that doesn't go away. No matter how often I have a crippling hangover.

It's not fun, piecing together the night before, wondering what I've said to who, and how to get out of it. Sometimes I have to send a grovelling text. Or decide not to see someone again. Maybe forever. I suppose Bob comes into this category. He saw me at my worst, for sure. Definitely better for Raf that we split.

No matter how many times I tell myself that, it still hurts. But never mind that now. Getting up this morning is going to be bad enough, without rehashing the mess of guilt and regret that is my divorce. I put out a hand blindly for my phone, but it's not where it always is, on the bedside table. Because I'm not at home.

Bloody hell, I'm at Rachel's stupid castle. In the middle of the sea. Is it the Atlantic? I gave up geography at fourteen, part of my strategy to get up and out. All I needed was enough grasp of the compass to go south, and shake the money trees down there. Well, I've done that, and a lot of bottles have fallen out on me.

I'm never going to drink again.

I fumble more and find my bag. My fingers know their way to the paracetamol in the side pocket without being asked and I chew the pills down dry, the bitterness making my face scrunch. After a while I can open an eye and see the welcome sight of a huge glass of water. Too late to ease the path of the pills, but it will take the taste away. I glug it down, some running onto the pillow. Now I worry. Did I put the glass there – or did someone else put me to bed and pour it for me, knowing full well how badly I'd need it? God, I hope I haven't made a total tit of myself in front of Raf. That's all the excuse the lad needs never to speak to me again.

I look down. I'm undressed. That's a good sign. But I haven't made it into my nightdress. Not so good. I'm just in last night's granny knickers, necessary for that tight dress. I call these my iron ladies. Not a pretty sight. I pray even harder there were no witnesses. But no, there won't have been; other people only take off shoes. Unless they're perverts. So present company in this castle mostly excepted, though there are a couple of question marks – and one big leering tick.

Now chunks of the night are coming back to me. They're not too bad. Relatively speaking. I don't think I was awful. No, no, I really wasn't. In fact, I don't think most of them would have noticed I'd had a drop too much. Everyone was drinking, not just me. I more or less remember leaving my clothes in that heap over by the door, now. Thank God.

The flash of appetite is another sign of recovery. What are we doing about breakfast? I'm sure Rachel has organised something. It might have been on that email but I have no intention of attempting to find it now. First, I need a shower. I think we kept to champagne, which makes it surprising that I feel this bad. A wash will put me right.

I didn't bring a dressing gown. I stick my head out of the door and immediately spot Tom, peering round the corner of his and Gita's room. Had to be him, didn't it? I retreat, and sit on my bed, head in hands.

There's a knock. I stiffen. 'Come in.'

But it's Gita. 'You OK?'

'Been better,' I mumble gracelessly.

'Here, have this,' she says, proffering actual coffee.

'Have I told you you're a bloody goddess?' My eyes are brimming with gratitude as I sip away. It's scalding, but immediately things are better.

'Not often enough. Why don't you nip and have a shower? Tom's just finished.'

For a second, I hesitate, then I see a fluffy towel on the floor, presumably where I threw it last night. Shall I ask her?

'Did … did I behave myself?'

'What? Last night? Don't you remember? You were the life and soul.'

Just as that's sinking in, Gita expands. 'You were completely fine. No dancing on tables. No dropping any clangers. No eyeing up the hostess's new husband.'

'As if.' I shudder. Then I remember. Rachel talking about eye colour. *Raf's*, to be precise. Shit. Why did she suddenly mention that? All right, it's easy enough to spill a secret when you've been a little, shall we say, over-served on the wine front. I've done it myself. I've said harsh things, to Bob, of course, and also to Raf. But Rachel wasn't even tipsy. Did she realise what she was saying? I shake my head, then remember why that really isn't a good idea.

I turn back to Gita, taking in the purple, bruise-like shadows under her eyes. She hasn't done her make-up yet. 'Is it me, or is all this a bit more of a strain than we'd bargained for?'

Her shoulders slump, then she flexes them. 'I'm putting it down to first-night nerves. I just hope my lot will behave.' For a second, I think she is just talking about her girls, but then my mind flashes to Rachel in that dress last night, and the look Tom was giving her. How does Gita stick it? I study her and there's something in her eyes. Maybe the worm is turning? I can't wait to see how that plays out, Gita finally taking Tom down for his behaviour. Then she's speaking again and I try to concentrate. The coffee is helping. 'Tonight's feast is going to be *great*, you'll see. And Rachel's got plenty planned before then. You'll love it.'

Organised fun. My favourite. *Not*. I let out the groan I've wanted to unleash since I opened my eyes. Gita just laughs. 'Scoot along now. Otherwise my girls will get in there and you'll have missed your chance. The teens alone take at least four hours apiece and Ruby is even worse.'

'Can't be the only bathroom in the castle,' I grumble as I pick up my sponge bag.

'It's the only one within easy walking distance.' Gita smiles, and for once the grin I return is genuine. At last, I'm beginning to feel I might just enjoy this.

Chapter 13

Rachel

Mount Tregowan, 31st October

Of course I've wondered what to do with them all, how to fill in the time before my special moment comes. The one I've been waiting so long for. That has to be in the Great Hall, and as close to midnight as I can get it. Just for the drama.

So today, before the feast, I'm going to keep my guests busy. We're going to have a little hunt, all over the island. People will be finding clues, building up a picture. I hope it will point them all in the right direction – without, crucially, giving the game away. I wouldn't want that. I won't be cheated of my big reveal. And its consequences.

I can't help but notice how much the group has frayed. People are wandering off at tangents, and even if they aren't physically distancing themselves, they're mentally all over the place. Once or twice, I've wondered quite simply if these people, my great friends, even get on anymore. I suppose a little of the blame lies at my door. I've been so busy with other things, I haven't had time to bring everyone together. But it shouldn't all fall to my lot, should it?

Realistically, there was always bound to be some tension within the couples. I mean, years on, things get tired, don't they? We can't all be love's young (*ish*) dream, like me and Ross. I think of him and smile. But even with me, Vicky and Gita, things aren't as they were. I suppose many years have passed, and when I've seen the girls (girls – they're not that anymore, of course, but what else can one call them?) it's been over the course of a dinner or a drink, not for hours on end.

I'm not regretting the whole thing, of course not. But part of me wants to fast-forward to tonight. That's going to be the fun bit, for me, anyway. Till then, I'll need to get everyone fed and watered, then out and about. I want them to get to know Mount Tregowan properly.

And, of course, it gives me more time to do what I like best: sit in my tower, surveying the mortals scurrying around my island like ants, and planning my next step.

All that sounds cold, but it's not. I'm only interested in justice, in putting things right at long last. There will be consequences, and things will definitely be uncomfortable at first. But I want to help us all to move on, and to help everyone understand the part they'll be playing in my future. I need to give tonight the best possible chance of success. And this is the way to do it.

Bear with me. Like all my most cunning ideas, it's going to pan out beautifully.

And collateral damage isn't such a big deal, is it?

Chapter 14

Gita

Mount Tregowan, 31st October

In the end it was Tasha who had read through the instructions properly and marshalled us all for breakfast, just in time. Everything was laid out in yet another large room just off the entrance. We were led there by a different maid. I'm not even sure how many of them there are. Tom might know – I've seen him giving them the odd glance. Or two. But I'm not going there. This weekend is our chance to reconnect.

I'm impressed with Tasha, I must say. Sometimes she's more like me than I am myself. She rapped on our door, good and early. We didn't need to disentangle ourselves, which was lucky I suppose. 'Are you decent? Time to get up and get breakfast,' she trilled.

'Can you wake your sisters?' I pleaded.

'They're already up,' she said, before striding back to her own room.

'Am I this bossy?' I asked Tom, my eyes still shut.

'No comment, m'lud,' he mumbled.

'Cheek,' I said, mock-whacking him with a pillow.

Just as well I checked on Vicky and got her into action. Tasha couldn't quite have taken that on. But Vicky's always fine after she's eaten something.

I can't help exchanging a tiny smug glance with Tasha when poor Jane trails down to breakfast with Geoff, just in time to see the staff clearing the last of the plates. She looks around mutely and it's Tasha who tells her, 'The email did say breakfast until 10.30. There's a coffee machine, though.' Geoff almost tuts at that and strides off after the maid. He's back a few minutes later, all self-satisfied, telling Jane it's sorted.

'It's like a hotel … but not,' Jane says quietly to me, and I signal agreement with my eyebrows. I don't feel right criticising Rachel overtly. She's hosting us all, for goodness' sake. The least we can do is obey her rules.

I've never pegged Jane as a rebel before; she always seemed too meek. But she's pretty unconventional, now I think about it. I suppose creatives have a different take on things. Even today, after moaning about being stuck in her fleece last night, she's in something pretty much identical now, a sweatshirt and some sort of jeggings. I understand the need for comfort, of course I do. But this is Rachel, after all. Her dress for the last Met Gala turned into an Internet meme. She really doesn't do casual.

Speaking of our hostess, there's been no sign of her yet. I'm happy to linger over my excellent coffee – there's a clever little machine dispensing barista-type brews, and flasks of hot water for tea – but Nessie and Ruby are getting restive.

'Muuum, there's no mobile signal *at all*.' Ruby's tone is bewildered. How could anyone do this to her? Actually, I'm a little surprised myself. I think my phone was connected last night. I take it out, and sure enough, there's nothing now, not a single bar.

'You two can go out and chase a signal – there's bound to be a spot where the reception is great,' says Tom.

I'm about to say *be careful*, but Tom gives me a look. 'Let them live a little, for God's sake,' he says. I suppose he's right, I shouldn't transfer my own anxieties onto them. And nothing bad could happen here, could it?

Ah, here's Raf, sauntering in. He's keen to grow his personal trainer business so we're soon discussing all his latest ideas. It's lovely chatting to him, I hope he and Vicky will get a chance for that proper heart-to-heart today.

I'm worried about Vicky. She's drifting farther and farther away from us, her friends. She's been putting off our catch-up lunches for ages, now. She hasn't really been the same since Raf left.

Things are spiralling; anyone can see that. She was late to our last lunch, with Rachel. I didn't say anything then, I knew she'd be furious. But as soon as she sat down, I could smell why. That tell-tale waft. Vodka.

It sounds melodramatic, but sometimes I think she is in danger of disappearing altogether. Maybe she thinks she's protecting her little secret, though it couldn't be more obvious if it tried. Raf hasn't said a thing to us, but I'm sure her drinking is the reason why he moved to Bob's. And why he spends time with us.

Poor Vicky. I want to help her.

But will she just shoot the messenger?

Chapter 15

Vicky

I feel better once I've grabbed a few things from the buffet. It's not *Downton Abbey*; no kippers under silver domes, but there's fancy granola, fruit. An array of cheeses and hams, very continental. And those dinky packets of cereals I used to hanker after as a child. No chance of those for us; my mother only lugged home the monster own-brand boxes.

Normally I'd dig in, bit of everything, but today I'm just after portable booty. I snag a few croissants and pastries, wrap them in napkins, and fill my travel cup right up to the brim with the coffee. It's hard manipulating the big front door with all this stuff, I have to put it down to fiddle with the catch. A maid glides into view and whisks the bolts across before I can even ask. I'm embarrassed. I wonder if she saw my hand shaking? Does she think I'm a lush? I look away and mumble my thanks.

Outside, the wind is still up but it's a bit less mad than it was on the beach yesterday afternoon. God, we've been here forever already. The place is beginning to feel curiously familiar.

Now where shall I sit, to have my breakfast? I look around, and despite myself I gasp at the view. I mean, it's breathtaking. I can see white horses on the waves nearest us. The sky is a piercing blue. It looks almost as good as it did in the picture Gita showed me of that surfer lad, though it's pretty brisk.

God, I hope Raf won't try surfing here – those rocks below look lethal, sharp as knives. I don't want to peer down anymore; it's making me dizzy. So I look around instead. There's a path skirting the castle, and rockeries built between the boulders, allowing whatever plants can stand the wind and salt to lodge and grow. I can see it's been professionally done, with great cushions of tessellated greenery. I've seen stuff like this on Instagram.

Here, at the point furthest from the mainland, round the back of the castle and facing straight out to sea, is a bench. I sink onto it gratefully. The rocks on either side act as a natural windbreak. It's a bit like being at a hair salon, inside one of those old-fashioned dryers. There is noise all around you – wind, waves – but you can tune it out. I prise the top off my coffee and take a long swig.

This is heaven. And it is Rachel's. I've envied her before, more often than I care to admit. But today I really understand for the first time the difference money can make. Imagine owning this, a chunk of the world that is yours and no one else's.

Well, apart from her husband, of course. And those middle-aged children. Rachel, with kids at last. I snort to myself as I remember their faces. Penny, so twitchy, and Roderick, with that slightly moist look. *Good luck bringing those up, Rach.*

There's a cough right behind me. I turn, and of course it's Roderick. Had to be. For a dreadful moment I wonder whether I spoke out loud. I say hi, to cover up. 'Just enjoying this amazing view.' It's hardly original, but we can't ignore each other, or the sea, I suppose.

'I love this spot. It was one of my mother's favourite places,' he says, sitting down next to me. I suppress the instinct to scoot over to the far end of the bench. I hope he can't smell any backwash

76

of alcohol. They say it leaks out of your pores for hours. Yes, I've read all the stuff on those websites that try to put you off. It works brilliantly until about 6 p.m. every night.

I search for something to say, latch on to his melancholy remark. 'You must miss her.'

To my horror, he fishes a tissue out of his pocket and stems his brimming eyes. 'Every day.'

Oh God, I'm so bad at this. And hasn't she been dead for years? 'I'm sorry, love, I didn't mean to make you …'

'It's not you,' he says indistinctly. 'It's just … this weekend.'

'Ah.' Oh dear. I don't think any of us gave Rachel's newly acquired in-laws a thought, least of all worried about their sensitivities. I rack my brains for a sympathetic comment. 'It must be so difficult.'

It's lame enough, but does the job. 'You're very understanding,' he says, turning watery eyes to mine. I'm not, but now isn't the time to disabuse him. What do I do next? Try and get him to talk about his dead mother? No, that's a bit amateur therapist, isn't it? Plus the idea of more tears appals me. Change the subject? Thank goodness, before I have to decide, footsteps crunch round the corner. Gita, I hope – she always knows what to say.

But it's Penny. Christ. This could turn into a real gloomfest. I've had my reservations about Rachel, over the years, but I feel sorry for her, lumbered with this pair. 'Morning, Penny. Well, erm, I'll leave you two to enjoy the view.'

I'm expecting some sort of encouragement to stay, after all they can sit here any time and I'm a visitor. But there's a leaden silence and so I get up awkwardly, collecting my half-eaten breakfast, and off I go.

Just before I'm out of earshot, I hear Penny saying angrily to Roderick, 'Look, you're not going to weasel out again, are you? She's going to tell everyone. We have to do it first. We simply *have* to deal with Daddy tonight.'

Chapter 16

Gita

Mount Tregowan, 31st October

I'm always dreaming of moments like this. Work is hundreds of miles away; the girls are busy who knows where. And Tom and I are together, for once. He's dominating the table, manspreading everywhere, paper flung wide. But I smile.

'What?' He looks up.

'Nothing, just thinking how lucky I am. How lucky *we* are to be here.'

He drops his warm hand onto mine for a second and it's all worth it. But, while I ought to be relishing this little bit of us-time, I can't help it. I start worrying about the girls, my mind full of cliffs, winds, seas … I'm a city girl who's produced three more city girls; you hear so many stories of selfies taken on the edge of promontories … I hope Tasha and Ness are keeping an eye on Ruby.

When I'm at work I've trained myself not to fret, and concentrate on my newspaper family instead. But at weekends I switch back. If I can't see them, something's missing. I feel the family is as fragile as a house of cards or a pile of bone china plates. One slip and the lot could come crashing down.

I suppose I can guess what they're up to, roughly. Nessie and Ruby will be waving their phones around to try and magically attract some internet beams; Tasha, going through a secretive phase, will be snatching a solo walk.

We've always tended to lump the girls together, making them into a little team against the world. But Ruby is so much younger. She's not the teenager she's longing to be at all. I turn to Tom. 'Do you really think it's safe? For Ruby to be out there, without one of us?'

He flips down the top of the paper. Rachel is so tactful, she's got copies of mine in as well as the rest. Briefly I wonder how they were delivered. I suppose the causeway must have been open this morning? But Tom is speaking.

'Course it's safe. Apart from the wild animals and quicksand.'

They say a shared sense of humour is key. But this is our child, after all. 'Maybe I'll just go after her.' I push my chair back. But he's up before I've got to my feet. 'I'll do it, don't you worry.'

When he's gone, my mood plummets. I know it's ridiculous, I wanted to make sure the girls were OK. And it's also great that Tom's a concerned dad. All the same ... But before I have time for too many regrets, here's Rachel. I've always loved the way she comes into a room. As if she owns the place. Which she so often does.

Her legs are endless. Those low-waisted jeans would make me look like one of Snow White's roommates. And that silk blouse is perfect, the quintessential dress-it-up, dress-it-down staple that's always on the paper's fashion pages and never in my own wardrobe. I feel wistful for a moment, then remember her bypass. Thank God I'm not so hung up on externals.

'The croissants were so delicious.' I smile as Rachel slides into the seat Tom has just vacated. 'My waistband is already feeling tighter.' I'm not joking – I'm glad the serving staff have removed my plate. The tell-tale pile of crumbs was almost as high as Mount Tregowan itself.

'Pastry chef. He's the best. You won't believe what the food was like when I got here,' says Rachel. 'I was just outside, having a chat with your Nessie. Such a lovely girl.'

What on earth can Rachel and Nessie possibly have to talk about? And, though I love her dearly, I can count on the fingers of one finger the times when my Ness has been described as 'lovely.' 'She's very moody at the moment,' I say carefully. 'I hope she was polite.'

Rachel just smiles. 'Oh, hormones can play absolute havoc, can't they? We have a lot in common, Nessie and I. You'd be amazed.'

'I really would be,' I say, racking my brains. I suppose there is a bit of an emo/gothic interface. That must be it. Rachel's got her cryptic smile on so I won't get any joy out of her even if I dig. She does love being enigmatic.

'And isn't this view incredible?' she asks.

I turn my head obligingly. She's right, it's spectacular. 'What's this treasure hunt about, later?' I ask idly, taking a sip of my second divine cappuccino. Even her coffee machine is amazing. I feel another fleeting pang for Roderick. He probably thought he was managing this place really well, till Rachel showed up.

'Oh, you'll see.' Her wink takes away some of the sting of being out of the loop, but not all. After a lifetime in journalism, I have a simple need for information.

'Are there numbers on the clues, or something? One for each of us? How many even are we, this weekend?'

She's laughing one of her silvery laughs, as though I've just told the best joke in the world. 'Can't you guess?' she twinkles. I look blank, and she leans over to me, even though we're alone in the room. 'It's Halloween, Gita. How many do you think?'

I sit back in shock. No! Even Rachel wouldn't tempt fate like that … would she? I start totting up in my head, wishing Vicky were here to do one of her lightning tallies. I finally get there, Rachel smirking all the while.

'Oh my God, Rachel. You can't be serious,' I remonstrate, but she's smiling from ear to ear and despite myself I join in, trying to quash my dread. I'm not superstitious, really I'm not, but I hope Rachel knows what she's playing at. On Halloween night, really? *Thirteen.*

I'm just about to speak when someone pokes their head around the door, then retreats. No mistaking those features, it was Penny.

'I always think of that line in *Shrek*, "Why the long face?"' Rachel whispers, then giggles behind her hand. Somehow even this is musical. I join in – though I spare a thought for poor Penny.

'When have you ever watched *Shrek*?' I ask.

'Those weekends with you, when the girls were babies, don't you remember? The bigger two, anyway.' *The bigger two.* She ought to remember Tasha's name, at least. She's her godmother. She jetted in for the christening, centre stage in all the photos. Then nothing, until the *Shrek* weekend, three full years later, when Nessie was on the scene. Honestly, what is she like? But then I think of the solid silver christening set stashed in the attic, the sporadic but lavish birthday gifts for Tasha (always a year or two too young, but fine to pass on to her sisters) followed now by very welcome clothes vouchers which I'm always tempted to snaffle for myself. I bite my lip.

'*Shrek* was on repeat on the telly. Honestly, that's the only way we got through it. Vats of cheap white wine, *Shrek* and nappies! It was hard work, but I loved it,' Rachel smiles heroically, Florence Nightingale after a really tough stint in the Crimea.

Her forty-eight hours of hell was my life, for year upon year. And then we did it all again with Ruby. I shake my head very slightly. Shards of Rachel on that weekend are coming back to me, through the haze of time and sleep deprivation.

'I've brought you this little crate of Pouilly Fumé,' she'd trilled, oblivious to the fact that I was breastfeeding and couldn't drink. She has only herself to blame for the wine. Then, after the babies' bedtimes, I found her snorting cocaine off the coffee table where Tasha played with her dolls. 'Are you sure you won't have a little toot? It would definitely mellow you out?' she said, all eyebrows. She and Tom stayed up late both nights, while I dragged myself off to bed. Neither put in an appearance for the 3 a.m. feeds.

'A long time ago, now,' I say, and turn to look out of the window. This side of the castle has picture windows. There's mist in the distance, where the French coast should be. I'm not sure whether Rachel did this revamp herself, or whether some past Tregowan thought he'd like a bit more light on his cornflakes. 'This place must be amazing in a thunderstorm.'

'Oh, it is. You'll see, later,' she says.

'What do you mean?' I'm instantly alert.

'There's a big one coming tonight. I can't wait.'

I stare at Rachel. The Cornish coast has, in the last two years, been swept by a series of devastating gales, ripping through the one train line, isolating the area from the rest of the UK, causing terrible flooding and wrecking local businesses. We've covered it in the paper. I turn back to the sea. Is it me, or are the waves mounting higher? 'Should we get the others in?'

'Of course not! Let them enjoy it. The fireworks won't start until later.'

'Ooh, I love fireworks,' I say, feeling five again. The prospect encourages me not to freak out about the weather. It might never happen; systems get blown off course, don't they? And Rachel does exaggerate. I make a decision to relax. Fireworks would be brilliant. Ruby's not mad about the loud bangs but Tasha and Nessie absolutely adore them.

'You have such a wonderfully literal mind, Gita. I've always loved that about you,' Rachel says softly.

'Is that a compliment?'

'Of course it is! I'm so pleased you're here,' she says. I can't help feeling she's changing the subject. But I'm the same. I'll do almost anything to swerve a confrontation.

I said *almost*.

Chapter 17

Vicky

Mount Tregowan, 31st October

OK, so I'm getting fresh air. That's what they all say, isn't it? What the doctor ordered. Obviously I'm not going anywhere near a doctor. I know what their first question always is, to a woman my age. 'How many units …?' Then that look. Always the look. Like they *know*. And they double anything I say.

Right, I'm striding onwards; I'm getting a walk. That's what's down on the email, apparently. I tried to make Tasha tell me the whole programme when I was collecting my breakfast, but she just hugged the information to her chest. 'Perhaps you should go for a walk now, Vicky,' she said, looking me up and down. What did she mean? How rough do I look? But she was off again. 'Then there's a treasure hunt, and we reconvene at the house afterwards. No, I'm not telling you about the evening now, you'll only forget.' When I remonstrated – I'm forty-five, not ninety-five, and I'm not her mother so she's got no excuse for treating me like I've got one foot in the care home – she pointed out I was perfectly at liberty to look at my own copy of the email. Of course, she knows that none of us can get a proper connection today.

I can't lose my temper with someone else's child. I can't even lose it with my own. Not anymore. The lad just won't stay near me for long enough. Admittedly, I was pretty sharp with him before he left home. Not intentionally. But when I've had a few ... well, stuff leaks out. So here I am. Alone.

Every now and then a gust of wind comes which suggests it means business. I look at my phone again, thinking I'll just check the weather app – then I realise it's useless here. How can Rachel stand it? How can she stay in touch with her pals, *Gwynnie* Paltrow and the rest, if both her mobile signal and the internet are up the bloody spout?

Funny how like Gita Tasha has turned out, but somehow with the caring filter turned off. Maybe that's the bit she gets from Tom. I wonder if people think Raf and I are similar? Doubt it. Though we're both stubborn, that's for sure. But he's nothing like his dad, thank God.

Gita sold this place to me on the grounds that Raf would love it, but these look like the wrong kind of waves, not cresting but heaving up and down, more restlessly with every minute.

From my vantage point, I can see a small walled garden below, on a sort of terrace cut out of the rock. Even this late into the season, there's something flowering down there, a splash of bright purple against the gunmetal sea and the dreary boulders. I feel recovered enough to totter down there to have a closer look. And what else is there to do?

Back home, I'd still be tucked up in bed, with Gita's paper, and coffee and Nurofen on an intravenous drip, till I felt strong enough to venture out and start it all up again. But now I'm outside, I can't help enjoying the wind on my face. I don't think there's been a real breeze through Canary Wharf's skyscrapers for years, though on a good day, you'll certainly hear the rustle of £50 notes. My hair is blowing everywhere and the salt air is stinging my cheeks, but it feels … healthy. Perhaps I should get out of the city more?

Oh, who am I kidding? The feeling is going to last as long as this walk. But I'm enjoying this: the odd sensations of my feet slipping on rocks and the cries of seagulls far out at sea. Now, am I taking the winding sandy path, or the steps cut out of the rock that we clambered yesterday? There's no contest; the steps will be quicker, more direct. On the way down, at least. I can take the winding path on the way back, save myself from the hill.

I'm still a bit below par, and I really don't want to lose my footing. Who'd have thought Rachel, who had twenty-five pairs of Christian Louboutins in her uni flat (I counted them, to great hilarity, one boozy night), would now be making us go on country rambles?

Thank goodness, there's a handrail, bolted into the rock. Looks like a new fixture. The Cadogan zillions strike again. The air is so fresh. I start to feel restored, cheerful even. This is why people like the seaside. It's hard to hang on to gloomy thoughts when you can see the gulls wheeling, the underside of their wings as white and crisp as company reports against the louring sky. *No, don't come any closer, you bugger.* God, they're scary when they're near, all claws and eyes. It's flown further out, now. Maybe its dead black gaze is fixed on an unlucky fish beneath that shifting surface.

The wind whips round and I almost lose my footing; I clutch the rail, move more slowly. I need to concentrate. Soon I've reached the level where the walled garden must be. It feels like I've been walking for hours. I check my watch; seven minutes precisely. I stop, bending over. Stitch. When did that last happen?

Just as the pounding in my head is subsiding, there's something in my peripheral vision. Moving fast, coming my way. Jesus, it's a boulder – a good-sized one – hurtling down the side of the mountain towards me.

As my heart thuds in my ears all I can do is cower, pressing myself into the rockface, making myself as small as possible, and hope it'll fall past me or over me or away from me. And if it hits me, I pray it won't be too hard.

Then the boulder smacks into the cliff just above me and its trajectory changes. Thank God. It whistles straight past me and onto the winding path below, before rolling downwards, much slower now. That impact on the steepest bit of the mountain must have absorbed a lot of its speed.

'Jesus!' I'm trembling, still pressed into the side of the mountain. I slowly become aware of the pain in my hands and peel them off the rough surface. I can see its imprint pitted into my skin. Better that, of course, than a massive rock on my head.

Now the fear has subsided, anger rushes in. Is the cliff crumbling – or did someone chuck that my way? It fell from somewhere up there. Was it the first level, nearest the castle, or the next one down? Impossible to tell, though from the speed at which it was travelling, I'd say it had fallen a long way. My neck is hurting, as I lean out to see. Up on the next level, I could swear someone steps back, out of sight.

I'm inching forward again when Tasha suddenly greets me from the garden entrance. 'Aunty Vicky,' she says, all smiles. Then, looking more closely, she steps forward. 'Are you OK?'

'Did you see that boulder?' I ask her, ashamed to find I'm breathless, almost shaking. Tasha's looking blank. 'Did you hear it crashing down the side of the mountain?'

'Oh. I saw a stone or something falling – was that it?'

She must be kidding. A stone? Next she'll be saying it was a pebble. But something stops me. Is she right? Am I getting things out of proportion? Still feeling the effects of last night? I squint down at the path below again, and now I'm not even sure I can see the boulder. It must have rolled into that scrubby undergrowth at the side of the path. I put my hand to my chest, feel my racing heart. Well, my body certainly feels it's been under attack. But then, it's led me astray before.

'Are you all right, Aunty Vicky?' she asks again.

I look at Tasha, still a bit uncertain. About the boulder, and about that name. I'm not sure Gita's attempts to get the kids to call her friends 'aunty' ever really worked. It makes me feel a hundred years old. They're so grown up, and in Tasha's case, so gorgeous. Close to, while I'm feeling jaded, her skin looks unfairly wrinkle-free, spread like silk over pretty features. Did I ever look that good, even at her age? I'm really, really never drinking again.

I take her arm. 'Show me this garden, then, love. Didn't know you were interested in plants?'

She gives me a look. Neither of us know one end of an allium from another. Raf once grew cress, or tried. The sandwiches were gritty with un-germinated seeds. 'Yummy,' we told each other, before I sneaked the lot into the bin once he was asleep. The lad grumbled for a few days but it was a mercy killing. I know enough to acknowledge this garden is pretty, with the patchwork of plants I spotted from up above. 'Do you think Aunty Rachel gets it all in a job lot from the garden centre, like Mum does with our window boxes?'

Nice to know Gita is no more green-fingered than I am. And that Rachel is an honorary aunt too. Bet she hates that.

The garden isn't big. The rock walls are head height, and cut out the roar of wind and sea. The silence seems suddenly loaded, ominous. 'Feels a bit like a church or something, doesn't it?' says Tasha, as we stroll. I look at her in surprise. I've grown used to teenagers not noticing anything but themselves. But maybe that's just lads? Or one in particular.

Then I notice something. Behind the purple bushes, there is a row of slabs, poking up at odd angles. There is writing etched on them, furred over with some sort of plant mould, lichen is it? Names, dates. God, they're headstones. One is a little less ancient than the rest. I kneel and brush the moss off it. 'Lady Tregowan ...' I read aloud.

'What? That's Rachel, isn't it? She's not dead! Is this some kind of weird joke?' asks Tasha.

I feel a prickle of dread for a second, then reason kicks in. 'No, no, it must be the first Lady T, Ross's previous wife. Look, *Evelyn*,' I read out. 'She died ages ago. Here's the date: 1985.' As I uncover the numbers – and take stock of the fact that this little graveyard is one of the few places Rachel hasn't got round to gussying up – something she said at our Soho lunch comes back to me. Some horrible accident, with Penny in the car.

You can see how it might have happened, on this island. The narrow paths, the sweeping turns. With that falling rock, they've nearly done for me already. I get up and brush off my trousers.

It's a funny place for a graveyard. Funny place, full stop. I suppose that little building further on is a chapel. When we reach the gap in the wall at the far end, I can't get out fast enough.

Then a gust of wind comes from nowhere, catching Tasha's skirt. She's dressed for an Instagrammable walk in Richmond Park, and the gossamer fabric flies up, reds and blues flashing as she wheels round.

It breaks the mood, but it's not just relief in our shrieks of laughter. There's a touch of hysteria, too.

Because there's something about this place that is seriously giving me the creeps.

Chapter 18

Rachel

Mount Tregowan, 31st October

Oh dear, I'm not sure this is going as well as I expected. Even Gita, my friend through thick and thin, seems prickly. Well, she has so much to put up with.

All the more reason to get on with things. This weekend is going to be a breath of fresh air. A new start, not just for me, but for everyone I've gathered here.

The secrets and the lies, the evasions and half-truths. How have they all lived with them? For me, just that little further away, it's more than clear that they need this. A storm, a rocket up their backsides. Well, as usual, I'm the one who'll make things happen.

And, at the same time, I'll be clearing a path forward. Into a new future, for me and for the Tregowans.

I hope they're all getting on well with my little hunt. It's started in earnest now – even Gita has finally made it outside. That'll give the staff time to deliver tonight's costumes to every room.

Yes, I did put it on my email, my expectation that everyone would join in with tonight's theme. But I know this bunch. Half of them haven't even pretended to read the small print I dictated so carefully. And the ones that have scanned it have not acted on it. Not properly, anyway. Never fear, I'm here to fill the gaps. They won't look as spectacular as me – that would be no fun – but each guest will be getting a cape dropped off at their room. It'll be hung either from the hook behind the door, or on the front of the wardrobe, or even be draped across the bed. The maids are under instructions to make them utterly unignorable.

I had them run up while my own costume was being finalised. They're less sumptuous than mine; of course. I'm generous, but I'm not crackers. It's human, to have a little vanity, isn't it? And I'm definitely that. *If you prick us, do we not bleed?* Funny how that line flashes into my mind. I can see the way my father's mouth would twist as he said it, and the triumph in his eyes as he finished it off. '*And if you wrong us, shall we not revenge?*'

Maybe not the best bedtime story he could have picked. I would have preferred Jane's cutesy mice, if they'd been available then. But Mummy made it plain it was a privilege to have him sitting there, even for five minutes, at the cost of my night's sleep. 'Daddy's so busy, dear.'

I knew what he did, at least. He spun money from straw, like Rumpelstiltskin. There was plenty of it when he started, thanks to forebears who snapped up unconsidered trifles of art all over Europe. There's oodles more now. Tucked away here and there. And displayed on walls, via my clever foundation. My job is to keep it all safe.

I know the cloaks are an additional expense, something I could have parked on the goodwill of my friends. I do know the value of money, though so many people assume I don't. But when you're going all out in other ways, you want the small details to be perfect too. It can always be written off against something, as a business expense. My accountants are clever. And I am cleverer still.

I know my friends. Even if Vicky *has* brought something, it'll be tat she's found on the Internet. She's bound to be sneery about the

91

whole idea of dressing up, say it's posh or elitist or something. As for Jane, the jury's still out on her ability to source evening wear.

No, I'm sure they'll love the robes when they see them. I can't resist slipping mine on now. I pirouette in front of the mirror. As the black silk velvet catches the weak midday sun, it shines like the pelt of a panther. Something with claws, for sure. The satin lining is slippery and cool, in contrast to its scorching red colour. As I swing round I see a tiny figure outside on the path down below, arrested for a moment. They must have caught sight of my kaleidoscope of red and black. I step back from the window. Damn, I don't want my secrets to get out too soon.

I drop to my knees and crawl close to the window again. Peeping up over the sill, I look down towards the walled garden, seemingly as timid as one of Jane's silly mice. But I am not.

As I thought, it's Tom. Something glints. Are those binoculars, in his hand? I didn't bargain for that. Oh well, a cat can look at a king, as they say. Or a queen, in this case. It's not going to help any of them in the long run.

This is one cat and mouse game that I have no intention of losing.

Chapter 19

Tom

Mount Tregowan, 31st October

Of course I haven't been on Ruby's case, as Gita demanded. The girl will be fine. Do her good, in fact, to knock about this place on her own for a bit. Not that she will be on her own; she'll be shadowing one of her sisters, begging to be included. 'Me too!' has been her signature tune since she could first waddle after Tasha and Ness.

I was an only child. Odds are I would have been solitary by nature anyway. I grew up satisfied with my own company, and the full beam of my mother's love and pride. Least said about my father the better. Still, there was no shortage of role models. Spider-Man. Batman. The Hulk, even. Loved those comics. OK, they were all loners with, shall we say, some problems in conforming ... but I've never had trouble convincing people I fit in. 'Team player', my appraisals always said.

I've been out an hour or so, I suppose, having a look at the terrain. Now I'm taking a squint round the outside of the castle. The bolts on the back door are pathetic. Rachel really

93

needs to up her security. I take in a great lungful of the salty air, saunter a bit further off. Standing here you get a great view of the island, sides falling away, like being on top of a volcano. Good to get a proper lay of the land. I turn back and look back up at the castle.

For a second, I'm distracted by a flash of something red, high up in one of the top windows. Which room is that? I wonder if there's a plan of the place online? The visitors' website? Then I remember the stupid lack of internet access, and sympathise with my techno-junkie daughters.

I pause, but only for a moment. I need to keep my eyes on the goal. And I found out plenty, just skirting the walled garden earlier. My own daughter, who'd have thought she had such a talent for subterfuge? Nose to nose with Rachel, of all people? Not going to lie, if it had been Tasha with a secret, I'd have been less surprised. She's at that age, and there's only so much adolescents ever tell a parent – and only so much a parent really wants to know.

But Nessie? I can't help laughing. It must be some sort of gothic surprise they've got planned for the party tonight. Rachel's always had a thing about Halloween, and God knows, Nessie dresses for it every day. Gita'll get a jolt when she finds out about this little pairing, that's for sure.

I pick up my backpack, sling it onto my shoulders again, look both ways – this place is crawling with eyes – and head off on the meandering path. I don't want to bump into anyone else, not while I'm so intent. The waves are already getting up. Last night's gales were nothing. According to the forecast, we're in for it big-time tonight.

I haven't felt this tingle of anticipation for a long time. It's a bit like the feeling I get, spotting a fit woman across a room. There's a twitch, a tug on a wire that starts in me, but connects to her. Or maybe it starts in her, and just draws me in. It's exhilarating, primeval.

I shift uncomfortably, setting my sights more firmly ahead.

Don't want to get distracted now. Which way will I go? The decision clears my head.

Stretching my hamstrings briefly, I pick up the path again, pushing myself this time. The sandy surface between boulders causes me to slip as I take the corners.

I like to think I've always been methodical, but now, like my fitness, I've stepped everything up a level. I've never shied away from a hard path. In fact, I relish it. Not going to lie, I love thinking on my feet. Makes me feel more alive. Helps me face my demons.

There've been a fair few of those, recently. But I have a feeling I'm going to be laying them to rest at last.

It's a good job I've just had that thought. Round the next bend I almost knock Ruby off her feet. A stone or two is dislodged, and skitters down onto the next level. I grab her shoulders.

'You gave me quite a turn, young lady.'

Ruby's bottom lip quivers. 'Daddy, what's the matter? Why are you so cross? Why is everyone so horrible here?'

She gets me every time. I enfold her in a hug. 'What do you mean, honey? I thought we were all having a lovely weekend away?'

Shit, she's sobbing in earnest now. 'Nessie told me to burger off, and I haven't seen Tasha for hours – she told me I couldn't play with her and her friend.'

'Her friend? Who's her friend?' I try and keep my voice light.

'She wouldn't say,' Ruby mutters damply into my jacket. Then comes that cry so universal to younger siblings – the point where I usually let Gita take over. 'It's not fair.'

'Life isn't fair,' I tell her, with the ring of authority. *Don't even get me started on it.* I feel her slight recoil. This isn't the everything's-lovely tack her mother takes. She looks up, enormous eyes fringed with sparkling teardrops. *Shit.* It would take a better man than me not to promise my daughters the world.

'Don't worry, love. We'll find them. We'll sort this out, you see if we don't.' I take her sticky hand in mine, and start doing just what I didn't want: traipsing around the island with a kid in tow, sorting out a pointless battle when one that's worthier of me is creeping up faster and faster.

Wasting precious, precious time.

Chapter 20

Gita

Mount Tregowan, 31st October

After Rachel wafted away to tweak her plans, I took my coffee outside for five minutes. There was a bit of a breeze, but no more than that. So much for an epic storm. I couldn't see Tasha or Ruby, but in the end I did glimpse Ruby, hand in hand with her daddy. Now I've crept back inside to savour the last of my cappuccino in peace. And have a think.

Rachel's definitely got something up her sleeve, and I'm trying not to mind that she's keeping it quiet. It's frustrating. I pick up the newspaper and concentrate on that instead. Then Penny pokes her head around the door again. I try not to think of Rachel's *Shrek* quip. Poor woman, it's her own home, yet she's tiptoeing while we galumph around, taking over the place.

'Rachel not with you?' she says in that high voice. Some Tregowan long ago must have been a soprano. Or a castrato, though that would have stunted the family tree somewhat.

'She had to check on the arrangements,' I say with a smile, putting down the paper. 'I'm having coffee. Why don't you join me?' Immediately I feel silly; I've invited her to sit at her own table. But she just looks grateful and sidles into the seat.

'I won't have another, it makes me so jumpy,' she says. Her leg immediately starts to shake. Her fingers get to work pleating a napkin and her forehead is no less concertinaed. Either she's been on an intravenous drip of caffeine already this morning – or something is really bothering her.

'It must be difficult having all of us milling about the place,' I venture.

'Difficult?' She raises her head, as though she's been miles away. 'Oh, that's not difficult. Not at all.'

I wonder how I can ask, *so what* is *difficult, then?* But I wait instead. As any journalist knows, silence can be the deadliest interviewing weapon. People can't help themselves; they rush to fill it.

'Do you get on with your family?' she asks me in a flurry.

'My kids?' I say in surprise.

'No, no … the wider family,' she says. There is white showing all around her pupils. It's disconcerting.

'You don't mean my husband? Of course I get on with him.' I clear that one up straight away. 'My relatives, though. I would say, not always. My grandparents had very high expectations …' I don't need to go into how far my parents let them down. Even now, the divorce is only spoken of in a hiss. 'And my girls don't always get on as well as they're doing now.' She wrinkles her brow. 'Bringing up children … has its challenges. Do you have any yourself?' I know the answer but still feel I have to ask the question.

'No. No. That was never on the cards,' she says, waving her hand as though pushing the idea away. She knocks over the sugar shaker and I pick it up. 'It's good to have young people around, though.' Her smile is an afterthought, not even reaching her nose, never mind those gooseberry eyes. I decide to mention the elephant in the room – though Rachel would kill me if she heard that description.

'It must be an adjustment, having a new member of the family in your midst,' I say gently.

Penny shies like a thoroughbred refusing a fence. 'Oh … Rachel. Well, of course, we're grateful for all that's she's done for this place. And for Daddy.'

We're both remembering all that kissing last night. I don't want to think about everything Rachel's doing for Daddy, and I'm certain Penny doesn't either.

'I had a stepmother,' I lean forward to confide. Where did that come from? I wasn't going to go there at all. I hardly ever talk about it. Remarriage is a badge of shame in my world.

'Did you?' Now Penny's eyes light up. 'And was she … wicked?'

'Aren't they all?' We both laugh. The atmosphere eases. Poor Penny, she's been yearning to bitch about Rachel. I would have burst, if I hadn't had friends to offload to about my stepmum. She didn't last long – my father is now an elderly reconfirmed bachelor – but it was no fun. I was in my twenties, but I took it as hard as a child half my age. Ironically, Rachel heard a lot about her. I wonder if she remembers, whether it's made her any better in the role? But then, Penny must be pushing fifty. Surely she should be over it.

'It's years since my mother died. But I think about it – and her – every day. You see, I was with her. When it happened.' Penny looks down, and that straight line of a mouth quivers, like a blip on a heart monitor. I reach out to try and pat her hand, but she knocks her napkin to the floor and stoops to pick it up instead.

I googled the family, when Rachel told me her happy news. You'd expect no less of a journalist. So I already know what she's talking about. Car accident. Coastal road. It reminded me of Princess Grace of Monaco. With the former Grace Kelly, you could picture the sugar-pink convertible, the warm breeze ruffling blonde hair, a fluttering Hermès scarf – then the horrible screech of brakes and grind of metal. Here in Cornwall, things would have been less glamorous – a wet road, a muddy estate car, a couple of posh ladies in Barbour jackets – but a tragedy nonetheless. One that has left its mark on Penny. Her eyes are now as sad as a medieval painting.

'It must have been terrible. But at least you were there in her last moments.' I always try to comfort, communicate. But it seems to have been exactly the wrong thing to say. Penny gives me a horrified look, scrapes her chair back, and more or less runs out of the room, colliding with Roderick as she does so. *Great. Well done, Gita.*

I pantomime distress and apology to Roderick, but he shakes his head, squeezing into the chair she's just vacated, pushing it back from the table. 'I take it Penny's been reminiscing again? She's like the Ancient Mariner with that story. You know, she *stoppeth one of three.*' He says it with heavy jocularity. If he were one of my girls, I'd tell him off for his lack of sympathy. As it is, I shrug and apologise some more.

'I feel awful. I strayed into something that's obviously very … raw.'

'That's just it,' says Roderick tersely. 'It wouldn't be raw, if she didn't keep picking away at it. She wants us to speak to my father about it. *"Put things right, at last,"* she keeps saying. But what's the good of that? Father did what he could, years ago. We can't go back on any of that now. And he's very clearly put it all behind him.'

'I suppose Rachel … appearing, that's bound to have stirred up some issues.'

'Issues! Ha. Well, yes,' he concedes. 'More coffee?'

I nod mutely. That's about as close to emotions as we're going to stray, I assume. And the next few minutes of conversation bear me out. Once a maid has appeared as if by magic to take away the empties (this *must* be my last cup, I'll be as twitchy as Penny if I carry on), Roderick steers us onto safer and far more boring territory with the ease of a public schoolboy well versed in avoidance. As soon as I can, I gently extricate myself.

'I should check on the girls! They've been gone so long,' I say, throwing down my napkin. I'm hoping he didn't spot me outside only twenty-odd minutes ago. I've certainly been eyeing the skies ever more yearningly while we've been discussing event footfall and ticketing. Unfortunately, after last night, Roderick thinks I have a burning curiosity about the inner workings of this place.

'Oh! Yes, certainly. We can pick this up again later. You should get out there while you can. Make the most of it.'

I decide to ignore the warning that yet more statistics will shortly be coming my way, and focus on the last part of his sentence. 'Make the most of it? Why? That sounds a bit dire. What on earth is going to happen?'

Roderick starts. 'Happen? Nothing's happening, apart from this blessed party. I just meant the thunderstorm.'

I raise my eyebrows. 'Rachel mentioned one, but I assumed ...' I'm not sure how to tell him, if he doesn't already know, that his stepmother loves hyperbole. She alarmed me to start with, but of course I rationalised. For Rachel, a drop of rain is a typhoon. A leaf moving on a tree is a force nine gale. But perhaps I was wrong.

'Oh yes,' he says, with an unmistakable gleam of satisfaction. 'She isn't exaggerating. Not at all. There's a huge storm coming. A tempest.'

'Oh, I hope it won't ruin the fireworks.'

'Fireworks? Did Rachel say we were having fireworks? Oh, I see. No, she meant it will *be* fireworks, when the storm hits. The lightning will be as spectacular as any show you've ever seen. We're going to be battered within an inch of our lives.'

'And that's a good thing?' I'm disappointed. And a bit annoyed with Rachel. I was looking forward to *oohs* and *aahs* and Catherine wheels.

'What?' He seems to shake himself out of some private train of thought. 'Oh, well. It'll separate the men from the boys, all right.'

I suddenly realise there are only five on the island – Roderick

101

himself, Tom, Raf, Geoff and Ross. I'm puzzling over who's in which category, when he speaks again.

'I just meant, if you've never experienced a storm on Mount Tregowan before, then you've never seen what nature can truly do. It's like nothing else, you see.' There it is again – a gleam from those cat-like eyes.

Then he leans forward, and half-whispers, half-hisses at me. 'It's like the wrath of God.'

Chapter 21

Vicky

Mount Tregowan, 31st October

Tasha is constantly twitching round, admiring the views (which are amazing) or fidgeting with her skirt. After another aimless turn, I just come out with it.

'Look, shall I leave you to potter? You're not in any hurry, but I'd like to get back inside before this wind pulls my hair out.' I'm joking, but it's getting up now, and in the distance I can see some greyish clouds gathering. Funny how, in London, I can go for months without looking out of a window, occasionally checking my phone for the temperature if I think I might need a scarf, but here we are literally surrounded by weather. It feels like being stalked by something wild, uncontrollable.

Tasha is trying to adjust her face so she doesn't show too much delight at the prospect of me sodding off, when we turn a corner and come slap bang into Tom and Ruby. I take a step back in shock and nearly fall. After the rock earlier, I'm on edge, that's for sure. But Ruby, bless her, runs forward and hugs me. Over her head, I avoid Tom's eyes as usual and he says, 'There we are! Told you I'd find Tasha for you, Ruby love.'

I can tell from his hearty tone that he's about to do one of his disappearing acts, but I want to go first – and I don't want him coming with me. I disentangle Ruby, though the embrace feels like a welcome confirmation that I do have a good mothering gene somewhere after all, and announce brightly to the group, 'Well, I'm off back to the house.' Then I stump away before anyone has a chance to follow.

I can't help it. As soon as I'm round the corner I have to pause, try to get my pulse back under control. I look around. Close up, the rough-hewn shape of the boulders seems somehow elemental. I think again about that near miss. What was all that about?

Surely there's no one here who wishes me ill? I have my moments, but I'm a nice enough person really … Oh God, introspection isn't good for me. I'm finally starting to relax again, when I hear something that makes my heart lurch.

A footstep on the path behind me.

Chapter 22

Tasha

Mount Tregowan, 31st October

Where is he, where is he? Dad turning up like that has properly scared him off. And Aunty Vicky before that. Just when we were getting somewhere. Just when we were finally sorting some things out …

We must talk. Otherwise there's a danger he'll get it all wrong. He might not even believe all those things I said. And I meant every word. I feel it again, just at the thought of him, that bubble of happiness, that Christmas-morning joy I used to get when I was a kid. Before I realised the rustling and swearing was Mum and Dad, dragging the stockings upstairs, trying not to argue again.

Raf – I love saying his name, even just to myself. I feel all melty as I think about him. *Raf.* But I'm not going to drift off into a daydream about him. I'm trying to be practical, actually help him with his work, now that I'm an influencer. Nessie would kill herself laughing if she could hear me call myself that, but even she has to admit I'm soaring now on my Insta. Over 7k followers, and more by the day. And I haven't had to flash the flesh, like some girls do. Well, not much, anyway.

I think Raf was impressed, when I told him about it earlier. He pretended not to be, but now I'm getting sponsorship, it takes it to a different league. It's just a few things at the moment, a discount code or two, a pair of trainers, a swimsuit. But they're brands I actually like, so it's not lying when I recommend them. I told Raf he should do the same.

As a PT he could be getting way more business, putting some routines on TikTok. He'd get free stuff, too; the latest weights and that. He can be so old-school though. When I suggested it he suddenly looked … disapproving.

Wait, could he just be jealous? That's just popped into my head, but I know I'm right. I smile. I do have a lot of male followers, it's true. It's not something I think about much at all, the number of fit-looking boys signing up. It's a compliment, but a lot of them might just be pretending to be single. The messages they send … It's hot air, isn't it?

It puts a whole different slant on things if he *is* jealous. Aw, so cute. But he should know better. He's never had any competition, not since that lame parents' do last Christmas. I mean, we've known each other forever. Since birth, really. But something happened that evening. Since then, I've known we are meant for each other. We just clicked. It was amazing. Like I was broken at birth, and he glued me back together. He was so easy to talk to, not like other boys. And when we first touched … It still gives me shivers.

Something weird is happening this weekend, though. Suddenly we can't chat like normal. I miss that. If I didn't know better, I'd say he was getting cold feet.

Some of it is people popping up all over the place here, getting in our faces. No privacy. Maybe we should just accept that, though? Come out of the shadows. I don't want us to be a secret; not after all this time. I never wanted it, really. My mum may be a pain sometimes but I usually tell her everything – the stuff she needs to know anyway. This feels like a sort of invisible mattress that's got stuck in between us. Keeping us apart. It feels wrong.

And it's not like she wouldn't be happy for me. Take the other day. 'I'm worried you're working too hard, all these study sessions with Rebecca. You need to let off steam, find a boyfriend,' she said earnestly. Little does she know that 'Rebecca' is actually Raf. Raf's dad, Bob, is fine with me being round there. Boys' parents are so much cooler than girls' parents.

It was Raf who said it would be more exciting as a secret. He was right; it felt so tingly. When we met up, I was breathless, dizzy with it. But now … We should stop hiding. I'll talk to him about it. As soon as I can find him. This island is like a maze. From the top, you can see down, spot everyone. But once you're on the paths, the high walls keep people on their own tracks, in a rat run or something. It's beginning to get to me. It's like we're trapped.

I turn another corner, and suddenly the place goes from creepy to amazing again. It's another of those views out to sea. It reminds me of Highway 1 in the States. We went on a family road trip when I was younger. Two, maybe three years ago. Mum and Dad were getting on, and even my sisters weren't too much of a pain. We went from LA to Big Sur, and round every bend was a view that had me grinning; surf pounding, the blinding sky of California and, out in the ocean, leaping blue-black blurs. Only dolphins playing. How cool was that?

The colours aren't as vivid here and the sea is much louder. Maybe it's the wind, and those massive waves further out, but everything seems angrier than California. When I peer over the edge – oops, not too far out – the sea is literally beating the rocks below. Like it hates us all.

To think this is Aunty Rachel's now. How great must it be, owning your own island? Even if it's a bit of a cold and unfriendly place.

I call her Aunty, but Rachel's not a real relative, not like all

Mum's great-aunts who are always bugging her. I could count the number of times I've seen Rachel on one hand. Well, until recently. She's super-glam. It feels good to sort of have her in the family. It's Mum who always refers to her as 'Aunty Rachel', but she's actually my godmother. Sometimes friends have mentioned her, when she's been in a photo alongside some megastar at Cannes or the Venice Biennale, and I've been able to say, 'Oh yeah, my godmum.' I try and be offhand, like it's just one of those things, but I see why Mum gets such a thrill from it. Even after all these years, she has a huge girl crush. Though if you say that, it makes her furious.

What I can't get over is the fact that they're the same age. Don't get me wrong, Mum looks great. But she's a mum; that's the first thing you notice about her. Rachel, though. She looks better than most of my friends. She must work out constantly. I slide a hand down my belly, suddenly realise my thighs are rubbing together as I walk. I've let things slip.

I hope Raf hasn't noticed I'm looking chunky. Maybe that's the reason he still wants to hide us? I look down, scuff a few pebbles out of my way, my sight blurry suddenly. Then I hear a cough. God, it's bloody Nessie coming round the corner. A moment's inattention and she's caught up with me. Typical. 'Have you found any clues?' she asks, in that voice that's one second from a whine.

I blink. Then I remember. The treasure hunt. There were meant to be numbered clues everywhere. Surely they would have leapt out? 'No. You?'

She shakes her head. She's trying that casual thing again, but I know she's dying for us to do this together. I think about walking on, but then … Well, actually – why not? Just this once. Raf is nowhere to be seen. I might as well have her company.

And to tell the truth I don't want to wander around here on my own. It's creepy. We can have a laugh like we used to, bitch about the grown-ups in our little gang of two. We'd hide under the covers when Mum and Dad were 'discussing things' at the tops of their voices. We'd tell each other stories. Lots of happy-ever-afters with princesses who stayed at home to cook and clean, and princes who put the bins out without being asked *every single time*.

'Shall we look together?' I say. Ness's smile lights up her face, banishing all trace of her boring emo pose. I realise I've actually missed this and we have an awkward hug.

'Yeah, why not, Miss Hippy Chic,' she says – but she means it nicely. We walk off arm in arm. She's not nearly as noxious when she's being true to herself.

We're a team again, and I feel like we're invincible, or something.

As though nothing could ever go wrong.

Chapter 23

Tom

Mount Tregowan, 31st October

Having Ruby in tow is not ideal. Too old for a piggyback, she's trailing along behind, happy as Larry – but she's slowing me down. And her incessant chatter is cutting my concentration. She has Gita's endless curiosity about stuff that doesn't concern her.

Every now and then I try and be all educational, just like Gita, and ask Rubes the name of a plant or a bird. Her answers have me in stitches. By the time she says 'phoenix' when I point to our umpteenth gull, she's got us both gasping. 'Isn't it funny, the way they look like their eyes are painted on?' she says, watching one swoop dangerously close. I'm more concerned about those razor claws than the eyes, as the bird comes at us. I put my arm over her thin shoulders and pull her away.

By the time we reach the bottom of the winding path, even I am tiring, and Ruby has been quiet for a while. She sits on one of the rocks marking the edge of the causeway, chest heaving up and down. Quite a hike for a little 'un. 'Why does the path disappear?' she asks the moment she's got her breath back.

'It's the tide,' I say absently, scanning the sides of the entry point, looking back at the steep steps cut into the rock, and the contrasting ribbon of path with its deceptively gentle slope. Whichever route you pick, it's quite a way back up to the castle. And, down here, there is literally nowhere to go – except into the sea. Just as I think that, a more ambitious wave hits the rocks and the spray flies up, catching Ruby smack in the back.

Luckily she finds it hilarious, though once the giggles wears off, her wet clothes are going to bring her mood right down. If Gita were here, she'd be clucking about pneumonia, freaking the child out. I just strip off my jacket, remove her sodden top, and wrap her up. The sleeves hang down, the hem is level with her knees. 'Do you like my new dress?' she asks, and I laugh.

Encouraged, she simpers and twirls. 'I'm Rachel, I'm wearing a beautiful ballgown,' she lisps.

'Enough, now,' I say quickly, grabbing her arm and getting a handful of empty jacket. I adjust my grip. 'We'd better get a move on. It's a long way back up that hill.'

She looks, too, craning her neck. High above us, we see the sheer face of Castle Tregowan. Behind it, a massive bank of grey and purple cloud has built up. When did that happen? I'm surprised, though I knew the storm was coming. Suddenly Ruby seems more of a titch than ever. 'Come on,' I say.

I should have known better. Ruby may be small, but she's stubborn as any mule. 'We were having fun! I want to stay here.' Christ. I turn to her, ready to let fly, but her bottom lip is already wobbling. I don't want to be Angry Dad. 'Let's see who can get up to the next level fastest,' I say with false brightness. 'On our marks, get set, go!'

That's more like it. Ruby shoots up the steep steps like a greyhound out of a trap. She won't keep that up for long, but it gives me time to look around. Soon I start the long climb myself. But by then, Ruby is nowhere to be seen.

'Ruby?' I shout upwards. The wind howls and the seagulls

screech in answer, out at sea. Nothing from my daughter. No sound of her feet on the stone steps, and when I touch the metal handrail, there's no vibration. It's still, and cold.

'Ruby!' I shout again. Then I start to take the steps two at a time.

Chapter 24

Gita

Mount Tregowan, 31st October

When Tom burst in, looked wildly around, and then asked me, all casually, if I'd seen Ruby, I didn't need any further prompting. I shot up and ran straight out onto the hill. *'Yes, of course I'll keep an eye on her,'* he'd said to me.

Now I'm standing on the edge of the steps down to the jetty and I can see … absolutely nothing. These intertwining pathways make it hard to find people. Was some Tregowan ancestor trying to repel visitors? My mind is windmilling from one thought to another, but behind them all, there's a single phrase repeating. *Where's Ruby? Where's Ruby?* Where the hell has she disappeared to?

She's nine years old, she's alone on the island with a storm coming. And she can't swim.

'Don't keep pushing it,' Tom used to say, when he got back from the local pool at the weekend, with Ruby's sausage of costume and towel suspiciously dry. 'She'll do it in her own time.' I'd throw together a lunch and get on brightly with the day, but of course I worried. Ruby's resistance to swimming has been monumental. I hoped peer pressure would do it, when they had lessons at school. Years of villa-and-pool holidays got us no further. Then Tom even booked her a private course. Nothing doing.

Now here we are, surrounded by a vicious-looking, freezing cold sea, and my baby is all alone out there. One step too far on any of the paths and she could be in the water. Vicky comes up to me as I'm craning out.

'Whoa, careful there. What are you looking at?'

'Looking *for*. Ruby's missing,' I say, turning to her.

'Shit.' Now she's leaning out, much further than I was, and I grab her jacket at the back. 'Anything?'

'Nope,' she says, planting her feet back on the path. 'Let's go down and look. The stairs intersect with the circular path on every level. We can split up, take one path each. That way we'll cover the whole place.'

Vicky's clear plan ought to be a comfort. Instead, terror leaps into my throat. I was half-expecting her to say I was being ridiculous. And usually she's too muzzy-headed to deal with anything except her beloved numbers. 'She hasn't been missing long,' I offer, and she looks shifty. 'What is it?'

'I was walking down there earlier, and a boulder nearly knocked me off the path,' she says. Her eyes are wide.

'Do you think something could have accidentally hit Ruby?' I say immediately. She glances away. 'Hang on. You mean … You can't be serious? You think it was … deliberate?'

'It missed me by a whisker,' she says.

Now there are iron bands around my chest.

'Listen, Ruby will be fine,' she says. It's probably the tone she used to reassure clients when Lehman Brothers collapsed. It does nothing for my blood pressure. 'Let's just get down there.' She sprints for the steps. I'm left with the circular path. She means well, but surely *I* should take the quicker route? Ruby needs me, not her. But I start to jog round anyway. Arguing will waste more time. When our paths intersect, we're both out of breath.

'Anything?' I say, when I can speak. Vicky's fringe is plastered to her forehead but her short cut is finally looking like a good choice. My longer hair is flying everywhere. She shakes her head.

'Let's try shouting,' I say, screaming Ruby's name down towards the foot of the hill, where I can see the waves spraying up now, lashing the sides of the island. The wind wrenches the words out of my mouth. Maybe the gulls hear me; nothing else will. Vicky and I look at each other, and then my most undemonstrative friend, with her lifelong phobia of public displays, not only grabs my arm, but pulls me in for a full hug.

Oh God. This is bad.

Chapter 25

Rachel

Mount Tregowan, 31st October

I put down my hairbrush. The one hundred strokes thing is old-fashioned, but it reminds me of my first nanny. I zone out when I'm doing it. There's so much said about mindfulness techniques, these days. People have forgotten the ancient self-soothing rituals.

Not that there's a reason for me to be tense. Everyone's cloaks and wigs are now in their rooms. But it's annoying they're not oohing and aahing over them. They're all still scattered around the island. That wasn't the idea. They should have been back in the Great Hall by now. But they seem to be enjoying wandering off piste in all ways, these friends of mine.

I pick up the gold brush again, draw it through the silken strands of my hair. I admire the effect in the mirror. Then I crane forward. I hope that's not a wrinkle. Despite myself, the brushing ritual, I'm still on edge. My big night is looming. I don't want a thing to go wrong.

Why are they taking so long over the hunt? Those laminated numbers were in position this morning; the servants made sure of that. But where are they now? I stride the few steps over to the picture window and look down. I can't see a single one. They were large, square A4 signs, big enough to be visible up here (of course I checked). They can't all have blown away, though I can see from the way the clouds are scudding that the wind is really picking up. If I didn't know better, I'd think that someone had deliberately been all round the island and thrown the numbers into the water. That's not playing the game. Not my game, anyway.

I catch myself frowning again. This will never do. This is my special weekend, my celebration. I've been so excited, putting it together. All I require is a little co-operation. Is that too much to ask?

Of course it's not. But then I'm used to being let down. I brush again, standing at the window, smoothing the hair over my shoulder. Now it's crackling with static. I watch the strands rise irresistibly towards the brush. The laws of nature. We subvert them at our peril. I throw the brush on the bed.

Movement catches my eye. What are they doing down there, my ants, my playthings? I heard a splash, earlier. And I can see people darting around now. Tasha is easy to spot, her skirt wheeling, Monroe-style. It's not subtle, but I was a teenage girl once – I can forgive her. The other sister is with her, my little emo pal. Hope she's not tiring herself out. Gita and Tom are on the level below. That's the first time I've seen them together for longer than a couple of seconds, I realise. Even from here it doesn't look good. They are squared up to each other. Jaw sticking out, shoulders hunched forward. And that's just Gita. She looks riled enough to commit murder. If I were Tom, I'd step away from the edge a little. I'm not thrilled they've brought their squabbles to my door. Domestics happen to the best of us, but keep it behind closed doors, please, people.

Who's that right by the foot of the mount? It must be Roderick. He looks like a cannonball from this angle. Ah, there's Penny twitching into view. They're never apart for long, my little

Tweedledum and Tweedle-doolally. If it weren't for Roderick, Penny would be in the Priory by now. The long-stay car park, if you know what I mean.

A knock. What's that? People know I'm not to be disturbed up here. Unless it's Ross ... but he wouldn't break in on me. Oh, it's one of my team. All hand-picked from my other places. The livery is a new touch, and I like it.

'*Ruby* is missing, you say? Oh, yes. Gita's youngest. Right, I'm coming,' I say. 'Straight away.'

I slip on my robe, plait my hair into a satisfyingly thick rope and curl it quickly onto my head. I barely stop to check my eyeliner, refresh my concealer. Wait, those little pumps I got from Stella McCartney ... ah, in the closet. I'm ready. Not that there's anything I can really do.

I wonder now if it was her I heard, earlier. That, well, I don't want to say *splash*. But there was something. If you have a calming regime, you don't want to interrupt it for just anything, do you? One hundred strokes doesn't mean seventy-eight.

Was it the sound of a child falling? Or was it just a slightly bigger wave, breaking on the rocks down there? Now I think about it, it was probably just that.

I march down the stairs, one hand out, feeling the coolness of the stone as I follow the corkscrew from my chamber to the guest floor. There are wet towels discarded on the landing. It's those teenage girls, but really! I hope I'm not going to have to have one of *those* talks with the staff. Well, it can wait until tomorrow. As I descend to the Great Hall, I hear raised voices.

Oh, fabulous. Just what I didn't want. Some sort of crisis, overshadowing everything. Look, I know a missing girl is serious. But she's not gone far, surely? That wave *was* just a wave. She can't have been unsupervised for long. I know Gita. Those girls don't get away with that much. Not really.

No, she'll have a handle on everything. Of course she will. These goose bumps are just from the chill. The temperature is dropping, that's all. I don't want any disruption, not tonight. It will be fine. Unless …

Unless she put Tom in charge? Did she? No, she wouldn't have. But as I burst in through the velvet entrance (one of my better ideas) the first person I see is Gita, her face already blotched with tears. She runs towards me, clutches at me. Over her shoulder, I lock eyes with Tom. Damn.

'Tom?' I say, but Gita breaks in. 'It's Ruby. He's *lost* her.'

Chapter 26

Gita

Mount Tregowan, 31st October

I'm lying in a tangle of sheets, my mind full of images. I remember sitting at the breakfast table, looking into Rachel's perfect face. My only worry then was my croissant blow-out. Now I feel as though I've aged ten years. I must look like I've piled on twenty.

It's Rachel's fault, like this whole bloody weekend. I shouldn't have taken that tea from her. 'I've put in a little something for the shock,' she said. I assumed she meant sugar. 'Go on,' she encouraged me. When I took a sip it wasn't sweet, or too hot either, so I gulped it down. The sedative must have started working at once, because when I looked at her, her smile was as wide and weird as the Cheshire cat's.

Thanks a lot, Rachel. My child has gone missing and you put me out of action. All right, it didn't knock me out for that long, under an hour. But still. What the hell was in there? It can't have been legal. But maybe someone else suggested it? Actually, Penny's a nurse, isn't she? It was probably her. Whoever it was, I'm angry. I should have been out there. Searching.

I was dimly conscious of people coming in and out of the room … Tasha, Tom. At one point the curtains were blowing around like crazy. Or was that the drug, too? I shake my head. I'm groggy, but things are clearing now. Tasha's sitting beside me, telling me the exact order things happened in. I don't know how I'd have got through this without her. But I wish she'd tell me faster.

'So?' I prompt. 'Was there any sign? Of Ruby?'

'I'm telling you, Mum. I ran down again to the water …'

'All alone? With the storm coming? Oh, Tasha!'

'No, no, in fact, Dad and Raf were with me.'

'And?' I prompt. 'What did you see? Anything? Anything at all?'

Tasha gives me a look and I try to calm down, fight the panic. She starts again. 'So, everyone was out on the hills by this stage. It's funny, you can see people much more clearly from the top, and the bottom. But when you're in the middle … you're sort of the filling in the sandwich. Hidden …' She realises that it's not the moment to find the island droll. Not when I'm thinking it's my mortal foe, the cause of my loss … but I'm doing my best to hold it together. Tasha may seem like an adult sometimes, but I can't burden her with my emotions which, at this point, are frankly raging.

'Well, we decided to follow the path all the way round. And that's when we found it.'

I'm leaning forward again now, despite my bone-weariness, the heaviness of my head and legs. 'What?'

'Ruby's little backpack. You know, that one she drags round everywhere …' Tasha glances away. I know her eyes are filled with tears. I know, because mine are too. I swallow a few times before I get it out. 'The one with the unicorns?' Now she gulps, and nods.

Time passes before she can take up the thread again. She's adopted a business-like tone, which makes her young voice seem suddenly harsh. 'So we went straight on up again. I mean … she wasn't there.' We both look at each other, eyes wide. The horror is getting closer. The horror that we still don't want to talk about.

121

'What did Daddy do next? Surely he called someone? The coastguard … the local police? *Somebody*,' I say, trying to keep my voice steady.

'He tried, of course he did. The landline is out … the storm, you know? And we couldn't get a signal with the mobiles, Mum. We tried. We really tried.'

Now I'm patting her back, trying to comfort her, while my mind whirrs. 'Did you see anyone else? While you were doing all this?'

She shrugs, almost silhouetted now by the windows. 'There were people around, yes. We bumped into that Roderick, Rachel's new brother …'

'Stepson,' I correct her absently. It hardly matters, now of all times, but I'd still hate my daughter to say the wrong thing. It's an easy mistake, Rachel and Roderick are about the same age. In a less topsy-turvy world, they really could have been stepsiblings.

'And erm, Penny, too. I even saw Rachel out there.'

'Rachel? Really?' I suppose I should be glad she was worried enough to venture out. 'Did you speak to her?'

'Just for a second. She said she was going to check on deliveries.'

'Deliveries? Wait, you mean there's some sort of warehouse down there?'

'No, it's just a boathouse. Where they tie up the ferry boat and store supplies.'

'I didn't even know there was a boat,' I murmur, though I suppose Jane used it last night. A second later, I've finally mustered the strength to fling the covers back and get out of bed. The first step sees me lurch and nearly fall. I put out an arm and Tasha catches me. She wants to steer me back down, but I shake her off, get my shoes on. Luckily I was fully dressed when Rachel gave me that Mickey Finn.

God, it's getting dark already, and my girl is still out there. The view would be spectacular, if I could give it a moment of my attention. Clouds are being thrown across the sky as the wind pushes the waves ever higher.

I rush out into the corridor, and run straight into the person I want to see least in the world. Tom.

Chapter 27

Tom

Mount Tregowan, 31st October

I can't believe Gita sometimes. She's crashed out all afternoon – no fault of her own I suppose – then gets an idea and doesn't for a second think that I will have already searched that fucking boat shed. Twice, three times, maybe four. What the hell does she think I've been doing?

There isn't a structure on this island I haven't scoured. The chapel, next to the walled garden. I've been over it like fucking Hercule Poirot on speed. Nothing. The two outhouses at the back of the castle, full of pots and gardening shit. Nothing. Then the castle itself. Ruby doesn't usually pull this kind of stunt – but what child wouldn't want to play hide-and-seek in a castle?

'She's too much of a wuss to have gone anywhere dark or creepy.' Nessie shrugged, when I ran up to her.

'Come on, Nessie. Now, of all times?' I said through gritted teeth. She pretended she didn't know what I meant. But the later it gets, the more the whole island seems dark and creepy, even to me.

I haven't got time for this, I'm exasperated and exhausted.

But of course I can't give up, nor rest. What I don't need is my bloody wife trying to second-guess my efforts. *Well, thanks, Gita, but maybe I know Ruby better than you. Yes, you're a great mother. But when do you have time to actually see the girls? Or listen to them, for that matter.*

Of course, I'm not going to say all this to her now. *But it's coming, Gita. And soon.* Now, I just throw my hands up in the air and stalk out again, into the increasingly ferocious wind.

I'm not a superstitious guy, but looking at the last of the daylight being blotted out by rolling inky clouds, I'm not going to lie, I feel a shiver that's nothing to do with the temperature. I would make promises, to be better, to try harder. To turn things around. But we aren't at that point yet. Are we?

Then Tasha bombs out of the front door, sliding to a halt as she sees me. Her face is a mask of worry, a younger version of her mother's distress – even though I'm angry with Gita, I can see she's not in her right mind now. Behind that, for a second, I see something else. But it's gone.

Ah, here's Raf loping along. Was he the shadow I saw? He's been pretty good all afternoon. Useful. None of us wants to say it, but things can only get more difficult, as night really starts to fall. Soon we won't be able to see our hands in front of our faces. He has a torch, and he's passing another to Tasha. I put out my hand for it and she obediently hefts it over. I turn it on and the yellow beam makes the gravel look alive, an arc swinging up to the trees streaming to the left in the wind. I button my jacket up and feel more in control than I have for a while. 'Right. Back down and up again? Another circuit?'

The kids nod dumbly, then Raf speaks up. 'Shall we go round the other way to you? That way we'll cover the lot between us.'

It's not a bad strategy. I agree, and we set off, the youngsters peeling away on the sloping path. I look grimly down at the steep steps. How many times have I been up and down them already? I shake my head, and start to shout. 'Ruby? Can you hear me?'

Over on the other path, I hear the almost-echo as Raf and Tasha take up the call. 'Ruby? Where are you, Ruby?' The wind snatches Tasha's voice but Raf's is good and deep and strong. She must hear that at least. She must. She must hear us.

Where are you, Ruby? Where are you?

Chapter 28

Vicky

Mount Tregowan, 31st October

This escalated so fast. Tiresome kids' game, to every parent's absolute worst nightmare, in under two hours. While Rachel's island has morphed from billionaire's playground to prison-cum-death trap.

God, Ruby has certainly upstaged her big sisters. No mean feat when one is as beautiful as Tasha and the other as strange as Ness. I'm a wreck, and I don't even want to think about poor Gita. A little girl, missing, on an island. Where someone almost brained me this morning. And a girl who, it turns out, can't even swim.

There must have been a moment, this morning, when that bloody causeway was open and escape was possible. We should have run when we could. I was probably clutching my head and groaning at the time, or sleeping it off. We really missed our chance. As a very minor plus, all this has banished the last of my hangover.

I dread to think what I'd be like, if it was nine-year-old Raf missing. At that age, he was such a confident little lad. I tried never to take my eyes off him, while pretending he was free as a bird.

I stop myself – I don't want to be that person. But an unsupervised non-swimmer? That's two counts against Gita already. And she's been zonked out, while the rest of us have raged around the island – but I suppose people deal with stress in different ways.

Anyway, I'm glad Raf has risen to the occasion. I'm in my room, resting from the search, and I've just spotted him from the window, going off with Tom and Tasha to scour the grounds again. They've been tireless.

Where can the bloody girl have got to? And I've only caught sight of Rachel once this afternoon. I can't help thinking that if one of my guests was missing, I'd maybe stick my head out of my turret and have a little look. But I suppose we've got all the servants, not to mention Roderick and Penny, wandering about yelling. It's hardly been the tranquil break we were promised. No sign of Ross either. I don't even want to think about why he might be exhausted.

Maybe Rachel is fuming because her treasure hunt got upstaged. No one seems to have found any of the numbers, which is weird. Oh well, perhaps she'll tell us more at the dinner tonight. Or will it be cancelled if Ruby …? God, this whole thing has killed my appetite. And that's a feat in itself.

Hang on, there's a commotion down below. I stick my head out of my door and there's Gita in the corridor, upright, but looking like death on a stick, poor love. We look at each other. 'Something's just happened, hasn't it?' she says fearfully. 'Have they … Have they found her?'

We run to the head of the stairs, look down below. Thanks to the high ceilings it's a long way and it's already dusk. I can't make much out but there's a kerfuffle, for sure.

I can see the pale pearl-grey uniforms of some of the staff. They're milling about … Are they dragging something? Looks like a tarpaulin. Gita lurches forward. I instinctively put my arm across the stair. Then I realise I can't stop her. She needs to be down there. I let her go first and we both run.

At the bottom, it's pandemonium. Everyone seems to be clustered around: Tom, the girls, Raf looming over everyone. When did he get so tall, my lad? Behind him is little Roderick and wait, there's Penny. Normally she's so hesitant, but now she shoves her way through.

'I'm a nurse, let me get to her.' People melt out of the way. Gita, on my side of the crowd, tries to barge through as well but she's less successful. Tom blocks her way, tries to take her in his arms, but she beats him off, fists pummelling. 'Let me see, let me see … Is she …?' She can't bear to say it and I can't bear to hear it either. I'm on the edges of the group now, but I want to bury my head, not push to the front. I don't want to see Ruby, that little monkey, still and grey in death.

A silence falls as Penny gets to work, rustling the tarpaulin away. It sounds as though she's shifting the girl, turning her … Amazing that so many people can make so little noise. Even the stones of the ancient castle seem to be waiting, waiting. Then, there it is, a little spluttering cough – and a collective sigh. I feel the emotion at some deeper level before I understand it consciously. She's alive. My chest heaves. I hadn't even realised I was holding my breath.

The sea of bodies parts and I see her, the little figure like a doll, a starfish on the tarpaulin. Bedraggled hair. Lots of, what is that? Cobwebs, I think. And she seems to be wearing an adult's jacket, wet through. But, thank God, her face is working, she's sobbing. She's never looked so ugly but so beautiful. Even Penny, kneeling by her side, no longer looks neurotic and middle-aged, but like a penitent who's received God's grace, so radiant is the smile she bestows on us all.

'I don't get it – was she in the water?' I say to the person next to me. It turns out to be Tom. I take a step away, wishing I hadn't spoken. He'll be too caught up to answer. Who else would know what's been going on?

Suddenly I hear Rachel's voice. A few of us look up. She's gliding down the stairs, in another of those silken gowns that would look stupid on anyone else. She flicks a switch and suddenly the hall is flooded with light. 'Cobwebs all over your hair, Ruby? And what's that in your hand?'

I crane to look. Christ … She's right, Ruby's clutching some sort of old knife. Like a letter opener … but posher.

'Looks like our Ruby found the priest's hole in our chapel, and thought she'd take a little souvenir. The Tregowan dagger, no less.' There's more than a hint of annoyance in Rachel's voice. She's definitely unamused by Ruby's escapade. I'm not the only one who bristles.

'She could have died!' It's Gita, stepping towards her, fists bunched, face red. It may be the first time in history she has openly confronted Rachel.

'Died? I don't think so. Isn't it more that everyone got into a bit of a panic? Completely understandable, of course.' The caveat doesn't take the sting out of Rachel's words one bit. 'She's absolutely fine!' She descends the final stair, turns to the prone figure and her voice goes sing-song, artificial. 'Aren't you fine, Ruby honey?'

Now she actually swishes over. Everyone steps back. She towers over the girl, then bends gracefully to pull Ruby into a sitting position at last and then, most audaciously of all, scoops her into a hug, prising the ornamental dagger away from her. Gita, who has been holding back as any mother would, wary of broken bones, convulsions, complications, gives Rachel a look I've never seen on a human face before.

Then Rachel releases Ruby as fast as she gathered her up and sweeps away again. 'I'm so glad everything's been sorted out. And don't worry, I'll get this put back right away,' she says, waving the dagger. 'See you all later for drinkies, before our special feast.'

She even shuts one eye in a wink. Jesus Christ almighty.

Chapter 29

Gita

Mount Tregowan, 31st October

I want my mood to be one of jubilation, now Ruby's been brought back safe. But all my joy at finding my baby threatens to burn away, unless I'm careful. I take some deep breaths.

Ruby's tucked up in our bed, with a hot chocolate, and Tom and I are sitting on opposite sides of her, each patting or stroking her arm or leg. I hate to say it but she's actually gone straight back on her phone, some game that isn't affected by the lack of signal.

The phone is a case in point. She shouldn't have one; not at her age. As Tasha and Ness are always reminding me, they were twelve before they got theirs. But I came home from work one day to find eight-year-old Ruby glued to this rose-gold thing with all the bells and whistles. A newer model than my own.

'I had to. She was at a playdate and needed to get in touch.' That was all the defence Tom offered. And, of course, Tasha and Nessie don't have a go at him about it. They save it up until I get home and gripe at me instead.

'Ruby, love. Why did you go in the priest's hole? And take that ... thing?' She frowns and redoubles her concentration on the string of blobs. Though I'm so angry with Tom I could kill him, I silently beseech him to have a go at least, not just lie there like a dummy. He shifts awkwardly.

'Ruby, Mummy's right. We need to know what happened.'

She sighs like a middle-aged businessman having to explain himself to pesky underlings. 'She told me to.'

'Who?' I say, but Tom overlays my question with a much louder one of his own. 'Told you to do what?'

I give him the eyes again and I ask, much more gently. 'We won't be cross, hon. I promise. Just tell us who you're talking about.'

'*Dur,*' she says. 'Who do you think?'

I shift on the edge of the mattress. I'm going to have backache tomorrow, but that's the least of my worries. 'We don't know, love. That's why we're asking.' My tone of sweet reasonableness is almost literally killing me. Tom flicks a glance at me and leans away.

Now he clears his throat. 'It's like this, Ruby. Sometimes even grown-ups aren't right, and it's OK to tell us, even if they've asked you to keep a secret ...'

Ruby looks up briefly and meets my gaze. She breaks in before he can really get into his stride. 'It was that lady, Mummy's friend.'

I think hard. 'Aunty Vicky?' Ruby rolls her eyes. I try again. 'Not Aunty Jane?' Unlikely – they hardly know each other, thanks to Jane's thing about children. Ruby shrugs, having evidently got to a gripping bit of her game. I resist the temptation to rip the phone from her little hands and throw it across the room. 'Not ... Aunty Rachel?'

She looks at me again and her eyes widen. She shakes her head again, but infinitesimally this time. She probably knows I don't want it to be Rachel. Or she could just be bored with this whole conversation. I'm not sure, but for me, the pieces drop into place. It fits. With Rachel's performance just now on the stairs. Suddenly it's all the proof I need.

I don't wait to ask another thing. I just leap up off the bed and I am out of the door before Tom can try and stop me.

Chapter 30

Rachel

Mount Tregowan, 31st October

I suppose I might have guessed it would happen, but it's still a rude interruption to my preparations for my big night when Gita crashes through my door.

She looks deranged, I'm sorry to say. The sedative seems to have worn off completely. Maybe I should have given her more.

I sit at my dressing table, but I don't turn around. I just watch her in my mirror. Her chest is heaving. Quite the Victorian heroine. She really should do more high-impact training. There aren't *that* many steps up to my tower.

'Why did you do it?' That's the question hurled at me. I put down my pot of Crème de la Mer and turn round slowly.

'Gita! What is this? I've no idea what you're talking about.'

Suddenly she's coming at me with a snarl on her face. Not so much broody hen as tiger mother. 'Please explain yourself,' I say, taking the precaution of getting swiftly to my feet.

Once we are both standing, she's lost her advantage. I have a couple of inches on her, I'm stronger by miles, thanks to my one-on-one sessions with Tracy Anderson, and there's a panic button on the wall behind me. What's more, I know she adores me; she always has. She wants this to be sorted out. She doesn't want to blame me for anything.

'Are you denying you told Ruby to hide in the chapel? And take that knife?'

Oh! So *that's* what she's so worked up about. '*Of course* I'm denying it,' I say. 'The Tregowan dagger is not a toy.' I watch the emotions surge over her face: fury, disbelief, incomprehension. Frankly, I'm astonished she thinks I'd do anything like that, and I tell her so.

'Who did, then? Ruby said one of my friends told her to do it.'

'One of your friends. That could be any of us on the island.'

'Not really, I asked her. About Vicky and Jane. And I hardly know Penny, I wouldn't describe her as a friend ...'

'But does Ruby know that? And why would Vicky, Jane or I wish Ruby any ill? We all love her,' I say, eyes wide.

Gita stops and thinks. It's almost comical, the way she switches tack. Two seconds ago, she was about to tear me limb from limb. Now she's the rational woman I've known all these years. 'Do you think it was Penny?'

I give her a look. 'There's something you need to understand about Penny. She's ... damaged.'

'What do you mean? She's highly strung, but that's understand-able, I mean, the accident ...'

'That accident was years ago. Anyone else would have got over it. But you're right, it's still affecting her. Don't you think that's odd?'

'What are you getting at? And what possible reason could Penny have had for getting Ruby to hide?'

'Where do I start?' I say. 'Listen, come and lie down,' I add. Gita hesitates for about a second before we both flop onto my bed, billowing with silks and cushions. It's the way we always used to chat, at uni, squashed up together on those narrow halls-of-residence singles. We swore they made them titchy so no one could have sex without falling off. But they were plenty big enough to snuggle up and exchange confidences. That's what we do now on my sumptuous four-poster.

'What do you know, about Penny's crash?'

'Well, you said there had been a car accident on the island, you mentioned it at lunch that time. And last night. And she was talking about it this morning. Roderick did say she never stops. It was a bit disloyal of him.' Gita sniffs.

'He's right.' I adjust a pillow behind me. Gita's always been one for family solidarity – and she's living with the consequences. 'Well, this is *entre nous*,' I say. Gita nods, all ears now. 'Penny was just a teenager at the time. She shouldn't have been driving. Particularly not on the island.'

'*Penny* was driving? I thought it was her mother?'

'Exactly,' I say. 'It should have been. It was like this …'

'But there aren't even any roads here,' she interrupts.

'Ross had them replaced with paths afterwards,' I explain patiently. 'No one's driven here since. The point is, she shouldn't have been at the wheel that day; it was illegal. So after the impact, her mother swapped places with her, so her precious little girl wouldn't get the blame. Neither realised how bad her head injury really was. Getting up and moving into the passenger seat was what actually killed Evelyn Tregowan.'

'Oh my God! How awful,' says Gita, eyes round. 'That's so sad. No wonder Penny's so odd … But I still don't see how that connects with Ruby?'

I sigh. 'She's got some weird salvation complex. She spent years nursing, but it got too much for her. Every time someone died on her watch she went into a tailspin. With Ruby, I bet she got her to hide, just so she could find her and "save" her. After all, only the family knows about the priest's hole. It's where the Catholic Tregowans hid their bits and bobs during the Civil War and after. Crucifixes and wafers and our lovely dagger. Penny always wants to be the heroine of the hour. It's a sort of … atonement complex.'

Gita is silent for a second, processing. Then she says slowly, 'God, it does fit. She rushed forward, saying she was a nurse. It looked like she was checking Ruby's airway, bringing her back to life … but if Ruby never went into the water, she was probably just cold and in shock. You mean, there was no need for any of that charade? I was so grateful to her. That's evil! Bloody woman! I'm so sorry, I thought *you* … well, it doesn't matter. But Penny should be getting some sort of treatment. Either that, or I'm calling the police.'

I put a hand on her wrist. 'Don't. They'd lock her up for good this time. You don't want that on your conscience. Ruby's OK, after all. Poor Ross. Believe me, he's tried everything.'

I carry on, knowing Gita can't resist insider information. 'He thought he was doing the right thing, hushing it up all those years ago. He still doesn't talk about it, but you know how it is in small communities. People were queuing up to gossip about it as soon as I got here. The coroner was a great friend of the family, Penny had her whole life ahead of her … But fudging things did her no favours. Between them, her mother and father really did a number on her. Like Larkin says.' I try a smile at Gita. I know she's now remembering our favourite poem from our English course.

Gita sighs. I can tell she's torn. Penny's little drama frightened her out of her wits, and Ruby was clearly petrified too. But she came to no harm. 'Ruby's fine now, isn't she? And I'd consider it a personal favour if you didn't take this any further. It will just embarrass poor Ross.' I look at her beseechingly.

For a moment, she holds firm, and then, as I knew she would, she concedes. 'All right. But if Penny steps out of line again, I really think you ought to have her committed. And if she lays another finger on any of my family …'

Gita's face suddenly turns ferocious, and I realise yet again how powerful the maternal instinct really is. I'm going to be relying on that when we have the next of these little chats, Gita and I. But she'll see reason, just as she has now.

Woe betide Penny, though, if she pulls another of her stunts. I wouldn't fancy her chances.

Gita, my lovely gentle Gita, looks like she'd cheerfully strangle her with her bare hands.

Chapter 31

Tom

Mount Tregowan, 31st October

I'm glad Gita has gone storming off. It gives Ruby and me a chance for a bit of a breather. She's still deep in her phone, but I can tell from the way her shoulders go down an inch that she's now relaxed. We just lie for a while and chill.

Finally I look at the time on my own phone. The movement doesn't escape Ruby. Her eyelids flutter. She's braced for what's coming. But I have to leave; I want to get out there and see what actually went down.

'Look, Rubes, do you mind if I pop out for a while? I need to check on something …' Immediately she's grabbed my wrist. 'Ouch! You need to trim those nails, honey.'

'You promised you'd cut them for me. Last week, remember?' I rack my brains. She's got a point. It didn't seem the most pressing item on my agenda. Little did I know she'd be digging them right into me a few days later.

'I'll do it in a bit,' I start to say, then I stop myself. 'That's if we've got nail scissors here.' Gita is right. Promising them stuff in the moment is easy. It can come back to bite you, though. Or leave tiny crescent marks in your skin.

'Why don't you just go? You know you're going to.' She's sulky now, chin down, avoiding my eyes, glued to the screen. I swing my legs to the floor as she speaks in a much smaller voice. 'But what if I get taken again?'

I look at her, hard. 'You didn't get taken, though, did you? You went and hid.'

'Did I?' she says, eyes now fixed on mine, wide and scared. I rather wish she was looking at that cascade of fruit instead.

'You know you did. In the old chapel.'

She looks me over again, head to toe, suddenly curiously like Gita, then returns to the game. I'm sick of being found wanting. I won't take it from a nine-year-old. I take a step towards her, but then Tasha bursts in on us. 'I need the straighteners.'

Immediately Ruby is off the bed and turning on her sister. 'No! I was about to do *my* hair.'

'Christ. I'm not getting stuck in the middle of round 101 of hair wars,' I tell them. Is Ruby even old enough to use those things? I'm sure Gita would have a view but I'm just glad of the opportunity to edge out as they square up to each other.

There's no one around as I pad down the stairs. I couldn't get my jacket; that would have drawn attention to my flit. As I pass the window I can see I'll get drenched. It's black out there now, no sign of whitecaps. I'm not sure if the wind has died down, or whether the waves are breaking on the other side of the island. Life in a London suburb doesn't prepare you for every eventuality.

I plod along as silently as possible, trying not to look furtive. I don't know who's more shocked when I almost run into Jane as I cross the hall. Looks like she was coming out of the small room to the side of Rachel's beloved Great Hall. I say 'small', but of course you could fit the downstairs of our house in it. It's some sort of pretentious library, the Laird's lair. Is Ross in there? I try and see over Jane's head. The light is on, but there doesn't seem to be anyone at home. Proves nothing, where Ross is concerned. She shuts the door behind her.

'Looking forward to the party?' she asks in that stilted voice, as though she hasn't spoken for hours. Maybe she hasn't. I haven't really seen her since this morning. Did she even turn out to search for my little girl? Gita has always insisted she's got some kind of allergy to kids.

The party? I've semi-forgotten that it's even happening. 'I suppose so,' I say, then realise that's borderline impolite. It's what we're all gathered here for, on Rachel's dime, isn't it? 'Erm, yes. Should be good.' A bluff, hearty tone should cover everything. 'And where are you off to?'

Jane looks startled. Have I been too abrupt? Too transparent in hoping she's going to heave herself upstairs, move out of my way? 'Oh, er, just getting ready,' she says. If I didn't know better, I'd say she was being shifty. We exchange another wary glance. God, she's not going to mention old times, is she? I cast around, find the ideal topic at last. 'Geoff getting on OK, is he?' He's another I haven't seen much of, though he was there when Ruby was brought in, I remember.

She gives me another of those uncertain looks, like I'm going to jump on her or something, and she actually edges past me. 'Um, yes. He's fine,' she says, speeding up as she reaches the stairs. 'See you later.' She scuttles up them as though she has the hounds of hell at her heels. Funny how people change. She really wasn't bad-looking at uni.

I'm almost at the front door when there's a dry cough behind me. Christ, what now? I turn, reluctantly. It's Ross. He must have been skulking in his library with Jane all along.

Now what was all that about, I wonder?

Chapter 32

Jane

Mount Tregowan, 31st October

God, I ought to have been braced for it. In fact, I've been lucky it hasn't happened before. But coming upon Tom unexpectedly has thrown me into quite a tizzy.

This is what comes of leading such a sheltered life. Encounters that most people shrug off without a thought make me hyperventilate. I hope Geoff thinks I'm out of breath because of the stairs. 'All right, old thing?' he says mildly as I erupt into our room.

I wish you wouldn't call me that. Naturally I don't say a word. My penances are many and varied. 'Of course. I've … hardly seen you today. What have you been up to?'

He looks up from fiddling with his tie. He's wearing that corduroy jacket I hate. I wish I'd taken more notice when he was packing. I suddenly wonder whether Rachel is expecting us to be in black tie evening dress. Oh God, Geoff is going to look absurd. No, she would have said. Unless it was in that blasted memo?

'Have you read that email? The one about the arrangements?' I ask him.

'Of course,' he says. 'She's provided those.' He gestures at the bed and I notice the pile of dark velvet. I thought it was some kind of fancy bedcover.

I step forward, lifting the two heavy capes, running my hands over them. The scarlet linings shriek when I shake them out. God, they're absolutely gorgeous. She has an eye for design, Rachel, I have to give her that. There are wigs, too. I twirl one cloak over my shoulders, like the woman in that Scottish Widows ad.

'Silly, that's mine,' he says. 'Look, it's trailing on the ground.'

I give him a little smile. He's about a centimetre taller than me, but I've always asked for help with high shelves. It's a courtesy of a sort. A fantasy, though one of the tamer ones a married couple can have. Anything to keep him sweet, I suppose. God, secrets can turn you inside out, and back again.

'Do you think … couples should tell each other everything?' I say to him. As soon as the words are out, I wonder what on earth I'm doing, how many careful years of fabrications I may be tearing down. But I should have known better.

'Of course. And we do,' he says. His tone is so sure that it shuts me up as efficiently as a slap around the mouth. I turn to the dressing table and start dragging my brush through my hair, tears rising unbidden. *Ouch.* I should have attempted this last night. I've washed my hair, but it looks like the sea-spray is here to stay. In the mirror, our eyes meet for a second, then dash away from each other like my own nimble mice.

When the gong sounds this time, it's less like some bonkers stage play and more a familiar part of this weird castle life. It's been the oddest day – all revolving around Gita and her child, of course – and now we have to face whatever Rachel has in store.

'That's just the first gong, darling,' Geoff says, reassuring now as he drags me in for a hug. 'You've still got time to get yourself all glammed up.'

I thought I'd already done that. I hesitate, then disengage so I can peer into the mirror. Apparently I need more make-up.

I fidget with the mascara wand. Rachel's cloak is like a bin-bag on me and I realise it will completely cover the dress I spent so long choosing. I wonder if everyone has these capes, or whether Rachel just doesn't trust me to get it right. I suppose I can't blame her after last night's fleece, but I don't want my nose rubbed in it. I sigh. Suddenly the whole weekend seems like a nose-rubbing of epic proportions. And that horrifying mention, out of the blue, of my long-ago abortion, my worry that Vicky heard it all. 'Why did we even agree to come?'

'Don't be silly,' says Geoff. 'You're going to look gorgeous, my darling. And we're having … quite a time. Look at this place. It's how the other half lives. You never know, maybe they want to give me some business.' I see a gleam in his eye that hasn't been there for those long weeks and months of worry. Whatever has been gnawing at him seems to be dissipating in this strange place, despite the near-death of a little girl and a gathering storm that is now trying to take the roof off Rachel's castle. If he can block it all out, and think only about the positives, I suppose I can.

'You're right,' I say. As long as he's on my side, as long as he never knows, I can get through anything. Rachel has promised to keep quiet. And, if Vicky heard, why would she ever say anything? Unless she drinks too much. Then all bets are off. She doesn't realise what she's saying or who she's hurting. I remember her shouting at little Raf, way back at Ruby's christening. He must have been all of ten. 'Stop whining, lad, no wonder Daddy left,' she yelled – just before she passed out.

But I can't go on thinking like this. I've spent my life held hostage by this damned secret. I deserve an evening off. Now Geoff is sweeping around the room, his own cape easily as long as mine. I squash my worries and try and look mysterious and gothic – and carefree – as I get up and join him in a little impromptu swishing. I can play-act for a few hours, can't I? And then opt for an early night.

Yes, it'll soon be all over. And tomorrow, thank Christ, I'm going to take Geoff and get the hell out of this place. No one can stop me.

Breathless, I whirl to a halt. 'I've just remembered, I left my handbag downstairs. So stupid. I'll just nip and get it.'

'Do you want me to fetch it?' offers Geoff, ever the gentleman. 'And I can finally have that little chat with Rachel.'

'With Rachel?' For a second, I'm surprised. I didn't think they were exactly on 'chat' terms. But then I remember that time, a couple of months ago, when I went for a Sunday walk, and came back to find Geoff on the phone. To Rachel, of all people. He was pink in the face, with that shiny, wrung-out look he gets when dealing with difficult clients.

Geoff flung me the receiver as though it were radioactive, and scuttled off outside 'to look at the runner beans'. Rachel and I had a desultory conversation and signed off. She was just about to get on a flight, and had just been with *the most fabulous* people. Talking to me in our little cottage must have been the dreariest of contrasts.

I suppose I've been preoccupied too. The blow from the publishers, all my usual regrets. Now I remember Geoff was saying something when I walked in. It sounded like: *'You wouldn't dare.'* It finally strikes me there might be a connection, with whatever has been eating away at Geoff these past months.

If he can get things sorted out at last, I'm all for it. So I leap at his suggestion. 'Oh, could you fetch it, darling? That would be so kind. Then I can keep on getting ready.'

He takes off his cloak, blows me a kiss, and shuts the door carefully behind him. Once he's gone, I take a deep breath.

I do hope I'm doing the right thing.

Chapter 33

Geoff

Mount Tregowan, 31st October

I don't like to deceive my wife, in fact I consider subterfuge abhorrent. But occasionally, things crop up that she simply doesn't need to know about. I bracket keeping them from her with my other essential duties as a caring husband, in that I am helping to preserve her all-important peace of mind. Regrettably, what I am about to do falls into that benighted secret category.

I am in my stockinged feet as I descend, and I am therefore all but silent. I find Jane's handbag sitting at the foot of the stairs and pick it up. Just as I am approaching the door to the library, hoping to be granted a brief audience with the 'lady of the house', who should shoot out but Rachel herself.

'Oh, it's you, is it?' she says, in perhaps not the friendliest tone. 'You do look silly with that bag. You'd better come next door.'

I follow obediently, and find myself in the morning room. I can't help noticing it is, in fact, afternoon – but I guess that a jest on the subject will fall on stony ground.

'I suppose you want to talk about the obvious?' Her question unfortunately doesn't suggest an open mind or even a receptive ear, for that matter. But it may be the only chance I get.

'Many thanks for letting me take this opportunity …' I begin.

'Oh, for heaven's sake, can you get on? I've got to do my make-up. It's my big night, tonight,' she says, not quite suppressing a yawn. As she seems to be caked in cosmetics already I am surprised there is space for more paint, but I decide now is not the moment to venture that opinion.

'You must realise, it's all been a terrible …'

'Mistake?' she breaks in, then laughs. For a woman in a tearing hurry to cover herself with rouge, she really spins her cackles out. Her manners are beyond appalling.

'A clerical error, I was going to explain. You see, these things are easily done, the work of a single moment of inattention on the part of a junior colleague …'

'I'm pretty sure Jane told me you're a one-man band in that titchy office of yours.' Rachel sniffs. 'So don't try and blame anyone else. Ross says …'

'You've told your husband?'

'Don't squeak! For God's sake, Roderick's voice is bad enough. Of course I haven't. Yet. He just says in general, don't deal with the little people … and now I see why. But I *will* tell him. Unless you sort things out.'

I swallow. 'I also wanted a moment with him. To ask whether there were any legal services I could offer whilst I'm here …'

Rachel's second peal of laughter is still ringing in my ears, long after she has swept out of the morning room and up the stairs.

When I've collected myself sufficiently to leave the room, I bump straight into Vicky. By the looks of things, she has been celebrating young Ruby's return to the fold in her own room. With rather too lavish a hand. She sloshes her drink all over me.

'Whoops! Doesn't matter, though, does it? Got to get changed, Geoffy. Chop chop.'

I don't bother trying to explain that I am already in my evening attire. I am about to go back upstairs when she grabs my arm.

'Just want to say, I really admire you. The way you're taking it.'

I look at her. Do I even want to know what she's talking about? We're standing in the corridor but she carries on as loudly as though addressing the crowds at Speakers' Corner.

'About Jane's, *you know*, op. Back in the day.'

I just look at her blankly, but she sails on.

'Lot of men might have seen her as damaged goods. The way she could never stay up the spout afterwards. But you've been fran … frab … fantastic.' She claps me heavily on the back and lurches up the stairs.

I am left staring after her, still clutching Jane's bag, a succession of images in my mind. Jane, white-faced, bent double in pain yet again. The folding away of another miniature sleepsuit, destined to remain forever untenanted. Vicky cannot possibly mean what she has just said.

I am amazed I am managing to stand upright. Because the metaphorical rug has been pulled right out, from under my very feet.

Chapter 34

Rachel

Mount Tregowan, 31st October

There. The final touch. I put my eyeliner down and get up, ready to step into my robes. There's a rap at the door and Ross appears, agitated.

'What is it, darling?' I say, going over to him. We embrace and, yet again, I realise I must get him started urgently on yoga. He needs more fluidity in his core. I can't be hugging a mop.

'Two things, my love. That little girl, Jane. The one in the erm, unsuitable clothes … she wandered into the library. Thinking of settings for a book, she said. Seems nervous about tonight. Something about one of your previous parties.'

The very idea of Jane's mice cavorting in a place like this. I snort. 'I suppose it's her outfit. She's got nothing to fear this time; my cloak will cover a multitude of sins. Although yes, now I think back, the silly thing did really overdo it, last time I had a Halloween thing. She had to get her stomach pumped. I wouldn't dream of referring to it – it was too ridiculous. Why on earth would she bother you about it?'

Ross's eyebrows raise a centimetre. 'Ah, I think she finds you a little ... intimidating.'

I laugh, but he goes on. 'And then I'm afraid there's Penny,' he mutters into my hair. I pull away a centimetre and gaze into his eyes. Usually he can't resist the swimming-pool depths of mine. But he just stalks off and stands by the window. I return to my dressing table. A flash of lightning strikes, then fades out over the sea. The storm is still a way off. But it's drawing ever nearer.

'Penny? What's her problem?' I adjust my tone enough for this to come out honeyed. He looks over at me but it's dark again, I can't see his expression. And vice versa.

'All that business with the child just now. It took it out of her. Brought back memories. I'm not sure she's up to – tonight. A tray in her room ...'

I rush to his side. 'Ross, no! She has to be part of the family group. Don't you see? I've been planning this for so long. You know that. She mustn't spoi ... *spend* any time worrying about all that. Everything worked out fine with Ruby, didn't it? I've had a word with Gita. Nothing to worry about there. Penny will enjoy herself tonight. Really she will. It's important, darling. For all of us.' I kiss him, and of course he concedes.

I send him on his way, to break the bad news to Penny. I can just see her thin features bunching, like the hood of a cagoule in bad weather. No one in this country seems to have heard of injectables.

God, that brings me to Jane. I hope she's going to make an effort tonight, not be a wet blanket about something that happened twenty years ago. All right, I shouldn't have mentioned the termination. I wouldn't have thought it mattered. Everyone must have known years ago. Then she was twitchy about her mouse books, too. She's turned into such a prima donna, I'm beginning to wonder why I asked her at all.

I thought Jane and Vicky were huge friends, but they don't seem to be hanging out much. Vicky's a bit off as well. And as for Jane's husband, I'm glad I caught him skulking outside Ross's study, before he worked up the nerve to go in. The cheek, suggesting he might ask Ross for work! I don't think so. Ross has got lawyers aplenty, and they're all better than Geoff.

He and Jane do serve one useful purpose, of course. They make up the numbers. I'm amazed people still haven't noticed that there are thirteen of us yet. Vicky particularly. She can't be too sozzled these days to perform simple addition, can she? Maybe it'll hit her when we sit down to table this evening. I kept last night to a buffet especially so the penny – ha-ha – wouldn't drop, but I'm beginning to feel none of this lot would appreciate my whole Halloween theme even if I asked them to stand up and be counted. And Gita, the one person I've told, seemed to think my idea was horrifying, instead of brilliant. Never mind. Pearls before swine.

Even these cloaks, though. Will they get that? I hope they do. I hope the events of that party twenty years ago – everything other than ditzy Jane ending up in A&E – haven't faded completely from their minds. Surely Gita will remember? She was so starry-eyed, madly in love with Tom. I had to prise her off him to pick up the costumes beforehand. 'Why are you buying so many cloaks?' Gita asked, once we'd bundled them all into my car.

'Hiring, honey, not buying. Do you think I'm made of money?' Gita lowered her eyes at that. Mentioning my fortune is always like flatulence at a funeral. All right, we're a couple of decades on from that night. And she's had three goes of baby brain. But won't the brand-new, lovingly made cloak in her room jog that memory?

It's almost as if none of them want to cast their minds back.

But I'm sorry, they're just going to have to.

Chapter 35

Vicky

Mount Tregowan, 31st October

I was that pleased about Ruby, I admit it. Been toasting her in the privacy of my room. Then popped downstairs for paracetamol – got a feeling I'm going to need some tomorrow. Finished my packet this morning.

Bumped into Geoff. Seemed a bit off. But he and Jane must have discussed everything, in the last, what, twenty years. Yeah, course. Close couple like that. Geoff did look a picture with that handbag.

Race back to my room for just one more sip and Tom is in the corridor. When isn't he hanging around in the shadows? I slam my bedroom door on him and stand with my back to it. My hand touches something soft and warm and I wheel round. It's a cloak, swinging from the hook.

I don't like it, the way people wander around my room at will. I'm used to my space being my own, 'specially since Raf left. If I leave my cereal bowl on the counter at 6 a.m. before going to work, it's there to greet me when I get home.

I switch on the light at last, calm my breathing. The bed has been turned down. It's just Rachel's house elves whisking around. But my eyes dart to the bedside cabinet all the same.

Now I'm looking at the cloak more closely. The velvet is shiny like polyester, though I'm sure Rachel would die at that idea. Inside, the lining is so red it hurts my eyes. God, it's lush. I slip it over my shoulders. The satin is cold as a knife on my arms.

Instantly, I'm having a flashback. To one of the (many) other times I've been so drunk I've blacked out. I've read all about it. More aversion therapy. Apparently once you've sunk enough alcohol, your hippocampus, the memory-maker, becomes paralysed. The brain becomes incapable of recording. But explain these splinters of the past that come back to me, then. My faulty showreel.

This cape, but so many years ago. And Tom, the smell of him, sharp, feral. His sweat. The way our bodies contorted, on a pile of other capes. The plunge, taking the plunge, as his arse rose and fell between my legs. How could a thing that was so wrong, feel so much righter than right? Then the shock, as I opened my eyes for a second, seeing another face, over his shoulder. A perfect oval swimming into focus, with mouth and eyes stretched round. That shows how long ago it was – her features were fully mobile. Then a flick of long blonde hair as she turned. I hadn't heard the door open, but I definitely heard it close, as Rachel left. Then the room was silent, apart from his panting.

Christ. I turn my head, so sharply I crick my neck. But it's not as simple as that, shutting stuff out. How many years ago was that? I can't kid myself. I know all too well. And since that day, the skulking around, the weight of the unspoken, lies between me and Gita. Rachel, too. And Tom's sly eye, mocking me. The duty to keep on turning up, keep on being friends. My reason for never drinking again. And the reason I'm reaching into the bedside drawer now, pulling out the flask of vodka, slugging back some more.

Sometimes things come along that you haven't planned for. You just have to make the best of them. Hunker down, keep quiet, respect the boundaries. That's what I've told myself over the years. But I've been wrong. I've taken on all the guilt – I should have got angry instead, a long time ago.

The cloak is still round me as I crash onto the bed. I sink my fingers into the silk and satin, digging my nails into it, twisting and pulling, trying to rip and tear. But it's too well made, the seams braided and bound, the fabric expensively woven.

Damn, damn, damn. Damn and blast. Scarlet dances across my vision, rivers of blood, of revenge. Sharp as those shards of memory. I've kept the secret – I've been forced to. They have all made me. And look what it's done to me. I don't want this anymore. And I'm not going to take it.

Rage finally rises in me at last, pure and cold as tempered steel. They say confession is good for the soul. But stabbing may be even better.

Chapter 36

Tasha

Mount Tregowan, 31st October

I hear the gong go a second time and I know that's the signal to assemble downstairs. But I literally don't know if I could actually move right now.

I don't know how long it's been since Rachel tapped at my door. I suppose it was lovely of her. She must have had so much to get ready, but here she was, checking on us kids, after the whole Ruby business.

So I welcomed her in. She sat herself down, right here on my bed. And what she said ruined my whole life.

'I just wanted to see how you're doing, after all the fuss over your sister,' she said. 'It's lovely to see how well you're all getting on. Raf, too. You must have seen so much of him over the years.'

I scooted over to make room for her, shoved myself up against the edge of the bed. I'd just been watching a bit of Netflix, decompressing. It was really stressful, the search. But it felt great to have Aunty Rachel there. She slid along so that we were propped up next to each other on the pillows, like friends. It kind of felt natural. Well, she's been round those few times, while Dad's been working from home.

There was one of those silences, like someone's waiting for something. Then I realised she wanted an answer about Raf. 'Yeah, well, Mum and Vicky are friends so we've seen them on and off,' I said, non-committal. Then I had a thought. 'Do you want to see my Instagram?' All the online tutorials say you should maximise your contacts. Aunty Rachel must have billions of followers.

'I was thinking earlier, what a handsome pair you and Raf make,' Rachel said.

'Do you think so?' I couldn't help smiling. I remember thinking it might even be a treat to talk about him.

'Yes. Such similar colouring, your hair, your eyes. Even the way you carry yourselves.'

I could feel myself frowning now, trying to picture us. 'Raf is way taller, of course. And so buff. I don't work out nearly as much as I should,' I said.

Rachel shrugged. 'Oh, maybe. I meant on a deeper level.'

She was losing me now. 'OK. So, about the dinner? I should mention Nessie is a pescatarian, if Mum hasn't already said …'

'The chef will have that under control. But with Raf, do you feel that connection? As well as having an *aire de famille*, as they say in French?'

'*Famille*? Family? We don't see that much of them. Aunty Vicky's always working, Mum says. And she can't talk …'

'I'm an only child, you see. It's a burden. So I just wondered.'

I was silent for a second. Then I turned to Rachel. The creamy skin. The big eyes. The expression in them. Interested, even a bit … envious. Why on earth would Rachel – ahem, Rachel *Cadogan* – envy me? There was that sense of expectation in the air again. I blinked.

'Wondered what?'

She paused for a second, and I thought she wasn't going to

speak at all, was just going to let me dangle there. Then she carried on.

'Why, what it's like to have a brother, of course.'

I just looked at her, like I was an idiot, like I'd been struck dumb. Somewhere, I could hear Rachel carry on talking, though her words hardly registered anymore.

'Tasha? Tasha! Are you OK? *Don't tell me you didn't know.*'

Chapter 37

Jane

Mount Tregowan, 31st October

Geoff walks back in and throws my bag on the bed. Immediately I know something's happened. Normally he'd bring it over to me, probably give me a kiss as well. He's only been gone what, ten minutes? We were happy, swooping around like demented vampire bats in our cloaks. Now he won't look at me.

Not one of his moods, please. I've got enough to cope with. Amongst this crew, Rachel and the rest, I already feel fragile, off-centre, like a runner wrongly entered in a sprint when I'm better at marathons. Who am I kidding? This is a race I'm not qualified for at all.

I head over to the suitcase. Why didn't I hang up my dress yesterday? Or today, even? I can't believe I've left it in here. I pull it out, crumpled and forlorn. But suddenly Geoff breaks into my thoughts.

'I've just bumped into Vicky downstairs. While I was getting your blessed handbag.'

I look up. His tone is so cold.

There's a pause while I decide what my strategy should be. At home, he sometimes perks up if I carry blithely on and pretend not to have noticed anything. I'll try it here, get on with sorting myself out.

The cloak will cover a lot, but not everything. I want to be bulletproof against Rachel's raised eyebrow tonight. I pick up the dress and shake it, seeing if the creases will magically fall out. They don't.

'Why didn't you tell me?' Geoff says abruptly.

I sit down, trying not to listen. 'If I have a quick shower and hang the dress up in the bathroom, the steam will help, won't it?'

There's a silence. 'Did I remember to pack that spare pair of tights, in case I get a ladder?' I burble on. There's no reply. And an increasingly loaded quality to the silence. I give up, and turn to him. His face looks odd. 'What is it, Geoff? Aren't you feeling well?'

'I'm trying to tell you. Vicky said something, just now.'

I look at him properly. He knows my book has been put on the back burner. He even knows about the way I, um, overdid things at Rachel's last Halloween party, years ago. There's only one thing he doesn't know. Ice crystals form in my stomach. No. Not after all this time. So many years clotting and passing, month by month, miscarriage by miscarriage. Why would Vicky open her big mouth now?

Because she's Vicky, a little voice tells me. *Because she's a drunk.*

She's my friend, I tell myself. She couldn't … she wouldn't betray me. Would she? But another look at Geoff's face tells me all I need to know.

I swallow. I get up and bustle about, keeping my back to him. 'What did she say? She certainly seems a bit weird this weekend, don't you think? Maybe it's Raf giving her the cold shoulder … Or maybe we should all just admit it, Vicky drinks too much. Does your shirt need steaming? I can put it on a hanger with my dress if you like. I'm going to run the water really hot. That'll do the trick. Got to put our best feet forward … especially after last night …'

'Jane. Stop it. Just look at me. Is it true? What Vicky told me?'

For a second, our gazes lock, then my eyes skeeter away from his. I start rummaging loudly in my make-up bag for a lipstick I haven't brought and wouldn't use anyway. 'I don't know what she told you, so how can I say?' My voice is rising, my cheeks are heating up. I know he'll see through me. Country solicitor he may be, but he's had his share of lying, scheming clients over the years.

I raise my eyes to his, pleading for love, for understanding. For time to explain. But he is hard, unreachable. He's not my cuddly Geoff anymore. He's like a statue of the man I married, and looks about as forgiving as a lump of marble too.

I sink onto the bed again, the tears finally sliding down my face. Geoff – kind, tender Geoff – who even in these last few distracted months, when he's barely slept and has been chased by worries of his own, has always rushed to hug me when I've had a bad day, when I've had to queue behind a mum with a pushchair or passed one too many playgrounds. Now he looks at me, shakes his head once, and walks out.

He doesn't even slam the door. Somehow that faint and precise click is the loudest, cruellest sound I've ever heard in my life.

Worse than when I lay with my legs in stirrups, getting that baby scythed out of me. Or when Rachel idly cast an eye over my bank statement, lying open on my student desk long ago, and saw the payment to the clinic. Or all those doctors afterwards, saying they didn't know what was wrong. But *I* knew. A slip of the knife. That was all it had taken, to wreck my dreams.

It was one thing, Rachel getting an abortion. She was as casual about that as she was about any other purchase. No shame, no blame. No consequences. For me, it was so different.

Of course, I'd been madly in love. 'Don't tell anyone about us; it's more exciting like this.' His breath had been hot in my ear. Just another student, but I'd have done anything he said, amazed he'd picked me at all. It had been a very slow night in the Union bar. No witnesses, to my triumph in getting off with him, and his deciding to settle for slim pickings. Then back to his squalid shared flat. After he'd come, he'd rolled onto his back. 'You're on the pill, right?' he asked, towelling himself off with my T-shirt. I'd nodded numbly, but what had I known, barely out of my teens, fat, shy and, until minutes before, an unloved, unwanted virgin?

Six weeks later, I'd finally run him down in a corridor. 'Yeah, I'm late too, for a lecture,' he'd said, though he'd bragged before that he never went to any. Then three weeks after that, when the awful deed had been done and our baby was dead, there he was that wretched evening, at Rachel's Halloween party. Not even embarrassed to meet my eye. 'You're sorted now, right?' he said over his shoulder as he helped himself to another beer. So he had understood what I'd meant, all along. But he'd chosen to abandon me, and our child, to our fate. I don't even remember the ambulance, the hospital, and my date with a funnel full of charcoal, later that night.

All this should have been forgotten, long ago, and as dead as that baby and all the others. Why on earth has Vicky dug it up, now of all times?

I wish I could see her, in this moment, and tell her what I think of her, until my blood boils over, and my anger cascades out, overriding her vodka fug, her pathetic excuses. What will she say? *I was drunk. I'm sorry. A slip of the tongue.*

Maybe there should be another slip of the knife. My knife, this time. Maybe she should go from being dead drunk, to just being dead.

That's what I want right now.

Downstairs, the gong sounds yet again and I turn like an automaton, shrug my dress on at last. Who cares what it looks like? Wrinkled or immaculate, it's all one to me. I throw on the cape and jam the wig over my hair.

Let the charade begin.

Chapter 38

Gita

Mount Tregowan, 31st October

I'm still not on an even keel, after the business with Ruby. I'm looking at this place, and everyone in it, with new eyes. I know everyone will be thinking I'm the one to blame – the mother always is. I wasn't watching, at the crucial moment. And no, I can't forgive myself.

But Ruby does have two parents. And Tom was supposed to be keeping an eye on her. How could he have let it happen?

I suppose he was 'busy with other things.' As he so often is. As he's been for months. Along the way, his abs have re-emerged, like Aztec ruins rising from the rubble. He says it's his way to conquer the stress. But it takes all his energy. 'Do you still find me attractive?' I asked him the other day. 'Of course I do, darling,' he said, hugging me, but I saw his eyes dart away, like silverfish running under the fridge when the kitchen light is turned on.

I know it's irrational, but I'm angry with Vicky, too. For agreeing to come here. I know, I went all out to tempt her. I showed her those pictures, I told her Raf would love it. But that stuff I googled was so misleading. I just saw the sea as a backdrop to our frolics. Never, for one moment, did I think it would become an enemy, the thing that might have snatched my Ruby away. Or something that would enclose us so fully in its aggressive, inescapable embrace.

I look out of the window now, as I fiddle with my earrings. The sea is so high, it seems to have swallowed the bottom of the island. It's roiling up and down, like a bedsheet twitched from the dryer. Should it be doing that?

I turn away quickly, reminding myself that it wasn't the sea that nearly did for Ruby. She was in the chapel, drenched yes, but Tom says it was just a wave; she never went in the water.

Who has their own chapel? It's ludicrous, even by Rachel's standards. I want to go and see it, but there's no time. I've got to get ready for this stupid evening. 'It's all heraldic shields in stained glass, lots of those lance things …' Tom told me. *More* bloody lances, like that dagger thing Ruby had.

Of course it would come complete with a priest's hole. Trust Rachel. She's almost more of a goth than Nessie. Oh, my head is swimming. I'm still not right after this afternoon. Naps have always given me jet lag. I'm better staying on the go. I take a last look in the mirror. I wonder, not for the first time, what it would be like to be Rachel, to see all that expensive beauty gazing back.

But no, I'm just a woman with a job and kids and a husband who doesn't seem to like me much anymore. A husband who seems to prefer – hell, has always preferred – forbidden fruit. Other women. There, I've acknowledged it at last.

I feel the spectre of divorce hanging over me, the shame and the humiliation looming. I'm going to turn out exactly like my parents. And be treated, like them, as a pariah. I was hoping this weekend would be a chance to reconnect with Tom, salvage things. Save me from lawyers and settlements and toxic wrangling. It hasn't worked. I could kill him for all he's done. But then, I could kill so many people this evening.

I sling on a necklace and check the fit of my dress. Thank God for Spanx. But even so, there's a mountain ridge where the Lycra stops and the flab begins. It's a metaphor for my life. Nothing is as smooth as it seems.

Then I catch sight of the cloak. Well, small mercies. I can eat what I like tonight at least. And I am dying, literally dying, for a drink. For a second, I think about popping to Vicky's room for what we used to call a sharpener, or what Tasha and her girlfriends now call a 'pre'. Vicky will have a bottle somewhere. But it's not like the old days. There wasn't any shame then, in openly wanting to get pissed. Now we're supposed to have grown out of it. Well, Vicky hasn't, but I have – most of the time. I wonder if I ought to be more concerned about Vicky's drinking. But honestly, I don't have the spare capacity.

For a second, my mind goes to that Halloween party long ago. I got ready then with Rachel. 'Do I look OK from this angle, though?'

'You look as perfect from that angle as you did from all the others. You are 360 degrees of fabulousness, Rach. Let's go,' I'd begged her.

The venue was the college dining room, less posh of course than her Grand Hall here, but unheard of then as a student party rendezvous. We left our bags and coats in a little room just next door, furnished with metal coat rails and little else. She turned to me later that evening, after we'd had a couple of drinks. 'You look gorgeous too,' she said softly. 'And, um, Gita ...' Then Tom bounded up and the moment was lost.

I haven't thought about that night for years. Now I suddenly wonder what she was about to say. It was about Tom, I think. But it can't have been important. Can it?

Chapter 39

Vicky

Mount Tregowan, 31st October

God, it's been the weirdest day, what with the hunt that never was, Rachel's treasure nonsense, then the hunt that should never have been, for little Ruby.

I can't be the only one gasping for a large one, desperate to get this dinner started so we can all bloody go, first thing in the morning. Gita was talking, at one point, about making a long weekend of it. Looking at her face now, across Rachel's ancestral hall, I can see she's gagging to get her girls back onto the mainland. I'm going to flag down the first London-bound train that comes our way.

One of the silent waiters passes and I stick out a hand – and indicate my glass. It's as dry as the Gobi Desert. I decide to go and talk to Jane. She jumps a foot. 'I don't know how you've got the cheek to come near me,' she spits as I almost trip. 'Looks like you need to go and have a lie-down anyway.'

'No, I bloody don't,' I snap. 'Drat Rachel and her stupid Persian rugs.'

'*Shh,*' she wipes a bit of my gin and tonic off her cloak and looks meaningfully over to Penny. True to form, the woman looks like she's just this moment stopped sucking a lemon.

'God, she won't care; she hates Rachel. Mind you, you could use her face to curdle milk tonight,' I confide to Jane. She takes a step away and frowns. 'Where's Geoff?' I ask, looking round. 'Has he cheered up? He was acting weird earlier. Have you found out yet what's been eating him?'

Jane glares at me. For a second, I think she's going to ignore me. Rude. Then she just barks, 'Where's Rachel? Have you seen her?'

I cast a look around the room, and put a hand against the mantelpiece. The marble is smooth, reassuring. Where the hell is our hostess? Everyone's gone AWOL tonight.

Gita comes over, Ruby super-glued to her side. I'm not sure who is clinging more. 'You all right there, love?' I say to Ruby, bending down a little, then wishing I hadn't. 'We need some canapés or something,' Gita says to a waiter.

'Do you know what time the tide does its thing tomorrow?' I say to Gita, leaning back against the mantelpiece, feeling its chill through Rachel's cloak and my own asymmetric black number.

'Tom will know. He's gone full-on Bear Grylls today. There's nothing he can't tell you about this island.'

'No! Don't bother him. He's doing sterling service, keeping that fun-sucker out of our hair,' I say, waving in the general direction of Penny. Jane and Gita exchange a glance. 'Oh come on, girls. I don't mean it. But honestly, what is she like?' I say, *sotto voce*.

Just then Rachel's little stepson turns up. 'Rodney, Rodney,' I say, trying to make him feel welcome.

'Rode*rick*,' Jane hisses, but all I hear is *dick* and it's the funniest thing anyone's said all night. It's not until Tasha comes up to us that I shake my head and stop giggling.

'Are you OK?' Gita says, looking at her daughter. It's true, she's a bit blotchy.

'Thank God we're past the spotty stage now, ladies, eh?' I say to the others, but they just stand there like statues.

Tasha is saying something to me, but her voice is so low I don't catch it at first.

'And you've pretended to be my mother's friend, all these years, and never said a thing ...'

'What? Hang on, Tash, rewind please.' I step forward, to hear the girl better, but also to screen Gita. Because it's suddenly obvious to me, Tasha must have somehow found out about her dad's roving eye. 'Look, what your father gets up to is his business. Your mum doesn't want to know,' I hiss, forgetting I'm wearing such high heels. Jane and Gita prop me back up and I take a sip, try and style it out. Almost miss my mouth. But has Tasha finished? No, she bloody hasn't.

'But I'm talking about you, *Aunt* Vicky. And what *you* got up to.'

Oh. She must be on about my liking for the drink. Well, that's none of her beeswax. 'Easy to know all the answers when you're thirteen years old, isn't it, love?' I say, shrugging to Jane.

'I'm eighteen!' the girl wails, sounding five, now. I catch sight of Gita's face. She's not impressed with me. However much her daughter is making a tit of herself, of course she's going to side with her. Even against one of her oldest friends.

'Flesh and blood. It's always flesh and blood,' I say, disgustedly.

'Yes, and he's your flesh and blood, isn't he? *Raf*, I mean.' Tasha's little face is scarlet now.

I nod. 'Give that girl a prize,' I say, raising my glass to her.

'And ... my father's. That's right, isn't it? Admit it. Admit it to my mother. Raf's my half-brother.'

I say nothing, air where my jaw used to be. I look at Gita, but her eyes are round and her head is shaking from side to side. She's backing away.

But she's not telling Tasha she's got it all wrong. She's not yelling at me to deny it. It makes me wonder if she's suspected, all this time. And has at last had her doubts confirmed.

Meanwhile Jane looks like I've hit her round the gob, God alone knows why. I turn back to Tasha, and see pain as well as twisted triumph in her eyes. *Shit.* They were thick as thieves, her and my lad this morning. Too late, I get it. 'You ... and Raf?'

'Me and Raf. My *brother*. Thanks, Vicky. Thanks for nothing.' This time, even in my fug, I notice she doesn't call me 'aunty'. I take a step towards them, her and Gita and Ruby, huddled now, but then there's a voice on the stairs.

'Good evening, everyone.' It's Rachel, with that skull on a stick, her new husband, in tow. I turn to her, my fists bunched. I knew I'd heard right, last night. That casual little comment about my lad's eyes. Rachel couldn't let it rest, could she? She had to cause trouble. I rush towards her, then suddenly I catch sight of Tom, right behind her, with that smug smile on his face.

That bloody snake. It's his fault, after all. The shit. Taking advantage of my weaknesses, my liking for a glass too many and that soft spot I had for him – and exploiting Gita's trusting nature too. Suddenly I'm raging about all of it. Well, I'm going to swing for him now. He's had it coming for long enough. He's going to get it.

I grit my teeth and take a step forward.

Chapter 40

Rachel

Mount Tregowan, 31st October

Poor Vicky. We all knew, of course. But maybe not how bad things had got. Still, it doesn't take long for her to 'freshen up'. She's lucky she didn't break her nose, falling headlong like that. Drunks bounce, don't they? And, once she's tottered out of the loo, looking greener than Tasha's emerald dress, she's ready to go into battle again. I can see it.

Too late, though, Vicks. We're now all seated at my lovely long table. I see her hesitate and swallow. Her throat must be like sandpaper after all that upchucking, but it's worked, just like it used to at uni. 'The Romans did it,' she'd point out at parties. 'They built special rooms for it.' Well, Vicky, my loo is not a vomitorium. And we've all grown past that shit. Or the rest of us have. She pulls out her own chair, waving away the server, and subsides. She's furious with me – I did glean that much from her ramblings. But who can she really blame, but herself?

I smile down the table. It feels good to have everyone here, all present and correct. Granted, the day has been full of more 'alarums and excursions' than I would have liked. Funny how my mind keeps drifting back to uni tonight. I remember the lecturer who first droned that phrase, and how Gita and I leapt on it. Every party after that was dissected for its share of *alarums and excursions*. And none had more than mine.

But tonight, I sense we all want to just enjoy the simple pleasures. I nod and more Cristal is poured. I hope those girls are appreciating it. Both Tasha and her mother are tucking in like it's lemonade. Tasha's had a shock, poor child. She won't look me in the eye. I hope Gita's not riled all over again. I'll speak to her later, smooth those ruffled feathers.

Raf, on the far side of the table, seems to have annexed his own bottle. Like mother, like son. I suppose it's a lot to take in. Even the backs of his ears are burning red, though why he should be embarrassed I don't know. It's his mother's little slip, not his. Well, hers and Tom's. I sip from my own flute, but only fizzy water tickles *my* nose. Honestly, this lot are so short-sighted. Even Tom, the ha-ha *professional*, is incapable of clocking the obvious tonight. He's got a lot of explaining to do – that's for sure.

I suppose it is down to me, as usual, to lance the boil, and release the ill will swirling around this table. But first I shall focus on higher things. The highest of them all. Love, not to put too fine a point on it. The one thing that eluded me for years, but which I've found on this funny little mountain. I raise my glass to Ross, all the way down the other end of the table. He's turned to speak to Penny. I cough, and his head shoots round. He salutes me and we both sip.

I look at Penny, her funny sour face, and I have a little idea. Quite a lot of tonight has been scripted – I'm known for my meticulous preparation – but I can improvise when I need to. 'Penny, have you asked Tom about all that business with your mother?' I call out. 'You know he could investigate for you?'

I love the colour Penny's gone, a shade paler even than dear Vicky, post-vom. Her mouth is hanging open but it's Tom who speaks. 'I do have a job, you know, Rachel,' he drawls. He even tries that eyebrow thing, trying to look laconic. I don't know how the others fell for it, long ago. He's got more *fromage* going on than Harrods' cheese counter. I can't resist.

'But do you, Tom?' My words fall into a sudden silence. Gita looks my way, as stricken as though I've ripped off her dress and revealed her pants. We could leave it there – but Tom won't be able to. He's always on the attack. It's the way he was made.

'What do you mean by that? If you've got something to say, spit it out,' he says. 'Of course I have a job.'

He asked for it. 'That's not quite what I heard,' I purr.

Vicky stares hard at Tom, almost the first time she's glanced his way all weekend. Raf looks confused, as well he might after guzzling that much champers. Tasha looks as miserable as her goth sister. Ruby, bless her, is nearly asleep, thumb in mouth. Jane seems to be in her own private hell, and that lump of a husband of hers just appears confused. I pity the bumpkins who run to him for boundary advice and whatnot.

Tom tries to style it out, shrugging as though I'm crazy and turning to Gita. She looks poleaxed. She's always hated being confronted by the truth, but she doesn't say a word. It's Geoff who finally pipes up. 'What do you mean, precisely, Rachel?' he says.

'Tell them, Tom. They call it gardening leave, don't they? Or maybe it's different at the Met? Body-under-the-patio leave?'

'Window-box leave in my case,' he says heartily, trying to take the sting away. 'I've never been much of a one for gardening.'

'Oh, silly me,' I say. 'They probably say it's a suspension, don't they? Or maybe … just a straightforward sacking?' Now Tom's face is like thunder. And, right on cue, the first real-life peals of the coming storm crack right above us.

Gita leaps on it to divert us all. 'Oooh, thunder, girls. Shall we count to see how far away the storm is? One, two, three …' she starts intoning, but the girls just stare at their father.

'Is this true, Dad? Have you been sacked?' This time it's Nessie who speaks. 'Why didn't you tell me? You kept saying everything was fine.' Her strange features twist and suddenly she's crying. I might have known she'd be teary. And she's set off her little sister again. Damn. I'll have to press on with the main event. Back to the sideshow later.

I tap my spoon against my glass. The staff are scurrying around, taking away the main course, the wild Alaskan salmon and the wagyu beef. Now the plates are being swapped for the special golden chargers with the pumpkin border. Laid across each one is a long brass skewer, copied exactly from the Tregowan coat of arms. They impale a parade of perfect berries, interspersed with exquisite mini macarons. Oh, and there's a dollop of sabayon on the side. Simply delicious.

I tap again, more loudly, and everyone swings to me. I can tell Gita wants to launch into some sort of protest so I get up quickly, gathering my cloak around me with a fluid gesture. 'I just wanted to thank you all so much for coming,' I say, my words sprinkling onto a multitude of expressions. 'And I wanted to make a little announcement, before we get sidetracked. We don't want our dear Tom to grab all the attention, do we? Even though he's pretty good at getting his way with us ladies – am I right, girls?' I can't help exchanging meaningful glances with my friends.

'Well, *this* very special bit of news is all mine … and my dear husband's.'

I glance over at Ross again, and he's sitting bolt upright, a polite smile on his face. On either side of him, the ugly steps bristle in anticipation.

Oh, this is going to be so much fun.

'Everyone, please raise your glasses, to the ancient and noble family of Tregowan.' I wave my glass aloft. 'And … to its newest addition.'

I let my cloak fall open and I caress my stomach in the unmistakable gesture of mothers-to-be over the millennia, just as there's another almighty thunderclap overhead. This time, the lightning

172

wastes no time at all in striking. It's immediate, and comes with a curious fizzing sound. And then, to my eternal annoyance, my moment is cruelly cut short.

All the lights go out.

PART TWO

PART TWO

Chapter 41

Geoff

Mount Tregowan, 1st November, Ten minutes past midnight

The horrible realisation that one among our number is dead ought to act like a pall upon the room. A dignified silence would be the only decent response to such an outrage. I regret to say that the exact opposite is happening here; there is complete and utter pandemonium in the Great Hall. The storm raging above us does not help one bit.

'Sit down! Sit down!' It takes me a few moments even to hear Roderick, let alone to register that no one is taking a blind bit of notice of him. Whether it is Vicky, drunkenly lurching about, or Gita's youngest daughter, weeping and shrieking hysterically, there is movement and noise everywhere. Everyone is on their feet; most are running around in the manner of decapitated poultry.

All except one of us, that is. There is a single, silent figure in our midst, at the centre of all the wild gesticulation, cries and shouts. It is not for some minutes that we begin to realise who, exactly, it must be.

It comes down to this. There were thirteen of us at the table, when Rachel began this supremely ill-advised so-called Halloween Feast. There are now twelve. And a body.

Rachel's university chums are all present and correct, their partners and offspring, if applicable, ditto. Her new, if one can call it that, family is hale and hearty. No, the corpse, I note with infinite regret, belongs to none other than our beautiful, eccentric, and some would say, wilful, hostess herself. Rachel Cadogan. Or, more properly, the second Lady Tregowan.

It takes some others round the table rather longer to make this deduction. The ceaseless movement and caterwauling do not, apparently, help people to reach logical conclusions. But, nevertheless, I now hear the word *Rachel* issue from more than one mouth. I am just wondering whether I should step in, reintroduce a bit of order, as Roderick has signally failed to quell the commotion, when there is a sudden and authoritative bark from the side of the room.

'Right, silence please. And nobody move.'

It is Tom. I suppose all that police training must be coming to the fore. 'Not a moment too soon,' I murmur in approval, and receive a frosty glance from him for my pains.

'Step away from the body, there,' he says, and Roderick and his sister shuffle back. They are closest to Rachel, and seem to have been inspecting her, ah, remains.

'Penny is a nurse,' Roderick quavers in outrage. 'She was just checking for a pulse.'

'And is there one?' says Tom drily. 'I can't help thinking all this noise might have woken Rachel up. If anything was going to.'

At that, there is another wail from young Ruby, and Gita starts to escort her out of the room. 'Take the others, too,' Tom tells his wife, nodding his head at his older daughters. 'As for the rest of you, everyone keep clear. And do *not* touch anything.'

Vicky puts down her glass with a fumble, and the wine goes all over the tablecloth. She giggles helplessly. 'Jane, could you help Vicky to bed?' Tom says, raising an eyebrow. I step forward too.

'Not you,' says Tom abruptly. 'All the men, I want us to quickly check the castle's locks and bolts. Then I suggest we all try and get some rest.'

I look at him in some astonishment, and there is an equally shocked murmur of protest from the others. None of us, quite obviously, is going to get a wink of sleep in this place tonight. Tom cannot seriously imagine that someone got in from outside. From whence, exactly? We all know the castle has been surrounded by rough seas for hours, and we are now in the eye of a storm. No one can have got in. No one can get out. We are, to put it quite simply, trapped.

I am as brave as the next man, I hope. But I must admit I am not particularly keen on traipsing around the dark and sinister corridors of this castle at the present moment.

Because there is, as we all now know, a killer in our midst.

Chapter 42

Gita

Mount Tregowan, 1st November

We're huddled in the library. Ross's domain, Rachel calls it. *Called it.*

Most of us have been here all night since ... it happened. Penny and Roderick were with us for a bit, but they've gone to their own rooms now. I suppose it's that stiff upper lip thing. God, I don't care about looking *British*, doing the right thing. I just want us to be safe. I got the girls to bed right after it happened, insisted they had to sleep, but then I immediately regretted it. What if the killer came back? Because someone *murdered* Rachel; that much is terrifyingly obvious. So I bundled them downstairs with their duvets and we've been camped out down here ever since.

It seems like safety in numbers, but that's an illusion. There are only twelve of us in the castle now, no longer Rachel's unlucky thirteen, but that doesn't make me feel one tiny bit safer. There's still a psychopath somewhere. And not out there, on the wind-lashed island. *Somewhere in this place.*

Here we all are, grim and gritty-eyed, with our hostess, the reason we're all here, the only thing most of us have in common, lying dead and cold in another room. I want to leave now, this minute, run out of here screaming and never come back. But we can't go anywhere. The sea beyond these walls is wild and swirling, waves crashing right up to the windows. The storm hasn't died down at all. The landline is still dead, and there's no mobile reception either.

We've got no choice; we have to wait for the tide. Then Roderick, before he went to his room, kept shaking his head at the waves and making dire predictions that we wouldn't even be able to cross in the morning. 'It's happened before. Adverse weather conditions,' he said, with a sort of subdued glee. He couldn't stand Rachel, that much was plain from the start, but I think he ought to hide his delight better than this. She's *dead*, after all.

God, I can't believe it. I can't, I can't. She can't be gone. She was more alive than all the rest of us put together. How can she be there, all alone in the Great Hall, cold and still, with her cloak – that silly bit of finery, so Rachel – now serving as her shroud?

I went in to see her just now. The girls were sleeping fitfully at last, and Tom just nodded at me, and whispered, 'You go. I've got this.' He knew I'd want to pay my respects. Despite everything, despite Vicky and her little bombshell over Raf, I decided I could trust him to keep an eye on them – for five minutes. He slipped up big time with Ruby earlier, but he's their dad after all.

They say people look like they're sleeping. She doesn't. She looks … dead. And so ungainly, hunched over the table like that. We couldn't move her; Tom said not to, but it seems wrong. I was only in there for a minute, but every detail is seared on my mind.

Someone – Ross, maybe, or one of the staff – had tried to spread a napkin over her hunched shoulders, to hide that dreadful skewer, but it just made things worse, tenting absurdly. She looked like some sort of hunchback, and under the wig you could see her poor pale face. She'd have hated this ridiculous, clumsy death. She was always so graceful.

181

So little time has passed, but already she was waxen, changing from flesh, into something halfway to stone. Her velvet robe was draped on the back of her chair – did someone take it off her, thinking she could be resuscitated? I didn't like to get too close.

Should we all gather in the chapel, say a prayer? If I were talking to Penny, I'd discuss it with her. But I can't bear to look at the woman, let alone speak to her. I can't forgive her for luring Ruby into the priest's hole. All right, I ought to feel compassion – she obviously has mental health issues. Perhaps I'll ask Roderick. If I can bring myself to. I can't forget that gleam of delight in his eye earlier, after we found Rachel.

But something else is puzzling me about Rachel. I couldn't help noticing it. Once I'd got over some of the horror of her huddled there, so awfully, awkwardly dead. We didn't see much of her dress last night, because of the cape. But slumped across the table like that, I could see the simple black satin gown. Beautifully cut, it goes without saying. Her stomach, though. Looking at her from the side. It was flat. There was no sign at all of a baby bump.

Then the night we arrived, her sea-green slip dress was so clingy. She was in amazing shape, no belly then either. Was she wearing some sort of next-level shapewear? Or was she just sticking her tummy out a mile last night on purpose, before the lights went out? For effect. I mean, I dread to think what I'd look like if I relaxed my stomach muscles in public, after three kids. I'd definitely look as though I was ready to pop the fourth. She must have been doing that, jutting her hips forward, when she made her announcement. Typical Rachel. Always so dramatic.

I'm looking back now, trying to see if there were any clues that she was pregnant. I think she was drinking champagne with the rest of us. I remember seeing a glass in her hand, certainly. But whether she actually sipped from it … Then it would be quite Rachel to go her own way. Everything she did showed it. Rules were for other people.

The first time I ever got into a car with her, I immediately wished I hadn't. 'No entry sign? What no entry sign?' she said, foot crashing down on the accelerator as we whizzed the wrong way down one of those rat-run roads behind her flat in Knightsbridge. God knows how she ever passed her test. If it hadn't been a UK driving licence, I'd say money must have changed hands.

I'm sad she didn't say anything to me about the baby; we were best friends for so long. I suppose not getting a wedding invite was a clue to how things had shifted, but I've got the childcare T-shirt after all. Loads to pass on. Was she already pregnant at that Soho lunch two months ago? She barely ate. Was it morning sickness ... or just Rachel? Or the bypass. At breakfast yesterday she was the same as usual. Glowing, gorgeous. God, it was only a few hours ago. Life turns on a knife edge. Oh. Wish I hadn't thought that. Suddenly the image of that wicked skewer pops into my head, embedded deep in Rachel's slender neck.

Poor Rachel. So much to live for, suddenly. A new husband, a new life here (though I shudder at the idea, I hate this place now) and a new baby, too. Mind you, she wouldn't have known what was about to hit her. A baby throws everything up in the air. Tom and I were sure we were going to redefine parenthood. I had everything organised before Tasha's birth, the Baby-gros arranged by colour and size ... three weeks later, with no sleep, we looked as though we'd been hit by an asteroid. And those little onesies, piled in the never-ending washing basket. I don't think I've seen the bottom of it since.

Rachel would have had help, of course. Hot and cold nannies on tap, I've no doubt. She would have needed them. I feel disloyal saying it. But really, she *was* a bit old for a first baby. Or maybe that's just me. I had mine in my twenties and thirties. I love my girls but Lord, the sleepless nights, the toll on your body. Did Rachel really want to do all that at forty-whatever? And Ross? Whatever age he is, it's definitely too old. Not to mention he's got that funny pair of grown-up children already.

But she won't be doing it now, will she? And nor will he. That baby has been snatched away with her. Gone, without a trace.

Ross must be devastated. Funny thing is that I caught a glimpse of his face last night just after Rachel put her hand on her tum and gave us that cat-got-the-cream smile. He was aghast. Granted, that's sort of his default expression. Arched eyebrows, puckered mouth. Tasha had a teacher once with a face like that. 'I've got Miss Cat-Bum as my form mistress this year,' she trilled. Not nice, but I knew immediately who she meant. I don't know if I've seen Ross crack a smile yet. I don't suppose I will, now.

Oh, Rachel. My eyes brim over again. Ross has got every excuse for looking pretty horrific right now. But if he were ever going to smile at his wife, last night would have been the moment. Surely. He must have wanted children. They'd have talked about it.

What am I saying? No, they really might not have done. That's Rachel all over. That *was* Rachel. I'm the one who likes to communicate. She just acted. She'd never had to wait for anything, any approval, any back-up. She came into her money so young. Her parents must have been younger than we are now when they died. Private planes sound so glamorous, don't they? But that Kennedy boy and his wife. Then there was a footballer recently …

Rachel didn't seem scarred by it. It's not right to say that coming into zillions must have softened the blow of being orphaned. But she never seemed to have a phobia about flying. She always did have that recklessness about her. Devil-may-care, they say. Well, don't care was made to care.

It must have been so liberating, being free to forge ahead at her own pace. That's what extreme wealth buys you, I suppose. Granted, half the time she made mistakes. A lot of her guys … and then a few business deals over the years … went awry, too. But with a financial cushion the size of a small country's GDP, it didn't ever seem to matter overmuch.

Children aren't like that, though. They're a joint venture, right from the off. Even Vicky has had to collaborate over the years with Bob – who really is a shit – because they have Raf together. Or so we thought. No, I'm not ready to think about all that yet, with Tasha. One horrible mess at a time. Betrayal on that scale, my husband, and one of my best friends … No, no, no. I have to shove it away. This is Rachel's moment.

Would Rachel have gone ahead with this without involving her husband *at all*? I sneak a look over at him. Unfortunately, our eyes meet and I have to look away again. God, this is all so awkward. But in that short glance I see he's aged too, since last night. He looks grey, deeply lined, vicious furrows on his face. Roderick is by his side again. He must have come back down when I tiptoed in to see Rachel. Both look off-kilter. What am I saying? Of course they do. We all do. I think the sun is coming up, though it's hard to be sure. The sky is still full of ink-black clouds and the rain is pelting the windows, rapping like hail or gunfire. Won't this storm ever blow itself out?

I wonder if any of us got any proper sleep at all. I know I hardly did. As for Tom, no sooner had I got back from the morning room just now then he was off. 'Where are you going?' I hissed over Ruby's head.

'Just checking everything's … locked up,' he said. God, the idea that someone might have got in from outside … might still be in the castle … I must admit it's a comfort to have him around. He's let me down horribly over the years, I can admit that now, but at least he's a proper man. Ross looks like he couldn't get out of his chair even if he had to and Roderick is the type I'd watch like a hawk if I had him on my team. He talks the talk – endlessly – but I imagine he's carried by his employees.

I dart another glance, this time to the left and right. We're all huddled in here. Roderick, staring straight ahead. At least he's not smirking anymore. Raf is pacing restlessly. Can't Vicky tell him to sit? But Vicky's still drunk, not even bothering to hide it. Well, what has she got to lose, now? I'll never respect her again, that's for sure. She has plenty of sorrows to drown. Her coffee cup is full of, ahem, clear liquid, which she's sloshed over her shoes at least twice.

The girls are awake now, at my side, not knowing what to do with themselves. Tasha is about a million miles deep in misery. I can't even begin to imagine how she's feeling. I shake my head. Why didn't Tom see what was going on with her, in all that time when he was home from work? He should have let me know she and Raf were getting so close. But he's oblivious to anything that doesn't touch him directly. No, no, I'm not going to give in to all that.

I've forbidden all the girls from posting on social media. Tasha is too heartbroken, and Ruby I hope is still too young, but I don't want any slips. Terrible that I even have to say it out loud, but I do. For them it's like breathing.

Tom's just come back. It's a relief. All right, he's been a shit, but I still worry about him. It's inbuilt. But as soon as he sticks his nose round the door, Geoff pipes up. 'Maybe, Tom, you and I should, ahem, do some more to secure the scene, as I believe they say? We are both the representatives of law and order here, are we not? I know we've, erm, left the body *in situ*, as it were, but is the door to the Great Hall actually sealed? Are all the exits covered?'

Tom just stands there, probably astounded at being bracketed with Geoff. So I jump in. 'Tom isn't that kind of policeman, though. He does fraud investigations. He's not a crime scene person, whatever they call them.'

'CSI,' Tom says absently. 'I'm really not sure about this, Geoff ...'

Then, wonders will never cease, Ross raises himself from his semi-coma in his chair. 'You know, I rather think that might be just the ticket? If you wouldn't mind, ah, Tom? Taking on those duties yourself? Just until the proper authorities get here from the mainland.'

Tom shrugs. 'Well ...'

Roderick chips in. He always seems to be trying to get into his dad's good books. Poor man, late forties and still after a pat on the head. 'I agree, Tom, you're best placed to sort this out. Just temporarily. We don't want to mess up the investigation. When the staff get here, in a while, they'll want to start cleaning and so on.'

'OK then, if we're all agreed?' Tom looks round and everyone nods, apart from Vicky, who buries her head in her cup, and Geoff, who stalks over to the window, no doubt peeved at being excluded. I admit, I give Tom a little smile. It seems to be the encouragement he needs. 'I'll get to it, then,' he says, all business.

So the Great Hall is now out of bounds. And Tom will have anything that might be construed as evidence locked up tight somewhere. I really don't know what. Things that might have fingerprints on? And the twelve skewers that weren't used as murder weapons, I suppose. God, even saying that makes me remember that horrible napkin tent on Rachel's back, and I feel sick.

After sorting out all that, Tom says he'll go down to the jetty, to see what the tide is up to, what the damage has been from the continuing storm. The wind is still whipping the island like a punishment.

Part of me wishes I could lash out at Tom the same way. For all his transgressions. But I've got to try and keep myself together. We only had a minute, last night, before we all took our seats at the table. And I was too angry to say a word. But Tom swore blind that whatever went on with Vicky twenty years ago was a one-off. And he had no idea about Raf. While Tasha is reeling, I need to be a support to her. It's not the time to tackle my husband. We've got enough to deal with as it is.

For a second, my mind flicks to Rachel, to what her advice would be. She must have thought I knew. Now I'm even wondering if at some level I did. Rachel would have a take on it. For a second, the loss hits me. A wave of sorrow. I'll never hear that voice again, persuading, cajoling, always getting away with – well – murder. *Rachel, Rachel. I can't bear it. I can't bear that you're gone. With*

your wildness, your wilful ways, your inconsistency and your charm.
I loved you so much.

But there's something else that keeps creeping in under the grief. It's insidious, unwelcome, but I can't keep it at bay.

This book-lined room was comfortable and elegant, when everyone first migrated to it, shocked and baffled, in the middle of the night. But it's getting more claustrophobic by the second. The jumble of bedclothes, my girls' bits and pieces, my own handbag and pillow and blanket aren't helping, but clutter isn't the problem. My sideways glances are being met by other covert peeps and diffident looks. All of us are doing it. All of us feel it. This prickling of the skin, this urge to hide – and yet this urgent, desperate necessity, to stick together.

Because one of us has blood on their hands.

Chapter 43

Vicky

Mount Tregowan, 1st November

This is the weirdest situation ever. The atmosphere was bad enough before Rachel died. When the lights went on, when I saw she'd been killed, my first reaction – after the horror – was astonishment. If Gita had finally killed Tom, now, that would have made perfect sense. Or if Gita had killed Penny, for what the silly mare had done to Ruby. Or if she'd even killed me, over the whole Raf thing. And that's just Gita.

Geoff was looking like he could cheerfully have stabbed Jane, after getting in such a grump before dinner. Jane's a deep one. I don't even know who she'd like to kill, maybe Geoff, maybe someone else, maybe even me, but I'm sure it would be somebody. Tasha could have gone for my lad, for the incest (though that's hardly his fault) or for her own dad, even. I'd have been in that queue too. Bloody Tom, the trouble he's caused me.

Penny looked like she could have killed *her* dad, most of the evening. I'd even overheard her saying something pretty threatening about Ross to Roderick: *'We have to deal with Daddy tonight.'*

It was probably to do with the car accident she's always banging on about. And Rachel was gearing up for some sort of announcement, too, not just the baby thing. I know what she was like when she had stuff to spill, that certain look in her eye.

But in the end, out of everyone, it was Rachel who turned up dead. Now here we are, minus the hostess with the mostest, and surprise surprise, the mood has not improved. In fact, it's toxic enough to finish the rest of us off easily. All of those other conflicts, festering unresolved. As usual, Rachel has overshadowed us all. And now she's left us stuck here, desperate to escape but completely unable to. Rats in a trap.

I suppose we're all thinking it, aren't we? We've all watched enough crime dramas to know the drill. *Whodunit.* Who had means, opportunity and motive?

Well, all of us had the means, right in front of us. Rachel's stupid skewers. A matching set of murder weapons, presented to us literally on a plate.

Opportunity. We had that, too. The lights went down, and someone got up. I wish I knew who. But it was black as pitch. I heard the noises. Did the front door open? Then that strange little scream. Was it Rachel? Such a tiny sound, and a matching wound … but it was more than enough. All that life, leaking away. The blood. God.

As for motives for doing away with Rachel, well, most of us have one. Take me. I should have known, as soon as I turned and saw her, gawping at me and Tom doing the nasty years ago, that the secret would come back to bite me one day. Even now, I don't want to believe she told Tasha about Raf out of malice. She may have assumed people knew. But it's probably just that she never really thought much about other people, and their little lives and feelings. She made that loud comment about Raf's eyes on our first night here. She put two and two together and, selfish to the end, didn't see a single reason to shut the hell up.

No wonder Raf's been giving me such a wide berth. He must

have thought I'd be angry about him hooking up with Tasha anyway, even before … Well, I suppose it's out there now. Even before he knew he might be Tom's son.

I mean, it's not definite. Raf *could* still be Bob's son. Or Tom's. I suppose that's no defence, though. It probably just makes me look like a slag. More of a slag. What can I say? Nobody minds when it's the plot of *Mamma Mia*, when Meryl Streep's been putting it about. But when it's me, suddenly everyone's got a view.

Bloody Tom. There's always been something about him. A charm, a way of getting what he wants … whatever it might be. And for however short a time.

I could blame Rachel, I suppose. I could say it was her fault for throwing that other stupid Halloween party, all those years ago. For inviting Tom, knowing I was fighting my attraction to him. I didn't like him; I pretty much hated him. But yes, I fancied him. Rotten. Why did I ever confide in her? She was leaky as a sieve. Hang on, is that another motive for me right there?

I've often seen red about Rachel – who hasn't? But to kill her … Over my lad's wrecked romance. Come on. He's twenty. It's not ideal, obviously, is it? Suspected incest. But Christ, they didn't know. He'll get over it. I got over that Tom business, after all.

I take another sip from my cup, and catch Gita's eyes on me. I know what she's thinking. Aside from that long-ago betrayal and its flesh and blood consequences. She thinks I'm on the sauce already. Well, she's actually wrong. This is water. After last night, not even I can face the booze again. Never say never, of course. But not for the foreseeable. Drinking out of a cup is a good cover.

Someone here has used that unholy trinity – means, opportunity, motive – to do something unspeakable. If they think that I'm three sheets to the wind, well then, all to the good. But I'm watching. I've got my eye on all of them. I hope I can keep it up. As soon as I said just now I didn't want a drink, of course the craving started. But I'm clamping down. *Think about something else, think about something else.*

For the moment, my money is on … I scan the room. Old Tregowan hasn't spoken, for hours. He seems almost as withdrawn as Rachel herself is. *Rachel.* I catch myself tearing up. But no, it's shock, as much as actual pain. There's nothing to be gained from more crying. I breathe in, man up.

Could Ross have done it? It's not impossible. The whole marriage was odd. Maybe he was having regrets? And she was so indiscreet. Was she blabbing a bit too much about things he wanted kept quiet? Perhaps he did it for his kids. They definitely hated her.

That makes me think of Roderick and Penny themselves. How did they feel about Rachel's announcement? The prospect of a new little Tregowan erupting onto the scene? That's a question. Whatever else is going on in their heads, they must have grown up with the idea that this island was rightfully theirs. Rachel must have been a large and glamorous spanner in the works.

Had Rachel wriggled her way into Ross's will? Not that she needed the dosh. But people with money tend to be good at getting more. And then she'd just announced an heir. Suddenly this place would have been divided at least three ways, maybe four. I doubt the stepkids loved that idea. Yet Penny was snivelling away last night, after the lights went up and the discovery was finally made. If the number of tears shed indicated genuine sorrow, then she's beating the rest of us by litres.

Still, here's a thought. If Rachel had made a will, and left everything to her new/old husband, then Penny could honk her nose on twenty-four-carat gold tissues for the rest of her life and not make a dent in that fabulous fortune. Shouldn't she be smiling from ear to ear? I wonder where she is. I thought we were all supposed to be corralled here, by order of the great Tom. But there's one law for us, and another for the likes of Penny, as usual.

At least Roderick is sitting here, doing his duty with the plebs, phone in hand. He's stabbing the buttons and sighing. Why bother? None of us are getting a signal. Anyway, don't tell me his little sinecure of a job needs his input, on a Sunday when the island is already closed for business anyway? He's outsourced all the grunt work surrounding the murder to Tom. What, exactly, does he have to sigh about? A tiny rival for his inheritance has been removed, a massive fly in the ointment is gone forever, and now his precious family stands to get a lot richer. It would be unseemly to look pleased but this false mourning isn't fooling any of us.

The most surprising reaction comes from Nessie. She's a goth, so you expect doom and gloom. But she looks genuinely stricken, poor lass, her perpetual black for once like real mourning. She hardly knew Rachel, and Rachel, with all her glitz, was as far removed from a teenage emo as they come. Like I said, weird.

Tom has been striding around, all manly decision, since the lights went up. But it has got us precisely nowhere. Finally, it gets too much for me and I just go ahead and say it. 'When the hell can we get off this fucking island?'

Gita winces. Is it the swearing within earshot of her dainty daughters (they've let rip with worse, I'm sure) or the fact that I'm voicing what everyone else is thinking? She gives me a look that could eat through titanium.

That's the end of all our nice little lunches, isn't it? Hard to forgive my transgression, even if it is ancient history. The years of secrecy I piled on top of it just make it worse. She ought to be angry with Tom – it takes two, and he's been living with her all this time. But it's much easier to hate me.

Well, don't worry, Gita. I hate myself, too. Why do you think I drink? Today that's added to my usual remorse after a well-lubricated evening, and the pain of losing Rachel is a blood-soaked cherry on top. It's a nasty cocktail, one that even I would turn my nose up at.

All right, I belly-ached hard enough about dragging myself to meet Gita in Soho all those times. I often wondered what on earth we'd find to say to each other. It was a bit like when I took Raf to museums when he was little. I grew up surrounded by closed pits and drunks. I wanted him to feel at home in galleries. 'You'll love it when you get there,' I'd say.

'Won't,' he'd say stubbornly, little arms crossed. But then he'd chatter on about seeing the pharaohs or whatever all the way home.

I put off my lunches with Gita, but actually I always did love seeing her. The shadow of Tom came between us, though. No matter how thoroughly I tried to drown his ghost, he haunted me.

Ugh, that makes me think of Rachel, her crumpled body a few doors away. And reminds me that I need answers. I turn to Roderick. 'You know about the tides, don't you? You can tell us. When can we cross that damned causeway?'

Roderick looks up slowly from his phone. For a second, it seems he's going to blank me completely, but I take a step towards him, and catch my foot in the rug. Once I've steadied myself on a chair he looks at me. 'That depends. As you can see, the weather is a factor.'

'Twice a day. I thought the tide went out twice a day?' I shake my head at him.

He laughs but the sound is mirthless. 'Have you even looked out of the window recently? It's *really* not going to be safe today.'

Somehow, the implication is that I'm too drunk to focus. And I resent it. I go over and have a look. Christ on a bike, he's right. It's mad out there, the waves higher than ever, lurching and crashing. The rain is falling thick and fast. The paths are awash. But that causeway, whenever it emerges, is still our only means of escape. Jane comes to join me, though she pointedly stands a little aloof, then Raf. We all watch in silence as another thousand or so litres of water are dumped on us, partly brine, partly rain.

Finally Raf turns away. 'Well, as soon as that causeway does appear, I'm going to try and get across.'

'No! No, you can't,' I say, going closer and trying to take his arm. He shakes me off as though I'm a gnat. 'You heard what

194

Roderick said. It's not going to be safe. What about those waves?' I wail, hating myself. I sound pathetic.

'Someone's got to try. Not you and the girls and so on,' he says, looking respectfully at Ross and Roderick. 'But I'm a strong swimmer.'

'What about Tom? He could do it?' I suggest. To my mind, he's definitely expendable. But Gita is the first to protest. Of course.

'Tom's needed here – he'll have to liaise with the police.' She's grasping at straws. I suppose I shouldn't be surprised she's still got his back; she's put up with so much shit over the years, what's a bit more? But I don't want my lad to take the risk.

'Maybe we should all just stay put, until the water dies down? We don't want to take any chances.'

'You were the one saying we had to get off, two minutes ago.' Raf's tone is dry. Now he comes over to me and gives me the briefest possible hug. It's not enough to mollify me, not nearly, but it's the closest we've been all weekend. It might just stop me from trying to stop him with every fibre in my body, the way I want to. 'You know I can do it. It has to be me.'

At this point, Gita does say, 'I don't think you should, Raf. It's too rough.' And from the sofa, Tasha sobs harder, which I suppose is her way of adding her mite. Raf smiles politely at Gita, avoids Tasha's eyes and allows Roderick to take him to one side and start explaining tides to him. Poor lad. Those seas are going to be deadly enough without Roderick boring him to death beforehand.

I sit down and cover my face with my hand. I don't want him to see me crumble. I know Raf's right: he's the fittest, he's the only one with a ghost of a chance, but I hate it. I hate all of this. I sip from my cup, forgetting it's water. Damn. But the annoyance helps me spring up again.

'Right. Then we should all get ready, so we can go the moment you've fetched help.' I look around, checking for assent. But everyone avoids looking at me. What's the matter with them?

'What are we waiting for? Are you all packed?' I say to the girls.

Gita immediately slips a protective arm around them, draws them closer, as though I have the plague – or worse. I swivel from Gita to Roderick, but he looks sheepish too.

'Look, Vicky. Why don't you just go and … lie down?'

'Me? Why should I? I'm not tired. What are you trying to say?'

Gita sighs. 'You seem a little … emotional. A sleep might do you good. You know, while Raf goes to the mainland.' It sounds anodyne enough. But I catch a glimpse of Nessie's face. Little tragedy-faced bitch is hiding a sneaky smile.

'Jesus! I'm not drunk, if that's what you mean,' I thunder. Gita makes a big deal of shrinking away from me again, taking her girls with her like some sort of fucking mother hen. I'm not having it, I'm not. I'm advancing on them all, about to give them a piece of my mind, when there's a cough from the doorway. It's Tom, with a very strange expression on his face. Raf takes the opportunity to sidle out without another look in my direction.

'Roderick? You're needed upstairs,' Tom says. There's something ominous about his tone. It sends a chill right down the back of my neck.

I'd say there's absolutely nothing good awaiting Roderick up there.

Chapter 44

Jane

Mount Tregowan, 1st November

Every time I think this weekend can't possibly get any worse, something completely ghastly happens. Actually, ghastly doesn't even begin to cover it.

If I could draw this scene, how would I do it? I look around the little group of us, collected in this room, huddled almost. The colours have changed. Friday was gold and sea-green, yesterday was Rachel's glamorous thundering black and red, but today? Today we're all grey, flotsam and jetsam left behind after the great storm has taken our princess away.

We are not the people who clinked glasses on Friday, that's for sure. That little soirée, my awkwardness over my fleece, already seems like several lifetimes ago. Even last night, with Rachel glittering and gloating over us all, with her announcement ...

The triumph in her voice. The way she looked directly at me as she said it. That tiny, twisted smile. I ought to be sorry she's dead. I ought to feel ... all the sorrow in the world. A young life. Well, youngish. A cruel death. A friend, gone. A person who was

197

so much larger than even her own huge life. But instead I have to hide my expression from the others.

Because I'm really rather pleased.

It would have been better if it had been Vicky, drunken spiller of beans, the lurching clown of our group. But Rachel was a fucking bitch too. I'm glad she's gone. There, I've said it. The way she smiled right in my face. I don't know why I ever confided in her about my feelings for Tom. Although she was a total egomaniac, forever full of clunking name-drops about the people she'd seen and the hotspots she'd been to, she was also a strangely brilliant listener. The way she fixed her eyes on you. It was such a compliment. Rachel, with the world at her feet, hanging on to your every word.

I suppose I found it intoxicating. She cornered me at one of Gita's little dos. Ruby's christening, in fact. Vicky wasn't the only one who'd had a glass too many that day. It was purely medicinal, for me, under the circumstances. Ruby was so gorgeous I could hardly bear to look at her. Silky black hair from her mum, utter physical perfection from her dad. Rachel had jetted in from Barbados or the Bahamas and was about to sweep out again, to St Helena or St Kitts, when she wedged herself down next to me on a sofa.

'You're keeping a low profile,' she said, fixing me with those eyes. 'These things are such a bore if you don't like kids, aren't they?' After a beat I nodded, wondering how on earth she'd made that leap. It must have shown in my face. 'I'm sorry, how dumb of me. You *do* like them. I'd wondered, after … what happened.'

Bang went my stupid hope that she'd forgotten all about my abortion. And my total humiliation at her long-ago Halloween party too, being hauled off to get my stomach pumped. I froze, while she carried merrily on. 'But you haven't had any more children. Is it Geoff? Does he have a … problem?' she whispered this last bit, and we both looked round to where he was chatting to Tom, or trying to. Tom, as usual, was letting his eyes rove over Geoff's head as he nodded along. Gita had a lot of very attractive young mum friends. Tom was the king of suburbia, surveying a herd of MILFs. Geoff was talking earnestly, gesticulating with his glass, and as we watched, he sprayed Tom with spittle.

'It's me,' I found myself saying in a rush. 'What I did … It left me with … problems. We're keeping on trying.' Rachel had been so sweet, on the surface. But I've had years to regret my naivety. She'd even spotted the way my eyes flicked involuntarily over to the source of all my pain and shame. Tom.

Oh, she was no fool, Rachel. She put it all together, there and then. My quick fling – well, not even that. It was just a cheap fuck, then an expensive trip to the abortion clinic. And when I'd seen Tom with Gita, at Rachel's party a few weeks later, it had been too much. Love's young dream – they'd been all over each other, and looking just perfect together. I'd almost ended it all, drinking myself to oblivion and beyond. You see, I'd been consoling myself with the thought that it wasn't me, it was him. But Rachel's party proved that, with the right woman, with *Gita*, he had no problem with commitment. Or so it then seemed.

Rachel never forgot; that much was clear on Friday night. Talking so loudly, so explicitly, when anyone could have heard. In front of Vicky. Her knowledge had made me sweat. A sword of Damocles, hanging over my head. Over my marriage. I thought the worst had finally happened, when Vicky told Geoff. It was almost a relief. But then, last night, Rachel gave me that pointed, triumphant glance when she made her proud announcement. My jealousy cut me like a knife. And I realised Rachel would always find a way to wound me.

Oh, why did I ever agree to come? I must have been crazy. But I suppose I thought if I were here, at least Rachel couldn't talk about me behind my back. I wouldn't have put it past her, not at all. She might have mentioned it even more loudly, so not just Vicky but the whole room could have heard. Then she'd just do one of those 'What have I said now?' little shrugs. And for her, that would have been that.

As it is, my peace of mind, my reputation, my *everything*. My life with Geoff. It's all been destroyed.

Just as well she won't be speaking ever again. Silent as the grave, that's Rachel now. God, I'm horrifying myself. I'm not that person, am I? I'm nice Jane, who draws the nice, nice mice. I'm not gorgeous and glamorous and fertile beyond my years, but I have nieces and nephews and a full life and I have, or had, a loving husband ... I need to hang on to all that, tighter than ever.

I should feel sorry for Rachel, dead with her baby inside her. Who knows, she might have craved that child, as I have yearned for my own over the years. Maybe it made her as mad as I am. Maybe all this is because of what she did, how she did it, and who she did it to.

I look around again, seeing the slumped shoulders, the apparent dejection. What if all of these people are hiding things, just as I am? What if no one is really sad she's dead?

It's hard to unlock people's hearts. Ironically, Rachel was gifted at it – but only for her own reasons. I do it sometimes, with my illustrations. People ask me why the mice are sad. Well, children ask me. Their parents never notice. Now we're the mice, lost and aimless, with the cat dead in the next room. We all have sad faces. But one of us is just pretending.

She played with us. She was merciless. It got too much, for one of our number. Someone has turned the tables on Rachel at last.

Suddenly Roderick bursts in on my thoughts. We all look up automatically. His face is grey. God, what now?

'She's dead,' he says, his face crumpling. *Wake up, Roderick,* I think. *She's been dead for hours.*

But it's Gita who snaps, 'We know.' I look over. Her milk of human kindness act is definitely souring. She turned on Vicky just now, and I couldn't have been more shocked. Now Roderick is getting it in the neck.

But his grief is suddenly visceral. Real. 'Not *her*, not *Rachel*,' Roderick almost spits, as though he can't get her name out of his mouth fast enough. 'It's Penny. Penny's dead,' he wails, then collapses into a chair, head in his hands. His blubbering is unmanly and, I hate to say it, repellent.

My God, I think. It can't be true. Can it? Not Penny?

Not another one.

Chapter 45

Gita

Mount Tregowan, 1st November

I can't help it, I find myself running out of the room and up the stairs. It's not as though I ever liked Penny that much. And, after what she did to my little Ruby, I positively loathed her. But dead? How can that be true? I need to verify the information, check my sources. I need to see this with my own eyes.

As I go, I almost collide with Raf, loping down the stairs to the front door with his wetsuit in his arms. It's almost as cumbersome as a dead body. He must be just about to try the causeway. I'm afraid we're pretty awkward with each other, super-polite, each stepping gingerly round the other. What's the etiquette for dealing with your husband's newly acquired illegitimate son? I'm going to have to get to grips with it. But I'm just not quite able to rise to the occasion now.

Raf has a slightly odd look on his face, preoccupied, even a bit noble. I've seen Tom with the same expression on the rare – let's face it, very rare – occasions when he decides to do something selfless.

Raf can't have heard about Penny. I falter for a second, then decide not to delay him. There's only a short window with the tides, and Roderick might well have got it wrong about his sister. He's certainly not behaving rationally. I quickly lean in and try and give Raf a hug. He's being very brave, after all, doing this for us. He steps back, not sure what I intend, but then smiles. He's a nice boy, when all is said and done. And his parentage is not his fault. 'Good luck, honey,' I say to him, and he smiles. 'Nothing to it,' he says, a bit more jauntily.

I hope he's right, but I barely have time to worry, taking the stairs two at a time as soon as he's passed me. I suppose I ought to stay with the girls, get them through this further shock. But I'm doing this to protect them. How much more can we all take? Ruby – thank God, she was restored to us. Then Rachel, taken instead. Now this, with Penny. What the hell is going on?

Is there a maniac on the loose? Or is it more sinister still? And where on earth is Tom? It's him I'm really rushing to find. Whatever happened years ago, however angry I am with him, we need to leave this place. We need to communicate, make the decision together, and then act on it. It's not safe. Not for the girls. Not for us. Not for anyone. At this moment, more than ever, I really need him.

My thoughts are whirling as I career on up the stairs. Penny's room is on the floor above ours, the floor that leads to Rachel's eyrie at the top of the castle. How did the woman feel, about her new stepmother lording it over her, being promoted right to the top of the heap? It's irrelevant now. Tom says I have a mind obsessed with trivialities. He says a lot of things. I tell him it's my job; I need to keep up with everything, know what's trending. Maybe it's one of the reasons I stayed in touch with Rachel over the years. Well, I wish I hadn't now.

I get to Penny's door, and stop. I'm breathing hard. Now that I'm here, I'm not so sure I really want to find out what's behind it.

Come on, Gita. Big girl now, I tell myself. A mantra that's got me through a hundred sticky board meetings, seen me arguing for pay rises when there's been a company freeze. That's pushed me, if not exactly through the glass ceiling, at least right up there so my nose is pressed hard against it. I put my hand on the brass doorknob. It's polished to a mirror shine. Of course it is.

I swallow and push it open. Tom is standing by the window, but I don't even register him. My eyes fly to the bed. Penny is there, curled into a foetal shape, on top of the covers. I know immediately it's true; she's dead. Skeletally thin in life, she is haggard now, a literal bag of bones. Her lank hair is partly over her face, but can't disguise the trail of vomit that leads to a pile of the stuff beside the pillow. It's yellowy-green. Suddenly the acrid smell hits me, together with the implications of what I'm seeing, and my stomach heaves. I bend over. Tom is by my side, helping me out of the room.

In the corridor again, my back against the reassuring firmness of the wall, I hang my head. Beads of sweat are standing out on my brow, Tom is holding on to me. I want to shake him off, but I'm concentrating so hard on not throwing up. Eventually I have myself under control. I nod to him and he removes his arms. Immediately I slump and I realise it's only him who's been keeping me upright. I rub the circulation back in, knowing there will be bruises tomorrow.

Finally I look at him. 'Christ, Tom.'

'I know, Gita, I know.' He moves as though to take me in his arms properly. I decide to acquiesce. It does feel comforting, and I need that. But it doesn't wipe away everything that's gone on this weekend. Not by a long chalk. I push him away an inch or two, so that I can speak.

'What are we going to do? Two people dead … I don't understand what's going on.'

'I know, love. I know. It'll be OK. It'll all be over soon. We've just got to stick together. We'll get through this.'

I look into Tom's eyes, as I have so many times before.

He's right. We're stronger together. We always have been, and always will be. Maybe I have to believe that.

What choice do I really have?

Chapter 46

Tom

Mount Tregowan, 1st November

Poor Gita – seeing Penny is a shock. Rachel last night was bad enough. For a few seconds there, I think she's actually going to faint. She's reported on worse, over the years. But seeing these things in real life isn't easy.

It's been a while for me, too. But you expect the unexpected in the police. I decide to move her away from it all. Our room is probably best. I put my arm round her but she's a bit aloof. I suppose I deserve it; there have been a few revelations this weekend that I could have done without. Don't get me started. Still, once she stumbles a couple of times on the stairs, she forgets to hold herself stiffly and I help her in and sit her down on the bed.

'Head between the legs,' I murmur. She turns to me mutely and gives me a bit of a stare. I hold my hands up and stride over to the window. God, women. One thing on their minds.

I gaze out blindly. Then I realise what I'm seeing. Not just the massive waves and black clouds that have become almost standard. No, there's something else moving down there. A tiny blob, far below, on the jetty. I suppose I must have leaned forward; Gita is suddenly off the bed and right beside me. 'What? What have you spotted?' she asks me. I realise, from her shrill voice, that she's probably hoping for a boatload of riot police, at the very least. It's more prosaic than that. Just a kid, little more than a teenager, alone against the might of this storm. Not going to lie, it doesn't look like a fair contest to me. Or is that the sudden realisation that he's my son talking? I can't deny, I've always wanted a boy. And he'd be perfect – if it wasn't for the relationship with my Tasha. We've got bloody Vicky to thank for that.

Gita cranes out of the window. I point, and she follows my finger. 'It's Raf.'

She gives me a look and moves a few centimetres away from me. We're going to have to have a talk about this. But not now surely? She swallows, then says, 'I saw him going downstairs earlier, on his way out. I can hardly see a thing out there, it's so wild. Is that really him? Right down there? Why isn't he moving?'

'Waiting for the right moment,' I say. Looks obvious to me.

'He's being so brave,' she says. 'But God, he's so young.'

Young and foolish. If I didn't have so many responsibilities, I'd be down there myself, making a better job of it. Sparing the boy – my boy – from risking his life. Why is he hesitating? But as it is, I'm stuck here watching with my wife.

'He's doing the right thing. He'll get help, then we'll all be able to get away,' I say to her comfortingly. She sags against me for a second. Then she seems to remember everything that's been said and done this weekend and she stands a little straighter.

'Look at the pounding that jetty is getting,' I breathe, marvelling at the raw power of the waves, but she's getting fidgety, craning to see, shaking her head.

'You brought your binoculars, didn't you?' she asks. I find them on the bedside table. She holds out her hand and I pass them across. But she can't get the hang of them at all, so I adjust them for her and hand them back. *You're welcome.*

The causeway has appeared; that much is obvious even with the naked eye. And I can see the little figure down there – hesitating, hesitating. I lean as close as I can to the pane of glass, feeling its chill against my forehand, my hands. 'Jesus,' I say. Gita turns to me.

'He should have gone earlier. Now he needs to wait a while. It's not safe,' I explain. Though most of the path has emerged from the sea, freak waves are lashing across it and breaking everywhere, metres high. It's spectacular, deadly. Anyone on it would be dashed away in a second.

Raf is still dithering, shifting weight from leg to leg. He's aching to take the plunge, trying to judge his moment, a sprinter more than ready for the starter's pistol. It's painful to watch. It must be even worse to be down there, in the wind and rain, trying to estimate the next move of something as unpredictable as the sea.

If he goes too soon he could be drowned in a moment, but if he waits too long, the pathway will disappear again.

'God, I can't watch, I can't,' says Gita, and she shuts her eyes. I shout, I can't help it, and she opens them just in time to see a tiny black figure being hit, full on, by a wave the size of a house.

'Oh my God! Did you see that? Did you see? Will he, will he be OK …?' While she jabbers, I'm straining every sinew to see him, but that little stick man has been swallowed whole. There's no sign. It's as though he was never standing there at all.

Gita looks at me and gulps. Her face is flushed; she is too overwrought to cry. I turn back to the window for a second, and see another massive wave crashing over the path. No one and nothing could have stayed upright under that barrage. *Shit, shit, shit. Poor kid.* This feels like the universe's revenge on me. No sooner do I learn I have a son, then he is swept away. It's amazing how much it hurts. Bloody Vicky. Damn her, this is her fault.

'He lost his footing,' I say quietly.

Gita can't process it immediately. 'He's a great swimmer. He'll make it, won't he?'

I look at her. To me, the truth is obvious. But, as so often happens, that's not what she wants me to say. I turn back to the window. 'If anyone can make it, he can. Don't worry.' I put my hand on her shoulder. When it meets no resistance, I draw her towards me. She looks numb. I wonder what she'll say to Vicky now? I doubt any of them down there will have been watching. Too wrapped up in the Penny situation. They're probably all clucking around Roderick.

'We should get back down,' I say.

Gita nods. 'There's nothing we can do here,' she says in a small voice. She follows me down the stairs. 'What shall I say to Tasha?'

'Don't say a word,' I tell her. Easier that way. 'After all, we don't know anything for sure,' I say. Though I'm afraid I have few doubts.

We've just witnessed another tragedy, in an already catastrophic weekend.

Chapter 47

Gita

Mount Tregowan, 1st November

Tom and I trail down the stairs together. It hits me that this is virtually the only time we've spent alone together as a couple all weekend. Viewing one corpse and seeing someone else probably becoming one … It could hardly be less romantic, could it?

And I'm not looking forward to meeting Tasha's eyes, after just seeing Raf disappearing under that tidal wave. This is one thing I don't want to communicate with my family about.

Abruptly, I stop Tom in his tracks. 'Let's sit here for a bit. I don't think I can face them yet,' I say. He looks at me but sits down obligingly enough on the stairs, legs wide. I perch two steps down and lean against the wall. It's comforting to feel the old bricks against my cheek. They've stood here through the centuries. They will have weathered storms like this before, outside the castle at least. I doubt they'll ever have witnessed the mess inside before.

I can't face thinking about Raf at the moment. I need a distraction. Penny, that strange unlucky soul, will just have to do. I remember her body, distorted in death. 'What do you think happened? With … Penny?' I ask him.

Tom shrugs. 'We should keep an open mind. I mean, if it were my investigation …'

He tails off. It's not his investigation, is it? But I suppose his training is not to shut down any lines of inquiry too soon. And not to let anything slip to civilians – even if you're married to them. I'll have to work this out on my own. Luckily it all seems pretty obvious. We've reported on cases like this, every newspaper has. I think of that tidy pile of sick and again my own gorge rises. 'It must have been an overdose. But why? I wonder if she really wanted to kill herself … or just, you know, make a gesture.'

A murderer has a fit of remorse and takes their own life. It happens more than you'd think. Our usual line is that they're escaping justice. 'It was guilt, must have been,' I say slowly, piecing it together, thinking out loud. 'She was nervy enough even before. It must have been Rachel's announcement. Maybe it caused one of those "moment of madness" things.' We use that headline a lot too.

Tom pauses and shrugs. 'Rachel did have it all,' he says heavily. Sounds like he agrees with me.

'Rachel was … *Rachel.*' I nod. 'Such a force. I suppose Penny thought Rachel had taken her father away, her one remaining parent. And then, last night – the baby. That must have been devastating. She would have lost everything. Or she might have feared she would.'

'Was she the resentful type? Penny, I mean?' Tom seems tentative, but I nod vigorously.

'Oh, *definitely*. From what I saw of her, anyway. But would that really have pushed her to the point of … stabbing? And then killing herself in remorse?'

Tom sighs. 'Murder's been done for less.' I look up at him, thanking God I don't have to be involved in his world. Journalists just report, we're not usually faced with the crime scene. I'm still not ready to see everyone yet, and Tom seems content to linger,

211

too. He's probably relieved I'm speaking to him at all, even if it's about such grim topics.

I cast my mind back, trying to remember what Penny was like last night, after the lights went back on. Was she distraught? Did she seem guilty? Was there anything off about her demeanour? But I was so busy, overloaded with my own horror, and worrying about the girls, that I didn't really have any attention to spare for the others. And, of course, I was furious with the blasted woman, after the Ruby business. I certainly wasn't in the mood to comfort her. I draw a blank. Maybe her remorse grew, as the hours went by. Until finally, in the early hours, she'd had enough.

Wait a minute, though. There might be an easy way to clear it all up. 'Did she leave a note? Did you find anything?'

Tom shakes his head. 'A lot of suicides don't, though. It's a myth that everyone wants to get stuff off their chest. Some write a couple of words. A lot don't put anything down on paper at all. Maybe they think the gesture is clear enough. She did leave something, though.'

I look at him, and he continues. 'Under her pillow. A stack of A4 posters, with numbers on.' I'm puzzled for a moment. 'The treasure hunt, remember?'

'Oh, yes.' It's all coming back. 'Poor Rachel, she was so pissed off. It was completely wrecked.'

'Well, now we know who did that.' Tom shrugs.

I think about it. It seems to seal the case against Penny. The hunt, Ruby … then Rachel. Guilt, remorse, anger. Maybe even the sanest woman would have found that emotional cocktail overwhelming. 'Terrible. And what did she take, to …? I mean, it looked like pills …' I remember the stench of vomit and put a hand over my mouth. There was a little bottle on the bedside table. Funny how much you remember when you cast your mind back. Things you've only seen for a second, that you don't consciously register. And yet they're there, somewhere deep down, all the time.

'Antidepressants, looks like. I mean, she was clearly a bit of a mess.' Tom traces a corkscrew at his temple. I'm sure that wouldn't pass the Met's sensitivity training – if it has any. But I get what he means. She was definitely highly strung, no argument there.

'And painkillers, too. I found these in her bathroom.' Tom pulls a packet of pills from his pocket. Diazepam. Even I know that's strong stuff. 'Shouldn't that be in an evidence bag or something?' I ask.

'Strangely I didn't bring that many on our pleasant seaside weekend,' Tom says with a lopsided smile. I sigh.

'Christ. I'm sorry, Tom. I can't believe it's turned out like this.' And I can't believe *I'm* apologising to *him*. I don't need to spend a fortune on therapy to know I'm still scarred by my parents' divorce. And I'm desperate to keep my own marriage together, no matter what. More fool me, I suppose. But Tom seems to relax immediately.

'Don't be silly,' he says. 'It's hardly your fault.' I can tell he's pleased I've said it. And tacitly I've let him off the hook. Again. But everything going on around us is so dreadful. This can't be the time to pick away at our relationship, on top of everything else.

'Thank God you're here, anyway. Can you imagine what it would be like, if the girls and I had been all alone here, with a killer?' I shiver suddenly. I wonder if it's the shock. The *shocks*.

'Well, listen, don't worry, you're safe. Now, go back to the girls. I'll run down to the jetty, see if I can find any sign of Raf. Hopefully he'll be halfway to the mainland by now,' he adds heartily. He stands up and pulls me up with him. As I move towards the library door, I glance back.

'Don't worry too much,' he says, planting a kiss on my forehead. He says it with that smile I've seen for more than twenty years, the one that first reeled me in, the one that so often infuriates me. The one that, today, I have to put all my faith into.

'OK,' I say obediently.

In truth, I'm thrilled to be getting far away, from the horror that is now poor Penny. What a thing to do. Well, both things.

Killing Rachel, and then herself. I just thought she was point-lessly neurotic. Turns out she had good reason to be such a bag of nerves. All that deranged hatred, in one bony frame. It doesn't bear thinking about. And I can't forget that she was the one to lure my Ruby to the chapel, too. We had such a lucky escape, there. The woman had a lot on her conscience.

But at least it means the worst is over. We just have to tough it out for a bit longer. I close my eyes on the memory of that little black stick figure disappearing under a huge wave, and I tell myself the police are going to come. Soon. And we'll be able to leave.

And never, ever come back.

Chapter 48

Tom

Mount Tregowan, 1st November

I'm pottering about in the admin office, just off the kitchen, going through the motions until the local boys get here and start their inquiries. There could be a miracle, you never know. Raf might just get through. If he does, I want to have things sorted. Even if he doesn't, when this storm eventually blows itself out, the telecoms will come back up, and we'll be able to get away at last. The others have asked me to secure the scene, and I've done what I can. Happy to help.

And speaking of help, Rachel's staff are all in the clear. They're lodged in an outbuilding just behind the castle. The castle itself was locked up tight last night before Rachel ... before the first death. She made my job easier by dismissing the lot of them for the evening, so she could make her big announcement 'amongst friends'. The staff quarters are password-controlled and the CCTV shows no one left until they started setting up for breakfast. I've seen a few bodies in my time – occupational hazard of coppering – and Penny was dead well before then. Early hours of this morning, we can safely say.

I mean, it's not great for the Tregowan family, that's for sure. Murder is bad enough. The knowledge that one of them committed it, and killed herself? Hard for them to accept. But to do old Ross justice, he seems to have taken it in. Shocked, but he isn't denying the obvious. Penny's death bears all the hallmarks of a suicide. The motive is clear, and of course explains Rachel's death.

Not going to lie, it's neat. The Cornish police will want to go over every inch. Fair play. They'll have to establish why Penny suddenly let rip. Did Roderick know that his sister was so unstable? Should Ross have got her shipped off to a treatment centre?

Plenty of questions. Above my paygrade, guv. But I'm in little doubt that everything points one way, like a large red arrow, right above the closed bedroom door of a tragically misunderstood, overwhelmed and damaged woman. Penelope Tregowan.

Maybe Penny didn't seem like the violent type. But, thanks to Rachel's theatrical choice of dessert, she had ready access to the skewer. Well, we all did – but we weren't all teetering on the brink of a breakdown. Even her father and brother will attest to that. Fragile mental state, dating from the time of her mother's accident. And then the added stress of Rachel erupting into the tight family circle. Add Rachel's pregnancy, bringing Penny's own mother right back to the forefront of her mind again. Enough to tip her over the edge.

I've been listening, you see. Talk in the shadows, here on the island, and on the mainland too. About that car accident long ago. Rachel herself was pretty indiscreet about it, on our first evening here. I'm pretty sure Penny overheard what she was saying. Neither Ross nor his son want all that raked up again. That much is clear.

People have long memories, in places like this. And Rachel, before she died, wasn't shy about confiding her theories. She always loved a grisly story. She'd mentioned it to me before, when she popped round during that 'gardening leave' she insisted on telling everyone about. While Gita was at work. But it made a lot more sense once I'd met Penny for myself.

'You know Penny's mother insisted they swap places?' Rachel said it slyly, watching for my reaction. '*After* the crash. So Lady T put herself behind the wheel, even though moving basically killed her. All so Penny could drag her stick insect body through life, scot-free.' Those may not have been her exact words. She was smooth, was Rachel. But that was the gist.

In my view, the coroner was at fault. The post-mortem on her mother must have showed injuries consistent with her being in the passenger seat, hitting the windscreen. Drivers have a distinctly different pattern of wounds after a crash, coming from contact between the sternum and steering wheel.

Photos of Penny afterwards show her in a neck brace, but with strapping to the torso too. Broken ribs, I'd diagnose. Typical driver injury. When I googled the accident, the old crime scene pictures came up. Someone in the local force should have been sacked for that alone. The car windscreen showed spiderweb fractures, radiating out from a point of impact. That would have been the first Lady Tregowan's head, giving her the bleed on the brain that was to finish her off, after swapping places. Her magnanimous gesture, preventing her daughter from taking the rap for dangerous, underage driving, ended up in a lifetime of shame and guilt for Penny.

'Poor Penny, even all those years of nursing didn't make her feel any better.' Rachel had shrugged, sitting on our sofa. Of course we talked about other things, Rachel and I, during those few visits. But the Tregowans' ancient history was on her mind.

Did Rachel tell Penny she knew the truth, or just let her accidentally overhear all those hints she kept dropping? It must have been torture. Penny was twitchy enough when we arrived. Then the news of the baby would have been enough to get her to the brink.

I turn to look out of the window. My desk is against it, facing into the room. Behind me is the useless Wi-Fi connector for the whole castle. The mobile signal, patchy at best yesterday, is non-existent today.

Here, on the ground floor, the water looks even higher than it does in the sitting room above, where the others are waiting. I bet they're wondering how long it's going to be, now. Our deliverance. Whether Raf will get through. Or whether the waves will be less dangerous when the second tide eventually comes.

And the big question, the one that's on all our minds: whether Penny was really the one.

And, if she wasn't, whether we'll ever get away from this place alive.

Chapter 49

Vicky

Mount Tregowan, 1st November

Weird, the way Gita bombed out of here, abandoning her girls. You'd have thought she had the devil at her heels. And now she's slipped back into the room, avoiding my eye completely. Yet she seems relieved about *something*. What does she know that I don't?

Naturally she's not saying a word; she just gives her girls a reassuring smile and pats Ruby's knee. I think about it. What could have calmed some of her fears? It must be to do with Penny's death – something that's clarified things, not made them worse.

Suddenly I get it. Even a woman in knots of anxiety the whole time, like Penny, would not spontaneously drop dead. There's only one explanation that makes sense of Gita's attitude. And fits all the facts. Penny must have stabbed Rachel, then decided she couldn't live with herself – or the consequences – afterwards. *She killed herself.*

Well, it's not great – that's the understatement of the century – but I suppose it beats having a psychopath in our midst. I smile tentatively at the girls and get a few lukewarm flickers back. Jane is still giving me the cold shoulder but she seems to have relaxed. No one is brave enough to look towards Roderick. The thought that his sister was a killer is not going to cheer him up at all, if it's even crossed his mind as a possibility. He's still sniffling away in his chair. I'm glad Rachel saw fit to kit this room out with a large box of tissues. She always did think of everything, though even she can't have foreseen this shitshow.

I take another sip from my cup. Gita tracks me. She doesn't quite sigh in disappointment, but I feel the judgement. *Thanks, Gita. Thanks for thinking I'm a hopeless drunk.* I'm stone-cold sober now. Though I am beginning to feel a massive glass at lunchtime might be just what the doctor ordered. And the least I deserve. I'm already anxious about Raf's mission. 'What time does the tide go out?' I ask the room. There's silence.

'Hello? Anybody? Just want to know when my lad will be setting out,' I say a little more loudly. Gita looks at me incredulously.

'Haven't you been watching?' she asks, almost crossly.

I shrug. 'Apparently not,' I say. 'Do you know?'

'For your information, the tide has been and gone. The causeway's covered again, now.'

'So he's off, already?' I can feel the relief coursing through me. 'He should be there soon. We shouldn't have too long to wait, now. Before help gets here.'

Gita just looks at me for a moment. Then she replies. 'Yes. Shouldn't be long now.' She turns away. Something's off, but I can't work out what. And I'm too tired to puzzle at it, after the night we've all had. 'Thank God, we won't be on this godforsaken rock much longer.' There's a movement from Roderick and I shut up. I keep forgetting. This is his home, not just some sort of posho theme park gone wrong.

But I really mean it. I need to be away from here. I don't want to think about Raf out there, anywhere near those waves, dark grey-green, shifting and turning and looking about as cold and horrible as water ever could. Rachel's pretty paved pathway has vanished again under all that brine, has it? I can't help shivering. There's a place for sea salt, and it's on a nice bag of chips on the front at Middleton or Horden beach. A million miles from here. I don't even want to wait for my lad to get back. I want to save him the trouble of the return journey. I want to leave now, too.

'This is stupid,' I say, then try and change my tone. The last thing I want to do is sound like one of Gita's whining girls. 'Doesn't Rachel have a boat or anything?'

Roderick raises his eyes from his snotty tissue for long enough to give me a baleful look. 'The Tregowan family has a boat, yes of course,' he says with some semblance of dignity. 'You might remember your friend Jane arrived in it on Friday night.'

'Must have missed that somehow,' I say. I'd had a couple by the time she and Geoff turned up. 'Well, what are we waiting for, then? Let's bloody go and get in it,' I say, levering myself to my feet. The cup sloshes and Gita tuts but I don't care, it's not going to stain. Everyone else stays put and stares at me as though I'm an exhibit at the zoo.

'Come on, you blithering idiots! I can't believe I'm the only one who wants to get away … get back to normality. Gita, don't you want to save your girls?'

'Shut *up*, Vicky,' she hisses at me, and reaches across to Ruby, as though her touch can obliterate my words.

'Let's not do anything precipitate,' Geoff pipes up. He's been silent so long, I'd almost forgotten he was here. But now I turn on him.

'Precipitate? *Precipitate?* We've been sitting here, waiting to be picked off for hours …' I start.

'Come now. The news about, erm, poor Penny … It puts paid to those concerns,' he says in that dry way.

'Well, even if she did bump off Rachel and then top herself,' I rail, as Roderick flinches in his chair, 'I certainly don't want to stay marooned here with their dead bodies. Do you?'

I seem to have hit a nerve, finally. Geoff looks round the

221

room, as though waiting for volunteers, then finally says, 'Well, as Jane and I arrived by boat, I do know exactly where it's tied up. I suppose I *could* venture forth and see whether there's any possibility of …'

Jane turns on him. 'Oh, don't be so ridiculous, Geoff. We're in the middle of a storm. It was rough enough coming on that thing on Friday afternoon. It would be total madness putting out in that tub in this weather. Even going outside to look is a waste of time.'

Well, that seems to have done it. Geoff, on his dignity, marches across the room and addresses everyone but Jane as he grasps the door handle. His knuckles are white. 'I'll be back shortly,' he says, shutting the door sharply behind him.

'I'm glad someone's seen sense. But what's got his knickers in a twist?' I ask with a chuckle. Now Jane does the same number on me.

'As if you didn't know. Why did you say that to him? *Why?*' She's screwed up her face and she's advancing towards me. Wow. No more Mrs Nice Mice. She looks demented.

Luckily, Roderick pipes up at the same moment with a very strange sound. After a moment, I realise it is a reedy, warbling laugh, teetering on the wrong side of hysteria. 'You people! Bickering amongst yourselves. What do all your petty quarrels matter? Haven't you learned anything from this weekend?'

Thank God, it's enough to distract Jane. Her narrowed eyes turn on Roderick instead. 'Yes, that's right, that's right,' he says, almost frothing at the mouth now. 'Tear yourselves apart, why don't you? But you don't know anything about real suffering. Not like my sister, or my mother … you're not worthy of sitting in their places. Get up, get up!' By now he's yelling at Gita and her girls. Their sofa must have been the spot where the late Penny, and the even later Evelyn, used to perch themselves.

'Roderick!' The voice is as sharp as a gunshot. 'Pull yourself together, boy.' It's Ross, breaking his long, anguished silence. 'What would your mother think?'

Roderick has already started to blub again and I'm trying to look anywhere but at him. We're spared the rest of the dressing-down, thank goodness, when Geoff erupts back into the room. The little hair he has is slicked around his head like seaweed, and drops of water scatter and fall onto his shoulders from his pate. His face, though, is the shocking thing. He looks as though he's aged ten years. Jane dashes forward, and he seems too numb now to shy away from her as he was doing before.

'Are you all right, Geoff? What happened? What did you see out there?'

There's silence for a few beats, as Geoff looks around, blindly, clearly trying to compute what he's just witnessed. Finally he speaks, in a strange, hoarse whisper.

'Someone's scuppered the boat.'

Chapter 50

Gita

Mount Tregowan, 1st November

You can cut the atmosphere in the library with a knife, once Geoff's made his pronouncement. It's not helpful; it really isn't. All right, I realise it's a horrible shock. I mean, I want to know who did it as much as anyone else. Try as I might, I just can't see Penny whacking the bottom out of the boat, no matter how deranged she must have been last night. She wouldn't have had the strength.

But it's too horrible to think about, and it's not good for the girls. Everything was sorted, with the finger pointing at Penny. The last thing they need now is to think there might be someone else out there who wishes us ill. Someone up to their neck in evil, to have done something so awful and destructive.

I take a breath, to steady myself, and smile reassuringly at the little faces on either side of me. Anyway, as Jane pointed out, we couldn't possibly have sailed off in that boat. The waves are mountainous. And it wouldn't have been big enough for all of us anyway.

'The boat being scuppered, Roderick,' I say to him, cutting across Vicky, who is lurching around, drunkenly asking people if they did it. As if anyone's going to stick their hand up. 'That doesn't mean other boats can't get to us, does it?'

He looks at me blankly and for a moment I worry he's going to burst into tears again. His glance darts to his father, as though dreading another telling-off. His eyes are red and moist, like Ruby when she had that galloping conjunctivitis. I can hardly hold his gaze. I want to give him antibiotic drops, but of course in this case that would do no good at all. This is no bacterial infection. This is something else. This is sudden death, and we're all stuck with the symptoms.

But the prospect of giving me a lecture on something really dull seems to perk him up. '*Scuppering* just means someone's taken an axe to it, made a hole in the bottom so it's no longer seaworthy. Of course another boat could still put in here. Potentially. But it all depends on the weather,' he says, his squeaky voice petering out as everyone turns to the window.

I don't even bother to say I already know what 'scupper' means. I think we've all been pretty well acquainted with the meaning, this afternoon. But, like the boat itself, that won't get us anywhere. Nothing will, from the looks of things. Sea and sky are charcoal-grey now. Rachel would probably have had a spectacular dress made in that shade already, from some couture house I could only dream of. She'd be appearing, round about now, and swishing about in her frock for us all to admire. Horror and disbelief pounce again. She's not here anymore. Now my own eyes sting.

'What about the next tide?' I say to Roderick desperately. I don't want to break down again. Vicky's already asked this question but she's hardly going to remember. How she has the nerve to sit here with us, nursing her vodka, after Tasha's heartbreak, after what she did to me, I just don't know. But that's Vicky all over. *Balls of steel*, Rachel used to say.

225

Roderick looks at me, surprised. 'Tides? You and I discussed all that on Friday,' he bleats.

'A lot has happened since Friday,' I say heavily. 'I can't remember a word of that conversation. And no one was really listening earlier, either.'

He nods nervously. I feel bad. Talk about kicking him when he's down. I hope he's not as delicate as his sister was. Heaven forfend he pulls the same trick as her. Suicide lays such a cruel burden on those left behind. God, imagine his father. In one weekend, he's lost his wife and his daughter. And his baby-to-be. The poor man. But Roderick is speaking again.

'As I said earlier to, to, *her*—' he indicates Vicky, who salutes him ironically with her cup '—the next low tide will be in the late afternoon. That's if the storm hasn't thrown things too much.'

'It won't have disrupted the gravitational pull of the earth, will it?' Nessie's voice drips with sarcasm. I whip round to look at her. It's the first time she's spoken for hours. She's slumping in that way I can't bear. I just about resist the temptation to tell her to sit up straight. I hope she's not sickening for something. She looks pale, but that's par for the course these days.

For a second, I wonder about that dry, knowledgeable tone she's used. But she's always loved the planets, my Nessie. Her first school project was a model of the solar system. I ran around in my lunch break sourcing tennis and ping-pong balls for her to stick onto wires. She was devasted when her friend with the stay-at-home mum got a gold star for hand-knitting the entire galaxy. She's older and wiser now, and she's got a point. I look towards Roderick.

He manages a weak smile. 'Of course it won't have changed anything fundamental. But if the sea is really rough, the causeway can be pretty much impassable anyway. You know, rogue waves sweeping across. Dangerous.' Again, I see that stick figure disappearing under the weight of water, and instinctively glance at Vicky. But she's got her nose buried in that damned cup once

226

more, oblivious to what might have happened to her son. I tell myself it's just as well – and shush the voice that says she has the right to know.

Roderick is still craning out to sea. 'It's possible it might be improving,' he says. Maybe he's seeing something different from me. I just notice the constant shifting of the sea and the sheets of rain. 'The police might try to reach us in a launch, I suppose,' he goes on. 'But all the same, I doubt they'd find anyone who wants to sail out past the rocks on a day like today. Our own boatman wouldn't dream of it. The Tregowan Needles, the locals call them. They're notorious, the Needles.' He chuckles drily. It grates on me. Surely he realises how inappropriate it is, for one of his family to be laughing about sharp pointed objects, at a time like this? But he's oblivious. 'They might just decide to wait until the conditions are better.'

I glance towards the window again. I'm beginning to wonder if this storm will ever end. There's some sort of bird out there. Looks too dark to be a seagull. It's being tossed around like a rag. How can he say this is an improvement? Then I remember how awful it was last night, and earlier. Pray God the wind drops, or the waves calm down. Something needs to give.

I start to wonder. A helicopter, maybe? But with this gale, it would be blown off course. And where could it put down anyway? There isn't any room. The whole of the top of the island is pretty much taken up with the castle, just with a little apron of garden in the front and then the walled area by the chapel on the level below. Neither look big enough to land a chopper. And both would be perilously close to the edge of the island, the sea and now these Tregowan Needles. I wish Rachel were here. If anyone could organise a way off, she could.

I must have tutted out loud. Tasha looks across at me – poor, pretty, heartbroken Tasha. God, I've got my work cut out with her, and she doesn't know the half of it. She's just as oblivious as Vicky. *All the king's horses and all the king's men.* The thought of the endless bolstering, the patient listening and propping up that I might soon need to do. It makes me yearn to be at work. Far, far from all this. I suddenly remember Rachel last night, with her meaningful look at everyone – me, Vicky and even Jane. Her insinuations about Tom, and the situation with his job. Damn Rachel. I don't believe there was anything between Tom and Jane. For God's sake. But damn Vicky, too. I look across at her, and she's clutching her cup as if her life depends on it. I suppose it does.

Vicky feels my eyes on her. 'OK, Gita?' she says with an ingratiating smile. I can't be as angry with her as I want to be, about Tom long ago, when I know that her son might already be dead. So I'm not going to ask her how she could have done it to me. I can see the explanation, her excuse. It's right there in her hand, as usual. But still, she remained silent, all these years. And what about poor Raf himself? If he's still alive, how will he and Tasha ever get over all this? God, I hate secrets. How has everyone else managed to suppress so much, all these years? Communication, that's the key to making things work in life. And how can you communicate successfully, if you're hiding things? From other people, and from yourself?

But Vicky has finally sensed something, through her fug of booze. Something about my reticence, the way I'm not attacking her as I could. And perhaps even the fact that Raf isn't back yet. Her eyebrows shoot up. 'Raf?' she says. Funny the way we still understand each other, even after all this. Even when we don't really want to. Suddenly she's on her feet and at the door.

'Tom said we should all stay here ...' I say to her back. She whips round and smiles crookedly.

'We both know what Tom can do, at this point,' she says, and she slams the door behind her.

Chapter 51

Vicky

Mount Tregowan, 1st November

Don't think about a drink. Don't, don't. Even though it might sharpen things up. The first one often does. But then the second blurs everything. I know that, I do. I do. I'm not going to. I have to keep focused.

Where the hell is Raf? When exactly did he leave this room? The way he edged out … He did give me that tiny hug, though. That warms my heart. Did he set off immediately, to swim to the mainland? Or did he wait? Does he know enough about the tides? Was the water calm enough?

There are too many questions, and I can't answer any of them. I should have gone down, to the pier. To see him off. To make sure everything was OK. But he didn't want me there, my lad. Christ, what sort of mother am I?

He's been avoiding me all weekend, especially since it came out about him and Tasha, and me and Tom. I understand how dreadful it was for him. For them both. But it might not even be true. That's the thing.

Yes, there's a chance that Tom is his father. Bob and I did carry merrily on after Raf's birth, 'trying for a brother or sister', as people coyly put it. And nothing happened at all. But, while that's odd, it's not proof positive. Raf *could* still be Bob's. He and Tasha could be freaking out for no reason.

Admittedly, I'd be the same. Much has changed in the past twenty years, but incest is still a taboo. If I'd been open right from the start, then, well, it would never have happened. But if Raf had said a word to me about Tasha, I would have told *him*. I never saw any sign of interest between them. But then, I wasn't looking. Why would I? I suppose I always hoped they got on. But, with Raf treating me like a leper, I haven't had the chance to see more.

And Gita. Oh God. I know I should have said. I know I've let the years rush by, blurring my stupid mistake, hoping it was all forgotten. But you can't bury a six-foot man, as Raf now is. One night, that's all it was, and not even that. It was ten minutes of madness. Less. I was drunk, of course, and Tom was predatory. Those were the days when he really put it about.

He was the best-looking boy on campus, by far. And he knew it, every second of every day. He was a peacock, bursting with testosterone. We were all drab and desperate, by comparison. I loathed him, outwardly. But inside I was as wet and willing as the rest. And I suppose at some horrible level I enjoyed getting one over on Gita, perfect Gita, with her stratospheric grades, her kindness, her beauty and her charmed life already rolling out in front of her. It was just a tumble, a fumble. I didn't want anything more from him. And very soon I wanted a lot less. Then I took up with Bob and, even though we argued about what day of the week it was and which way was up, right from the start, I held on to him for grim death and said nothing.

Rachel had to be the one to walk in on us. When she burst through the door, to dump someone's coat on the rail, I had my back to her. Well, I was astride Tom, on the floor, trying to avoid carpet burns from the cheap nylon pile in that drab little room right next to the fancy college dining hall. I whipped my head round for a second and saw her, and then, I sometimes think, I saw his face change, become even more avid, as we screwed away. Did he know she was there? Even pant out her name? I just can't remember. But he could have. Easily. She threw the coats, I know that, because they clipped me round the shoulder, and she disappeared in her absurd Halloween cloak, a version of the one she wore last night. Tom came in one last expansive thrust. The timing didn't escape me. I assumed she was yet another scalp he'd quite like.

Then, when I dismounted, he immediately sloped off, was reunited with Gita, and the rest is history. I drank enough to blot the world out, let alone him, my crushing sense of guilt and even Rachel's looming face. Jane upstaged me in the bad behaviour stakes, getting her stomach pumped. I'd almost forgotten it, or at least pushed it right to the back of my mind, by the time I realised I was pregnant. Bob and I had just become an official thing, boyfriend and girlfriend, just like Tom and Gita. It wasn't easy, being pregnant and finishing my finals. I had Raf right after leaving uni. How could I have said anything at that point?

I need to talk to Gita about it, I really do. But what can I say, after all these years? I can't even pretend it was nothing. Raf is the proof that it was a seismic event. Except, he actually *might not be*. He could still be Bob's son, he could. It's a shred of hope that I cling to.

Anyway, it's more important that I reconnect with Raf than have it out with her. Gita has waited twenty years to hear the story, she can last a few hours more. But I need to be near Raf. I know he went ages ago, but if I wait down by the pier, I might see him coming back. Hopefully with the cavalry we need right now.

Downstairs, out in the hall, I rummage through the rack by the door, trying to find a jacket that will do. I throw on the first that looks as though it will fit. One of the staff comes out of the kitchen, but backs away when she sees me. They're avoiding us now. Well, we're all avoiding each other.

I fling open the door, and the wind rips my breath away. I thought the turmoil in my head was bad, but this is nuts, like being put through a washing machine spin cycle. I'm pinned for a moment on the threshold, watching the clouds being yanked across the leaden sky like grey rags on strings. The air is heavy with a seaweed tang. I want this wildness to purge all my regrets. But I know even this isn't scourge enough. So I plunge on, and go to where the paths start. The one that traces the island's curves, and the one that cuts straight down to the sea.

Which one will Raf have taken? The meandering trail, or the fastest route? I don't hesitate, going straight downhill towards the reckless sea. Though I am so far away from it, up here, it seems suddenly as though it's lurching up to meet me. I grip the handrail with all my might, and wait for the dizziness to pass off. For a second, I feel as though I might plummet right from the top of the mountain, to those cold grey depths. No, it will not take me. Life will not get the better of me, let alone the sea. For a second, I pat the pockets of the jacket. If it were mine, there'd be a hip flask somewhere. A quick nip of cleansing vodka would put fire in my veins. But thank God, it's not my coat, and that reflex has to go unfulfilled. My body wants it badly but I tell myself no. I lift my head up again to the scudding clouds, make a resolution, and then start my descent.

I'm going to wait for Raf. I'm going to sit there until he comes. I'm finally going to come clean, explain everything. Make him see that, all along, I've only tried to do what's best for him.

The thought chugs through my mind, pushing out visions of drink. It sustains me down and down the steps, slick as they are with the spray from the sea and the endless spatters of rain. A few times I nearly slip, but my rictus grip on the railing – itself unpleasantly slimy – saves me from tripping and falling. It takes me ten minutes to get down to the foot of the hill, with the weather worsening at every step.

By the time I've reached ground level, I'm out of breath and it's raining in deadly earnest, chilling me to the bone. The skies are suddenly going a deeper shade of charcoal, while the waves crash over onto this rocky promontory I'm standing on. I don't like it. I don't like it at all.

Worst of all, there is no sign of Raf. *Well, what was I expecting*, I ask myself, as I pace this way and that. I walk round the island as far as I can, coming to the pier Roderick mentioned. I suppose this is where Jane arrived on Friday night, when she missed the causeway. She always was a bit dozy, in her own little world. I suppose even at uni she was dreaming about mice in tutus. I love Jane, but thank God I didn't have to read that stuff to Raf; he was straight Captain Underpants all the way. Give me a fart joke over a prancing rodent any day.

These thoughts keep me distracted until I come right up to the little boat shed. Like everything else here, apart from the Tregowans themselves, it shows signs of having been recently tarted up by Rachel. It's all painted in Farrow and Ball, and has a brand-new padlock keeping it shut. I peer in through the window. It's so dark. But the torch on my phone reveals the disappointing truth – just a few piles of rope. I go over to the boat, upturned on the pier. This must be the one they were talking about earlier. Sure enough, there's a hole knocked right through the bottom, the wood all jagged. No sign of what was used to do the damage. Thrown into the sea, no doubt. And right by the side of the boat, hidden from sight until now, I suddenly see a pile of sodden clothes.

My heart stops in my chest. Oh Christ. Goose bumps start right at my knees, then sweep my body. I feel my hair standing away from the nape of my neck. I'm shivering even in this too-hot, oversized jacket.

That's Raf's sweater. He was wearing it when I last saw him.

In fact, I bought it for him for Christmas, last year. When I saw he'd actually brought it here, I thought we had a real chance of a reconciliation, of some sort. Since then I've been waiting for my moment. The right time.

How stupid I've been. Any of the minutes we spent together on this island would have done. Because one thing is now clear. These are Raf's jeans, his socks, his shoes. His watch. God, oh God, oh God, his phone. I fall to my knees, and gather everything – his precious belongings – to my chest. I bury my face in them, the sopping-wet denim, the mushy drenched fleece which, even though it still smells faintly of my lad, gives me no succour. I look out and into the evil sea. A gull flies right past my face, screaming at me, and for once I want to scream right back.

I tell myself it means nothing. He would have had to take his kit off, to get into his wetsuit, to go across. He couldn't take his phone, could he? One drop of water and you have to cocoon the blasted thing in dry rice and hope and pray the battery will survive. He had to leave this stuff behind. He's a fit young lad. He's reached the mainland by now. No, definitely. For sure. He's getting help; he's talking to the police. He's explaining everything that's happened here. That will take some time.

He's not dead, he's not dead. But it doesn't matter how often I chant it to myself, or scan the horizon for any sign: a swimmer, a boat, anything at all. Deep in my heart I know. The sea has taken him. My little lad is gone. Into this water, away from this world. Away from me.

And it's my fault. Because I never told him about his father. Well, even now I hedge. Who his father *might* be. I had twenty whole years to sort that one out. But instead I dodged it, drank it away, avoided the question in Bob's eyes, kept my distance from Tom, held Gita at arm's length. God, it would have been so much easier to stick one of Raf's hairs in an envelope, get it tested and face the truth for once. But I've been a coward. Such a coward.

And, worse than anything, I brought him to this island, where Rachel has forced everything into the light.

My face is wet, but whether with tears, seawater or the rain pelting down, I don't know and I don't care.

Rachel, Rachel, thank God you're dead, I shout to the sky.

Because if you weren't, I'd fucking kill you right now.

Chapter 52

Jane

Mount Tregowan, 1st November

It's been an hour, more or less, since Vicky trailed back to the house. She was a changed woman, a drowned rat. That Louise Brooks bob, so severe, was plastered to her face. It immediately made her look more vulnerable, less of a bulldozer. It was as though all the bluster had beaten out of her, by the winds and rain. And her discovery.

I feel for her. I do. She must be beside herself, worrying about Raf. He's been gone ages, now. No one wants to say anything, but it must be too long, surely? And he is a lovely boy. I suspected Tasha might be keen on him, on our first night here. Not that it was surprising. Same generation, same level of gorgeousness.

And, now that I know, of course I see the resemblance. To Tom. Their eyes have the same spacing, they have very similar chins and they share a certain stance that, in Tom, is bulletproof arrogance and in Raf is endearing braggadocio. I wonder where the dividing line falls? Maybe at the point where you start to go round impregnating people you shouldn't be messing with.

You'd have thought Vicky would have mentioned something, in all this time. I thought we were such good friends. But you don't really know people until something like this happens. And I suppose I can't talk. I didn't confide in her, either.

But I did see what flashed between the two of them, Tom and Vicky, when she burst back into the room where we've been sitting all this time. It's like some interminable dentist's waiting room, for all its book-lined luxury, for all its views onto Rachel's glorious bloody island and her sea.

One glance was enough. Her terror for her boy, Tom's immediate reassuring expression, as steadying as an arm around her, as though he'd said the words aloud, *don't worry, he'll be fine*. If Raf hadn't been their son, then that lightning transmission could not have taken place. I don't know if I was the only one who saw, or whether my own, still more troubled connection with Tom means I am super-sensitive to the nuances. I looked away. It was too painful to gaze on.

People think I don't know the pain of losing a child. But they're wrong. I know it better than almost anyone. That first baby, Tom's, scraped out of me so long ago. And then all Geoff's attempts. Each one of those was as worthy of love and remembrance as anyone else's child. They didn't have the chance to live and breathe, to move and make a difference in the world, but they were, each one of them, my little bundles of potential, all the more precious because they were denied their chance.

I wish I could say that my grief rises up and helps me distract Vicky from her fears. But it remains locked within me. People don't see that I am a mother too, if only of the dead. They have never given me leave to mourn. The few times I admitted to having a miscarriage, people would say, 'Oh, you can try again.' But the child I'd lost wasn't just a sudoku puzzle that didn't come out right. It was a soul, a piece of my heart. So now I cannot help others. My sorrow is locked in me, like a tear that trembles on an eyelash but will not fall.

Geoff comes over to me, where I stand pretending to look out of the window on the worsening weather. God, this grimmest of weekends just had to be accompanied by the worst storm in living memory. I try my hardest not to flinch away when his hand comes down on me, as I know it will. I ought to be glad, that he's giving me this sign of reconciliation, of forgiveness. But instead something in me shrivels away from him.

Geoff, of all people, understands the depths of my misery, plunging further than the fathoms now pressing on Rachel's stupid causeway, and stretching beyond Finistère on the French coast opposite us. It wasn't for nothing that the Romans called it the 'end of the world'.

I don't want Geoff's sympathy and forgiveness anymore. It's just another burden on my shoulders, like his pudgy hand. God, I shouldn't say that about him, but at times like this I can't deal with his compassion. I feel the need to be punished, the way I know I deserve. Especially when, in the still watches of this sleepless night, I finally decided to clear the slate completely. I whispered my confession to Geoff – that the baby I had aborted was Tom's. I don't know how he can have come round so quickly.

I should be grateful to my husband, for his forbearance now, and for all he's done in the past. Not least his many attempts to impregnate this diminishingly attractive body, when all along I've known it was futile. Whatever those doctors did with their little metal sticks long ago, whichever bits of Tom clung inside me and had to be scraped away, they took the spark of life with them, in a torrent that leaked through pad after pad, for months. I've always known it was hopeless every time since then, that not one of my children would live long enough to see the light of day.

If I'd only left Tom's seed to grow, the harvest would have been a child as healthy and strong as Raf was, or as beautiful as Tasha, Nessie or Ruby. A child to be proud of, a child to love. Instead Geoff and I are ... where we are. 'The products of conception,' say the textbooks. Margaret Atwood, in *The Handmaid's Tale*, was more realistic. Unbabies. Shredders. That's what our nursery was filled with, before we painted it over.

Geoff presses his hand down harder and tries to turn me towards him. I concede and bury my head in his sweater. My eyes are dry and his arms are a prison, but at least it gives me time to think.

And, finally, to feel. I start praying for Raf, though to whom I'm not sure. I hope he makes it. Surely he will? That strong young man should be able to battle through even seas like these. But, like the rest of us, he's been put in mortal danger.

Rachel loved to cause a ripple. Well, she's got a tidal wave now. Marooning the incestuous pair, these star-crossed lovers, here on her island must have tickled her to death.

Quite literally, as it may have turned out.

Chapter 53

Tom

Mount Tregowan, 1st November

I've come down to the office again, mainly to get away from Vicky. She's drunk. On the verge of hysteria. I don't much want to be sitting with Gita and my daughters when she finally blows.

Down here I'm trying to avoid looking out of the window. Will Raf make it? If anyone can, he will. Suddenly a memory comes to me, a swimming gala with Tasha and Nessie ages ago. Raf was there, and beat everyone in his year hollow. I was impressed. Maybe that should have told me. Another winner. Chip off the old block. Vicky has given me some weird glances over the years, but I never cottoned on. Maybe she's right: I didn't want to. It'll be an irony if I lose my only son, the day I found him.

I'm almost glad when there's a tap at the door. It's Ross Tregowan, of all people. I see his head first, poking round with his tongue flicking out nervously. I start back. Hope I've got my game face back on by the time he sits down in front of me, but the resemblance to a lizard hasn't gone away. Up close, the sagging neck and downward-drooping eyes don't improve matters. What's he after? I thought he'd pretty much become a living statue in the library with the others. But maybe he wants access to one of the rooms he asked me to seal?

'I'm very sorry for your loss,' I say formally.

'And yours,' he barks.

'Sorry?' Is this about Raf? Has he heard something I haven't?

'Well, you'd known Rachel longer than I had. All of you. I imagine you're feeling it too.'

Oh, Rachel. Right. I adjust my notebook. 'Ah, yes. I suppose I was also thinking of, erm, your daughter …' It seems almost bad manners to draw her to his attention.

'Poor dear Penny. Yes. A double blow.' He bows his head. But I think we both now know where his daughter was in Ross Tregowan's own personal pecking order.

'Were you surprised? About Penny, I mean.' I don't want any more misunderstandings. 'Was it … in character?'

Tregowan swallows. His Adam's apple bobs and I think about tennis balls stuck in drinking straws. I look away. 'Put it this way. Between us, she'd been … fragile for a long time.'

Fragile is said in those inverted commas which means, pretty much, insane. Looks like Tregowan is of that generation that sees mental health issues as moral failings.

'I understand it was after her mother's death …?' I let the sentence hang delicately, so Tregowan will fill me in. But it's uphill work. And I'm still none the wiser about why he's really here. It's his castle, though. He has every right to pop up where he pleases. Suddenly he becomes a little more expansive.

'Such a difficult time. My first wife, Penny's mother, she was quite a free spirit, you know.'

As opposed to rules-are-for-the-little-people Rachel? Looks like Tregowan has a type.

'Evelyn loved nothing better than careering around the cliffs, here or on the mainland.'

'But you can't drive on the Mount?'

241

'Oh, not now.' Tregowan looks out of the window, plucking absently at the loose, mottled skin on the backs of his hands. I focus on my notebook. 'I changed everything after she died. Evelyn, I mean.'

'The crash was here?'

Tregowan nods. There's a pause. 'Penny felt such a terrible burden of guilt. But it wasn't her fault. Not really. She was a novice driver, you see. Evelyn encouraged her to take chances. She loved risk.'

'I thought your wife was driving?' I frown. But we both know the truth.

'Oh, of course.' Tregowan dismisses it. 'Now, was there anything else?'

'I thought you wanted to ask me something?' I shrug at him, wondering if the weekend has caused him to lose his own marbles, or whether he was like this before. 'But wait a minute, you're confirming that Penny's guilt about being in the driving seat finally caused her to kill herself?'

'Well. I'm not saying anything, dear boy. But Rachel did drop that little hint last night. She had a sense of mischief ...' His voice peters out, as he realises what he's said. We've all had a taste of Rachel's idea of fun. It was expensive, like everything else about her. This weekend it's cost her own life, and her stepdaughter's.

'Did you know about the baby?' I lean forward. 'Your baby?' I hadn't intended to ask, none of my business, but the man seems so ... bloodless. Rachel and his daughter are both gone and he's somehow blaming everything on his first wife. Does he bear no responsibility for the way things have turned out?

'The baby?' He blinks slowly, his expression cold. I wouldn't be at all surprised to see a third eyelid flick across. 'I'm sorry, I must, er, get on. Duties ...' he says. His upper lip is so stiff it's got rigor mortis. But perhaps he considers my questions inappropriate in an underling. He pushes his chair back, but doesn't get up. 'If that's all?'

Again, I shrug. I'm not sure what to make of him. He's at the age when dementia starts … I feel another prickle of disgust at Rachel. I suppose it's not completely impossible that she actually loved the guy. I run an absent hand over my torso as I look at him. But if she didn't, then she was shunning younger, fitter men to pleasure a desiccated ruin. And, from what I've seen just now, she must have been willing to watch his mind slip away too. I hope the title and the island were worth it.

Well, I'm still a policeman at heart. I want justice. It sounds lofty. It isn't; it's the business I've been in, all these years. All right, this situation is complicated. By Rachel, by all our relationships with her. With everything that's gone on this weekend. And the stuff that happened twenty years ago. Stuff that leached out into our lives, like battery acid corrupting everything it touched. Like poison. But I've still got my eye on the prize, despite everything. I want to see this wrapped up, and quickly, with an outcome that does the least damage possible to the living.

Ross Tregowan is still sitting there, a blank expression on that face. 'I just want to get one or two things clear in my mind,' I say to him, leaning forward across the desk. 'To sort things out – beyond any reasonable doubt.'

He sighs, just once, and we get down to it.

Chapter 54

Gita

Mount Tregowan, 1st November

It had to happen. My reckoning with Vicky. To have her betrayal heaped on top of Rachel's death is almost more than I can stand.

We've been through so much together, over the years. Her rotten marriage, to Bob, for instance. And now of course I'm beginning to see why *that* fell apart. All this time, I've assumed he was the bad guy, the unreasonable one. Even though I know Vicky herself can be impossible, I've made endless allowances for her. But a secret this big, at the centre of their relationship? It's clear they never stood a chance. No man could put up with the suspicion that his son was not even his.

But the thing is, it was never obvious. Did Vicky pick Bob on purpose, because he was just a watered-down version of my Tom? Slightly shorter, a little more brash, definitely less charismatic. He is Tom Lite – I see that now.

And I can admit it, I feel a fool. All the time we've spent with Raf, marvelling at the way he fitted so easily into our family, the way he cleaved to us and not to Vicky. He loved it at our house, with Tom and me. He was part of the family. Literally.

Tom's told me he knew nothing about the situation with Vicky. Aside from the actual impregnation, for want of a better word. It still astounds me. They've never seen eye to eye, in all these years, he and Vicky. But something aligned, at least once. Below the belt.

Antagonism often conceals a spark. Elizabeth Bennet versus Mr Darcy, and all that … God. Tom was sheepish, earlier. 'It was twenty years ago. I was a dick then,' he said, literally hanging his head. No one's disputing that. The question is whether he's changed.

Now, after all the years of silence, he suddenly can't shut up about it. 'She was available … she made that plain. It was a shag. It meant nothing. Less than nothing. Not that it excuses my behaviour, not that it makes it any better …'

But of course it does make it better. The more he runs her down, the more likely I am to forgive him. At the moment. While it's all at this raw level. At some point, intellect will kick in and I'll have to take a long, hard look at Tom. For now, he can't slag her off enough for me. Why does it work this way? Why am I willing to blame another woman for my own husband's failure?

I can answer that in seconds flat. Because I want to keep my family intact.

Oh, it's all too much to deal with. I envy Vicky, taking refuge in her beloved booze. I wish *I* could drink all this away. Rachel, gone. Penny, too – not that I care an awful lot about her. Is that terrible? No, under the circumstances I can let myself off. I didn't know her until forty-eight hours ago and it turns out she was a murderer. I can't mourn that kind of person. But Raf. I don't want to include him in the same breath as them, the dead … but he's been gone too long now, surely? I'm beginning to believe he can't have survived. That wave must have taken him.

The last time he was at our house, he gave me a bunch of flowers. 'What's that for?' I asked, trying to conceal a leap of pleasure. He was so good-looking, such a delight to have around. 'Just … for having me here,' he said, with that smile. Tom's smile, I now see. It was shouting at me all the time, the truth. But I was blind.

I suppose he saw me as his mother-in-law, in all but name. He and Tasha clicked at some deep level, and no wonder – they were like calling to like. It turns my stomach. My poor girl. How will she be able to look at herself in the mirror? How can Vicky? How could she do this to us all?

I look across at her. 'Gita …' she starts, but I turn my head away.

This is horrible, but maybe Raf going missing is actually the best thing that could have happened to Tasha. For just a second, I even think to myself: *if only Vicky could disappear the same way.* What is happening to me? This place is making me into a monster. God, I regret giving in to that invitation. Why did I bring us here?

'Gita,' says Vicky again. I force myself to glance over. It's as good a time as any. The girls have gone to the loo, together in a posse. Roderick is lying down upstairs. Ross is having a walk. I don't know how he can, in this weather, but I suppose he's used to it. If I were him I'd worry about being blown away, but in the circumstances … Jane and Geoff have gone off together, no doubt to their own room. So it just leaves me, and my erstwhile friend.

She's a mess. Her features have that blurry look drunks get, lumpy underneath, like porridge. Usually, I'd have some compassion. Now I wonder if we were ever really close at all.

'What I don't understand is why you didn't tell me.'

To give her credit, she doesn't pretend she has no idea what I'm talking about. 'How could I? You were in love. You wouldn't have listened. It was a mistake. Yes, a drunken one. But it was once and never again. And anyway, you knew full well the kind of shit Tom was. *Is.*'

'Shut up, shut up,' I say. My hands are over my ears. I don't want what she's saying inside my head.

'Come on, Gita. It's not like he hasn't kept it up. Do you

think he's been faithful to you, for one second, throughout your relationship? Your marriage?'

'You don't know what you're talking about.'

'Him and me, that was a one-night thing. On my side. But he carried on giving me the eye. For years. Why do you think I avoided him?'

'Um, maybe because you were ashamed?' My eyebrows are virtually on the ceiling. But she hasn't finished.

'He liked to have someone on the back burner. Come on, you must have known, Gita. I always assumed you did. And what about Rachel?'

Goose bumps stand up on my arms. 'What do you mean, Rachel?'

'Surely you were aware? When your girls were tiny … And he spent so much time with her, in the last few months.'

'Wait. How do you even know that? Unless you were still carrying on with hi—'

Vicky cuts me off. 'Raf said. You know he was always round at your place.' She swallows. It rankles, does it? Good. 'He said sometimes Rachel was there. Didn't you know? Tom never said a word to you?'

My head is spinning, now. Surely not both Vicky and Rachel? What is going on? No, no. I take a breath, get centred. 'It was probably a work thing.'

'Work!' Vicky snorts. 'If that's what you want to call it.'

'For your information, Tom's involved in investigating art fraud. Money laundering, that stuff. And Rachel has … had, her art foundation. It would have been about that.'

'Whatever. What can I say, if you're determined not to hear? I suppose you've had to practise selective deafness a lot over the years. Blindness, too. Heaven forfend you should make a clean break, like I did. You would have lost the huge house in the suburbs, I suppose, and the girls' schooling. I hope it's all been worth it.'

The words are bubbling up in me but I clamp down. Vicky carries on. 'I thought that was why you spent so much time at work. Dumping the girls with nannies or whatever. And look how that's worked out.'

Now my intake of breath is harsh, involuntary. I can't believe she's bringing my daughters into it. 'You're saying I'm a bad mother? You? You're saying that, with that cup of vodka in your hand? And if you really want to look at things, look at *Raf*. He couldn't wait to get out of that door. Risking his life, to get away from you.'

Oh God! What a thing to say. I've gone too far, and I know it. Lashing out at my old friend, who's almost certainly just lost her son. Even if she is a sozzled psycho-bitch. I clam up, just shake my head. Luckily she's too drunk to focus properly on what I've said.

'Listen, Gita,' she goes on, her words running into each other. 'I've never had him tested. The DNA. Bob might be his dad ... There's every chance.'

But both of us know. 'Why didn't you say something to me? Over all these years? I could have forgiven you.'

'Could you?' she asks me. Our eyes meet. She's right. This runs too deep. The betrayal has been bad enough, but the ramifications of it ... OK, she never wanted Raf and Tasha to fall in love, but the irresponsibility. The damage inflicted on my beautiful daughter. An innocent young girl.

'Why didn't you say anything, when you knew where things were going, between the two of them?'

'You forget.' Her voice is full of sorrow. 'I didn't know. I had no idea. I've scarcely seen Raf, these past two years. I blamed Bob. Now I wonder if it was Tom ...'

'Don't blame Tom for this! If he'd had the least idea, don't you think he'd have stopped them?'

'I suppose he would. But I honestly didn't know they were becoming close – Raf and Tasha. Let alone ... you know. Really. I couldn't have stood by. I would have had to say something, risk our friendship. But Raf said nothing to me. Maybe he was embarrassed,' she stumbles on hurriedly before I can erupt again. 'You know, they're so coy about first love, teenagers, well, young adults. I knew he was at your place a lot. It hurt. I couldn't bring myself to raise it with you. I preferred to hope. That he'd come back. That he'd get tired of playing happy families with you all. That we'd be the unit we'd once been.'

'Weren't you worried Tom would say something to him?'

Vicky couldn't sound more incredulous if she tried. 'Are you kidding? Mr Avoidant? Not in a million years. And we never discussed the possibility. That Raf ... Not once. You've got to believe me, Gita.'

My shoulders sag. I realise, finally, that Vicky had no intention of causing this mess. She's just been doing what all drunks do. Drowning her guilt and her responsibilities.

'Have you spoken to Bob?' I ask quietly. 'Not about the father business ... Today. About Raf going for help.'

'Of course not!' Vicky's eyes are wide. 'We've been stuck here. In Rachel's bubble. I haven't given Bob a thought. And the phones are down anyway. Why would I try?'

I stumble over my words, continue slowly. 'Well ... um. In case he doesn't make it back?'

'What do you mean? Why wouldn't he make it?' There must be something more in my face this time, because Vicky lurches to the window. She looks out as though she's going to see Raf right there, larger than life, but of course there's nothing but wind and waves and bleak, bleak sky as far as the eye can see. She turns back to me, her face a picture of anguish. 'Gita? He's going to make it, isn't he?'

Despite myself, my anger shrivels and dies. It was only yesterday that I thought Ruby was gone, lost forever. Now Vicky is starting to feel that same winnowing pain. Whatever she's done, however flawed she may be as a friend and a mother, she needs a hug. As usual, it's like embracing a plank, but we both endure it. It's

249

better than being alone in, what did she call it? *Rachel's bubble.*

Yes, we've all been trapped in that. Until yesterday, it seemed iridescent, weightless, beautiful, like the pretty soap spheres my girls would blow long ago with little plastic wands.

Now all that gilded insubstantial nonsense, so quintessentially Rachel, has somehow become something horribly different.

Our prison.

Chapter 55

Geoff

Mount Tregowan, 1st November

I suppose I was expecting Jane to go to pieces at some point. She leads a very sheltered life and, knowing how fragile she is, I've always protected her as best I can. I can't say I'm not angry about, well, matters that have come to light this weekend. But, when I look at the rackety lot around us, I'm still glad she and I have each other.

I can tell she is beginning to find our confinement in the library wearisome. It makes sense to encourage her to get up and out. Often jollying her along, taking her for a little walk, can make all the difference. So I reach for her hand and pull her up. She looks at me in surprise.

As soon as we're outside the room, I clear my throat and begin the speech I've prepared. I've had time, while the rest of them have been coming and going with their endless shenanigans. It's something I do, to get things straight in my head. I take hold of her again. She turns to look at me.

'I've been thinking,' I begin. 'You know, it wasn't your fault.

What happened, long ago. I was angry when Rachel told me, yes. And jealous. After all, we've never got a baby to stick. It hurt, that you'd had that. And with Tom, of all people.' I wait for some sort of sign from her that she feels contrite – even that she's listening. I clear my throat and carry on. 'But we've been through so much. I'm not going to desert you now.'

I don't expect a rush of gratitude – I know my wife by now. But I think I deserve more than that tight, automatic smile. I hide my disappointment. She just needs time. Time to sort out her emotions. She'll pour them into her next book, even if she can't tell me about them. Yes, I do read them, assiduously. Of late, more and more mice have joined an exodus to the big and unfriendly city, leaving their snug little holes in the country.

She's looking up at me, about to speak at last, when someone comes round the corner into the hallway. Damn, it's Tom.

He gives Jane that up-and-down look, partly surprised, partly amused. I want to knock his block off, but I jam my fists into my trouser pockets. 'Hello, old man,' I say genially.

Tom eyebrows arch. 'How's it hanging?' he says to me. 'See you later.'

'Oh, where are you off to?' Jane asks, rather to my surprise. It's as though she doesn't need to stop herself, anymore.

'Yes, let's all sit down and have a, erm, catch-up,' I say, as brightly as I can under the circumstances. 'Clear the air.' We're outside the Great Hall and we all exchange a glance. No one wants to go in there.

'How about the office, downstairs?' says Tom, without marked enthusiasm.

A few minutes later, we're settling ourselves down. Tom has assumed the power position behind the desk but I'm ignoring the provocation. 'What do you think about all this business? From a, ahem, professional perspective?' I ask him. The light from the window must be going into Jane's eyes; I see her wince. 'Seems like a pretty open and shut case, doesn't it?'

Tom looks up from where he's been fiddling with a fountain pen, but he doesn't speak. God, he's a handsome bastard. Again I imagine how it would feel, ramming my fist into those white teeth. Pretty satisfying, I should imagine. Reluctantly, I go on. 'I mean, now that Penny's killed herself.'

'Is that what everyone's saying?' His tone is polite.

I look at Jane, who shrugs. 'No one's really talking about it. It's so bizarre, isn't it?' she says. 'It's only hours since Rachel ... That amazing mermaid gown, when we arrived! She was so sniffy about my fleece. And as for your gilet!' She turns to me. I don't know what she means. It's a perfectly serviceable garment. 'Then her blonde hair, and all the blood. The orange wigs ... Why did she want us all to wear those? And the cloaks?'

I look at her in concern. Why is she rambling like this? The whole weekend has really been too much for her. The sooner I get her away to some peace and quiet the better. Tom and I exchange a glance.

Tom plays with his pen again. 'Well, that was all very Rachel. Getting us dressed up. Out of our comfort zones. Into hers.' His voice is neutral, but what he's saying is not.

I look back, and I can't help remembering Rachel lying there, face down in her dinner plate. Although no one realised it was her. Not straight away. 'Perhaps she just wanted to sow confusion? Make us all look the same, play some sort of trick?'

'Maybe we should put our heads together, see if we can work all this out?' Tom says to me. 'Get the best brains working on it.' I notice Jane gives him a sharp glance, but for once he's making perfect sense. 'For instance, what did you do, when the lights went out?'

'Um, well. If memory serves ... I think I just sat there. Yes, I just stayed in my seat.'

'Was anyone else moving?'

'Well, someone certainly was. Unless Rachel reached round and stabbed herself,' Jane points out. She's my wife, and I'd never say a word against her, but I don't think either Tom or I appreciate the acerbic tone. Tom's smile is a line straight as the horizon. Not the one I can presently see outside. That is still buckling and bowing with waves as big as the Old Bailey.

'OK. Did you *hear* anyone?' he persists.

'Hear?' Jane suddenly speaks up, repeating the word. It's as though it's sparked some sort of memory. She has that look she gets when she's thinking about a new illustration. She does have very good recall. It's handy when I've lost my reading glasses.

'I *did* hear something. A sort of fizzing sound,' says Jane slowly, looking at me, and then Tom, and then back at her engagement ring. She starts turning it on her finger. I always used to say I'd replace the row of shyly winking diamonds with something more substantial, when I'd fully consolidated the practice. But she's got attached to it over the years.

'And Penny?' Tom asks. 'Did you notice anything amiss with her last night?' he asks.

'Apart from the fact that her new stepmother had just been stabbed to death with a skewer?' I say, with some jocularity.

Jane launches into speech as though she hasn't heard me. 'I mean, I don't pretend to know Penny, I'd never clapped eyes on the woman before this weekend. But she was nervous, highly strung. She was like that on Friday evening as well, it wasn't just the … Rachel thing. Her hands weren't dripping with blood, when the lights went up. Definitely no Lady Macbeth impressions. *Wouldn't* she have had blood on her? There was so much …'

'What? Oh, no. That was just on the floor,' says Tom, as matter-of-fact as if we're discussing a spilt glass of wine.

'On her, though?'

He shakes his head impatiently. 'No, the skewer was inserted very cleanly, looks to me like it was between two of the vertebrae. If it hadn't killed Rachel instantly, my guess is she'd have been a quadriplegic. It was a very neat job, I have to say. Which suggests a degree of medical knowledge …'

With a jolt, I remember something. 'Penny *was* a trained nurse,' I remind them both.

Tom nods with grudging respect. 'Did you notice anything else? When the lights came up?'

Jane is looking a bit queasy. She's always had a delicate stomach. The idea of the vertebrae ... or maybe it's the thought of Rachel, paralysed. I see her swallow uneasily. Despite the, deucedly uncomfortable revelations of this weekend, I still feel compassion towards my wife. I hope I won't have to rush her out of the room.

'I didn't notice anything,' Jane says. 'I don't know if I even looked in Penny's direction, to be honest. I was looking at ...' She gestures a closed fist, coming down hard, neatly conjuring up the skewer for us, and going green about the gills in the process herself.

'Were there fingerprints?' I ask.

Tom shrugs. 'The police will test for all that. But it would have been easy enough to use, I don't know, a napkin, say.'

'And the lights? How did they go out like that?'

'Easy,' says Tom, and he sits back expansively. 'Someone removed a bit of one of the flex casings from a sidelight, then threw water on it. It fused. Because every light was on the same old circuit, they all went out. Pouf.'

That explains the fizzing Jane heard. Cunning. Whoever did this has quite a practical bent. For the first time, I wonder about Penny. I can't see her knowing a lot about circuitry. But it's not the moment for me to add my two-pennyworth.

Suddenly it does all get the better of Jane and she's rushing past me, for the door. 'I'd better ...' I say to Tom.

'Yeah, yeah, go,' he says, suddenly dismissive. I try not to take his tone personally. I really can't approve of Jane's interest in the man, on so many grounds. Though I suppose she was a lot younger, and possibly stupider, then.

It's the only thing that makes sense.

Chapter 56

Jane

Mount Tregowan, 1st November

The cool of the bathroom is a comfort. I lean my sweaty face against the mirror, trying to control my breathing, trying not to catch my own eye, willing myself not to throw up.

I remember being so impressed with this room when we first arrived. The tiles are a deep, serene shade of lagoon-blue. The stacks of impossibly fluffy towels, the plush dressing gowns on the hooks – it was all so beautiful, like one of those swanky European boutique hotels. The kind of place Rachel flitted in and out of. I'm always hoping Geoff will want to stay in one when we go away, but he's much more a frilled valance and trouser press kind of man.

Now the towels are trampled, there are puddles of bathwater on the floor and the loo roll lies in soggy strips, as though it's been worried to death by the Andrex puppy. A sorry state. A bit like the island itself, I suppose. It's staggering how fast things can go downhill. When we arrived, the chatelaine was holding court; everything was sparkling and wonderful and gorgeous, from the

Great Hall to our hostess herself. Now she lies rotting and we're all running around like headless chickens. Or perhaps we should be.

Instead, we've actually been cooped up like battery hens in that bloody library. Raf is the only one who's been spurred into action. And, as the hands on the clock go round, I can't be the only one wondering if we'll ever see him again. It will truly be a crime against nature if the sea has swallowed that beautiful man-child.

I've got my breathing under control now and wiped the film of sweat off my face with a bit of dryish loo paper. I wonder what on earth that army of maids is doing? Are they all in shock? Or too busy being chased around the castle by Tom to do any cleaning? That would explain a lot.

The array of Aesop bath products, brand-new when we got here, have been plundered and scattered by Gita's careless children. I breathe in the expensive sharpness of mandarin and the soapy medicinal smell of rosemary. For a moment I imagine the Tuscan hillsides and sun-drenched orange groves they were plucked from, only to end up in this watery hellhole. I read the name of the hand soap from its black and white label. *Resurrection.* I almost laugh.

Well, that's not going to happen, is it, Rachel?

Chapter 57

Vicky

Mount Tregowan, 1st November

I can't believe we're all still crammed in here, lambs waiting for the slaughter. I walk over to the window. The sea has us cornered, as high as ever, cutting off any escape as surely as though we were floating in outer space or deep in some subterranean cavern. What time is it? It must be edging towards the second tide, mustn't it? Or is my gnawing fear about my lad playing havoc with my internal clock?

Where is he? Where the hell is he? I search the horizon, hoping against hope I'll suddenly see his head popping up above the waves, slick as a seal.

I remember that lesson I took him to, with Gita's girls. He must have been five, Tasha all of four, though she'd been having lessons for two years already. 'Now, you mustn't expect miracles. It's a slow process, learning to swim. They have these reflexes, as babies, but they disappear. It all needs to be relearned,' Gita droned. Honestly, even then I found it irritating. I didn't pretend to be a perfect mother *and* the ultimate worker bee, like she did.

I was holding things together, and that was plenty. We were on our own, already. Whereas she had an au pair in tow, bloody Tom at home, and an army of relatives just dying to help.

Anyway, Raf took one look at the water, jumped in and he was off. We looked on in astonishment. 'Has he got his foot on the bottom?' Gita asked, before having to concede he was a natural. Tasha did her best to follow him with her floatation swimsuit, but was soon out of her depth and whining. The instructor had to fish her out.

I must admit, I felt pretty smug that day. Raf did me proud. I've done plenty wrong in my life, but making him was my best move by far. However I accomplished it. I raise my coffee mug to him, and salute my beautiful, brave lad. I sip and the familiar oily taste strokes my throat, fire in its wake.

Yes, yes, all right. I've slipped. Again. I know I'm weak. But for God's sake, who would begrudge me a shot or two of vodka right now? Only a monster like Gita. My lad is out there somewhere – no one knows where. In my view, I'm clinging to my sanity pretty well, and if a little drink helps me, then so be it. I turn to glare at Gita, but of course she's already giving me the evils.

Well, I don't care. Tomorrow is another day for giving up. Today, I bloody well need this. I sip again and don't even realise I'm crying, till the tears plop into my cup. Suddenly there's a hand on my waist. I look down in surprise. It's Gita, her third finger encrusted with all the junk Tom's given her over the years, the wedding band, the engagement rock, the eternity rings. Prizes for looking the other way. Lies, told in hard cold stones.

She guides me over to a chair and I sit down gratefully. I might just close my eyes for a moment. The room is moving, as though we're on a ship. The waves, the bloody waves, surrounding this place, taking my lad, and now in here too. It's more than enough. If I could just sleep, I'd be able to unjumble my head. There's a ton of impressions, pictures. Little mice, so playful. One sneaking up behind another, and sticking a tiny shard of metal into a sleek furry neck. A joke, a game, it must have been.

But Raf, out there, despite all his skill. That water is ice. It's November now. All Saints' Day. Ha! Neither Rachel nor Penny were saints. My boy, though. He took off all his clothes.

'Wear a jacket,' I always told him. 'Wrap up warm.' I did the mother stuff, I did. It was a foreign language, but I tried to learn it for him. I couldn't learn 'wife', but 'Mum' I spoke. 'You won't feel the benefit. Don't treat this place like a hotel.' Well, he didn't. He checked out.

I feel myself drifting, between here and where he is. I open my eyes. Another sip – that might do it, send me after him for a while. To the place where I can forget. I look along my hand, to where I'm clutching my cup. I try and move it to my lips, but I'm so tired. I'll shut my eyes again. Rest. That's the thing. Rest in peace. Just for a while. Rest with Penny and Rachel.

I smile as they take me away with them.

Chapter 58

Gita

Mount Tregowan, 1st November

OK, so Vicky has now passed out cold. But at least we're all back in the room together. That leaves me with Roderick, who is pretty much a puddle on the floor, and Ross, who hasn't spoken since he got back from his walk. Jane seems to have sunk into a miasma of gloom, or is it shame? I didn't miss Rachel's significant look, just before she died, so I suppose I can't ignore the evidence of yet another of Tom's flings anymore. Why *wouldn't* he have slept with Jane, after all? He's got through the rest. But I can't be bothered with all that now. I need help, with this useless bunch of adults, and more particularly, with my girls.

They're not dealing with this well. I'm worried about Tasha. Her 'boyfriend', or whatever we have to call him, is still nowhere to be seen. I hate this, the waiting, the hoping. It would have been better in a way if we'd been certain he wasn't going to make it. Not knowing is terrible. With Tash, I have to keep up a pretence that everything's going to be fine. It becomes more difficult with every passing minute. She's not a fool. We need to be watching her like a hawk. Both of us, Tom and I. She's under my eye now. But I can't keep her cooped up here forever. She's just sitting here, alternately weeping, and checking her silent phone, as she has been for ages.

All right, I never expected any help from Vicky. She's not equipped for an emotional crisis. Give her a financial meltdown, and she'll be pushing buttons and righting the world in moments. But something that touches her like this … I mean, I understand. I was a mess, yesterday, with Ruby. And let's face it, Vicky doesn't need much excuse to start drinking. If there's a 'y' in the day, a vowel in the month … We definitely need to get her into rehab, when this is over.

But we're in the middle of something bigger here. I'm angry she couldn't stay sober a bit longer, when there's so much at stake. Our lives, for instance. We're stuck on an island in the middle of the sea with two dead bodies, and another one missing in action, somewhere out there. It was scary enough, even before the scuppered boat was found.

Penny was nervous from the moment we arrived on Friday, skinny and skittish and strange. By all accounts, she had lived on a knife edge since her mother's death, years ago. It was clear she loathed Rachel. And then, last night, there was Rachel's little bombshell.

But try as I might, I keep coming up with objections to the idea of Penny as the murder/suicide type. Penny was gawky, all elbows. I can imagine her trying to stab Rachel easily enough, but even with her medical knowledge, I have the feeling she would have messed it up. She was too clumsy. She looked guilty, all right, as soon as the body was found. She was on the verge of hysteria. But then, who wasn't?

Oh, I don't know. I just want it all cleared up. I have to admit that poor Rachel was asking for it. And she did always get what she wanted. Then Penny had that cupboard full of tranquillisers. I suppose we'll have to wait for the police. They'll sort it out. They must get here soon. Even if – God forbid – Raf didn't make it, then the tide will turn again at some point. Hopefully the waves will be a bit less deadly than they were earlier. I'm almost afraid to look out of the window. Even if it *is* as bad as it was before, I think we should take the chance. We need to get away from here. I'll carry Ruby. I'll carry all the girls. I'll drag everyone bodily off this island if I have to. But we have to leave.

When is the next low tide? Roderick ought to be keeping us informed. I look over. Damn, he seems to have fallen asleep as well. He doesn't even have Vicky's excuse of a skinful of vodka. I'm reminded of those snail trails in the garden in the morning, as I see the tear tracks on his cheeks. I pity him, I do, but it's not attractive. I suppose I can't entirely blame him for zoning out. It's one way to get through this. It feels as though we're sitting in death's waiting room. It's not as if any of us have much in common, without Rachel. And we weren't getting on even before she got stabbed.

Who was it who said, *Time and tide wait for no man*? Here we sit, twiddling our thumbs, waiting, waiting for the tides to turn. I'm beginning to feel, ridiculously, as though Rachel is the lucky one. At least she's left this place.

She always did love a captive audience.

Chapter 59

Vicky

Mount Tregowan, 1st November

When I wake up, I can hear the ghost of a snort ringing in my ears. I hope it wasn't me. I look around but no one seems to have noticed. I can feel something digging into my cheek. Great, it's my phone. I prod it, but it's run out of charge.

I heave myself up and look into the mirror over the fireplace. Yep, there's a red oblong right across my cheek. My hair is everywhere and my eyes look even grittier than they feel. None of that matters, compared to the ball of anxiety lodged in my chest.

I turn to the others, about to speak, but Gita puts a finger to her lips and nods her head over to Roderick. His face is in shadow but I see, now, that he is asleep. I hope he was the one who grunted, though he seems quiet enough. Gita's three girls are back, flanking her silently on the sofa. Tasha is avoiding my eyes. A bit of fellow feeling would be nice, though in the circumstances I suppose I can't expect that.

Nessie is sitting with an arm across her stomach, doing something on her mobile with one thumb. Ruby is deep in her own phone. Surely she's a bit young to have one? Though at times like these it must be a blessing. Times like these? What am I saying? This is unprecedented. Well, I bloody hope it is. I'm certainly not planning to be in this situation ever again. I knew it was a mistake leaving London. Christ, what an understatement.

I whirl around, looking at the foot of my chair, then broadening the search to the nearest coffee table, the mantelpiece itself, the window ledges … Gita catches my eye.

'Lost something?' she asks drily.

'My cup,' I say defiantly. She gives her head a sad little shake, but at least she keeps her mouth shut. I carry on with my search. I expect one of Rachel's bloody minions has nipped in and cleared up. There's a tray of coffee over by the window on a little banquette. I go over and clasp my hand to the pot; it's still warm. I pour myself a cup and sip it defiantly, looking straight at Gita. *Vodka is not the only liquid I consume.* She shuts her eyes, refusing to get the message.

'Before you drop off too, Gita,' I say. 'Has there been an update? When are we getting off this f … this island?' I try and keep it clean for Ruby's sake.

'While you were out cold?' There's a pause. I suppose she wants me to try and correct her. As far as I am concerned, it was sleep rather than a state of unconsciousness, but I'm not going to argue the toss.

'Yes! Yes, if you must, while I was *out cold*!' Roderick stirs uneasily in his sleep and I hiss the rest. 'So? Anything? What about the fucking *tide*, for example?' So much for my resolution. And of course Ruby looks up, electrified. Gita tuts.

Roderick is rubbing his bleary eyes now, but I'm past caring. 'When does it sodding go down? Roderick, you know, don't you?'

The pathetic little man looks like a vole in the spotlight, blinking and blanching. 'The tide?' It's as though he's never heard the word. Even though, from the way he was holding forth earlier in the weekend, you'd think he was the world expert.

'Yes, the frigging tide,' I say, glancing at Ruby again. 'When the hell does it go down? When can we get off this island?'

He looks at the window in bewilderment, then back at me again. 'But I don't understand. I thought someone had gone for help. That boy ... Raf.'

I'm suddenly furious. 'In case you hadn't noticed, he hasn't made it back, has he? He's probably died, trying to save us all, while you've been sat in that chair all afternoon snivelling.'

Roderick's brows disappear into his hairline, making him look more like a clown than ever. He shrinks back into his seat, and a couple of tears trickle down his cheeks, proving my point. God, I'd like to punch him. But then my anger leaves me and I'm horrified at my own outburst. I know it's just my terror for Raf. But I must try and get a grip. If only there was vodka in this cup. I slosh the coffee down in disgust, march over to the window again. The bloody sea, crashing this way and that. People pay fortunes for views of this stuff. Christ. I long for concrete.

I subside into my seat. Gita comes over, doing her best to bring comfort, despite herself. She puts a hand on my shoulder this time. But I feel so far away from human touch right now. I don't know who I hate more: her, myself, Tom – or Rachel.

'Why?' I say to her, trying to clear the hair from my face, to find the space for words. 'Why are we all still here? There has to be a way to get off this fucking rock.' I don't even register Ruby's excitement anymore.

'We're perfectly safe here. It's all good – it is, it really is,' she croons, stroking my hair. It's maddening.

'Perfectly safe?' I shake her off, incredulous, but she signals to me furiously with her eyes.

Aha. She is saying this not for my benefit, but for her daughters. She's trying to reassure them, pretend the situation's under control. But under the platitudes, I hear something else, loud and clear. Something she doesn't want to acknowledge.

Shit. It's blind terror.

266

Chapter 60

Jane

Mount Tregowan, 1st November

If I were drawing us, now, it would be as a nest of little mice, underground, while a cat sits above, waiting for some delicious whiskers to poke out. So it can pounce. That's the feeling I get.

But it's at odds with what I know.

What I know is this. The cat is dead and gone. We're here, on the island, with two corpses: the killer and her victim. The mystery is done and dusted, though the boat is a bit peculiar. Hard to imagine Penny taking a hammer to it. And when would she have had time? But never mind that, because we also have a boy unaccounted for, and the minutes ticking by, every one suggesting more strongly that there's another tragedy on our hands. Otherwise, this place would be swarming with police and we'd be on our way back to safety and sanity.

So many unhappy people, gathered on one rock. Praying for deliverance, or for our escape route to come clear again. If we dare to use it. The waiting is unbearable.

Geoff is one of the few who seem steady and certain. He's

convinced sitting tight is the right thing to do. Not that we have a choice. His anxiety levels seem to have abated hugely, from the moment we found Rachel dead. Which is very odd, when you think about it. I'd say that would be the time when you'd start fearing for your life, when the host of the party you're at is killed in highly suspicious circumstances. But no, Geoff has become more expansive by the hour. And now he seems to have got over Vicky's revelation about my abortion, and Tom's hand in it, as it were, in lightning quick time. I've even seen him smiling to himself when he thinks I'm not watching.

I'm trying not to let it worry me. I can't let doubt creep in, I can't. What possible reason could Geoff have, for being so pleased about Rachel's death? They barely knew one another. And how has he brushed past all the baby stuff? He ought to be incandescent, at the charade that's been foisted on him all these years, the fantasy that we could have had a proper family life together, with children and a future. What I've done is monstrous. But he doesn't seem to care.

Why was he saying 'You wouldn't dare' to Rachel on the phone that time? Pointless, as she *always* dared. And she did love a secret. She was a voracious collector. Art, jewels … nuggets of gossip. Did she know, somehow, what has been bothering Geoff all this time? I wish I'd had the courage to confront her on Friday night. Instead, I just fell victim to her legendary charm, and then one of her cruel indiscretions. And she fell victim herself, to murder.

I need to talk to Geoff. Just, not now. I'm glad Vicky has woken up. The snoring was embarrassing. As soon as she was finally awake, and even though she is understandably groggy, she pointed out the inescapable truth. The tide. We need to be ready, ready to go as soon as we possibly can. But there's so much swirling round my head right now.

I suppose grief pushes people into a passive state, even at the best of times. Sitting Shiva, as my Jewish mum would have done. Or holding a wake, like Geoff's Anglo-Irish relatives. It's all about being together, and doing very little. Well, we're covering all the religions here. Even Gita's girls are as meek and still and silent as the rest of us.

Tasha is still so pretty, despite her swollen eyelids and her intermittent descents into tearfulness. She has more salt water in her, it seems, than laps around this island. Nessie, the complicated one, seems to have turned even further inward than before. Every now and then, a strange expression flits across her face, darting like a swallow in summer. If I didn't know better, I'd say the girl has a secret. Ruby is hard to read too. I don't pretend to know much about children, despite all my efforts and all my books, but shouldn't she be wriggling more? She seems as glued to her phone as a kid twice her age. It's not normal, surely.

Oh well. All I need to concern myself with is our precious dogs. I should be getting them back from the sitter tonight. I sneak another glance at my watch. Time is doing that weird thing; at one moment, it's standing still, the next, a couple of hours have passed. Oh, please say we won't have to endure another endless afternoon on this island. With the dead bodies. And the living are no fun either. I must ring Bella; warn her that I won't be back for my babies. I get up.

'There's no signal,' says Geoff. Damn. I'd forgotten. But even so, I need to get out of this room, away from these people. I pretend I haven't heard, and nearly collide with one of the servants. Another tray, laden with yet more tea and several plates of delicious tiny biscuits. It's as though Rachel is looking down on us, making sure our needs are met.

Though now that I think about it, it's much more likely that she's looking *up* at us.

From somewhere very toasty indeed.

Chapter 61

Vicky

Mount Tregowan, 1st November

That's it. I've had about enough. It must be past three o'clock …
No, I am not going to sit here and drink tea and watch the winds
continue to rage. There needs to be some sort of Air Sea Rescue
thing going on. Don't these people understand? We now need to
be looking for Raf, as urgently as we should be vacating this island.

I bolt for the door, before anyone can stop me. Maybe I'm
being melodramatic. We're not under guard, it's not locked. But
somehow everyone's eyes have been restraining me, all this time.
Now I can't stand it anymore.

Out in the corridor, I hesitate for a moment. I'm going to see
Tom, immediately. But there's something I need to do first …

When I come to, the light has that grainy quality it gets not long
before dusk. I get up with a jolt. Don't tell me I've missed the
fucking tide? I grab my phone, but only twenty minutes have
passed. It's just because the clocks went back – last week was it?
Darkness comes earlier. There's still time.

God. I needed a drink, and that catnap. Though my head is pounding, I still feel better than I did earlier. And I'm full of Dutch courage. I shove all my stuff into my case – I'm going to be ready to leave even if no one else is – and then I head downstairs.

I hesitate outside the door, despite all my resolve. Seeing Tom has always been difficult. And events this weekend haven't made things any easier. In a different world, we might be working together to find our lad, our Raf. But of course it's not certain that's who he is, and anyway both of us made our choices long ago. I steel myself, and fling open the door.

Tom isn't at the desk. I hesitate for a second, then hear a noise from the back room. I tiptoe forward, stick my head round the door. It's a tiny annexe to the main office, floor-to-ceiling filing cabinets. It looks as though it's been burgled. Is this what Tom has been doing, all this time? When he could have been insisting we get organised, search for Raf?

Tom looks up, irritated, furious even, but – I hate to admit this – as handsome as ever. Maybe it's the light, I think, trying to minimise the pull. But he always was gorgeous. His eyes rake me up and down.

'Vicky. Sobered up, have we?'

In a moment, all kindly thoughts have vanished. *Tosser*, I think to myself. Always was. Some things never change.

'I need to talk to you. About Raf,' I say, but I'm looking over his shoulder as I speak. 'Should you be snooping through that stuff?'

'Just searching for something that might explain why someone wanted to hurt Rachel.' He shrugs, with that old half-smile. He holds my fascinated gaze, moves towards me, and suddenly I'm all too conscious of him.

'What was Rachel talking about, last night?' I bark at him, trying to break the spell. God, was it only last night? It seems like weeks ago. He comes forward, takes my elbows. I flinch, but his grip is gentle.

'Come and sit down, Vicky. This is all so difficult for you.'

'It's difficult for everyone,' I snap, moving away.

'Don't get defensive. I wasn't talking about your drinking. Though perhaps we should?'

His voice is gentle, understanding. I go over to the window, put as much distance as possible between us. Here on the ground floor, in the office, the view is less dramatic than from those majestic picture bays upstairs. But the sea seems closer than ever. It's moving like a children's rocking horse, hypnotic. Empty. How much longer can we wait for the tide? 'Where are they?'

'Where are who?' Tom says, a hint of amusement in his tone.

'The bloody *police*. The reinforcements Raf was going to fetch.'

'Maybe you should start to brace yourself, Vicky. Raf's a strong lad.' Am I imagining it, or is Tom's smile actually proud? He carries on. 'And in great shape. But he's been gone too long.'

It takes a second for his meaning to sink in. Then I realise. This isn't some sort of flirtation. Tom's being nice to me because he thinks … He thinks the worst.

Now he's putting his head on one side. 'Vicky, if he'd survived, we would have been off the island by now. That wave did for him. He's gone. You have to face it.'

'Wave? What wave?'

'Didn't Gita tell you?' he asks, his forehead creasing in concern. 'We saw it come over the causeway, sweep him away. I don't think he really stood a chance.'

Time seems to pass, seconds, minutes, I don't know. Then I'm shouting. 'She said something about him risking everything, getting away … I didn't take it in. Why didn't she make me understand? She's been sitting there, all this time, knowing this? It's incredible.'

Tom shrugs. 'You'd have shot the messenger, wouldn't you? Like you're doing now. Besides, what good would it do? We don't know anything for sure. We can only assume.'

I slump into the chair. He looks at me across the desk, his

expression so kindly now. 'Why didn't you tell him about me?' he asks softly.

'Why didn't you ask if he was yours?' I hit back.

'Come on, Vicky. It never crossed my mind. But you knew. Didn't you think it would be best to, um, share all that with him?'

'No, I fucking didn't, actually. Tell him his father took advantage of me when I could hardly say no? If you *are* his father, anyway. We don't know.'

Tom tuts. 'You may have been drunk that night, Vicky. Let's face it, it would have been surprising if you hadn't been. But you couldn't get enough of me. You were giving me the come-on the whole night; don't pretend otherwise. And when we were alone together, you were moaning away like some kind of porn star. That's why Rachel burst in. Surprising the whole party didn't come in with her, the racket you were making. Take some responsibility, for God's sake. Gita was your friend, after all.'

'And your girlfriend! And not long after that, she was your *wife*. What about your responsibility to her?' I snarl.

He spreads his fingers apart. 'The heart wants what it wants,' he says.

'The heart,' I say, and now I'm looking him up and down. With the contempt he deserves. 'How would you know? You don't have one.'

As I get up and leave, I hear him laugh. 'Takes one to know one, Vicky.'

I slam the door loudly enough to wake the dead.

Even Rachel.

Chapter 62

Gita

Mount Tregowan, 1st November

I sigh as Vicky erupts back into the room, gibbering about Tom and about what's coming to him. I really don't need my girls to hear any more nonsense from her. But she doesn't stop there.

'And is it true? Did you see Raf getting swept away by a wave?'

'Calm down, Vicky. Can you speak more slowly? I can't understand what you're saying,' I say, eyeing Tasha. This is the last thing she needs to hear right now.

Geoff gets up, and gestures for Vicky to take his chair. He's a nice man. I didn't think a lot of him before this weekend, but his calm courteousness has certainly made today easier. He always seemed such a windbag before. Maybe he needed a crisis to come into his own.

'Did any of you lot see it? See Raf being …?' Vicky asks.

Tasha sits bolt upright and I brace myself for more tears, but thank goodness Jane pours oil on the troubled waters.

'Vicky, don't you think we'd have said?' She hands Vicky a cup of tea, though it's probably a bit cold by now. Rachel's servants

274

haven't been in for a while. I don't know how anyone can go on using that china with the Tregowan sword on it.

'Try and take a breath, Vicky. I know it's upsetting—' I break in. I shouldn't have done. She turns on me.

'Upsetting? *Upsetting?* My lad could be fucking dead and you think it might be "upsetting"?'

'Vicky, lashing out at me won't help us find Raf. But feel free if it makes you feel better,' I say, resigned. Then there's a huge sob from beside me on the sofa and a minute later Tasha has shot to her feet and left the room. I glare at Vicky. 'Thanks. She'd just about stopped crying.'

'Well, I'm sorry if I'm ruining your daughter's day. Maybe if you'd been a better friend to me over the years, this situation would never have arisen.' Vicky has got to the dangerous stage; articulating each word with huge deliberation. Things can only go downhill – but I'm too infuriated to care.

'I don't know how you can talk to me about friendship. If you hadn't had sex with Tom behind my back, we wouldn't be in this mess now.' It's out before I can think better of it, and I don't even need to turn my head to see the instant reaction from Nessie and Ruby. Ruby lets her phone fall with a clatter, while Nessie gasps like a dowager dropping her lorgnette. Damn.

The fight goes out of Vicky and she slumps in her seat. But only for a second. She starts to pipe up again, but I break in quickly and cut her off. 'We've all been very preoccupied, lost in our thoughts …' I say. I look over at Roderick, who seems to be on the verge of tears again. 'We haven't really been in a state to notice much.'

'Oh, come on,' says Vicky. 'No one else saw a thing? I'm beginning to wonder if it happened at all.'

'I don't really see where you're going with this, Vicky. Where is Raf, if there wasn't a wave? He should have been back ages ago. And I hate to say it, but that water out there is cold. Really cold.' Ruby burrows into my side and I feel awful. I clasp an arm round her. But I can't shelter her from every unpleasant truth, however much I wish I could. There are too many of them at the moment. 'And as for the police,' I say with my head up, shaking Ruby just a little to bolster her spirit. '*Tom* is the police. And he's here. So we really don't need to worry.'

Vicky turns and gives me a baleful stare. She opens her mouth and I brace myself for another tirade. Honestly, she really needs treatment. Her worry about Raf would have anyone reaching for a drink, fair enough – but most of us would have the sense to keep it to just the one. Not Vicky. She's swaying now. Before I have time to think about it, Geoff has shot up and is settling her back in the chair again. She goes quiet. Thank goodness.

I ought to go and see if Tasha's OK. I ought to see if Tom needs anything, too. But I don't like to leave Nessie and Ruby, not while Vicky's like this. I look towards Jane. 'Would you mind keeping an eye on the girls for a bit? I just need to see how Tasha is doing.' For a second, I think Jane's going to refuse. She looks so surprised. I suppose someone with her aversion is never asked to babysit. But it's not exactly going to be full on. She only needs to sit there and carry on looking aloof, for God's sake. 'Just for ten minutes?' I plead.

'Of course,' she says, with a social smile, and edges herself between Nessie and Ruby in the place I've vacated, as though she's sitting between two unexploded bombs. A servant opens the door and comes in with the next tray. Coffee, this time. Nessie jumps up. 'I'll come with you, Mum, I'm dying for the loo.' She's not looking great. All this seems to have been a shock to her system. Once we're in the corridor, she bolts to the cloakroom and slams the door. I hesitate outside for a moment, wondering what's given her this dicky tummy. But Rachel's food was so rich, last night. All except the pudding. And that was enough to turn anyone's stomach. I feel stupid, loitering outside. So I plod up the stairs, to see how Tasha's doing.

All we need now is for her to get some crazy notion into her head; that she and Raf are star-crossed lovers, that she can't live without him. I'm dreading finding her missing, too. But, when I poke my head round her door, she's safely on her bed, deep in her phone. I come and lie beside her, and see she's scrolling through pictures of the two of them. Who knew there were so many?

'You didn't tell me about Raf,' I say gently.

She sniffs. 'You could see we really got on,' she says slowly.

'Yes. As friends. I mean, you've known each other forever. You've grown up like brother and sister.' God, I could cut my tongue out! I can't believe I just said that. But it doesn't provoke the storm that I brace myself for. A fat tear plops from each of her beautiful eyes, but she isn't hysterical anymore.

'We just understood each other. And then it became ... something more.'

'He's always been a lovely kid.' I lean closer to the photos filling her phone screen. So good-looking. So sweet. They look adorable together. Like siblings? I squint. I'm not a hundred per cent sure. There are similarities – but surely they come mostly from their easy-going personalities.

At this point, I can't work out whether it would really be a relief or not, if Raf has actually been swept away. Earlier I thought it might be, but I was so angry. I absolutely wouldn't wish such an awful death on anyone, especially poor Raf. Nor do I want to see Vicky suffer, whatever she has done. She may have multiple failings as a human being – and as a mother – but she doesn't deserve that. On the other hand, if he's gone, well, this is horrible, but it does solve some problems. The incest. The whole question of his paternity. And what to do about him and Tasha, going forward.

It would still leave my relationship with Vicky in intensive care, and with little real chance of survival. She did the dirty with my husband, whether Raf was the result or not.

And I can't acquit Tom, either. I mean, yes, Vicky must have been offering it to him on a plate. And no, most men wouldn't turn the opportunity down. But it was wrong. The thing with Jane wasn't great, either – but it was before we were officially together.

All right, it's a mess. Unfortunately, it doesn't mean I love Tom any the less.

I've worked hard, throughout our marriage. And I've held things together. Admittedly, I haven't looked as closely at some of our problems as I should have done.

When he came home that day, four, no five months ago, my heart sank. 'There's a glitch at work,' he said, his eyes not quite meeting mine. There'd been other times, when I'd had questions, and his answers had been quick. Too quick.

So I was pleasantly surprised when it was nothing to do with all that. 'Corruption,' he said. 'That's what I'm being accused of.' I could tell from the set of his mouth that he found the charges ridiculous. 'I'm going to fight this with everything I have.'

Of course I had no qualms at all about throwing my weight behind him, standing by him. He's not a bent copper. He's never been *corrupt*. I'm so angry with his accusers, I could kill them for what they've done to him, blackening his reputation. It's so unfair.

And he didn't know a thing about Raf, either. That much has been obvious. It's typical of Vicky not to have found out herself. She could have clarified the situation so quickly. Those DNA companies probably even provide an SAE, it's so easy, now. But no. She prefers to take refuge in a sort of half-life of uncertainty and shifting parameters. Keeping on the right side of Bob, I suppose. I don't know whether he's paid her any child support over the years – probably not, knowing him – but that would have stopped if he'd known Raf wasn't his. Not that Vicky has really needed any extra. She's managed to keep down a job all this time. Christ knows how. I wouldn't employ her to run a tap at this point.

I suppose that's how you get, when you prefer to look at the world through the bottom of a glass. Vicky hasn't been able to face reality for years. I thought it was just her inability to keep relationships going, long term. But maybe it was about Raf all along? Secrets do so much damage. I mean, I'd hate to see the state of Vicky's liver. But I bet her heart is no better, with all the poison she's kept in it for so long.

Tom's the opposite. All right, he's got his flaws. But he loves his family. 'You and the girls are everything to me,' he said, when he came home that day. I believed him. And I can't imagine him doing anything that would put us in danger. I've never cross-questioned him about what went on. It would be unsupportive. My job has been to take his side, not to niggle away at him. He's always tried to do the right thing by us.

And I'd still defend him, and our family, against anyone.

Yes, to the death.

Chapter 63

Tom

Mount Tregowan, 1st November

At the start of the day, there were question marks. I'm not sure anyone really saw Penny, nuts though she was, as quite crazy enough to take a skewer to her stepmother. But there's plenty of evidence when you start looking for it. Rachel would keep on blabbing about how Penny killed her own mother in the car accident. That's a cast-iron motive right there. A night of remorse, and her involvement in that stunt with our Ruby in the chapel, and you've got enough guilt to sink the sanest person.

But now Geoff is up there in the frame too. A little digging into his background, when Gita first said Jane had been worrying about him, turned up some interesting stuff. One of his clients – the richest – is an old family friend of Rachel's lot. And there were rumours that some funny business had gone on with her will.

Jane is pretty much away with the fairies, or perhaps with those twee animals she draws. I don't think she'd notice if she were married to one of the Great Train Robbers. But Geoff has all the sweaty hallmarks of a guilty man. Rachel would have been on to him; she had a nose for that kind of thing. Yes, there's a reason he looked a lot perkier the minute she was dead and cold. The threat of being disbarred, and prosecuted for embezzlement, had been miraculously lifted. His client had no other relatives; Rachel was the only one due for a slug of the fortune. That's how she knew the money had gone astray. And now she's not around anymore to moan about failing to receive it. Heaven knows she hardly needed the dosh – but that wouldn't stop her making the poor schmuck's life a misery.

Jane herself. Does she have a motive? I haven't turned anything up, except the surprising fact she's spent about fifteen of the last twenty years in fertility clinics, getting one treatment after another. Intriguing for a woman who, according to my wife, hates kids. She and I had that near miss, years ago. But then her period came, and that was that. Not for the first time, Gita seems to have got things arse over tit. But that doesn't give Jane a reason to kill Rachel. Unless I'm missing something.

Roderick had as good a motive as anyone for wanting to see the back of Rachel. He's run this island for donkey's years, just avoiding a loss, enough to more or less keep the bats out of Lord Tregowan's belfry. But in breezes Rachel and suddenly everything goes five-star. And, with her name attached to the place, they're getting the crowds to match. How galling must it have been, for the poor guy. Plodding along doing Daddy's bidding, when suddenly the game changes and it's the wicked stepmother at the helm.

As for Lord Tregowan himself, I'm not sure it stacks up. Yes, he might well have got sick of Rachel; that seems to be the inevitable outcome of all her relationships. She was strong meat; strong poison, I would say. Perhaps he didn't know quite what he was taking on. He probably wanted her money to prop up his castle, though no doubt there was a prenup. And he might well have wanted to shut her mouth about that car accident. It'll be interesting to see what transpires now. I don't know who her heirs are; the Tregowans or her foundation? If it's the former, I don't know why Roderick keeps on looking so miserable. He'll be able to build a statue to his mum and sis, and mourn by it night and day – or get on with a life of total luxury. Whichever he wants.

I'm afraid not even my own family emerges totally free of suspicion. I might well have wanted to prevent Rachel from yammering on about my work situation. Let's face it, who hasn't wanted to gag that woman over the years? Then take Gita herself. Rachel was the one who let it all slip about me and Vicky. That's crushed our daughter. And bingo, given Gita a reason to kill. If she were a psychopath, that is. I don't think for a moment she'd do it.

Tasha, now. Could she have offed Rachel, as revenge on her big mouth? I can't see it. It's not just that she's my daughter, and incapable of hurting a fly. If Tasha had stabbed Rachel after Raf disappeared, then it would make some sort of sense. She might have blamed Rachel for Raf's suicide mission. But that happened later. Tasha was shocked and devastated, yes. Homicidal, no.

How about Raf? Did he kill Rachel, and then volunteer to brave those dangerous waters, knowing he was unlikely to make it? But he wouldn't have killed Penny, throwing the blame her way, only to swim into oblivion the next day. What would have been the point of that?

Even Ruby has a motive, I suppose. Penny lured her to the chapel, almost giving Gita a breakdown yesterday afternoon. The woman was a menace. But a little girl, feeding an adult enough pills to kill her? And Ruby had no earthly reason to kill Rachel – and would have been incapable of pushing that skewer down with enough force to sever a grown woman's spine.

Who's that ramming the door, breaking my train of thought? Ah, Gita.

My first thought is, good. It's time we had a little talk. My second is: *Christ. What the hell has got into her?*

Chapter 64

Gita

Mount Tregowan, 1st November

It's funny, with kids. With having three, at any rate. You give your attention to whichever of them needs it the most at the time. Once that particular girl's crisis has been dealt with, whatever it is – anything from a lost toy to a broken heart – then you can look around at the others.

When I leave Tasha's room, safe in the knowledge that she'll be OK, not today, not tomorrow, but eventually, that's when it hits me.

Nessie. The way she's been, this whole weekend. And particularly today, with her inconsolable tears for a woman she hardly knows.

I thunder straight to the sitting room. There she is, back from the loo, hunched next to Jane with Ruby on the other side. I stare straight at her. 'Ness, can we have a little chat?'

She looks up slowly and, as our eyes finally meet, I get my confirmation. 'Sure, let me just finish this level of my game.'

'Nice try,' I say, charging over and yanking her arm. She doesn't make it a battle royal, maybe because everyone's looking at us.

I march her up to my room. Once the door is shut and we are both sitting on the bed – Rachel didn't seem to believe in chairs for guests – I just come out with it.

Damn it, I was right. In an instant, her face crumples. For a second, I feel bad. But then anger rises up. What the fuck has been going on? In my own house? Tasha and Raf was a disaster, all right. But now *this*? It is unbelievable. I don't know how it can have happened. Or what the hell Tom has been playing at. All these months at home, when I assumed that finally, I no longer had to worry about the kids all the time. There was a responsible adult in the house, to help them with homework, ferry them to clubs. To keep them safe.

Safe, my eye. I stare at Nessie. She sits there, reddening like an Englishman in full sun, shifting under my gaze. 'It's not what you think,' she starts.

Chapter 65

Tom

Mount Tregowan, 1st November

I suppose I've been expecting it to happen at some point. But when Gita erupts into the room, hair flying behind her like a black silk pennant, it's still a shock.

'What the hell have you got to say for yourself? What's all this, this, this *infernal* scheme of Rachel's? And don't tell me you didn't know about it.'

I might be six-foot-whatever, and in the best shape I've achieved since college days, but I'm not going to lie – I draw back in my chair. At this moment, my wife is terrifying. And, actually, magnificent. I feel a prickle of desire for her, probably the first for months. This is not the time, though. I clear my throat and shift in my seat.

'What are you on about, Gita?' I say. A mild tone sometimes works. Yep, not today. She's off. Why do women do this? Get so shouty? If they could just stay reasonable, keep a lid on their emotions … I sit in silence, waiting for Gita's storm to abate,

285

while outside the rain rattles against the windows. When there's a gap in her tirade, I finally get my chance.

'Look, you know what Rachel was like. When she came to me, I just had to …'

Then I realise Gita is staring at me as though she's never seen me before in her life. 'You're not saying you were, somehow, a part of this?' she says slowly, incredulously.

I backpedal. 'What? No, of course not. Look, you know I kind of cut out when you get above a certain number of decibels.' I spread my hands and smile, in the old way.

'Did you know or not? About Nessie and Rachel?' she says, speaking as though to a simpleton.

'Nessie and …? Nope, can't say I did.' My tone is airy.

Gita gets up and starts pacing the small office. I wish she wouldn't. I can concentrate better when she's in one place. 'I didn't even know they'd spent any time together, let alone cooked up this crackpot scheme … Is it even legal?'

'Now you've got me,' I admit. 'I thought you meant they'd had an argument, one of the times Rachel was round. What the hell are you on about?'

Gita gives me another piercing look. 'How many times, exactly, did Rachel come round? While I was out of the way?'

I look vague. 'While you were out at work, you mean? A couple, I think. She just hung out with the kids, really.'

'Did you ever ask yourself why? Why Rachel, who was always off to New York for this fundraiser or that, and who had just lumbered herself with this project.' She gestures out of the window, where the storm clouds are still banked high. I take it she means Castle Tregowan, and all who sail in her. 'Why would she keep on dragging herself to the suburbs to see our teenage daughters?'

'And Ruby,' I tack on. She glares at me for my pains and I stumble on. 'No, I mean, she's … she was Tasha's godmother … I thought you wanted her to be involved. Didn't you think it might be good for their careers, or something?'

Gita sighs. I've got her there. She was always obsessed with Rachel's celebrity status, not that she'll admit that. And she was keen for some of that stardust to rub off on her children. An internship for Tasha at the Cadogan Foundation, for instance. Her art career would be made.

'What about Rachel and Nessie?'

I shrug. 'I mean, I'd say they got on OK … Rachel was never really focused on kids, though, was she?'

Gita pounces. 'Right. Exactly. You said it. So why was she suddenly hanging out with ours?'

Sometimes it's better to concede defeat. 'You tell me.'

'Because she was hiring Nessie.'

She's got me now. 'What are you on about? Hiring her for what?'

'As a rent-a-womb.'

We both sit there, Gita fixing me with her huge chocolate eyes, me staring back like an idiot. I suddenly become aware of the drumming of the rain outside.

'What?'

'She's paid her to be her surrogate.'

I look at her blankly.

'Her surrogate. Her surrogate *mother*,' Gita is yelling again now.

'You're kidding?' Christ. *Christ.* That bloody, bloody woman.

'Kidding? I only wish I were,' says Gita, and suddenly there they are. The tears. Streaming down her face, and I do the only thing a husband can. We both stand up and I take her in my arms. Behind her back, my face darkens in anger. I can't believe this, I can't. Even from beyond the grave, Rachel is still fucking with us.

That bitch.

287

Chapter 66

Tom

Mount Tregowan, 1st November

It's a theatrical touch, calling everyone to drinks. All right, it's a bit early to start, nowhere near 6 p.m. yet. But I reckon we need a stiff one. And, as everyone's been in that room all day, it's just a question of ex̶c̶h̶anging teacups for booze. I'd imagine it will be welcome. Particularly to Vicky.

I think I can safely say I've cleared things up. A lot of truths have come out.

I'm still reeling from Gita's revelation. How Nessie could be so naive, I just don't know. But Rachel dangling the money for her to study drama at Julliard in New York, board and lodging paid, was enough to sign her up. I didn't even know she was interested in acting. Yes, the whole bloody thing is illegal – you can't pay a surrogate in the UK, only cover their expenses. And we don't even know if the foetus is Ross Tregowan's. God, I hope it isn't. He doesn't seem to have known a thing about the whole revolting idea.

It's a mess. Nessie doesn't know what she wants to do next.

Being a single mum in suburbia is not the same as dropping Rachel's spawn and, as Gita puts it, 'prancing around Manhattan in leg warmers'.

Anyway, shelving that for the moment – we still have five months to work it out – my job is to reassure people that it's all over. Rachel and Penny are dead, and Raf is almost certainly sadly gone now too. End of story.

It's not pleasant, but it's tied up with pink ribbons, at least. And all we have to do is wait for deliverance, when we can wheel our cases down that causeway, to the rest of our lives. Sure, we'll have to make some statements to my colleagues, the local boys in blue, but we know what we're saying. And what happened.

We can all drink to that.

I lift my own glass in a toast, and look round. 'To absent friends.' Everyone murmurs, but the atmosphere is subdued. Vicky downs her drink in one and holds it aloft. 'I need another to take the taste away,' she says. I come round and top her up, exchanging a glance with Gita. I'm glad we've got onto the same page again, more or less, my wife and I. Nothing like a massive crisis to get the family pulling together.

Nessie is huddled, looking like a baby herself, not Rachel's bloody baby-mother-to-be. Tasha has violet shadows under her eyes. Ruby looks a fully-fledged teenager, now. Roderick sags in his chair, keeping an eye on his father. Ross, meanwhile, is sunk in gloom, looking as old as Methuselah. Jane and Geoff sit on the banquette by the window, silent, but I see they're holding hands. Looks like they will come out of this stronger.

The atmosphere in the room is more settled, even though the storm is really getting up outside, the wind cracking and moaning and sounding like feet on the march. It makes it all the more cosy, here by the fireside. It feels as though we've come through the worst. As though we're turning a page, on Rachel and all her doings.

At last.

Chapter 67

Jane

Mount Tregowan, 1st November

As Tom holds forth by the mantelpiece, telling us all his conclusions, I realise it's the first time this weekend – maybe ever – that I've had licence to just sit and look at him. It's always been hurried glances before, with me desperate not to catch his eye, show him I'm still intrigued. And I've been in hiding from Geoff, too. The last thing I wanted was for him to guess there was something between Tom and me, and then to realise what it might be.

But all that's over now. Geoff knows the truth. Everyone else in the room probably does too, Vicky and Rachel were so indiscreet. Well, I don't care anymore. Even Gita, who's lorded it over me with her Madonna pose for twenty-odd years, no longer seems like such a perfect mother. One daughter has been committing incest, the other is apparently a teenage pregnancy statistic (I haven't missed all the shouting in corridors or the fact that Nessie has suddenly stopped hiding her little bump and is now sitting proudly cradling it) and the youngest is so neglected she went missing for hours yesterday. That's nothing to post about on Instagram, is it, Gita?

I turn back to Tom. His arm is relaxed, lying across the marble mantelpiece. Those biceps are certainly impressive.

His gaze sweeps past me. No change there. Today, however, he doesn't have such a huge audience to draw on. His eyes drift to Gita, via Geoff and Roderick. His daughters are deep in their phones, no doubt regularly bored to tears by Daddy's little chats.

I realise, suddenly, that this is a hard crowd for Tom to play. He's always at his best with strangers. Well, let's just say it – women. For them, he pulls out the stops. But he's already slept with all the adult females here who aren't actually dead. And while I think we can rule out Penny, who really knows about Rachel? Gita is the only one of us getting repeat performances. Looking at her now, she seems a tad weary. I can't say I'm surprised.

In the absence of willing fresh flesh to manipulate, Tom is having to branch out and try to appeal to the men instead. Neither Roderick nor Geoff seem to be lapping it up in quite the way he's used to.

'That's all very well,' says Geoff in his driest and most lawyerly voice. 'But until we get the toxicology reports, we won't really know if Penny was in the habit of taking antidepressants, will we?'

'She certainly was not,' pipes up Roderick. 'I know my sister and in recent years she's made stringent efforts to get off her medication,' he says, sitting forward.

'And how was that going for her?' says Tom rather cruelly, looking down on Roderick. It seems to rub the little man up the wrong way. He stands and marches over to Tom. But it's no contest. Tom is tall, taut, and looks ready to spring into action, whether that is delivering an uppercut to Roderick's quivering jaw or slapping on handcuffs.

Roderick backs away but carries on. 'I don't understand where that medication came from, that stuff she … took. She didn't use painkillers – she didn't need them – and we got rid of the Sertraline ages ago.'

'She probably didn't tell you everything. What sibling does?' Tom glances at his own daughters for a second and Tasha colours. She has sworn blind she didn't know a thing about Nessie's pregnancy – but then I heard her tell Gita she saw her sister and Rachel deep in conversation yesterday afternoon.

'All the same ...' blusters Roderick.

'Look, she had a thing about that accident with her mother. And she hated her stepmother,' Tom says in a voice of exaggerated reasonableness.

'But we need to keep an open mind about Penny, don't we?' I say, surprising myself. 'The police will be doing a proper investigation, after all.'

Tom whips round. I flinch, but he just laughs. 'Sure. Just stating the obvious.'

I swallow, but I stick to my guns, for once. 'But is it really so obvious? I don't know. I'm not sure we should prejudge the situation ...'

Geoff, bless him, chimes in. 'Jane's right. We need to present the police with the facts, when they come. Let them draw their own conclusions.'

'I ... agree,' says Vicky, slurring even more than usual.

Tom shrugs. 'You're quite right. You're *all* right,' he says. 'Let's just wait for the reinforcements to deal with everything. After all, we're all in this together, aren't we?'

There's that charm again, and I horrify myself by feeling a twinge of desire.

I might as well admit it: I still find Tom irresistible.

292

Chapter 68

Geoff

Mount Tregowan, 1st November

I suppose you see it all, as a country lawyer, a *community* lawyer. Some people like to dismiss us, look down on those of us who are content to stay below the radar, instead of prancing around in the big city. But there's a place for everyone, in this venerable calling, upholding the rule of law. I certainly like to think my work has made me something of a student of human nature.

I'm not going to bore my fellow guests with all my thought processes this weekend. That would not be my wont. But it's been abundantly clear, from the very outset, that something has been awry. 'Out of whack,' I suppose Gita's delightful daughters would say.

At first, of course I looked to Rachel, the cause of so much mayhem over the years. If anyone had the potential to kill in cold blood, it would be she. Gita is the one who sullies herself on that ghastly tabloid paper, but it was Rachel who really delighted in muckraking, with her love of gossip and her refusal to acknowledge boundaries. I'm afraid I have first-hand experience of the seamy side of her interests.

Her manic gaiety that fatal night was, I felt, leading up to rather more than an announcement about the arrival of a new heir to the baronetcy. Not to put too fine a point on it, so to speak, she was dying to plunge the knife into someone. It might even have been my good self. But then she rather spoiled my thesis by turning up dead. I remember the light shining off that skewer, when the chandeliers went back on again. You couldn't often say it about Rachel – fine figure of a woman if nothing else – but she was not, then, a pretty sight.

There've been one or two shocks since then, all right. Not least in the matrimonial department. I suppose I should know that spouses can lead very separate emotional lives. I've brokered enough divorces over the years. But I had no idea that Jane has been hiding so much. To be blunt, the fling with Tom. I suppose I can forgive her poor taste – and at least it predated his relationship with Gita. Vicky, of course, cannot say the same.

As for the thorny issue of the abortion, and the subsequent miscarriages. Well, all I can say is I wish she'd told me sooner, and that I hadn't had to hear it third-hand. We could have saved ourselves a world of pain and trouble. And I could have told her a little secret of my own.

I have no desire for children. Never have had. There, it's said. I bought into her plans, long ago, the preparation of the baby's room, all the folderol that went with it. That's what the ladies want, isn't it? But I never really warmed to the idea of losing my wife to maternity. Chaps get sidelined by their children; it's behind half the splits I see. I didn't wish to play second fiddle to some little usurper, no matter how adorable the outfits Jane lavished our funds on. I rather rejoiced at the negative tests that piled up in our rubbish bins. And I've enjoyed the fact that she's poured so much love into her rodent friends instead. I've even tolerated those mutts of hers, Dolly and Molly, biting my ankles and trying to trip me up.

Next step is to tell Jane. I'm biding my time; she'll be astonished, to say the least. I'll find a moment, when she is a little calmer. Dear old thing is terribly overwrought. Understandably.

Possibly more pressing, presently, is the question of the murderer in our midst. I'm going to allow myself a dry laugh at this point, though levity may seem out of place.

Does anyone still believe that Penny, that pathetic specimen of a menopausal neurotic, could possibly have planned an execution? Bringing about the preceding blackout alone would surely have been beyond her.

No, there is a much more obvious candidate available to us, if we only choose to look. Someone who certainly has the 'smarts' to accomplish such a deadly deed. And who yet remains the last person one would suspect.

It's not a conclusion that I relish, it is a matter of simple deductive reasoning. We were all provided with murder weapons and disguises by our hostess herself, in the shape of the skewers and cloaks. And we all had ample scope, when the lights went down, to pounce on her bare flesh. Each of us, barring perhaps Gita's younger two offspring, had a pressing reason to wish Rachel Tregowan was out of the way.

I include even her widower in this. He cannot have been unaware of the way his bride was spreading talk of his first wife's unfortunate demise, and her daughter Penny's role as inadvertent murderess. A secret that had been closely guarded for thirty years, a coroner's verdict that had perhaps been procured by underhand means, all were being exposed to scrutiny thanks to Rachel's habitual indiscretion.

It was the same inability to keep a secret that led to my own contretemps with Jane, and then the revelations about Raf. Even young Nessie might have been infuriated when Rachel seemed to be making their infernal deal public, without acknowledging the vital role of the girl's own uterus in proceedings. Who knows, anger at being written out of the story might have outweighed financial considerations, for a hormonal teenager. Nor was there any love lost between Rachel and her stepchildren, while Gita and Tom both had equal cause to want to protect his professional reputation.

Looked at like this, the wonder is that Rachel was not bristling with skewers like a moribund porcupine at the end of that tragic meal. But only one of us took, if I may be forgiven for putting it this way, the plunge.

There is, indeed, only one amongst us who, in common parlance, 'ticks all the boxes'. And I am now confident I know their identity.

I may look inert, I may have been side-lined by some on this weekend's guest list as the little lawyer from the sticks, but inside, I am a coiled spring. Ready and waiting for my moment.

Oh yes indeed, murderer in our midst. I have my eye *very much* upon you.

Chapter 69

Vicky

Mount Tregowan, 1st November

I've been thinking, while Tom's been chuntering on. I've got my eyes shut, so everyone will assume I've passed out again. *'Poor Vicky, she's a hopeless drunk, you know.'* Little do they all realise, I've got my wits about me, for once.

Because there are some aspects of this whole business that I just don't buy. All right, the Rachel/Penny axis, that makes a sort of sense. It's neat. But Raf? The way people have started looking at me, in a pitying way. It's like they're implying my lad knew when he set out that he couldn't make it. That just isn't right.

I'm not denying there are reasons why he might feel, well, despairing. The incest. I mean, Christ. And even the idea that Tom is – or could be – his father. It's bad. But it's not *that* bad. Not when you're twenty, with the world at your feet. No, Raf is a lad with inbuilt confidence so strong it's like his own personal life jacket. Or is that just his mother's desperate wish?

I've started to develop some suspicions of my own. I just can't see Penny, twiglet-thin and nutty as she was, running down to the pier in the middle of the night and knocking massive holes in that boat. So who did it, and why?

So for a while, my money has been on – tah-dah – none other than Ross Tregowan himself.

When you think about it, it makes perfect sense. He'd decided things weren't working out with Rachel anymore, but he'd still like her dosh, thank you very much. So he fitted up Penny, and got rid of two birds with one stone. He seemed to find Penny's personal struggles nothing but an embarrassment. The way he'd hushed things up about his first wife wasn't secret anymore. That gives him another juicy motive. Besides, no one watching him today would believe he was inconsolable about his poor daughter. As for the boat, I'd say he wanted to keep us here while the evidence trail went cold. He'd know exactly where it and a handy hammer were kept. His type always think they're above the law.

Except that, last time I went to the toilet, I found him. Ross Tregowan, standing right outside this room, with a lost look on his face and tears running down his wrinkly cheeks. It was a horrible sight. It wrung my heart. I couldn't quite hug him but I patted him on his lord-of-the-manor tweeds, and he scuttled off to his room. Whether it's Penny he misses, or Rachel going that's blown a massive hole in his life – a hole as big as the one in his boat – his upper-crust front has well and truly gone soggy. Poor old bloke. His secret's safe with me.

But, no sooner than Ross has disappeared from the frame, someone else has popped into my mind. And this time, I really think it's a runner.

I've known Gita twenty years. She thinks she can hide every problem behind a perfect facade, but there are some things that poke out despite her best efforts. Yesterday she was furious Tom hadn't got Ruby's swimming up to scratch. Today she seems pretty pissed off he didn't monitor Tasha and Raf.

I'm beginning to think some dark thoughts about my lovely friend Gita. There's nothing she wouldn't do, to protect those kids.

Look how angry she is now about Nessie – justifiably, I admit. What's the betting that, if Rachel wasn't already dead, she'd have been beaten to a pulp by Gita, for that alone?

I sit here, my mind whirring. Yet, try as I might, I can't quite get my suspicion of Gita to fit everything that's happened this weekend. I don't buy it that Penny killed Rachel and then herself. But I can't squash Gita into that role, either. Would she really have fed poor Penny an overdose? It might have been a mercy killing, in its way … but still, I can't see my conscientious, loving friend bending over the bedside, pressing pills on that poor skinny wretch.

It's a relief.

But if she didn't do it, then someone else did.

Who is it? Who, *who*? As I cudgel my tired brain for what seems like the millionth time, Tom speaks up from his position in front of the fireplace. 'Listen, folks. It won't be much longer now. Who's for another drink?'

Tom sweeps the room again with that commanding stare. Everyone is silent. But, as I watch through slitted eyes, one person's gaze swivels over and meets mine. And I'm sure I'm not imagining it, their eyelid closes, slowly, slowly, in a wink.

Just then, the door flies open – and someone bursts in.

Chapter 70

Gita

Mount Tregowan, 1st November

I've just spotted the weirdest thing. Geoff has just winked at Vicky, of all people, when the door is thrown back almost off its hinges. Then somebody erupts into the room.

It's Raf – Raf like a superhero, like an avenging angel, flying into the middle of a group which, only a minute before, had seemed inert and hopeless. Suddenly the energy around us changes, infected by his determination and enthusiasm – and the back-up he brings with him. I genuinely don't think I've ever been so happy to see the police before. I've even treated Tom's closest colleagues with a degree of caution – you never quite know where you stand, as the wife, when your husband's colleagues know more about him than you do – but now I just feel total gratitude. They are our liberators.

And, if I ever doubted Raf's parentage, that is put to rest forever. Raf is tall, furious, in command. Just like his father – the human rights barrister, delivering a blistering closing speech. Immediately, as soon as he's bounced into the room, Tasha looks like she's been plugged into the mains, completely reanimated. Raf's directing people here and there, he's pausing to give Tasha a brief (brotherly) cuddle, he's trying to detach Ruby from his leg. God, it's good to see him.

There is so much going on in the room, I don't really understand all of it. Not at first. Everyone's got to their feet, the girls are now hugging each other, jumping up and down, Geoff is stepping forward to speak to the duo in plain clothes. The uniformed police, three of them, are milling amongst us, moving purposefully.

Turns out Raf's survival is indirectly down to me. I showed Vicky those pictures of surfers, she emailed them to him – and he bought a special new wetsuit, a 6mm thick one built to withstand even Rachel's Cornish seas. If he hadn't, he'd never have survived for long enough in those grim waters to bring us deliverance.

Tom is in the centre of it all, slapping Raf on the back, talking earnestly to the policemen, smiling at me from across the room. Then he claps his hands. 'Just a small announcement. We'll all be making our way off the island shortly so I suggest that everyone gather their things in an orderly manner. Before we do that, and while my colleagues are here, I just wanted to share this new piece of evidence with everyone. I found it in the castle files.'

Tom rifles in his pocket, and pulls out something – a scrap of paper. I crane forward but it's too far away to see, and a few others are shaking their heads too. 'I'll just read what's on it, shall I?' Tom looks round and there's a chorus of assent. '"*I'm sorry, I can't go on.*" There. That's all but, as I think we can agree, it says enough, doesn't it? Poor Penny. Roderick, can you confirm? Is this her handwriting?'

Roderick steps forward, looking puzzled. He bends over the paper. 'Yes. Yes it is.'

There's a hubbub in the room. I feel relief course through me. Awful though it is, it's nice to know the mystery is laid to rest. It really was Penny.

But then Roderick looks up. 'This proves nothing, though. My sister ... was always writing stuff like that. I have notebooks full of it, from when she's been in clinics. She didn't mean it, and she never tried to take her own life. Not once. And this paper, it's yellow. It looks old. Someone's just ripped this out.' He snatches it from Tom, and passes it to a uniformed policeman, who studies it and looks quizzically at Tom. 'We'll be getting this checked, sir. With all the evidence,' the constable says.

Suddenly, in the uneasy bustle that follows, Ruby pipes up from the depths of the sofa. Her pure, clear child's voice cuts through the babble as efficiently as any knife.

'Daddy, I just want to know one thing ...'

'Not now, Ruby,' I try to shush her. 'This isn't the moment to bother Daddy. Wait till we're on the boat.'

'But this is about the boat, Mummy. The one that got broken. There's something I really *need* to ask Daddy.'

Tom and I exchange a glance. We both know Ruby will go on and on if he ignores her. He shrugs. 'All right then,' I say gently. 'Ask away, honey.'

'Why were you hitting the boat, Daddy? Yesterday, when we'd been on our walk.'

It feels as though the whole room swivels to look at our little girl. She is twirling her hair round a finger, and fixing her father with round eyes. 'What do you mean, love?' I ask her, glancing towards the officers, at Tom. At anyone. What on earth is she saying?

'I saw Daddy breaking the little boat, before Penny asked me to go in the cupboard,' says Ruby, then reinserts her thumb in her rosebud mouth.

Tom, in the knot of police colleagues, shakes his head with a wry 'What can you do with kids?' laugh. 'I think you've been having nightmares again, honey. Don't worry, we'll be home soon.'

Now Ness and Ruby are looking at each other, and at Tasha

too, and I realise how tight their bond is, how much solidarity they have as a group. They might squabble amongst themselves, yet they'll always stick up for each other against outsiders. But Tom ... he's not an outsider. He's their father. And he can't have scuppered the boat. Surely he can't.

Then Nessie is standing up, pointing at him. Her finger is shaking. 'You were always talking to Rachel, when she came round. Whispering. I heard you. About art. And you don't even like art.'

'You can't talk, young lady, about secrets with Rachel.' Tom laughs again. 'What is all this? My own kids. What are you even saying?'

'Yes, girls, come on now. Daddy's been working harder than anyone, trying to get us off this island,' I say.

Tom straightens up. 'Now then. Enough of this silliness. I'll just go and get our cases ready.' he says firmly.

And then he's moving towards the door. But his head is down and forward; his arms are pumping. Even when I've registered how fast he's moving, how determined he looks, I immediately start to rationalise it.

He's going to get our luggage. He's doing something practical, something useful. He's doing it for us. There's a reason why he's picking up speed. An explanation. An innocent one.

Because Tom can't have done anything wrong. He's a police officer, like these people who are here to save us. And he's our rock. He's the cornerstone my life is built on. He's my husband. He's the girls' father. He can't be running. He can't. He just can't be.

But he is.

Not for long, though. My husband, my Tom, the man I promised to love and cherish all those years ago, is almost at the door, when a foot is stuck out at just the right moment. Geoff, the dry-as-dust country lawyer, has brought him crashing to the floor. The world is upside down.

It isn't until Tom is expertly caught and cuffed, with the

beginnings of a bruised forehead from his collision with the fireplace, that I finally stop the endless rationalising, the making of excuses, the turning of blind eyes. And down it all comes, my life with Tom. The infinite adjustments I've had to make, to allow his behaviour to be normal.

He is actually being led off now. He goes, with just one backward glance at me. I know that expression so well. The irresistible little boy, caught with his hand in the cookie jar. Pleading for my forgiveness.

This time I turn away from him. I can't do this anymore. Would they have swooped on him so quickly, if he hadn't given himself away like that, trying to bolt? The stress of a lifetime of lies must finally have got the better of him.

We're all on our feet, now. I feel strange, lighter in spirit but heavier in heart. I walk like an automaton, gathering Nessie and Ruby, and we all start moving to the door.

Then Vicky, of all people, the woman with her emotions buttoned up tight into her sharp jackets, stops right in front of us and bursts into tears.

'I'm sorry. I'm so sorry about Tom. I know you must be in bits too. But seeing Raf again, bursting through the door like that … I really thought he was gone,' she says, her face working. She doesn't know whether to laugh or cry. And as for me, I have absolutely no idea anymore. I bundle her into a hug. We both need this. For once she relaxes and it feels healing. There's been so much that's wrong between us, but maybe, just maybe, things will come right someday. I break down and sob all over her in turn as the truth sinks in. Tom has been taken away. I'm not sure how much more I can take.

Then my girls are gently separating us, getting us both out. Around us everyone comes to life, not waiting for an invitation, scrabbling together belongings in double-quick time. Soon there is a ragged group of us on the pier, averting our eyes from the

CSI officers going in to deal with the two poor shrouded women we are leaving behind.

Miracle of miracles, the wind has dropped. The sea is like a millpond, mocking us with its complete docility. There's no trace at all of the madness and storms that have kept us all at bay, stuck on this rock. Raf could swim this in minutes, now, and I feel we could too. Even Ruby. But of course, I'm not going to chance a single member of my depleted family.

I can't quite believe it as we step carefully into the police launch, holding on as the boat sways. Is this freedom? Are we really being allowed to leave this place? Even though nothing will ever be the same again, this heady moment of liberation feels precious. I look behind me as the boat picks up speed. The water is only wild in our wake. The rest stretches out, serene, with the island set into it like a jewel lying on blue velvet.

There, high on the hill, is Rachel's castle, fully visible, now the clouds have rolled away. As I watch, the last of the sun catches the turret where she loved to sit. I can almost imagine her there, still. Would she be sad that we are opting out of her games, for good? Or did she accomplish what she set out to do? She changed everything, for all of us; that much is certain.

Ross and Roderick have opted to stay. I wonder what their life will be, left behind on the island, like driftwood washed up by the tides. I have a suspicion that eventually, each of them will be happier, in a way. Being stuck with each other will be so much less complicated than dealing with other people, with women and their moods and demands. I suppose they'll reopen to the public, after a seemly interval. I definitely don't think Ross will be making any more forays to Monaco, that sunny place for shady people, where he met our Rachel.

He was always out of his league with her. But now he can look forward to a quiet old age, with Roderick as his solace. And the merry ring of the cash register. People will be flocking to see the place where Rachel Tregowan died. There are enough of them with Rachel's own gothic, morbid streak to find the place horribly fascinating. I can just imagine Roderick laying on Halloween-themed parties to capitalise on the new notoriety of the place. All with that superior look on his face, of course.

As I set foot on the solid ground of the mainland at last, with my daughters safely on the path ahead of me, I can't resist one last glimpse at Rachel's island. The castle, aloof on its mound, is beginning to disappear into the gathering dusk. The roar of wind and sea is gone, leaving nothing but a beautiful, deep silence behind. But when I turn back, there's Tom, ahead of us on the path, his hands behind his back. Cuffed.

Now that I think about it, it's always been Tom's speciality. Hiding in plain sight. Whether it was the flirtations with the mums from school – *you're being paranoid, anyone can see it means nothing* – to conspiring with Rachel and then covering his tracks, he's been masterly at concealing his motives. Or I've been incredibly trusting and naive, take your pick.

He so nearly got away with it. Thank God for Raf, making it through. He'd begun to suspect Tom, realising how much he had to lose, but without direct proof he had primed the local police to stand back and watch Tom like a hawk, let him convict himself. And it happened, when Tom couldn't resist the urge to run. Even if Vicky hadn't started putting two and two together, even if Geoff wasn't working his own way round to the truth, Raf was onto Tom anyway. Brave, brave boy, swimming through the storm. The knowledge that he'd be breaking Tasha's heart – and mine – didn't deter him.

I still can't quite believe what Tom has been capable of. Stabbing Rachel to silence her, maybe. But coolly dosing Penny up? Making her the sacrificial victim to his own vanity and determination to get away with it?

Vicky. Jane. And Rachel herself, if Vicky's right. He betrayed me with them all. And betrayed them in turn. And hid the lot of it.

Maybe I was just so used to hiding my head in the sand. Maybe he chose me in the first place because I couldn't see through him. But, whichever way round it is, my ignorance is the truth.

I had no idea that he'd dipped into Rachel's cursed money pot, or that she had found yet another of his weaknesses. Her art foundation seemed above reproach. All those glittering soirees, all that press coverage. But of course it was the perfect vehicle for money laundering. Even a fortune Rachel's size had to feel the squeeze of a global meltdown. He must have been so excited, when he was first given the Cadogan Foundation dossier to investigate, and discovered what she was up to.

'I've got my grandfather to thank for all this,' Rachel used to say in interviews, implying the man was part saint, part business whizz. In fact, it seems he was wholly venal, stripping canvases from drawing rooms all over Europe as the jackboots moved in. And she carried on the family tradition, whitewashing funds from the worst crime families, so the Cadogans could always be seen at the best black-tie events.

Tom must have been crazy, thinking he could hold any of that over Rachel. She soon made sure there was plenty of proof that he'd been taking her bribes, suppressing bits of the police investigation. But she signed her own death warrant when she threatened to show it all to his bosses.

Ironically, he even used her money to pay for the swimming lessons that Ruby refused to take. No wonder he was so unruffled by our girl's refusal to dip a toe in the water. It wasn't his dosh he was wasting.

He really thought Rachel would be in his power. Silly man, it was the other way round. Rachel always kept the upper hand. Even in death. She had records in more than one place. I can't believe how stupid he was, thinking he'd covered his tracks, destroying files on the island. Did he really think it was that simple?

Vicky's smile is as wide as the beach, as she watches Raf lope along. She's confronted a lot of demons this weekend, I can allow her a little joy at the return of her prodigal son. It doesn't last long, she turns to me, suddenly serious again, and whispers. 'How on earth did Tom even kill Rachel? There was so little noise.'

I've been thinking about this. 'He did bio-med at uni in his first term, remember?' Vicky's eyes widen, and she nods.

'And fusing the lights?'

I shrug. 'He changed to electrical engineering, for the rest of his degree. Rachel had tarted up the castle a lot, but she hadn't bothered nearly as much with the bits that didn't show. You know what she was like. All fur coat and no knickers. The wiring was probably a century old. And he knew his way around a fuse box. He always tinkered with our electrics at home. I used to be pleased, it saved getting an electrician in.'

'Say no more,' says Vicky. '*Dodgy wiring*. He did make a point of using exactly that phrase.'

It doesn't give either of us much satisfaction, but it fills in a few more blanks in this hellish crossword puzzle.

'Right from the start, he was all over the castle and the grounds, doing recces, working out the terrain. He was so … sneaky.' But I don't need to tell Vicky that, do I?

'I can't believe the way he made us feel he was a bit reluctant to secure the scene, at the beginning. He practically got us to beg him. And all the time, he was destroying the evidence, binning documents, digging up Penny's so-called "confession". He fooled me completely. Again.'

My smile is rueful. 'You and me both.'

There's silence for a while, apart from the gulls, mercifully distant now. I think back to the aftermath of the first killing. Tom was so busy. No wonder. The golden hour, they call it in the police handbooks. Something strikes me.

'When I went up to Penny's room … you know,' I say to Vicky. 'He was so clever. He more or less talked me into saying out loud that it looked like suicide. And once the idea was in my head …'

308

'It then got into all our heads. Tom was good at that.' She doesn't say any more. She doesn't need to. Tom pulled whole flocks' worth of wool over my eyes during our time together.

I'm glad Rachel was what she was. I'm glad she was bold and brazen, right to the end. Of course I'm not thrilled to learn where her money came from, or that she knew it and added to it without, apparently, the slightest pang of conscience. But she never played by the rules. I suppose that's why she thought it was fine to drop that bombshell on Tasha, and then just walk away. I shouldn't forgive her for that. But my fury evaporated as soon as I saw her corpse.

At least she did the right thing in one way – by keeping enough documentation in New York and Nassau to show Tom's fingerprints everywhere. Only Rachel could have had the chutzpah to decide to unmask her blackmailer in front of his family and friends, as I'm certain she was about to do. And only Tom had the nerve to beat her to it.

We all had our dark secrets on that island, and our reasons to want to shut each other, and Rachel, up. But Tom, my once-beloved husband, was the only one with everything to lose if he didn't silence her permanently. His career, reputation, family, marriage. All of it was on the line.

Corruption. I should have known, when he first said that word, when he said that's what they were suspending him for. There was a whiff of sulphur in the air right then. I was just relieved it wasn't a woman. But corruption touches everything, every part of your soul. And it *was* a woman, all along. It was Rachel.

All that time I spent defending my marriage, preserving it because my parents hadn't managed to save theirs, I didn't once stop to wonder whether it was worth my efforts.

In my circle, other women always say to the wife who's discovered her husband's little peccadillos, 'It's his loss. You're better off.'

In this case, it's more than true. My girls and I will truly be a force, now. And, bizarrely, Rachel's little heir, in Nessie's belly, might well be the one to keep a roof over all our heads. Even after adjustments for all that wartime pilfering and current laundering, there should still be some money sloshing around in the Cadogan bank, shouldn't there?

Please let it be so, Rachel. I want to be able to thank you for that, at least.

Epilogue

Vicky

Central London, 6th March

I'm bang on time as I bound up the steps to our rendezvous. The girl with the iPad frowns at the seating plan and of course I do my usual, bypass her and saunter over. For a second, a flash of blonde hair mesmerises me. My heart stops. *No. Not another invitation I'm going to regret accepting.* It can't be, can it? But thank Christ, it's a lass half our age, at a different table. And she's not a patch on our Rachel.

I slip into the seat opposite Gita and we take a long look at each other. She is amazing, as ever. But is that a thread of silver winking out from that sheaf of black hair? I know she'll be scrutinising me in turn. And my smile will echo that touch of wariness I see behind her eyes. She's already ordered all the little snacks – olives, bread and those saucers of oil and spices. I tear off a hunk of bread, stuff a bit in, and push my shoulders down. *Relax.*

'So. How are you?' We say it at exactly the same time, and laugh. God, we've been through so much. Where to start? Well, in the obvious place. 'Have you seen Tom?'

Gita looks down. 'Yes. I've taken the girls along. Just once. I'm not sure I'll go again. It's hard … on us all.'

'Do you know what's going to happen? What he's going to plead?'

'I think insanity is his best bet,' she says. 'God, isn't that an awful thing to say? About my own husband.' She looks down and fiddles with the bread.

'Don't beat yourself up. You couldn't have known,' I say.

'I could. I just didn't *want* to. I wish … I wish he'd died on that island,' she blurts. Her bottom lip goes. If only I could be the sort of person who reaches across the table easily, to pat her hand. And then, I decide I can be. I touch her soft skin, smoothing the indentations where Tom's rings used to be. I do what I can to make the marks go away.

'If it's any consolation, I wish he'd died too,' I say, to get her to crack a smile. It works, but she still looks sad. 'On the bright side, you now have the book deal.'

She can't help pepping up a bit at this. Rachel was always catnip to the papers, and an inside track on her troubled story is going to be a sure-fire best seller. 'True. Anyway, how about you?' she says.

I raise my glass of sparking water, and toast her ironically. 'Well, as you can see, I'm loving my new regime. It's so easy. Not!' There's little that makes you crave a drink like the death of a friend, the revelation of a scandal you've been hiding for years about your child, and supporting a single mother with a jailbird husband. But I'm not about to throw away the painstaking progress I've made. I definitely can't go back to that rehab therapy room where I had to share my innermost secrets with a group of strangers. I was surrounded by addicts and junkies, but you could still have heard a pin drop when I told my sorry tale.

'You've done so well,' Gita says.

'One day at a time,' I intone. 'Anyway, the news on Raf was good at least.'

'I'll drink to that,' says Gita, and we clink our San Pellegrino glasses. I'm having a slice of lemon in mine, for the thrills. 'It's a shame he and Tasha didn't make it anyway.'

'I'm not sure you really mean that,' I say. I was relieved when Raf turned out to be Bob's after all – and of course I kicked myself for having shied away from the truth for so long. If I'd bitten the bullet earlier, I could have saved myself from so much guilt and doubt. And maybe Tasha and Raf would still be going out. But they're both so young. And, if the past few months have shown us anything, it's that relationships started in the dark do not prosper.

Both of us shift in our seats and I change the subject. 'Are you a bit clearer on all the money laundering stuff now?'

'I suppose I am,' says Gita. 'But you're miles better on the financials than I am.'

'It's my bread and butter, I suppose.' I shrug. 'And simple, really. Although organisations like Rachel's do their best to make it as complicated as possible, so you can't follow the trail. I always think it's more like tumble-drying than laundering. The money gets bounced from place to place, taking out all those inconvenient little wrinkles, until it's impossible to work out where it originally came from. And it's easier to do now that you can ping it around the globe electronically. Put simply, buying artwork for millions is a great way to churn your dirty money.'

'I don't get why Rachel ever got into it, though. She was rich from the start, it's not like she needed it.'

I sigh. 'If her grandfather hadn't got involved in dealing stolen pictures during the war, then the Cadogans would never have had to do business with the kind of people who need their money washed in the first place. But shifting paintings across Europe in the middle of it all, under the radar, must have been an expensive business. A lot of palms to grease. And people like that want their payback. I don't think they're keen on companies deciding to take the moral high ground later and go straight.'

'So it wasn't really Rachel's fault?'

'I hate to burst that bubble, but you knew Rachel as well as anyone. Better. She was well aware of what she was up to. By her generation, it was a tradition.'

Gita looks down at her menu. 'But she might well have wanted to get out of it all,' she says in a small voice.

'She might,' I say obligingly. But we both know Rachel didn't get out. She carried right on with the family business. And it meant enough to her that she was willing to throw Tom under the bus, when he tried to lean on her. But I can't think about him anymore, all that energy and rage bound up in a prison cell. Though I've spent two decades hating him, and I still can't believe the lengths he went to, I don't want to dwell on him there.

'Talking of Rachel … how's Nessie?'

'About to pop any minute. I can forgive Rachel a lot, but not that. Messing with my own daughters. Telling Tasha, *you* know, and then Nessie. It's beyond me how she thought she could get away with it.'

'She was ruthless,' I nod. 'Do you know what Nessie is planning?'

'For the baby? Not yet. You heard she's staying with Jane and Geoff? She needed a bit of space. Well, we all did. I had to get my head around the whole idea. Let things calm down a little.'

'Aren't you worried Jane will kidnap the baby?'

Gita laughs. 'Just wait until she finds out what it's really like, having a newborn around. Not quite like those well-behaved mice. I feel bad, though. I had her wrong all those years. I really thought she hated kids.'

'Don't tell me you regret sending her all those pictures?' I look Gita in the eye and she has to giggle.

'I know it was awful but it kept me sane. When the kids were so small and it was hard to keep things on track.'

'Have you thought about letting Jane and Geoff adopt the baby?' It would be such a neat ending. For all of us.

'It's not my baby.' Gita shrugs. 'I have to accept I can't smooth this out, however much I might want to. It's up to Nessie. Of course I'm going to support her, whatever decision she finally makes. But technically, it isn't even my grandchild. It's Rachel's. Ross Tregowan is refusing to get a DNA test. We might have to force him. Another battle on our hands.'

'Will the baby be Rachel's heir?'

'Heir to what? To all the crimes Rachel committed? To the awful things she provoked others into doing? It seems like a poisoned chalice to me.'

I nod. Though I notice Gita isn't saying no. There must still be chunks of Rachel's fortune that are pure as the driven snow. And that's another generation of school fees to find, after all. Another child that Gita will yearn to bring up in a picture-perfect way, even if she's just playing granny this time.

But, despite everything on her plate, I do sense the glimmerings of a new contentment from Gita. 'And how's work?' I ask her.

She smiles. With the book coming out, with her status as the late Rachel Tregowan's best friend verified beyond all doubt, and with her position at the newspaper iron-clad as never before, I can see that the past months have actually given her a stability she never had when Tom was roaming free. 'All good,' she says. 'Let's have a toast.'

I raise my glass.

'Absent friends?' Gita says, and for a moment, as the spring sunlight bounces off our glasses, it's almost as though Rachel is with us again, with all her wicked, effervescent charm.

She was my rival. Almost my nemesis. A troublemaker, par excellence. But always forgiven, and now forever in my heart. I miss her madly. I think Gita does too.

We clink.

'To our friend. To Rachel.'

_One year to the day after Lady Tregowan's death, it is rumoured
that two of her closest friends performed their own ceremony,
against the wishes of the Tregowan family, and scattered her
ashes on the causeway to her beloved Cornish island, Mount
Tregowan. No invitations were issued._

Acknowledgements

Thank you first of all to Abigail Fenton, Head of Digital at HQ, for spending these past months on Mount Tregowan with me. I am so grateful for all your support and encouragement. Thank you, too, to my wonderful, eagle-eyed editor Dushiyanthi Horti for all your patience and care and to Belinda Toor, Helena Newton and the team at HQ Digital.

As ever I've relied on my nearest and dearest to help bring this story to life. Thank you so much to my mother, Anita Freeman, for her uncanny ability to spot a mistake, to Lucy Woollatt for all her wise counsel, and to Clare Pillman and all my friends, for chats, dog-walks, Zooms and laughs along the way.

Keep reading for an excerpt from
Whisper Island ...

It was the perfect place to escape to.
It was the perfect place to
die.

WHISPER
ISLAND

USA TODAY BESTSELLER
CARISSA ANN LYNCH

Watch Me

The backbone of every triumph is built on two simple words: *Watch me.*

Like when my parents said I'd never make it to graduation, I whispered those words: *Watch me.*

And from that day forward, I never got in trouble at school. Never made another bad mark in class. Not because I believed them, but because I wanted to prove them wrong.

I'll prove so many people wrong.

Watch me.

When college after college rejected me, and a school counselor suggested that I might consider a different track, I shouted the words "Watch me!" to an empty hall of lockers and doors.

There are many more examples.

But all that matters is NOW.

Six of us are going to the island. Only one of us will make it back.

That one of us will be ME.

From the back of my mind came a familiar, snarky voice: *If you do this, you'll never leave that island. You'll never make it home again.*

But that voice was wrong, and I hadn't had a "home" in years.

As I stared in the mirror, eyes like two gaping holes staring back at me, I didn't say the words this time.

I didn't need to.

They were seared in my brain, writing themselves, like the unseen stylus of an Etch'n'Sketch engraving the words, deep and thick, across my cerebrum.

They rattled like a mantra, growing louder and louder, until they beat like a metal drum.

My lips moved silently in the mirror.

Watch me. Watch me. Watch me.

HOW IT STARTED

Chapter 1

Riley

Some might say we went too far.

After all, our plan was born in the span of one drunken weekend. Settled over shots of tequila.

But if you had to credit *one* person—or blame them—then I guess that one person was me. Ultimately, I was the one obsessed with puzzles.

I didn't want to hang out with them in the first place; just the mere junction of words like "group" and "project" gave my introverted ass an ulcer. I avoided people in college, determined to get the work done and get back to my lonely apartment.

But then there was Scarlett. Everything changed after Scarlett.

She was my bridge to the others, extrovert to my introvert. Follower of all things art and art-drama related, Scarlett had followed the same track as me since freshman year. We shared the same three courses on Tuesdays and an early Foundation studio lesson on Thursdays.

If not for her annoying charm and persistence, our friendship probably never would have gained traction. In fact, I *know* it wouldn't have, because there's no way I would have initiated one in the first place.

I'd always been a loner, having fewer friends than I could count on one hand.

When I went to college, I never expected that I'd make a friend, much less more than one of them. Certainly not friends as glamorous as Scarlett, Sammy, and Mia.

"Riley, right? With an *i* or a *y*?" asked the girl with the bright red hair and million-dollar smile. Her hair was twisted into galactic spirals around her freckled face. She wore fake lashes and blood-red lipstick that was often smudged on her straight white teeth. She had a nice smile; the sort of smile you see in toothpaste commercials.

"Riley with an *i*," I stammered, watching curiously as she plopped down in the seat beside me. Before I could get a word in edgewise, she launched into a noisy monologue about two influencers in the art world who were up in arms on Twitter.

When the girl named Scarlett—of course I knew her name before she told me; it was impossible not to know a person that loud—was done talking, she drew in a deep breath then asked: "So, whose side are you on? 'Cause this shit is important to me when choosing friends." She winked and smiled, something playful but serious behind that cutesy facade. Still, I got the sense that she meant it. I had no clue who these influencers were, and I didn't mess around on Twitter.

Scarlett had a big dimple on her left cheek which reminded me of my first, and only, friend in school. Her name was Sierra—"like the desert, not the singer"—and she'd treated me terribly. Just the thought of that bitch made me clench my jaw.

I cleared my throat, considering the five-minute soap opera Scarlett had dropped on my lap just then. There was obviously a correct answer here, but I wasn't sure what it was.

It was a dispute over plagiarism—one artist claiming another's work too closely resembled their own. *Nothing new in the art world.*

But both artists were clearly respected and well-known, according to Scarlett. I should know about this, but I didn't.

"Truthfully? I'd have to see both pieces to make a fair judgment," I said and shrugged.

When you don't know the answer, just tell the truth. That's an adage I've always lived by, and it usually works out. Not always, but often.

Scarlett's eyes widened. "Excuse me? You haven't actually seen *The Donovans* yet? Where the hell have you been, Rye?"

I wasn't a big fan of nicknames. But I found, coming from her, "Rye" sounded kind of ... endearing. *Sierra never would have called me "Rye", that's for damn sure.*

"I'm not much on social media," I admitted. Another painful truth-bomb. "I used to have an online journal, but I kept it mostly private ..."

Scarlett stared at me, bug-eyed and silent, like she was seeing me for the first time, an exotic animal at the boring old petting zoo.

"Wow. Just ... wow. You don't know what you're missing. The drama on social media alone is worth it, but the connections, Rye ... the connections are everything in this business. It's important to know who's who ... what's trending ... well, don't worry. I'll show you the pics after class so you can see what I'm talking about. I need to know whose side you're on and then I'll know if we can be friends." There it was again: the wink-y smile, making me instantly feel at ease. There was something about her I liked, even though we were nothing alike.

"Okay, sure," I said, laughing awkwardly. I couldn't help feeling embarrassed, always out of the loop and in the dark about all things current on the art scene. It wasn't the first time I'd heard the speech about "connections". Nowadays, my classmates were already building their online presence, some going so far as to sell digital services or be commissioned to do pieces already. But, for me, it was less about connecting and pursuing fame, and more about stroking a compulsion. I'd lived with obsession for decades.

I didn't do art because I wanted to; I did it because I *had* to.

When I tried to imagine my future after college, walking out of those doors with a diploma in Fine Arts, I couldn't see my art displayed on the walls of some fancy exhibition … *Maybe I'll teach.*

But the thought of standing in front of a classroom, even a small one, was terrifying.

No. That's not an option either.

"Hey, I hope I didn't hurt your feelings. I admire it. You're all about the art, glory be damned. Fuck what the powers that be are saying or doing …" Scarlett nudged me.

A flicker of a smile must have shown on my face.

"Yep. I was right about you," Scarlett teased. Before I could ask what she meant by that, she was inviting me to lunch.

Lunch, for me, usually involved grabbing a quick sandwich in the commons, then hiking the mile back to my car, where I would sit in the AC and scarf down my food, hurrying to start the trek back across campus to my last afternoon class. There was a cafeteria in the commons and an outdoor patio, but I never knew where to sit. I preferred eating alone in my car, anyway.

"Okay. I don't think I've ever seen you in the commons before, though," I said, skeptically.

Scarlett released a bellyful of laughter, loud and snort-worthy, catching the attention of classmates nearby. We were all waiting wearily for Mr. McDaniel to show up for class; he was often late, sometimes drunk, and he liked to keep us over while he finished his lesson, as though he had no concept of time.

"Nah, silly. Nobody eats in that shithole! There's this Irish pub downtown, a few blocks from campus, and Tuesdays are dollar beer days."

I thought about my next class, less than forty-five minutes after lunch. *Would I be able to make it back in time?* I hadn't missed a class all semester. But one thing that reassured me: Scarlett was in my next class. If she had to be back on time, then surely, she would make sure we both were.

So that's how it started.

Trailing behind her in the school parking garage, I was happy to climb in the passenger seat of her yellow Mini Cooper, Billie Eilish blaring all the way to the Irish pub, O'Malley's on 11th Street, nestled between a boarded-up bookstore and a hemp shop.

When Scarlett told the hostess that two more were coming, I couldn't hide my surprise and disappointment. As an introvert, it was hard enough connecting with one person, let alone three.

"Don't worry. Sammy and Mia are cool. You're going to love them, I promise," Scarlett said, as though she could sense the bubble of anxiety that lived under my skin. *It's always there, brewing and bubbling, waiting to be squeezed until it explodes from within.*

But in the end, Scarlett was right. Mia and Sammy were cool, and I was excited, in particular, to meet Mia.

After that day, afternoons at O'Malley's became a regular thing, even sometimes on our days off from classes. It was a tiny, claustrophobic space with slabs of wood for tables and the faint smell of beer and piss embedded in the mothball-colored carpet.

But it was less about the atmosphere and more about the company. These three women intrigued the hell out of me.

Mia, with her feathery black hair dipped in blue, her shapeless paint-stained tops, she wore the uniform of "artist" well. She was gorgeous, stunning even, with the type of beauty that seems reckless and easy. The kind that feels unfair.

Sammy was different. Neatly pressed, she often sported button-down shirts and starched khakis, never a hair out of a place in her neat brown bob. She wore thick black glasses. No makeup. Despite her lengthy school hours, she maintained the books for a popular smoke shop in town, and I could often smell the tangy aroma of nicotine on her hands. I still wasn't sure why she chose art instead of accounting. She liked numbers and she was the most organized of the group. Scarlett joked once that Sammy was our "Velma" of the group, which of course made her our "Daphne", seeing as she was the only redhead of the gang.

Mia and I had looked at each other then. "If they're Velma and Daphne, who's that make us?" she'd teased. We were both dark-headed, Mia and I, but unlike her with her natural, fuck-it-why-try beauty and strange blue stripes, I had to work hard just to look presentable with my thinning hair and ruddy complexion. The extra pounds I'd been carrying for months didn't help either. *The freshman fifteen,* they called it. More like the "freshman fifty" for me.

"I guess we're Scooby Doo and Shaggy, unless you want to be Fred?" I had teased, surprising myself when I got a laugh out of her. *Hell, maybe I can do this friend thing after all.* Mia had a great laugh; she would tilt her head back and open her lips as wide as they would go, then laugh from her belly.

Mia had taken an instant liking to me, which pleased me more than I cared to admit.

It was silly, the way the four of us acted. Getting sloshed during the middle of a weekday, cracking jokes about cartoons that showed our age, and listening to Scarlett's latest online gossip as though it were gospel. She liked to joke that Tuesdays were "church": "Come listen to me speak now, children," she often joked, taking the pulpit behind a table in a corner booth, lining up rows of tequila and bottles of beer.

But it was fun. Hell, it was so fun that I didn't mind missing the occasional class or being late anymore. I enjoyed feeling part of the "gang", even if it was only during school hours.

Mia was a painter, and the second she had walked in the pub, on that first day, I recognized her. How could I not have put two and two together? Mia was THE Mia Ludlow. Daughter of Cristal Ludlow, the famous local sculptor and painter whose work was easily recognized all over the country, and even internationally. But it wasn't just her mother's legacy that made me recognize her:

330

no, Mia's work stood for itself. She had been spotlighted many times all over campus, and in some local papers as well. She was already well regarded in the art world because of her mother, but the work itself justified the attention. *Destined to outdo her mother,* one headline had read, featuring a nightmarish portrait of Jesus she had made on lithograph paper.

But according to Scarlett, there was more to Mia than met the eye. More than the talent and the famous name—she had a reputation. Everyone knew that scandal followed the rich girl, but nobody seemed to care.

Sammy and Mia, despite looking and acting like polar opposites, had been friends since grade school, growing up in Cement Ville together and competing against one another in local art contests and fairs. Now, they were no longer rivals, but best friends and roommates, they liked to proclaim.

Sammy liked to keep Mia's humility in check. "Oh, get over yourself, Mia," she often teased, rolling her eyes and smirking as Mia shared photos of her current works in progress, a dilapidated version of Monroe Institute, our school. It resembled the campus, buildings and landmarks easily recognizable, but everything was lopsided and distorted, the upside-down, creepy version of real life. And it was done in dark gray acrylic paint.

Mia had this style beyond compare; she took normal everyday objects and destinations and turned them into hideous versions of themselves. For me, viewing her art was like seeing my own soul on display, although I'd never admit that to her.

When you live with anxiety and depression, it alters the view on everything. Looking at her work made me feel seen; there's no other way to explain it.

All her work was hauntingly beautiful and a little disorganized, like Mia herself.

"Mia's a genius," Scarlett explained that first day (although I already knew that, as I'd been following her work on campus and in the papers for years). "We love her, but she's always in her own head, working through next steps, planning her next project … We like to keep her in the present, and of course keep her humble." Scarlett winked across the table at Sammy. We all knew Mia had gotten into some trouble in her freshman year of college and she'd had to come back and do her freshman hours all over again … but we never talked about that. I waited for the others to bring it up, but they never did. Her talent and legacy overshadowed any of the hidden parts of herself …

All three were different, yet there was something about each of them … Mia's careless beauty and dark genius. Sammy's snarky jokes and studious, know-it-all attitude. And of course, Scarlett, with her gossip and wink-y smiles. The girls didn't kiss each other's asses, but I could tell they were close; teasing often, but in a way that you knew meant love.

I couldn't help wanting a small piece of that for myself.

By the time our sandwiches and beers showed up that day, it was half past noon. Still nervous about the time, I drank my beer too quickly, feeling loose in the lips and warm to the touch within minutes of receiving my meal.

"There's no way we'll get back on time," I told Scarlett. *Is that a slight slur in my voice?* I had wondered, cringing.

"No worries, Rye. We'll just have a couple more, then finish our food. We'll be twenty minutes late, tops, I promise. And, hey, what does Grossman care anyway? It's not like he takes roll. Plus, it's college. We pay for these stupid classes. We shouldn't have to go to every single one if we don't want to," Scarlett said.

"Huh. I never thought of it like that," I burped, slugging down another beer. It tasted awful and flat, lukewarm on my tongue, but at that point, I didn't care.

As usual, Scarlett was right. Grossman didn't notice when we snuck in late that day, or any other day after. She flirted with him, batting those hideous, spidery lashes, and he always let us slide. I quickly learned that Scarlett didn't follow rules—as fun as she seemed, she was also impulsive. A few days into our friendship, I

332

found her in the bathroom on campus, crushing up a pill with a razor. She snorted the entire thing in one fell swoop, then offered to chop me a line.

I shook my head and said, "No, thank you."

As the weeks went on, our Tuesday lunches turned into a regular thing. I stopped worrying about being late and started worrying about my friends. It's not that I was lonely or desperate for friends—the opposite, actually. The degree with which these women intrigued me was baffling, even to me.

Mia wasn't the only genius in the group. Over time, I learned more about Sammy and Scarlett's passions as well. Sammy had a knack for computers and graphic design, creating some of the most incredible images; you'd never know they weren't sketched by hand. And Scarlett, for all her talk of gossip and scandal, and her small drug problems, had quite the impressive social media following. I didn't sign up for Instagram, but I googled her. Nearly 50k followers, and she posted day and night. Discussing technique and the latest trends in the art world; she always had something to say that drew people in. Did she create her own art, or spend all her time talking about it? I often wondered if it mattered anymore. She had a way with people—a skill so foreign to me, I'd prefer to recreate the Sistine Chapel than try to imitate Scarlett's presence online.

Weeks became months, and somehow, the friendships continued until the end of the semester, much to my surprise and delight.

I'm not sure how our hangouts evolved from weekly lunch sessions into weekend sleepovers ... Well, that's not true. *I do.*

Again, it started with me. My suggestion.

"Tomorrow is Friday, y'all. Got any big plans?" Scarlett had asked one Thursday afternoon. We were piled into our normal booth in the back of the pub. The table was dirty, elbows sticking to the plastic placemats. Sammy, as usual, set to work, using her own pack of disinfectant wipes to clean off her space.

Scarlett nudged me, hard, in the ribs. "What are you doing this weekend, Rye?"

I tried to imagine how Scarlett spent her weekends. Images of that straw in her hand, residue fringing her nostrils, came to mind. I shrugged.

For them, weekends probably meant freedom and fun. For me, they were lonely. I looked forward to weekdays because I got to attend classes and see them, although admitting that seemed rather loser-ish now.

"Probably going to finish my puzzle," I said, finally. Normally, I wouldn't have brought up my puzzle craze, but I was tired, and too depressed about the impending weekend to care.

I expected them to laugh at me. After all, who spends their time doing puzzles? *Little old ladies, that's who,* I could imagine my old friend Sierra saying.

"Oh, damn. I love puzzles. I haven't done one in, like, I don't know … a decade," Mia exclaimed.

"Me neither," Sammy chimed in as she smudged the disinfectant wipe in a slow, methodical circle. "I like doing them online sometimes. Have you guys tried that puzzle photo app? You can take any of your photos and turn them into puzzles, then work them online …"

"Nah. I'd rather do a real puzzle. And a hard one too, like ten thousand pieces," Scarlett said, signaling for our waiter to bring another round of shots.

"You all should come over to my place. We could do a puzzle together," I said, an edge of hopefulness in my tone. It was like someone else talking, the words not my own. *Did I really just invite these girls over to my place—my tiny apartment with no working windows and few personal effects—to do puzzles together?*

I'd imagined inviting Mia over a thousand times, and the others too, but never this soon. And not like this.

"Hell yeah. I'm down. How about tomorrow?" Scarlett suggested.

A letter from A.M. Castle

Thank you so much for choosing to read *The Invitation*. I hope you enjoyed it as much as I loved writing it.

I started *The Invitation* during the first coronavirus lockdown in the UK. It was born out of my longing to escape from the hot, dusty city, at a time when travel was impossible. I've visited Cornwall many times but a couple of years ago I chanced on St Michael's Mount, and fell in love with it. Like my fictional Mount Tregowan, it has a tidal causeway and an atmospheric castle ... though any similarity ends there! If you're lucky enough to find yourself in that part of the world, do go and visit this wonderful place and perhaps you, too, will see Rachel's light shining from the highest turret on a stormy night.

I love hearing what readers think of my stories, so if you've enjoyed *The Invitation*, please leave a review. You can also get in touch here:

Website: https://www.alicecastleauthor.com

Facebook: https://www.facebook.com/alicecastleauthor/

Twitter: https://twitter.com/AliceMCastle

And do watch out for my next book …

Bye for now, and happy reading,

Alice

Dear Reader,

We hope you enjoyed reading this book. If you did, we'd be so appreciative if you left a review. It really helps us and the author to bring more books like this to you.

Here at HQ Digital we are dedicated to publishing fiction that will keep you turning the pages into the early hours. Don't want to miss a thing? To find out more about our books, promotions, discover exclusive content and enter competitions you can keep in touch in the following ways:

JOIN OUR COMMUNITY:
Sign up to our new email newsletter: hyperurl.co/hqnewsletter
Read our new blog www.hqstories.co.uk
🐦 : https://twitter.com/HQDigitalUK
f : www.facebook.com/HQStories

BUDDING WRITER?
We're also looking for authors to join the HQ Digital family!
Find out more here:
https://www.hqstories.co.uk/want-to-write-for-us/
Thanks for reading, from the HQ Digital team

If you enjoyed *The Invitation*, then why not try another utterly gripping crime thriller from HQ Digital?